J. L. de Lolme

The constitution of England, or, An account of the English government

J. L. de Lolme

The constitution of England, or, An account of the English government

ISBN/EAN: 9783742840745

Manufactured in Europe, USA, Canada, Australia, Japa

Cover: Foto ©Andreas Hilbeck / pixelio.de

Manufactured and distributed by brebook publishing software
(www.brebook.com)

J. L. de Lolme

The constitution of England, or, An account of the English government

NGLAND;

OR,

AN ACCOUNT

OF THE

NGLISH GOVERNMENT:

IN WHICH IT IS COMPARED,

WITH THE REPUBLICAN FORM OF GOVERNMENT, AND

THE OTHER MONARCHIES IN EUROPE.

BY J. L. DE LOLME, ADVOCATE,

MBER OF THE COUNCIL OF THE TWO HUNDRED IN THE

REPUBLIC OF GENEVA.

A NEW EDITION, ENLARGED.

Ponderibus librata fuis.——

Ovid. Met. L. I. 13.

NEW-YORK:

TED BY *HODGE & CAMPBELL*, AND SOLD

AT THEIR RESPECTIVE BOOK-STORES.

M. DCC. XCII.

CONTENTS.

BOOK I.

BOOK II.

CONTENTS.

THE Book on the Englifh Conftitution, of which a new Edition is here offered to the Public, was firft written in French, and publifhed in Holland. Several perfons have afked me the queftion, How I came to think of treating fuch a fubject? One of the firft things in this Country, that engages the attention of a ftranger who is in the habit of obferving the objects before him, is the peculiarity of its Government: I had moreover been lately a witnefs of the broils which had for fome time prevailed in the Republic in which I was born, and of the revolution by which they were terminated. Scenes of that kind in a State which, though fmall, is independent, and contains within itfelf the principles of its motions, had naturally given me fome competent infight into the firft real principles of Governments: owing to this circumftance, and perhaps alfo to fome moderate fhare of natural abilities, I was enabled to perform the tafk I had undertaken, with tolerable fuccefs. I was twenty-feven years old when I firft came to this Country: after having been in it only a year, I began to write my work, which I publifhed about nine months afterwards: and have fince been furprifed to find that I had committed fo few errors of a certain kind: I certainly was fortunate in avoiding to enter deeply into

ing that there was some connection and clearness, as well as novelty, in the arguments, I think the work was of some peculiar utility, if the epoch at which it was published is considered; which was, though without any design from me, at the time when the disputes with the Colonies were beginning to take a serious turn, both here and in America. A work which contained a specious if not thoroughly true, confutation of those political notions by the help of which a disunion of the Empire was endeavoured to be promoted (which confutation was moreover noticed by Men in the highest places,) should have procured to the Author some sort of real encouragement; at least the publication of it should not have drawn him into any inconvenient situation. When my enlarged English Edition was ready for the press, had I acquainted ministers that I was preparing to boil my tea-kettle with it, for want of being able conveniently to afford the expence of printing it, I do not pretend to say what their answer would have been; but I am firmly of opinion, that, had the like arguments in favour of the existing Government of this Country, against republican principles, been shewn to Charles the First, or his Ministers, at a certain period of his reign, they would have very willingly defrayed the expences of the publication.—In defect of encouragement from Great Men (and even from Bookfellers) I had resourse to a subscription; and my having expected any success from such a plan, shews that my knowledge of this Country was at that time but very incomplete*.

* In regard to two Subscribers in particular, I was, I confess, sadly disappointed.—Though all the Booksellers in Lon-

After mentioning the advantages with which my Work has not been favoured, it is however juſt I ſhould give an account of thoſe by which it has been attended. In the

don had at firſt refuſed to have any thing to do with my Engliſh Edition (notwithſtanding the French work was extremely well known,) yet, ſoon after I had thought of the expedient of a Subſcription, I found that two of them, who are both living, had began a tranſlation, on the recommendation, as they told me, of a noble Lord, whom they named, who had, till a few years before, filled one of the higheſt offices under the Crown. I paid them ten pounds, in order to engage them to drop their undertaking, about which I underſtood they already had been at ſome expence. Had the Noble Lord in queſtion favoured me with his ſubſcription, I would have celebrated the generoſity and munificence of my Patron ; but as he did not think proper ſo to do, I ſhall only obſerve that his recommending my work to a Bookſeller, coſt me ten pounds.

At the time the above ſubſcription for my Engliſh Edition was advertiſing, a copy of the French work was aſked of me for a Noble Earl, then inveſted with a high office in the State; none being at that time to be found at any Bookſeller's in London. I gave the only copy I had (the conſequence was, that I was obliged to borrow one, to make my Engliſh edition from ;) and I added, that I hoped his Lordſhip would honour me with his ſubſcription. However, my hopes were here again confounded. As a gentleman, who continues to fill an important office under the Crown, accidentally informed me about a year afterwards, that the Noble Lord here alluded to, had lent him my French work, I had no doubt left that the copy I had delivered had reached his Lordſhip's hand ; I therefore preſumed to remind him by a letter, that the Book in queſtion had never been paid for ; at the ſame time apoligizing for ſuch liberty from the circumſtances in which my late Engliſh Edition had been publiſhed, which did not allow me to loſe one copy. I muſt do his Lordſhip (who is moreover a Knight of the Garter) the juſtice to acknowledge, no later than a week afterwards, he ſent two half crowns for me to a Bookſeller's in Fleet-ſtreet. A Lady

firſt place, as is above ſaid, Men of high rank have condeſcended to give their approbation to it; and I take this opportunity of returning them my moſt humble acknowledgements. In the ſecond place, after the difficulties by which the publication of the Book had been attended and *followed*, were overcome, I bagan to ſhare with Bookſellers in the profits ariſing from the ſale of it. Theſe profits I indeed thought to be but ſcanty and ſlow: but then I conſidered this was no more than the common complaint made by every Trader in regard to his gain, as well as by every Great Man in regard to his emoluments and his penſions. After a courſe of ſome years, the net balance formed by the profits in queſtion amounted to a certain ſum, proportioned to the bigneſs of the performance. And, in fine, I muſt add to the account of the many favours I have received, that I was allowed to carry on the above buſineſs of ſelling my book, without any objection being formed againſt me from my not having ſerved a regular apprenticeſhip, and without being moleſted by the Inquiſition.—Several Authors have choſen to relate, in Writings publiſhed after death, the perſonal advantages by which their performances had been followed: as for me, I have thought otherwiſe; and, fearing that during the latter part of my life I may be otherwiſe engaged, I have preferred to write now the account

brought them in a coach, who took a receipt. As ſhe was, by the Bookſeller's account, a fine Lady, though not a Peereſs, it gave me much concern that I was not preſent to deliver the receipt to her myſelf.

At the ſame time I mention the noble Earl's great punctuality, I think I may be allowed to ſay a word of my own merits. I waited, before I preſumed to trouble his Lordſhip, till I was informed, that a penſion of four thouſand pounds was ſettled upon him (I could have wiſhed much my own Creditors had, about that time, ſhewn the like tenderneſs to me,) and I moreover gave him time to receive the firſt quarter.

of my fucceffes in this Country, and to fee it printed while I am yet living.

I fhall add to the above narrative (whatever the Reader may be pleafed to think of it) a few obfervations of rather a more ferious kind, for the fake of thofe perfons who, judging themfelves to be poffeffed of abilities, find they are neglected by thofe having it in their power to do them occafional fervices, and fuffer themfelves to be mortified by it. To hope that men will in earneft affift in fetting forth the mental qualifications of others, is an expectation which, generally fpeaking, muft needs be difappointed. To procure one's notions and opinions to be attended to, and approved, by the circle of one's acquaintance, is the univerfal wifh of Mankind. To diffufe thefe notions farther, to numerous Parts of the Public, by means of the prefs or by others, becomes an object of real ambition; nor is this ambition always proportioned to the real abilities of thofe who feel it; very far from it. When the approbation of Mankind is in queftion, all perfons, whatever their different ranks may be, confider themfelves as being engaged in the fame career: they look upon themfelves as being candidates for the very fame kind of advantage: high and low, all are in that refpect in a flate of primæval equality; nor are thofe who are likely to obtain fome prize, to expect much favour from the others.

This defire of having their ideas communicated to, and approved by, the Public, was very prevalent among the Great Men of the Roman Commonwealth, and afterwards with the Roman Emperors; however imperfect the means of obtaining thefe ends might be in thofe days, compared with thofe which are ufed in ours. The fame defire has been equally remarkable among modern European kings; not to fpeak of other parts of the World; and a long catalogue of Royal Authors may be produced. Minifters, efpecially after having loft their places, have fhewn no lefs inclination than their Mafters, to convince Mankind of the reality of their knowledge. Noble Per-

fons of all denominations ha[...]alogue.
And, to fpeak of the Country,[...]here is
it feems no good reafon to m[...]ward
to it; and Great Men in it, [...]who are
at the head of the People, are [...]y anxious about the fuccefs of their [...]printed
performances which they fome[...]lay before the Public; nor has it bee[...]an wifh-
ing that a compliment may be p[...]know-
ledge, that has ventured to give[...]cimens.

Several additions were made [...]he time
I gave the firft Englifh Edition [...]ore accurate divifion of the Chapters, [...]es and
paragraphs were inferted in it; [...]he 11th
Chapter of the 2d Book; and [...]ers, the
15th, 16th, and 17th, amounting to [...]nes, were
added to the fame Book. Thefe [...]chapters
never having been written by m[...]e been
inferted in the third edition mad[...]ranflat-
ed by a perfon whom the Dutch [...]oyed for
that purpofe: as I never had a [...]perufe
a copy of that Edition, I cannot [...]Tranf-
lator has performed his tafk. H[...]ed with
the copy-right of the Book, I have [...]our new
Chapters to it (10, 11. B. I. 19 [...]way of
taking a final leave of it; and in [...]mpletc-
ly to effect this, I may perhaps gi[...]nths, a
French Edition of the fame (whi[...]why I
have not done fooner,) in which [...]ntioned
additions, tranflated by myfelf, [...]
In one of the former additional[...]7th, B.
II.) mention is made of a peculia[...]ending
the Englifh Government, conf[...]narchy.
which is the folidity of the power [...]As one
proof of this peculiar folidity, [...]n what

Chapter, that all the Monarchs who ever existed, in any part of the world, were never able to maintain their ground against certain powerful subjects (or a combination of them,) without the assistance of regular forces at their constant command ; whereas it is evident that the power of the Crown, in England, is not at this day supported by such means ; nor even had the English Kings a guard of more than a few scores of Men, when their power, and the exertions they at times made of it, were equal to what has ever been related of the most absolute Roman Emperors.

The cause of this peculiarity in the English Government is said, in the same Chapter, to lie in the circumstance of the great or powerful Men in England, being divided into two distinct Assemblies, and at the same time, in the principles on which such a division is formed. To attempt to give a demonstration of this assertion otherwise than by facts (as is done in the Chapter here alluded to) would lead into difficulties which the Reader is little aware of, In general, the Science of Politics, considered as an *exact Science*, that is to say, as a Science capable of actual demonstration, is infinitely deeper than the Reader so much perhaps as suspects. The knowledge of Man, on which such a Science, with its preliminary *axioms* and *definitions*, is to be grounded, as hitherto remained surprisingly imperfect : as one instance, how little Man is known to himself, it might be mentioned, that no tolerable explanation of that continued human phænomenon laughter, has been given, as yet ; and the powerful complicate sensation which each sex produces in the other, still remains an equally inexplicable mystery.

To conclude the above digression (which may do very well for a Preface) I shall only add, that those Speculators who will amuse themselves in seeking for the *demonstration* of the political Theorem above expressed, will thereby be led through a field of observations which they will at first little expect ; and in their way towards attaining such demonstration, will find the Science, com-

monly called Metaphyfics, to be at beft but a very
fuperficial one, and that the Mathematics, or at leaft
the mathematical reafonings hitherto ufed by Men,
are not fo completely free from error as has been
thought *.

Out of the four Chapters added to the prefent Edition, two (the 10th and 11th, B. I.) contain, among other
things, a few ftrictures on the Courts of Equity; in
which I wifh it may be found I have not been miftaken:
of the two others, the one (19th, B. II.) contains a few
obfervations on the attempts that may in different circumftances be made, to fet new limits on the authority of the
Crown; and in the 20th, a few general thoughts are introduced on the right of taxation, and on the claim of
the American Colonies in that refpect. Any farther obfervations I may hereafter make on the Englifh Government, fuch as comparing it with the other Governments
of Europe, and examining what difference in the manners of the inhabitants of this Country may have refult
from it, muft come in a new Work, if I ever undertake
to treat thefe fubjects. In regard to the American difputes, what I may hereafter write on that account, will
be introduced in a Work which I may at fome future
time publifh, under the title of *Hiftoire de George Trois,
Roi d'Angleterre*, or, perhaps, of *Hiftoire d'Angleterre,
depuis l'année* 1765 (that in which the American Stamp

---

* Certain errors that are not difcovered, are, in feveral
cafes, compenfated by others, which are equally unper-
ceived.

Continuing to avail myfelf of the indulgence an Author
has a right to claim in a Preface, I fhall mention, as a farther explanation of the peculiarity in the Englifh Government above alluded to, and which is again touched upon in
the Poftfcript to this Advertifement, that a Government may
be confidered as a great Ballet or Dance, in which, the fame
as in other Ballets, every thing depends on the difpofition of
the figures.

duty was laid) *jusques à l'année 178—*, meaning that in which an end shall be put to the present contest *.

Nov. 1781.

POSTSCRIPT.

Notwithstanding the intention above expressed, of making no additions to the present Work, I have found it necessary, in the present new Edition, to render somewhat more complete the xviith Chapter, B. II. *on the peculiar foundations of the English Monarchy, as a Monarchy*, as I found its tendency not to be very well understood; and, in fact, that Chapter contained little more than hints on the subject mentioned in it : the task, in the course of writing, has increased beyond my expectation, and has swelled the Chapter to about forty pages beyond what it was in the former Edition, so as almost to make it a kind of a separate Book by itself. The Reader will now find it in several remarkable new instances to prove the fact of the peculiar *stability* of the executive power of the British Crown; and especially a much more complete delineation of the advantages that result from the stability in favour of public liberty †.

* A certain Book written in French, on the subject of the American disputes, was, I have been told, lately attributed to me, in which I had no share.

† For the sake of those Readers who like exactly to know in what one Edition of a book differs from another, I shall mention, that three new pages have also been added in the xviith Chapter, besides a few short notes in the course of the Work.

Thefe advantages may be enumerated as follows. I. The numerous reftraints the governing authority is able to bear, and extenfive freedom it can afford to allow the Subject, at its expence. II. The liberty of fpeaking and writing, carried to the great extent it is in England. III. The unbounded freedom of the Debates in the Legiflature. IV. The power to bear the conftant union of all orders of Subjects againft its prerogative. V. The freedom allowed to all individuals to take an active part in Government concerns. VI. The ftrict impartiality with which Juftice is dealt to all Subjects, without any refpect whatever of perfons. VII. The lenity of the criminal law, both in regard to the mildnefs of punifhments, and the frequent remitting of them. VIII. The ftrict compliance of the governing Authority with the letter of the law. IX. The needleffnefs of an armed force to fupport itfelf by, and as a confequence, the fingular fubjection of the Military to the Civil power.

The above-mentioned advantages are peculiar to the Englifh Government. To attempt to imitate them, or transfer them into other Countries, with that degree of extent to which they are carried in England, without at the fame time transferring the whole order and conjunction of circumftances in the Englifh Government, would prove unfuccefsful attempts. Several articles of Englifh liberty already appear impracticable to be preferved in the new American Commonwealths. The Irifh Nation have of late fucceeded to imitate feveral very important regulations in the Englifh Government, and are very defirous to render the affimilation complete: yet, it is poffible, they will find many inconveniences to arife from their endeavours, which do not take place in England, notwithftanding the very great general fimilarity of circumftances in the two kingdoms in many refpects, and even alfo, we might add, notwithftanding the refpectable power and weight the Crown derives from its Britifh dominions, both for defending its prerogative in Ireland, and preventing anarchy. I fay, the fimilarity in *many respects* between the two kingdoms; for this resemblance may perhaps fail in regard to some important points: however, this is a subject about which I shall not attempt to say any thing, not having the necessary information.

The last Chapter in the Work, concerning the nature of the *Divisions that take place in this Country*, I have left in every English Edition as I wrote it at first in French. With respect to the exact manner of the Debates in Parliament, mentioned in that Chapter, I should not be able to say more at present than I was at that time, as I never had an opportunity to hear the Debates in either House. In regard to the Divisions in general to which the spirit of party gives rise, I did perhaps the bulk of the People somewhat more honour than they really deserve, when I represented them as being free from any violent dispositions in that respect: I have since found, that, like the bulk of Mankind in all Countries, they suffer themselves to be influenced by vehement prepositions for this or that side of public questions, commonly in proportion as their knowledge of the subjects is imperfect. It is however a fact, that their political prepossessions and party spirit are not productive in this Country, of those dangerous consequences which might be feared from the warmth with which they are sometimes manifested. But this subject, or in general the subject of the political quarrels and divisions in the country, is not an article one may venture to meddle with in a single Chapter; I have therefore let this subsist, without touching it.

I shall however observe, before I conclude, that there is an accidental circumstance in the English Government, which prevents the party spirit by which the Public are usually influenced, from producing those lasting and rancorous divisions in the Community which have pestered so many other free States, making of the same Nation as it were two distinct People, in a kind of constant warfare with each other. The circumstance I mean, is, the fre-

quent reconciliations (commonly to quarrel again after-
ward) that take place between the Leaders of parties, by
which the moſt violent and ignorant Claſs of their parti-
ſans are bewildered, and made to loſe the ſcent. By
the frequent coalitions between *Whig* and *Tory* Leaders,
even that party diſtinction, the moſt famous in the Engliſh Hiſtory, has now become uſeleſs : the meaning of
the words has thereby been rendered ſo perplexed that
nobody can any longer give a tolerable definition of them ;
and thoſe perſons who now and then aim at gaining popularity by claiming the merit of belonging to either
party, are ſcarcely underſtood. The late *Coalition* between
two certain Leaders has done away and prevented from
ſettling, that violent party ſpirit to which the adminiſtration of Lord Bute had given riſe, and which the American diſputes had carried ſtill farther. Though this
Coalition has met with much obloquy, I take the liberty
to rank myſelf in the number of its advocates, ſo far as
the circumſtance here mentioned.

May, 1784.

THE

CONSTITUTION

OF

ENGLAND.

INTRODUCTION.

THE spirit of Philosophy which peculiarly distinguishes the present age, after having corrected a number of errors fatal to Society, seems now to be directed towards the principles of Society itself; and we see prejudices vanish, which are difficult to overcome, in proportion as it is dangerous to attack them *. This rising freedom of sentiment, the necessary fore-runner of political freedom, led me to imagine that it would not be unacceptable to the Public, to be made acquainted with the principles of a Constitution on which the eye of curiosity seems now to be universally turned; and which, though celebrated

* As every popular notion which may contribute to the support of an arbitrary Government, is at all times vigilantly protected by the whole strength of it, political prejudices, are, last of all, if ever, shaken off by a nation subjected to such a Government. A great change in this respect, however, has of late taken place in France, where this book was first published, and opinions are now discussed there, and tenets avowed, which, in the time of Lewis the Fourteenth, would have appeared downright blasphemy; it is to this an allusion is made above.

D

as a model of perfection, is yet but little known to its admirers.

I am aware that it will be deemed presumptuous in a Man who has passed the greatest part of his life out of England, to attempt a delineation of the English Government ; a system which is supposed to be so complicated as not to be understood or developed, but by those who have been initiated in the mysteries of it from their infancy.

But, though a foreigner in England, yet, as a native of a free Country, I am no stranger to those circumstances which constitute or Characterise Liberty. Even the great disproportion between the Republic of which I am a member, and in which I formed my principles, and the British Empire, has perhaps only contributed to facilitate my political inquiries.

As the Mathematician, the better to discover the proportions he investigates, begins with freeing his *equation* from *coefficients*, or such other quantities as only perplex without properly constituting it,—so it may be advantageous to the inquirer after the causes that produce the equilibrium of a government, to have previously studied them, disengaged from the apparatus of fleets, armies, foreign trade, distant and extensive dominions ; in a word, from all those brilliant circumstances which so greatly affect the external appearance of a powerful Society, but have no essential connection with the real principles of it.

It is upon the passions of Mankind, that is, upon causes which are unalterable, that the action of the various parts of a state depends. The machine may vary as to its dimensions, but its movement and acting springs still remain intrinsically the same ; and that time cannot be considered as lost, which has been spent in seeing them act and move in a narrower circle.

One other consideration I will suggest, which is, that the very circumstance of being a foreigner, may of itself be attended, in this case, with a degree of advantage. The English themselves (the observation cannot give them any offence) having their eyes open, as I may say, upon their liberty, from their firſt entrance into life, are perhaps too much familiarifed with its enjoyment, to inquire, with real concern, into its caufes. Having acquired practical notions of their government, long before they have meditated on it, and thefe notions being flowly and gradually imbibed, they at length behold it without any high degree of fenfibility; and they feem to me, in this refpect, to be like the recluſe inhabitant of a palace, who is perhaps in the worſt fituation for attaining a complete idea of the whole, and never experienced the ſtriking effect of its external ſtructure and elevation; or, if you pleafe, like a Man who, having always had a beautiful and extenſive fcene before his eyes, continues for ever to view it with indifference.

But a ſtranger, beholding at once the various parts of a Conſtitution difplayed before him, which, at the fame time that it carries liberty to its height, has guarded againſt inconveniences feemingly inevitable, beholding in ſhort thoſe things carried into execution, which he had ever regarded as more defirable than poffible, he is ſtruck with a kind of admiration; and it is neceffary to be thus ſtrongly affected by objects, to be enabled to reach the general principle which governs them.

Not that I mean to infinuate that I have penetrated with more acutenefs into the Conſtitution of England than others; my only defign in the above obfervations, was to obviate an unfavourable, though natural, prepoffeffion; and if, either in treating of the caufes which originally produced the Englifh liberty, or of thofe by which it continues to be maintained, my obfervations ſhould be found new or fingular, I hope the Englifh reader will not condemn them, but where they ſhall be found inconfiftent with Hiſtory, or with daily experience. Of readers in general I alfo requeft, that they will not judge of the principles I ſhall lay down, but from their relation to thofe of human nature: a confideration which is almoſt the only one effential, and has been hitherto too much neglected by the Writers on the fubject of Government.

CHAP. I.

Caufes of the liberty of the Englifh Nation.—Reafons of the difference between the Government of England, and that of France.—In England, the great power of the Crown under the Norman Kings, created an union between the Nobility and the People.

WHEN the Romans, attacked on all fides by the Barbarians, were reduced to the neceffity of defending the centre of their Empire, they abandoned Great Britain as well as feveral other of their diftant provinces. The ifland, thus left to itfelf, became a prey to the Nations inhabiting the fhores of the Baltic ; who, having firft deftroyed the ancient inhabitants, and for a long time reciprocally annoyed each other, eftablifhed feveral Sovereignties in the fouthern part of the Ifland, afterwards called England, which at length were united, under Egbert, into one Kingdom.

The fucceffors of this Prince, denominated the Anglo-Saxon Princes, among whom Alfred the Great and Edward the Confeffor are particularly celebrated, reigned for about two hundred years ; but, though our knowledge of the principal events of this early period of the Englifh Hiftory is in fome degree exaft, yet we have but vague and uncertain accounts of the nature of the Government which thofe nations introduced.

It appears to have had little more affinity with the prefent Conftitution, than the general relation, common indeed to all the Governments eftablifhed by the Northern Nations, that of having a King and a Body of Nobility ; and the ancient Saxon Government is "left us in ftory (to ufe the expreffions of Sir William Temple on the fubject) " but like fo many antique, broken, or defaced pictures, " which may ftill reprefent fomething of the cuftoms and " fafhions of thofe ages, though little of the true lines, pro- " portions, or refemblance *."

* See his Introduction to the Hiftory of England.

It is at the era of the Conquest, that we are to look for the real foundation of the English Constitution. From that period, says Spelman, *novus seclorum nascitur ordo* *. William of Normandy, having defeated Harold, and made himself master of the Crown, subverted the ancient fabric of the Saxon Legislation : he exterminated, or expelled, the former occupiers of lands, in order to distribute their possessions among his followers ; and established the feudal system of Government, as better adapted to his situation, and indeed the only one of which he possessed a competent idea.

* See Spelman, *Of Parliaments.*—It has been a favourite thesis with many Writers, to pretend that the Saxon Government was, at the time of the Conquest, by no means subverted ; that William of Normandy legally acceded to the Throne, and consequently to the engagements of the Saxon Kings; and much argument has in particular been employed with regard to the word *Conquest,* which, it has been said, in the feudal sense only meant *acquisition.* These opinions have been particularly insisted upon in times of popular opposition : and, indeed, there was a far greater probability of success, in raising among the People the notions familiar to them of legal claims and long established customs, than in arguing with them from the no less rational, but less determinate, and somewhat dangerous doctrines, concerning the original rights of Mankind, and the lawfulness of at all times opposing force to an oppressive Government.

But if we consider that the manner in which the public Power is formed into a State, is so very essential a part of its Government, and that a thorough change in this respect was introduced into England by the Conquest, we shall not scruple to allow that a new *Government* was established. Nay, as almost the whole landed property in the Kingdom was at that time transferred to other hands, a new system of criminal Justice introduced, and the language of the law moreover altered, the revolution may be said to have been such as is not perhaps to be paralleled in the History of any other country.

Some Saxon laws, favourable to the liberty of the people, were indeed again established under the successors of William ;

This sort of Government prevailed also in almost all the other parts of Europe. But instead of being established by dint of arms and all at once, as in England, it had only been established on the Continent, and particularly in France, through a long series of slow successive events; a difference of circumstances this, from which consequences were in time to arise, as important as they were at first difficult to be foreseen.

The German Nations who passed the Rhine to conquer Gaul, were in a great degree independent. Their princes had no other title to their power, but their own valour and the free election of the People; and as the latter had acquired in their forests but contracted notions of sove-

but the introduction of some new modes of proceeding in the Courts of Justice, and of a few particular laws, cannot, so long as the ruling Power in the State remains the same, be said to be the introduction of a new Government; and as when the laws in question were again established, the public power in England continued in the same channel where the Conquest has placed it, they were more properly new modifications of the Anglo-Norman Constitution, than they were the abolition of it; or since they were again adopted from the Saxon Legislation, they were rather imitations of that Legislation, than the restoration of the Saxon Government.

Contented, however, with the two authorities I have above quoted, (*Spelman* and *Temple*,) I shall dwell no longer on a discussion of the precise identity, or difference, of two Governments, that is of two ideal systems, which only exist in the conceptions of men. Nor do I wish to explode a doctrine, which, in the opinion of some persons, giving an additional sanction and dignity to the English Government, contributes to increase their love and respect for it. It will be sufficient for my purpose, if the reader shall be pleased to grant that a material change was, at the time of the Conquest, effected in the government then existing, and is accordingly disposed to admit the proofs that will presently be laid before him, of such change having prepared the establishment of the present English Constitution.

reign authority, they followed a chief, lefs· in quality of fubjects, than as companions in conqueft.

Befides, this conqueft was not the irruption of a foreign army, which only takes poffeffion of fortified towns. It was the general invafion of a whole People, in fearch of new habitations; and as the number of the conquerors bore a great proportion to that of the conquered, who were at the fame time enervated by long peace, the expedition was no fooner completed than all danger was at an end, and of courfe their union alfo. After dividing among themfelves what lands they thought proper to occupy, they feparated; and though their tenure was at firft only precarious, yet in this particular, they depended not on the king, but on the general affembly of the nation *.

Under the kings of *the firft race*, the fiefs, by the mutual connivance of the Leaders, at firft became annual; afterwards, held for life. Under the defcendants of Charlemain, they became hereditary †. And when at length Hugh Capet effected his own election to the prejudice of Charles of Lorrain, and intended to render the Crown, which in fact was a fief, hereditary in his own family ‡. he eftablifhed the hereditarifhip of fiefs as a general principle; and from this epoch, authors date the complete eftablifhment of the feudal fyftem in France.

On the other hand, the Lords, who gave their fuffrages to Hugh Capet, forgot not the intereft of their own ambition. They completed the breach of thofe feeble ties which fubjected them to the royal authority, and be-

---

* The fiefs were originally called, *terræ jure beneficii conceffæ;* and it was not till under Charles *le Gros* the term *fief* began to be in ufe. See BENEFICIUM, *Gloff. Du Cange.*

† *Apud Francos vero, fenfim pedetentimque, jure hæreditario ad hæredes tranfierunt feuda; quod labente fæculo nono incipis.* See FEUDUM—Du Cange.

‡ Hottoman has proved beyond a doubt, in his *Francogallia*, that under the two firft races of Kings, the Crown of France was elective. The Princes of the reigning family had nothing more in their favour, than the cuftom of chufing one of that houfe.

came every where independent. They left the king no jurisdiction either over themselves, or their vassals; they reserved the right of waging war with each other; they even assumed the same privilege, in certain cases, with regard to the king himself*; so that if Hugh Capet, by rendering the Crown hereditary, laid the foundation of the greatness of his family, and of the Crown itself, yet he added little to his own authority, and acquired scarcely any thing more than a nominal superiority over the number of Sovereigns who then swarmed in France †.

But the establishment of the feudal system in England, was an immediate and sudden consequence of that conquest which introduced it. Besides, this conquest was made by a Prince who kept the greater part of his army in his own pay, and who was placed at the head of a people over whom he was an hereditary Sovereign : circumstances which gave a totally different turn to the government of that kingdom.

Surrounded by a warlike though a conquered Nation, William kept on foot part of his army. The English,

---

* The principal of these cases was, when the King refused to appoint Judges to decide a difference between himself and one of his first Barons : the latter had then a right to take up arms against the King; and the subordinate Vassals were so dependent on their immediate Lords, that they were obliged to follow them against the Lord Paramount. St. Louis, though the power of the Crown was in his time much increased, was obliged to confirm both this privilege of the first Barons, and this obligation of their Vassals. -

† " The Grandees of the Kingdom," says Mezeray, " thought that Hugh Capet ought to put up with all their " insults, because they had placed the Crown on his head : " nay, so great was their licentiousness, that on his writ- " ing to Audebert, Viscount of Perigueux, ordering him to " raise the siege he had laid to Tours, and asking him, by " way of reproach, who had made him a Viscount? that " Nobleman haughtily answered, *Not you, but those who* " *made you a King.* [Non pas vous, mais ceux qui vous ont " fait Roi.]"

and after them the Normans themselves, having revolted, he crushed both; and the new King of England,
at the head of victorious troops, having to do with two
Nations lying under a reciprocal check from the enmity
they bore to each other, and moreover equally subdued
by a sense of their unfortunate attempts of resistance,
found himself in the most favourable circumstances for
becoming an absolute Monarch; and his laws, thus pro-
mulgated in the midst as it were of thunder and lightning,
imposed the yoke of despotism both on the victors and the
vanquished.

He divided England into sixty thousand two hundred
and fifteen military fiefs, all held of the Crown; the pos-
sessors of which were, on pain of forfeiture, to take up
arms and repair to his standard on the first signal: he subjected not only the common people, but even the Barons,
to all the rigours of the feudal Government: he even imposed on them his tyrannical forest laws *.

He assumed the prerogative of imposing taxes. He
invested himself with the whole executive power of Government. But what was of the greatest consequence,
he arrogated to himself the most extensive judicial power
by the establishment of the Court which was called *Aula
Regis;* a formidable tribunal, which received appeals from
all the courts of the Barons, and decided in the last resort
on the estates, honour, and lives of the Barons themselves;
and which, being wholly composed of the great officers of
the Crown, removable at the King's pleasure, and having
the King himself for President, kept the first Nobleman
in the Kingdom under the same controul as the meanest
subject.

* * *

  * He reserved to himself an exclusive privilege of killing
game throughout England, and enacted the severest penalties
on all who should attempt it without his permission. The
suppression, or rather mitigation of these penalties, was one
of the articles of the *Charta de Foresta,* which the Barons afterwards obtained by force of arms. *Nullus de catero amittat vi-
tam, vel membra, pro venatione nostra.* Ch. de Forest. Art. 10.

Thus, while the kingdom of France, in confequence of the flow and gradual formation of the feudal government, found itfelf, in the iffue, compofed of a number of parts fimply placed by each other, and without any reciprocal adherence, the Kingdom of England on the contrary, in confequence of the fudden and violent introduction of the fame fyftem, became a compound of parts united by the ftrongeft ties, and the regal authority, by the preffure of its immenfe weight, confolidated the whole into one compact indiffoluble body.

To this difference in the original Conftitution of France and England, that is, in the original power of their Kings, we are to attribute the difference, fo little analogous to its original caufe, of their prefent Conftitutions. This it is which furnifhes the folution of a problem which, I muft confefs, for a long time perplexed me, and explains the reafon why, of two neighbouring Nations, fituated almoft under the fame climate, and having one common origin, the one has attained the fummit of liberty, the other has gradually funk under an abfolute Monarchy.

In France, the Royal authority was indeed inconfiderable; but this circumftance was by no means favourable to the general liberty. The Lords were every thing: and the bulk of the Nation were accounted nothing. All thofe wars which were made on the King, had not liberty for their object; for of this the Chiefs already enjoyed but too great a fhare: they were the mere effect of private ambition or caprice. The people did not engage in them as affociates in the fupport of a caufe common to all: they were dragged, blindfold and like flaves, to the ftandard of their leaders. In the mean time, as the laws by virtue of which their Mafters were confidered as Vaffals, had no relation to thofe by which they were themfelves bound as fubjects, the refiftance of which they were made the inftruments, never produced any advantageous confequences in their favour, nor did it eftablifh any principle of freedom that was in any cafe applicable to them

The inferior Nobles, who fhared in the independence of

the superior Nobility, added also the effects of their own
insolence to the despotism of so many Sovereigns; and
the people, wearied out by sufferings, and rendered desperate by oppression, at times attempted to revolt.   But
being parcelled out in so many different States, they could
never perfectly agree, either in the nature, or the times of
their complaints.   The insurrections, which ought to
have been general, were only successive and particular.
In the mean time the Lords, ever uniting to avenge their
common cause as Masters, fell with irresistible advantage
on Men who were divided; the People were thus separately, and by force, brought back to their former yoke;
and Liberty, that precious offspring, which requires so
many favourable circumstances to foster it, was every
where stifled in its birth *.

At length, when by conquests, by escheats, or by Treaties, the several Provinces came to be *re-united* † to the

* It may be seen in Mezeray, how the Flemings, at the
time of the great revolt which was caused, as he says, " by
" the inveterate hatred of the Nobles, (les Gentils-hommes)
" against the people of Ghent," were crushed by the union
of almost all the Nobility of France.—See *Mezeray, Reign of
Charles* VI.

† The word *re-union* expresses in the French law, or
History, the reduction of a Province to an immediate dependence on the Crown.   The French lawyers who were
at all times remarkably zealous for the aggrandisement of
the Crown (a zeal which would not have been blameable, if
it had been exerted only in the suppression of lawless Aristocracy,) always contended that when a province once came
into the possession of the King, even any private dominion of
his before he acceded to the Throne, it became *re-united* for
ever: the *Ordonnance* of Moulins, in the year 1566, has since
given a thorough sanction to these Principles.   The re-
union of a province might be occasioned, first, by the case
just mentioned, of the accession of the possessor of it to the
throne: thus at the accession of Henry IV. (the sister of the
late King being excluded by the Salic law) Navarre and

extensive and continually increasing dominions of the Monarch, they became subject to their new Master, already trained to obedience. The few privileges which the Cities had been able to preserve, were little respected by a Sovereign who had himself entered into no engagement for that purpose; and as the *re-unions* were made at different times, the King was always in a condition to overwhelm every new Province that accrued to him, with the weight of all those he already possessed.

Bearn were *re-united*. Secondly, by the felony of the possessor when the King was able to force by dint of arms, the judgment passed by the Judges he had appointed: thus the small Lordship of Rambouillet was seized upon by Hugh Capet; on which authors remark that it was the first dominion that was re-united: and the duchy of Normandy was afterwards taken in the same manner by Philip Augustus from John King of England, condemned for the murder of Arthur Duke of Britanny. Thirdly, by the last will of the possessor: Provence was re-united in this manner, under the reign of Lewis XI. Fourthly, by inter-marriages; this was the case of the county of Champagne, under Philip the Fair; and of Britanny under Francis I. Fifthly, by the failure of heirs of the blood, and sometimes of heirs male: thus Burgundy was seized upon by Lewis XI. after the death of Charles the Bold, Duke of that Province. Lastly, by purchases: thus Philip of Valois purchased the Barony of Montpellier; Henry IV. the Marquisat of Saluces; Lewis XIII. the principality of Sedan, &c.

These different Provinces, which with others united, or *re-united*, after a like manner, now compose the French Monarchy, not only thus conferred on their respective Sovereigns different titles, but also differed from each other with respect to the laws which they followed, and still follow: the one are governed by the Roman law, and are called *Pays de Droit ecrit*; the others follow particular customs, which in process of time have been set down in writing, and are called *Pays de Droit Coutumier*. In those Provinces the people had, at times, purchased privileges from their Princes, which in the different Provinces were also different, according to the wants and temper of the Princes who granted them.

As a farther confequence of thefe differences between the times of the *re-unions*, the feveral parts of the kingdom entertained no views of affifting each other. When fome reclaimed their privileges, the others, long fince reduced to fubjection, had already forgotten theirs. Befides, thefe privileges, by reafon of the differences of the Governments under which the Provinces had formerly been held, were alfo almoft every where different : the circumftances which happened in one place, thus bore little affinity to thofe which fell out in another : the fpirit of union was loft, or rather had never exifted : each Province, reftrained within its particular bounds, only ferved to infure the general fubmiffion ; and the fame caufes which had reduced that warlike, fpirited Nation, to a yoke of fubjection, concurred alfo to keep them under it.

Thus Liberty perifhed in France, becaufe it wanted a favourable culture and proper fituation. Planted, if I may fo exprefs myfelf, but juft beneath the furface, it prefently expanded, and fent forth fome large fhoots ; but having taken no root, it was foon plucked up. In England, on the contrary, the feed lying at a great depth, and being covered with an enormous weight, feemed at firft to be fmothered ; but it vegetated with the greater force; it imbibed a more rich and abundant nourifhment ; its fap and juice became better affimulated, and it penetrated and filled up with its roots the whole body of the foil. It was the exceffive power of the King which made England free, becaufe it was this very excefs that gave rife to the fpirit of union, and of concerted refiftance. Poffeffed of extenfive demefnes, the King found himfelf independent ; vefted with the moft formidable prerogatives, he crufhed at pleafure the moft powerful Barons in the Realm : it was only by clofe and numerous confederacies therefore, that thefe could refift his tyranny ; they even were compelled to affociate the People in them, and make them partners of public Liberty.

Affembled with their Vaffals in their great Halls, where they difpenfed their hofpitality, deprived of the amufe-

ments of more polished Nations, naturally inclined, besides, freely to expatiate on objects of which their hearts
were full, their conversation naturally turned on the injustice of the public impositions, on the tyranny of the
judicial proceedings, and, above all, on the detested forest
laws.

Destitute of an opportunity of cavilling about the
meaning of laws, the terms of which were precise, or rather disdaining the resource of sophistry, they were naturally led to examine into the first principles of Society;
they enquired into the foundations of human authority,
and became convinced, that Power, when its object is not
the good of those who are subject to it, is nothing more
than the *right of the strongest*, and may be repressed by
the exertion of a similar right.

The different orders of the feudal Government, as established in England, being connected by tenures exactly
similar, the same maxims which were laid down as true a-
gainst the Lord paramount in behalf of the Lord of an
upper fief, were likewise to be admitted against the latter,
in behalf of the owner of an inferior fief. The same
maxims were also to be applied to the possessor of a still
lower fief: they farther descended to the freemen, and to
the peasant; and the spirit of liberty, after having circu-
lated through the different branches of the feudal subordina-
tion, thus continued to flow through successive homoge-
neous channels; it forced a passage to itself into the re-
motest ramifications, and the principle of primeval equality every where diffused and established. A sacred principle, which neither injustice nor ambition can erase;
which exists in every breast, and, to exert itself, requires
only to be wakened among the numerous and oppressed
classes of Mankind.

But when the Barons, whom their personal consequence had at first caused to be treated with caution and
regard by the Sovereign, began to be no longer so, when
the tyrannical laws of the Conqueror became still more
tyrannically executed, the confederacy, for which the ge-

neral oppreſſion had paved the way, inſtantly took place. The Lord, the Vaſſal, the inferior Vaſſal, all united. They even implored the affiſtance of the peaſants and cottagers; and that haughty averſion with which on the Continent the Nobility repaid the induſtrious hands which fed them, was, in England, compelled to yield to the preſſing neceſſity of ſetting bounds to the Royal authority.

The People, on the other hand, knew that the cauſe they were called upon to defend, was a cauſe common to all; and they were ſenſible, beſides, that they were the neceſſary ſupporters of it. Inſtructed by the example of their Leaders, they ſpoke and ſtipulated conditions for themſelves: they inſiſted that, for the future, every individual ſhould be intitled to the protection of the law; and thus did thoſe rights with which the Lords had ſtrengthened themſelves, in order to oppoſe the tyranny of the Crown, became a bulwark which was, in time, to reſtrain their own.

⸦⸦⸦⸦⸦⸦⸦⸦⸦⸦✦✦✦⸧⸧⸧⸧⸧⸧⸧⸧⸧⸧⸧

C H A P. II.

A ſecond advantage England had over France :—it formed one undivided State.

IT was in the reign of Henry the firſt, about forty years after the Conqueſt, that we ſee the above cauſes begin to operate. This Prince having aſcended the throne to the excluſion of his elder brother, was ſenſible that he had no other means to maintain his power than by gaining the affection of his ſubjects; but, at the ſame time, he perceived that it muſt be the affection of the whole nation: he, therefore, not only mitigated the rigour of the feudal laws in favour of the Lords, but alſo annexed as a condition to the Charter he granted, that the Lords ſhould allow the ſame freedom to their reſpective Vaſſals. Care was even taken to aboliſh thoſe laws of the Conqueror which lay heavieſt on the lower claſſes of the People *.

* Amongſt others, the law of the *Curfeu.* It might be

Under Henry the fecond, liberty took a farther ftride; and the ancient *Trial by Jury*, a mode of procedure which is at prefent one of the moft valuable parts of the Englifh law, made again, though imperfectly, its appearance.

But thefe caufes, which had worked but filently and flowly under the two Henrys, who were Princes in fome degree juft, and of great capacity, manifefted themfelves, at once, under the defpotic reign of King John. The royal prerogative, and the foreft laws, having been exerted by this Prince to a degree of exceffive feverity, he foon beheld a general confederacy formed againft him : and here we muft obferve another circumftance, highly advantageous, as well as peculiar to England.

England was not, like France, an aggregation of a number of different Sovereignties : it formed but one State, and acknowledged but one Mafter, one general title. The fame laws, the fame kind of dependence, confequently the fame notions, the fame interefts, prevailed throughout the whole. The extremities of the kingdom could, at all times, unite to give a check to the exertions of an unjuft power. From the river Tweed to Portfmouth, from Yarmouth to the Land's End, all was in motion : the agitation increafed from the diftance like the rolling waves of an extenfive fea ; and the Monarch, left to himfelf, and deftitute of refources, faw himfelf attacked on all fides by an univerfal combination of his fubjects.

matter of curious difcuffion to inquire what the Anglo-Saxon Government would in procefs of time have become, and of courfe the Government of England be at this prefent time, if the event of the Conqueft had never taken place ; which, by conferring an immenfe as well as unufual power on the head of the feudal Syftem, compelled the Nobility to contract a lafting and fincere union with the People. It is very probable that the Englifh Government would at this day be the fame as that which long prevailed in Scotland, where the King and Nobles engroffed, jointly, or by turns, the whole power in the State, the fame as in Sweden, the fame as in Denmark, countries whence the Anglo-Saxons came.

No sooner was the standard set up against John, than his very Courtiers forsook him. In this situation, finding no part of his kingdom less irritated against him than a-nother, having no detached province which he could engage in his defence by promises of pardon, or of peculiar concessions, the trivial though never-failing resources of Government, he was compelled with seven of his attendants, all that remained with him, to submit himself to the disposal of his subjects; and he signed at Runing Mead * the Charter of the forest, together with that famous Charter, which, from its superior and extensive importance, is denominated *Magna Charta.*

By the former, the most tyrannical part of the forest laws was abolished; and by the latter, the rigour of the feudal laws was greatly mitigated in favour of the Lords. But this Charter did not stop there; conditions were also stipulated in favour of the numerous body of the people who had concurred to obtain it, and who claimed, with sword in hand, a share in that security it was meant to e-stablish. It was hence instituted by the Great Charter, that the same services which were remitted in favour of the Barons, should be in like manner remitted in favour of their Vassals. This Charter moreover established an equality of weights and measures throughout England; it exempted the Merchants from arbitrary imposts, and gave them liberty to enter and depart the Kingdom at pleasure; it even extended to the lowest orders of the State, since it enacted, that the *Villain*, or Bondman, should not be sub-ject to the forfeiture of his implements of tillage. Last-ly, by the twenty-ninth article of the same Charter, it was enacted, that no subject should be exiled, or in any shape whatever molested, either in his person or effects, otherwise than by judgment of his peers, and according to the law of the land †: an article so important, that it may be said

* Anno 1215.

† " Nullus liber homo capiatur, vel imprisonetur, vel dif- " sesietur de libero tenemento suo, vel libertatibus, vel libe-

to comprehend the whole end and design of political societies ; and from that moment the English would have been a free People, if there were not an immense distance between the making of laws, and the observing of them.

But though this Charter wanted most of those supports which were necessary to insure respect to it, though it did not secure to the poor and friendless any certain and legal methods of obtaining the execution of it (provisions which numberless transgressions alone could, in process of time, point out,) yet it was a prodigious advance towards the establishment of public liberty. Instead of the general maxims respecting the rights of the People and the duties of the Prince (maxims against which ambition perpetually contends, and which it sometimes even openly and absolutely denies,) here was substituted a written law, that is, a truth admitted by all parties, which no longer required the support of argument. The rights and privileges of the individual, as well in his person as in his property, became settled axioms. The Great Charter, at first enacted with so much solemnity, and afterwards confirmed at the beginning of every succeeding reign, became like a general banner perpetually set up for the union of all classes of the people ; and the foundation was laid on which those equitable laws were to rise, which offer the same assistance to the poor and weak, as to the rich and powerful *.

" ris confuetudinibus fuis ; aut utlagetur, aut exuletur, aut
" aliquo modo deftruatur ; nec fuper eum ibimus, nec fuper
" eum mittemus, nifi per legale judicium parium fuorum, vel
" per legem terræ. Nulli vendemus, nulli negabimus, aut
" differemus, juftitiam vel rectum." *Magna Chart.* cap. xxix.

* The reader, to be more fully convinced of the reality of the causes to which the liberty of England has been ascribed, as well as to the truth of the observations made at the same time on the situation of the people of France, needs only to compare the Great Charter, so extensive in its provisions, and in which the Barons stipulated in favour even of the Bondmen, with the treaty concluded between Lewis the

Under the long reign of Henry the Third, the differ-ences which arose between the King and the Nobles, rendered England a scene of confusion. Amidst the vicissitudes which the fortune of war produced in their mutual conflicts the people became still more and more sensible of their importance, and so did in consequence both the King and the Barons also. Alternately courted by both parties, they obtained a confirmation of the Great Charter, and even the addition of new privileges, by the statutes of Merton and of Marlebridge. But I hasten to reach the grand epoch of the reign of Edward the First; a Prince, who, from his numerous and prudent laws, has been denominated the English Justinian.

Possessed of great natural talents, and succeeding a Prince whose weakness and injustice had rendered his reign unhappy, Edward was sensible that nothing but a strict administration of justice, could, on the one side, curb a Nobility whom the troubles of the preceding reign had rendered turbulent, and, on the other, appease and conciliate the people, by securing the property of individuals. To this end, he made jurisprudence the principal object of his attention; and so much did it improve under his care, that the mode of process became fixed and settled; Judge Hale going even so far as to affirm, that the English laws arrived at once, *& quasi per saltum*, at perfection, and that there has been more improvement made in them

Eleventh and several of the Princes and Peers of France, intitled, *A Treaty made at St. Maur, between the Dukes of Normandy, Calabre, Bretagne, Bourbonnois, Auvergne, Nemours; the Counts of Charolois, Armagnac, and St. Pol, and other Princes of France, risen up in support of the public good, of the one part; and King Lewis the Eleventh of the other,* October 29, 1465. In this Treaty, which was made in order to terminate a war that was called the war for the Public good *(pro bono Publico,)* no provision was made but concerning the particular power of a few Lords: not a word was inserted in favour of the people. This treaty may be seen at large in the *pieces justificatives* annexed to the *Memoires de Philippe de Comines.*

during the *first* thirteen years of the reign of Edward, than all the ages since his time have done.

But what renders this æra particularly interesting, is, that it affords the first instance of the admission of the Deputies of Towns and Boroughs into * Parliament.

Edward, continually engaged in wars, either against Scotland or on the Continent, seeing moreover his demesnes considerably diminished, was frequently reduced to the most pressing necessities. But though, in consequence of the spirit of the times, he frequently indulged himself in particular acts of injustice, yet he perceived that it was impossible to extend a general oppression over a body of Nobles, and a People, who so well knew how to unite in a common cause. In order to raise subsidies, therefore, he was obliged to employ a new method, and to endeavour to obtain through the consent of the people, what his Predecessors had hitherto expected from their own power. The sheriffs were ordered to invite the Towns and Boroughs of the different Counties to send Deputies to Parliament; and it is from this æra that we are to date the origin of the House of Commons †.

It must be confessed, however, that these Deputies of the People were not at first, possessed of any considerable authority. They were far from enjoying those extensive privileges which, in these days, constitute the House of Commons a collateral part of the Government: they were in those times called up only to provide for the wants of the King, and approve of the resolutions taken by him and the assembly of the Lords ‡. But it was ne-

* I mean their legal origin; for the Earl of Leicester, who had usurped the power during part of the preceding reign, had called such Deputies up to Parliament before.

† Anno 1295.

‡ The end mentioned in the Summons sent to the Lords, was *de arduis negotiis regni tractaturi, & consilium impensuri:* the Summons sent to the Commons was, *ad faciendum & consentiendum.* The power enjoyed by the latter was even inferior to what they might have expected from the Summons

verthelefs a great point gained, to have obtained the right
of uttering their complaints, affembled in a body and in a
legal way—to have acquired, inftead of the dangerous refource of infurrections, a lawful and regular mean of influencing the motions of the Government, and thenceforth to have become a part of it.   Whatever difadvantage might attend the ftation at firft allotted to the Reprefentatives of the People, it was foon to be compenfated
by the preponderance the People neceffarily acquire,
when they are enabled to act and move with method, and
efpecially with concert *.

And indeed this privilege of naming Reprefentatives,
infignificant as it might then appear, prefently manifefted
itfelf by the moft confiderable effects.   In fpite of his
reluctance, and after many evafions unworthy of fo great a
King, Edward was obliged to confirm the Great Charter ;
he even confirmed it eleven times in the courfe of his
reign.   It was moreover enacted, that whatever fhould
be done contrary to it, fhould be null and void ; that it
fhould be read twice a year in all Cathedrals ; and that
the penalty of excommunication fhould be denounced

fent to them : " In moft of the ancient Statutes they are not
" fo much as named ; and in feveral, even when they are
" mentioned, they are diftinguifhed as petitioners merely;
" the Affent of the Lords being expreffed in contradiftinc-
" tion to the Requeft of the Commons."   See on this fubject the Preface to the Collection of the Statutes at Large, by
Ruffhead, and the authorities quoted therein.

* France had indeed alfo her affemblies of the General
Eftates of the Kingdom, in the fame manner as England had
her Parliament ; but then it was only the Deputies of the
Towns within the particular domain of the Crown, that is,
for a very fmall part of the Nation, who, under the name of
the *Third Eftate,* were admitted in thofe Eftates ; and it is
eafy to conceive that they acquired no great influence in an
affembly of Sovereigns who gave the law to their Lord Paramount.   Hence, when thefe difappeared, the maxim became immediately eftablifhed, *The will of the King is the will
of the Law.*   In old French, *Qui veut le Roy, fi veut la Loy.*

againſt any one who ſhould preſume to violate it *.

At length he converted into an eſtabliſhed law, a privilege of which the Engliſh had hitherto had only a precarious enjoyment; and in the ſtatute *de Tallagio non concedendo*, he decreed, that no tax ſhould be laid, nor impoſt levied, without the joint conſent of the Lords and Commons †. A moſt important Statute this, which, in conjunction with Magna Charta, forms the baſis of the Engliſh Conſtitution. If from the latter the Engliſh are to date the origin of their liberty, from the former they are to date the eſtabliſhment of it; and as the Great Charter was the bulwark that protected the freedom of individuals, ſo was the Statute in queſtion the engine which protected the Charter itſelf, and by the help of which the People were thenceforth to make legal conqueſts over the authority of the Crown.

This is the period at which we muſt ſtop in order to take a diſtant view, and contemplate the different proſpects which the reſt of Europe then preſented.

The efficient cauſes of ſlavery were daily operating and gaining ſtrength. The independence of the Nobles on the one hand, the ignorance and weakneſs of the people on the other, continued to be extreme: the feudal government ſtill continued to diffuſe oppreſſion and miſery; and ſuch was the confuſion of it, that it even took away all hopes of amendment.

France, ſtill bleeding from the extravagance of a Nobility inceſſantly engaged in groundleſs wars, either with each other, or with the King, was again deſolated by the tyranny of that ſame Nobility, haughtily jealous of their

---

* Confirmationes Chartarum. cap. 2, 3, 4.

† " Nullum tallagium vel auxilium, per nos. vel hæredes
" noſtros, in regno noſtro panatur ſeu levetur, ſine voluntate
" & aſſenſu Archiepiſcoporum, Epiſcoporum, Comitum, Ba-
" ronum, Militum, Burgenſium, & aliorum liberorum hom'
" de regno noſtro." Stat. an. 24 Ed. I.

liberty, or rather of their anarchy *. The people, oppreffed by thofe who ought to have guided and protected
them, loaded with infults by thofe who exifted by their
labour, revolted on all fides. But their tumultuous infurrections had fcarcely any other object than that of giving vent to the anguifh with which their hearts were full.
They had no thoughts of entering into a general combination, ftill lefs of changing the form of the Government, and laying a regular plan of public liberty.

Having never extended their views beyond the fields
they cultivated, they had no conception of thofe different
ranks and orders of Men, of thofe diftinct and oppofite
privileges and prerogatives, which are all neceffary ingredients of a free Conftitution. Hitherto confined to
the fame round of ruftic employments, they little thought
of that complicated fabric, which the more informed
themfelves cannot but with difficulty comprehend, when,
by a concurrence of favourable circumftances, the ftructure has at length been reared, and ftands difplayed to
their view.

In their fimplicity they faw no other remedy for the national evils than the general eftablifhment of the Regal
power, that is, of the authority of one common uncon-
trouled mafter, and only longed for that time, which, while
it gratified their revenge, would mitigate their fufferings,
and reduce to the fame level both the oppreffors and the
oppreffed.

The Nobility, on the other hand, bent folely on the enjoyment of a momentary independence, irrecoverably loft

* Not contented with oppreffion, they added infult.
" When the Gentility," fays Mezeray, " pillaged and
" committed exactions on the peafantry, they called the
" poor fufferer, in derifion, *Jaques bonhomme* (Goodman
" James.) This gave rife to a furious fedition, which was
" called the *Jaquerie*. It began at Beauvais in the year 1357,
" extending itfelf into moft of the Province of France, and
" was not appeafed but by the deftruction of part of thofe
" unhappy victims, thoufands of whom were flaughtered."

the affection of the only Men who might in time support them; and, equally regardless of the dictates of humanity, and of prudence, they did not perceive the gradual and continual advances of the royal authority, which was soon to overwhelm them all. Already were Normandy, Anjou, Languedoc, and Touraine, re-united to the Crown; Dauphiny, Champagne, and part of Guienne were soon to follow: France was doomed at length to see the reign of Lewis the Eleventh; to see her General Estates first become useless, and be afterwards abolished.

It was the destiny of Spain also to behold her several Kingdoms united under one Head; she was fated to be in time ruled by Ferdinand and Charles the Fifth *. And Germany, where an elective Crown prevented the *re-unions* †, was indeed to acquire a few free Cities; but her

---

* Spain was originally divided into twelve Kingdoms, besides Principalities, which by Treaties, and especially by Conquests, were collected into three Kingdoms; those of Castile, Aragon and Granada. Ferdinand the Fifth, King of Aragon, married Isabella, Queen of Castile; they made a joint Conquest of the Kingdom of Granada, and these three Kingdoms, thus united, descended, in 1516, to their grandson Charles V. and formed the Spanish Monarchy. At this æra, the Kings of Spain began to be absolute; and the States of the Kingdoms of Castile and Leon, " assembled at Tole-" do, in the month of November, 1539, were the last in " which the three orders met, that is, the Grandees, the Ec-" clesiastics, and the Deputies of the Towns." *See Ferrera's* " *General History of Spain.*

† The Kingdom of France, as it stood under Hugh Capet and his next Successors, may, with a great degree of exactness, be compared with the German Empire as it exists at present, and also existed at that time: but the Imperial Crown of Germany having, through a conjunction of circumstances, continued elective, the German Emperors, though vested with more high-sounding prerogatives than even the Kings of France, laboured under very essential disadvantages: they could not pursue a plan of aggrandisement with the same

people, parcelled into fo many different dominions, were
deftined to remain fubject to the arbitrary yoke of fuch of
her different fovereigns as fhould be able to maintain their
power and independence.   In a word, the feudal tyranny which overfpread the Continent, did not compenfate,
by any preparation of diftant advantages, the prefent calamities it caufed ; nor was it to leave behind it, as it difappeared, any thing but a more regular kind of defpotifm.

   But in England, the fame feudal fyftem, after having
fuddenly broken in like a flood, had depofited, and ftill
continued to depofit, the noble feeds of the fpirit of liberty, union, and fober refiftance.   So early as the times
of Edward, the tide was feen gradually to fubfide ; the
laws which protect the perfon and property of the individual, began to make their appearance ; that admirable
Conftitution, the refult of a threefold power, infenfibly
arofe †, and the eye might even then difcover the ver-
dant fummits of that fortunate region that was deftined
to be the feat of Philofophy and Liberty, which are infe-
parable companions.

fteadinefs as a line of hereditary Sovereigns ufually do ; and
the right to elect them, enjoyed by the greater Princes of
Germany, procured a fufficient power to thefe, to protect
themfelves, as well as the leffer Lords, againft the power of
the Crown.

   † " Now, in my opinion," fays Philipe de Comines, in
times not much pofterior to thofe of Edward the Firft, and
with the fimplicity of the language of his times, " among
" all the fovereignties I know in the world, that in which
" the public good is beft attended to, and the leaft violence
" exercifed on the people, is that of England."   *Memoirs de*
Comines, tom. I. lib. v. chap. xix.

C H A P T E R III.

The Subject continued.

THE Reprefentatives of the Nation, and of the whole Nation, were now admitted into Parliament : the great point therefore was gained, that was one day to procure them the great influence which they at prefent poffefs ; and the fubfequent reigns afford continual inftances of its fucceffive growth.

Under Edward the Second, the Commons began to annex petitions to the bills by which they granted fubfidies : this was the dawn of their legiflative authority. Under Edward the Third, they declared they would not, in future, acknowledge any law to which they had not exprefsly affented.   Soon after this, they exerted a privilege in which confifts, at this time, one of the great balances of the Conftitution : they impeached, and procured to be condemned, fome of the firft Minifters of State. Under Henry the Fourth, they refufed to grant fubfidies before an anfwer had been given to their petitions. In a word, every event of any confequence was attended with an increafe of the power of the Commons ; increafes indeed but flow and gradual, but which were peaceably and legally effected, and were the more fit to engage the attention of the People, and coalefce with the ancient principles of the Conftitution.

Under Henry the Fifth, the Nation was entirely taken up with its wars againft France ; and in the Reign of Henry the Sixth began the fatal contefts between the houfes of York and Lancafter. The noife of arms alone was now to be heard : during the filence of the laws already in being, no thought was had of enacting new ones ; and for thirty years together, England prefents a wide fcene of flaughter and defolation.

At length under Henry the Seventh, who, by his intermarriage with the houfe of York, united the pretenfions of the two families, a general peace was re-eftablifhed, and the profpect of happier days feemed to open on the Nation. But the long and violent agitation under which it had laboured, was to be followed by a long and painful recovery. Henry mounting the throne with fword in hand, and in great meafure as a conqueror, had promifes to fulfil, as well as injuries to avenge. In the mean time, the People, wearied out by the calamities they had undergone, and longing only for repofe, abhorred even the idea of refiftance; fo that the remains of an almoft exterminated Nobility beheld themfelves left defencelefs, and abandoned to the mercy of the Sovereign.

The Commons, on the other hand, accuftomed to act only a fecond part in public affairs, and finding themfelves bereft of thofe who had hitherto been their Leaders, were more than ever afraid to form, of themfelves, an oppofition. Placed immediately, as well as the Lords, under the eye of the king, they beheld themfelves expofed to the fame dangers. Like them, therefore, they purchafed their perfonal fecurity at the expence of public liberty; and in reading the hiftory of the two firft Kings of the houfe of Tudor, we imagine ourfelves reading the relation given by Tacitus, of Tiberius and the Roman Senate *.

The time, therefore, feemed to be arrived, at which England muft fubmit, in its turn, to the fate of the other Nations of Europe. All thofe barriers which it had raifed for the defence of its liberty, feemed to have only been able to poftpone the inevitable effects of Power.

But the remembrance of their ancient laws, of that great charter fo often and fo folemnly confirmed, was too deeply impreffed on the minds of the Englifh, to be effaced by tranfitory evils. Like a deep and extenfive ocean, which preferves an equability of temperature amidft all the viciflitudes of feafons, England ftill retained thofe principles of liberty which were fo univerfally diffufed through all orders of the People, and they required

* *Quanto quis illuftrior, tanto magis falfi ac feftinantes.*

only a proper opportunity to manifest themselves:

England, besides, still continued to possess the immense advantage of being one undivided State.

Had it been, like France, divided into several distinct dominions, it would also have had several National Assemblies. These Assemblies, being convened at different times and places, for this and other reasons, never could have acted in concert; and the power of withholding subsidies, a power so important when it is that of disabling the Sovereign and binding him down to inaction, would then have only been the destructive privilege of irritating a Master who would have easily found means to obtain supplies from other quarters.

The different Parliaments or Assemblies of these several States, having thenceforth no means of recommending themselves to their Sovereign but their forwardness in complying with his demands, would have vied with each other in granting what it would not only have been fruitless, but even highly dangerous, to refuse. The King would not have failed soon to demand, as a tribute, a gift he must have been confident to obtain, and the outward form of consent would have been left to the People only as an additional means of oppressing them without danger.

But the King of England continued, even in the time of the Tudors, to have but one Assembly before which he could lay his wants, and apply for relief. How great soever the increase of his power was, a single Parliament alone could furnish him with the means of exercising it ; and whether it was that the members of this Parliament entertained a deep sense of their advantages, or whether private interest exerted itself in aid of patriotism, they at all times vindicated the right of granting, or rather refusing subsidies ; and, amidst the general wreck of every thing they ought to have held dear, they at least clung obstinately to the plank which was destined to prove the instrument of their preservation.

Under Edward the Sixth, the absurd tyrannical laws against High Treason, instituted under Henry the Eighth, his predecessor, were abolished. But this young and virtuous prince having soon passed away, the blood-thirsty Mary astonished the world with cruelties, which nothing but the fanaticism of a part of her subjects could have enabled her to execute.

Under the long and brilliant reign of Elizabeth, England began to breathe anew : and the Protestant religion, being seated once more on the throne, brought with it some more freedom and toleration.

The Star-Chamber, that effectual instrument of the tyranny of the two Henries, yet continued to subsist ; the inquisitorial tribunal of the High Commission was even instituted ; and the yoke of arbitrary power lay still heavy on the subject. But the general affection of the peole for a Queen whose former misfortunes had created such a general concern, the imminent dangers which England escaped, and the extreme glory attending that reign, lessened the sense of such exertions of authority as would, in these days, appear the height of Tyranny, and served at that time to justify, as they still do excuse, a Princess whose great talents, though not her principles of government, render her worthy of being ranked among the greatest Sovereigns.

Under the reign of the Stuarts, the Nation began to recover from its long lethargy. James the First, a prince rather imprudent than tyrannical, drew back the veil which had hitherto disguised so many usurpations, and made an ostentatious display of what his predecessors had been contented to enjoy.

He was incessantly asserting, that the authority of Kings was not to be controuled, any more than that of God himself. Like Him, they were omnipotent ; and those privileges to which the People so clamourously laid claim, as their inheritance and birthright, were no more than an effect of the grace and toleration of his royal ancestors *.

Those principles, hitherto only silently adopted in the

* See his declaration made in Parliament in the year 1610, and 1621.

Cabinet, and in the Courts of Juſtice, had maintained their ground in conſequence of this very obſcurity. Being now announced from the Throne, and reſounded from the pulpit, they ſpread an univerſal alarm. Commerce, beſides, with its attendant arts, and above all that of printing, diffuſed more ſalutary notions throughout all orders of the people; a new light began to riſe upon the Nation; and the ſpirit of oppoſition frequently diſplayed itſelf in this reign, to which the Engliſh Monarchs had not, for a long time paſt, been accuſtomed.

But the ſtorm, which was only gathering in clouds during the reign of James, began to mutter under Charles the Firſt, his ſucceſſor; and the ſcene which opened to view, on the acceſſion of that prince, preſented the moſt formidable aſpect.

The notions of religion, by a ſingular concurrence, united with the love of liberty: the ſame ſpirit which had made an attack on the eſtabliſhed faith, now directed itſelf to politics: the royal prerogatives were brought under the ſame examination as the doctrines of the Church of Rome had been ſubmitted to; and as a ſuperſtitious religion had proved unable to ſupport the teſt, ſo neither could an authority pretended unlimited, be expected to bear it.

The Commons, on the other hand, were recovering from the aſtoniſhment into which the extinction of the power of the Nobles had, at firſt, thrown them. Taking a view of the ſtate of the Nation, and of their own, they became ſenſible of their whole ſtrength; they determined to make uſe of it, and to repreſs a power which ſeemed, for ſo long a time, to have levelled every barrier. Finding among themſelves Men of the greateſt capacity, they undertook that important taſk with method and by conſtitutional means: and thus had Charles to cope with a whole Nation put in motion and directed by an aſſembly of Statesmen.

And here we muſt obſerve how different were the effects produced in England, by the annihilation of the power of the Nobility, from thoſe which the ſame event had produced in France.

In France, where, in confequence of the divifion of the People and of the exorbitant power of the Nobles, the People were accounted nothing, when the Nobles themfelves were fuppreffed, the work was completed.

In England, on the contrary, where the Nobles ever vindicated the rights of the People equally with their own, —in England, where the People had fucceffively acquired moft effectual means of influencing the motions of the Government, and above all were undivided, when the Nobles themfelves were caft to the ground, the body of the People ftood firm, and maintained the public liberty.

The unfortunate Charles, however, was totally ignorant of the dangers which furrounded him. Seduced by the example of the other Sovereigns of Europe, he was not aware how different, in reality, his fituation was from theirs: he had the imprudence to exert with rigour and authority which he had no ultimate refources to fupport: an union was at laft effected in the Nation; and he faw his enervated prerogatives diffipated with a breath *. By

* It might here be objected, that when, under Charles I. the regal power was obliged to fubmit to the power of the People, the king poffeffed other dominions befides England, viz. Scotland and Ireland, and therefore feeming to enjoy the fame advantage as the Kings of France, that of reigning over a divided Empire or Nation. But, to this it is to be anfwered, that, at the time we mention, Ireland, fcarcely civilized, only increafed the neceffities, and confequently the dependence, of the King: while Scotland, through the conjunction of peculiar circumftances, had thrown off her obedience. And though thofe two States, even at prefent, bear no proportion to the compact body of the Kingdom of England, and feem never to have been able, by their union with it, to procure to the King any dangerous refources, yet, the circumftances which took place in both at the time of the Revolution, or fince, fufficiently prove that it was no unfavourable circumftance to Englifh liberty, that the great crifis of the reign of Charles the Firft, and the great advance which the Conftitution was to make at that time, fhould precede the period at which the king of England might have

the famous act, called the Petition of Right, and another
posterior Act, to both which he assented, the compulsory
loans and taxes, disguised under the name of *Benevolences*,
were declared to be contrary to law; arbitrary imprisonments, and the exercise of the martial law, were abolished;
the Court of High Commission, and the Star-Chamber,
were suppressed *; and the Constitution, freed from the
apparatus of despotic powers with which the Tudors had
obscured it, was restored to its ancient lustre. Happy
had been the People, if their Leaders, after having executed so noble a work, had contented themselves with
the glory of being the benefactors of their Country.
Happy had been the King, if, obliged at last to submit,
his submission had been sincere, and if he had become
sufficiently sensible, that the only resource he had left was
the affection of his subjects.

But Charles knew not how to survive the loss of a power he had conceived to be indisputable: he could not reconcile himself to limitations and restraints so injurious,
according to his notions, to sovereign authority. His dis-
course and conduct betrayed his secret designs; distrust
took possession of the Nation; certain ambitious persons
availed themselves of it to promote their own views; and
the storm, which seemed to have blown over, burst forth
anew. The contending fanaticism of persecuting sects
joined in the conflict between regal haughtiness and the
ambition of individuals; the tempest blew from every
point of the compass; the Constitution was rent asunder,
and Charles exhibited in his fall an awful example to the
Universe.

been able to call in the assistance of two other Kingdoms.

* The Star-Chamber differed from all the other Courts
of law in this: the latter were governed only by the common
law, or immemorial custom, and Acts of Parliament; whereas the former often admitted for law the proclamations of the
King in Council, and grounded its judgments upon them.
The abolition of this Tribunal, therefore, was justly looked
upon as a great victory over regal Authority.

The royal power being thus annihilated, the Englifh made fruitlefs attempts to fubftitute a republican Government in its ftead. " It was a curious fpectacle," fays Montefquieu, " behold the vain efforts of the English to eftablifh among themfelves a democracy." Subjected, at firft, to the power of the principal Leaders in the Long Parliament, they faw that power expire, only to pafs, without bounds, into the hands of a Protector. They faw it afterwards parcelled out among the Chiefs of different bodies of troops ; and thus fhifting without end from one kind of fubjection to another, they were at length convinced, that an attempt to eftablifh liberty in a great Nation, by making the people interfere in the common bufinefs of Government, is of all attempts the moft chimerical ; that the authority *of all*, with which men are amufed, is in reality no more than the authority of a few powerful individuals who divide the Republic among themfelves ; and they at laft refted in the bofom of the only Conftitution which is fit for a great State and a free People ; I mean that in which a chofen number deliberate, and a fingle hand executes ; but in which, at the fame time, the public fatisfaction is rendered, by the general relation and arrangement of things, a neceffary condition of the duration of Government.

Charles the Second, therefore, was called over ; and he experienced on the part of the people, that enthufiafm of affection which ufually attends the return from a long alienation. He could not, however, bring himfelf to forgive them the inexpiable crime of which he looked upon them as to have been guilty. He faw with the deepeft concern that they ftill entertained their former notions with regard to the nature of the royal prerogative ; and, bent upon the recovery of the ancient powers of the Crown, he only waited for an opportunity to break thofe promifes which had procured his reftoration.

But the very eagernefs of his meafures fruftrated their fuccefs. His dangerous alliances on the Continent, and the extravagant wars in which he involved England, joined to the frequent abufe he made of his authority, betrayed his defigns. ⸗ The eyes of the Nation were foon opened, and faw into his projeſts; when, convinced at length that nothing but fixed and irrefiſtible bounds can be an effeſtual check on the views and efforts of Power, they refolved finally to take away thofe remnants of defpotifm which ſtill made a part of the regal prerogative.

The military fervices due to the crown, the remains of the ancient feudal tenures, had been already aboliſhed: the laws againſt heretics were now repealed; the Statute for holding parliaments once at leaſt in three years was enaſted; the *Habeas Corpus* aſt, that barrier of the Subjeſt's perfonal fafety, was eſtabliſhed; and, fuch was the patriotifm of the Parliaments, that it was under a King the moſt deſtitute of principle, that liberty received its moſt efficacious fupports.

At length, on the death of Charles, began a reign which affords a moſt exemplary leſſon both to Kings and People. James the Second, a prince of a more rigid difpofition, though of a lefs comprehenfive underſtanding, than his late brother, purfued ſtill more openly the projeſt which had already proved fo fatal to his family. He would not fee that the great alterations which had fucceffively been effeſted in the Conſtitution, rendered the execution of it daily more and more impraſticable; he imprudently fuffered himfelf to be exafperated at a refiſtance he was in no condition to overcome; and, hurried away by a fpirit of defpotifm and a monkifh zeal, he ran headlong againſt the rock which was to wreck his authority.

He not only ufed, in his declarations, the alarming expreſſions of Abfolute Power and Unlimited Obedience—he not only ufurped to himfelf a right to difpenfe with the laws; but moreover fought to convert that deſtruſtive pretenfion to the deſtruſtion of thofe very laws which were held moſt dear by the Nation, by endeavouring to aboliſh a religion for which they had fuffered the greateſt calamities, in order to eſtabliſh on its ruin a mode of faith which repeated Aſts of the Legiſlature had profcribed; and profcribed, not becaufe it tended to eſtabliſh in

England the doctrines of Transubstantiation and Purgatory, doctrines in themselves of no political moment, but becaufe the unlimited power of the Sovereign had always been made one of its principal tenets.

To endeavour therefore to revive fuch a Religion, was not only a violation of the laws, but was, by one enormous violation, to pave the way for others of a ftill more alarming nature. Hence the Englifh, feeing that their liberty was attacked even in its firft principles, had recourfe to that remedy which reafon and nature point out to the People, when he who ought to be the guardian of the laws becomes their deftroyer: they withdrew the allegiance which they had fworn to James, and thought themfelves abfolved from their oath to a King who himfelf difregarded the oath he had made to his People.

But, inftead of a revolution like that which dethroned Charles the Firft, which was effected by a great effufion of blood, and threw the ftate into a general and terrible convulfion, the dethronement of James proved a matter of fhort and eafy operation. In confequence of the progreffive information of the People, and the certainty of the principles which now directed the Nation, the whole were unanimous. All the ties by which the People were bound to the throne were broken, as it were, by one fingle fhock; and James, who, the moment before, was a Monarch furrounded by fubjects, became at once a fimple individual in the midft of the Nation.

That which contributes, above all, to diftinguifh this event as fingular in the annals of Mankind, is the moderation, I may even fay, the legality which accompanied it. As if to dethrone a King who fought to fet himfelf above the Laws, had been a natural confequence of, and provided for, by the principles of Government, every thing remained in its place; the Throne was declared vacant, and a new line of fucceffion was eftablifhed.

Nor was this all; care was had to repair the breaches that had been made in the Conftitution, as well as to prevent new ones; and advantage was taken of the rare opportunity of entering into an original and exprefs compact between King and People.

An Oath was required of the new King more precife than had been taken by his predeceffors; and it was confecrated as a perpetual formula, of fuch oaths. It was determined, that to impofe taxes without the confent of Parliament, as well as to keep up a ftanding army in time of peace, are contrary to law. The power which the Crown had conftantly claimed, of difpenfing with the laws, was abolifhed. It was enacted, that the fubject, of whatever rank or degree, had a right to prefent petitions to the King *. Laftly, the key-ftone was put to the arch, by the final eftablifhment of the Liberty of the Prefs §.

The Revolution of 1689 is therefore the third grand æra in the hiftory of the conftitution of England. The Great Charter had marked out the limits within which the Royal authority ought to be confined; fome outworks were raifed in the reign of Edward the Firft; but it was at the Revolution that the circumvallation was completed.

It was at this æra, that the true principles of civil fociety were fully eftablifhed. By the expulfion of a King who had violated his oath, the doctrine of Refiftance, that ultimate refource of an oppreffed people, was con-

---

* The Lords and Commons, previous to the Coronation of King William and Queen Mary, had framed a Bill which contained a declaration of the rights which they claimed in behalf of the People, and was in confequence called the *Bill of Rights*. This Bill contained the Articles above, as well as fome others, and having received afterwards the Royal affent, became an Act of Parliament, under the title of *An Act declaring the Rights and Liberties of the Subject, and fettling the Succeffion of the Crown.*—A. 1 William and Mary, Seff. 2. Cap. 2.

§ The liberty of the prefs was, properly fpeaking, eftablifhed only four years afterwards, in confequence of the refufal which the Parliament made at that time, to continue any longer the reftrictions which had before been fet upon it.

firmed beyond a doubt.   By the exclufion given to a family hereditarily defpotic, it was finally determined, that
Nations are not the property of Kings.   The principles
of Paffive Obedience, the Divine and indefeafible Right
of Kings, in a word, the whole fcaffolding of falfe and fuperftitious notions, by which the Royal authority had till
then been fupported, fell to the ground, and in the room
of it were fubftituted the more folid and durable foundations of the love of order, and the fenfe of the neceffity
of civil government among Mankind.

CHAPTER IV.

Of the Legiflative Power.

IN almoft all the States of Europe, the will of the
Prince holds the place of law ; and cuftom has fo
confounded the matter of right with the matter of fact,
that their Lawyers generally reprefent the legiflative authority as effentially attached to the character of King ;
and the plenitude of his power feems to them neceffarily
to flow from the very definition of his title.

The Englifh, placed in more favourable circumftances,
have judged differently : they could not believe that the
deftiny of Mankind ought to depend on a play of words,
and on fcholaftic fubtilties.; they have therefore annexed
no other idea to the word *King*, or *Roy*, a word known
alfo to their laws, than that which the Latins annexed to
the word *Rex*, and the northern Nations to that of *Cyning*.

In limiting therefore the power of the King, they have
acted more confiftently with the etymology of the word ;
they have acted alfo more confiftently with reafon, in
not leaving the laws to the difpofal of the perfon who is
already invefted with the public power of the State, that
is, of the perfon who lies under the greateft and moft important temptations to fet him himfelf above them.

The bafis of the Englifh Conftitution, the capital principle on which all others depend, is that the Legiflative

power belongs to Parliament alone; that is to fay, the power of eſtabliſhing laws, and of abrogating, changing, or explaining them.

The conſtituent parts of Parliament are the King, the Houſe of Lords, and the Houſe of Commons.

The Houſe of Commons, otherwiſe the Aſſembly of the Repreſentatives of the Nation, is compoſed of the Deputies of the different counties, each of which ſends two; of the Deputies of certain Towns, of which London, including Weſtminſter and Southwark, ſends eight,—other Towns, two or one; and of the Deputies of the Univerſities of Oxford and Cambridge, each of which ſends two.

Laſtly, ſince the Act of Union, Scotland ſends forty-five Deputies; who, added to thoſe juſt mentioned, make up the whole number of five hundred and fifty-eight. Thoſe Deputies, though ſeparately elected, do not ſolely repreſent the Town or County that ſends them, as is the caſe with the Deputies of the United Provinces of the Netherlands, or of the Swiſs Cantons; but when they are once admitted, they repreſent the whole body of the Nation.

The qualifications required for being a member of the Houſe of Commons, are, for repreſenting a County, to be born a ſubject of Great Britain, and to be poſſeſſed of a landed eſtate of ſix hundred pounds a year; and of three hundred, for repreſenting a Town or Borough.

The qualifications required for being an elector in a County, are to be poſſeſſed, in that County, of a Freehold of forty ſhillings a year †. With regard to electors in Towns or Boroughs, they muſt be freemen of them, a word which now ſignifies certain qualifications expreſſed in the particular Charters.

When the King has determined to aſſemble a Parliament, he ſends an order for that purpoſe to the Lord

---

† This Freehold muſt have been poſſeſſed by the elector one whole year at leaſt before the time of election, except it has devolved to him by inheritance, by marriage, by a laſt will, or by promotion to an office.

Chancellor, who, after receiving the same, sends a writ under the great seal of England to the Sheriff of every County, directing him to take the necessary steps for the election of Members for the County, and the Towns and Boroughs contained in it. Three days after the reception of the writ, the Sheriff must, in his turn, send his precept to the Magistrates of the Towns and Boroughs, to order them to make their election within eight days after the reception of the precept, giving four days notice of the same. And the Sheriff himself must proceed to the election for the County, not sooner than ten days after the receipt of the writ, nor later than sixteen.

The principal precautions taken by the law, to insure the freedom of elections, are, that any Candidate, who after the date of the writ, or even after the vacancy, shall have given entertainments to the electors of a place, or to any of them, in order to his being elected, shall be incapable of serving for that place in Parliament. That if any person gives, or promises to give any money, employment, or reward, to any voter, in order to influence his vote, he, as well as the voter himself, shall be condemned to pay a fine of five hundred pounds, and for ever disqualified to vote and hold any office in any corporation; the faculty, however, being reserved to both, of procuring their indemnity for their own offence, by discovering some other offender of the same kind.

It has been moreover established, that no Lord of Parliament, or Lord Lieutenant of a County, has any right to interfere in the elections of members; that any officer of the excise, customs, &c. who shall presume to intermeddle in elections, by influencing any voter to give or withhold his vote, shall forfeit one hundred pounds, and be disabled to hold any office. Lastly, all soldiers quartered in a place where an election is to be made, must move from it, at least one day before the election, to the distance of two miles or more, and return not till one day after the election is finished.

The House of Peers, or Lords, is composed of the Lords Spiritual, who are the Archbishops of Canterbury and of York, and the twenty-four Bishops; and of the Lords Temporal, whatever may be their respective titles, such as Dukes, Marquises, Earls, &c.

Lastly, the King is the third constitutive part of Parliament: it is even he alone who can convoke it, and he alone can dissolve, or prorogue it. The effect of a dissolution is, that from that moment the Parliament completely ceases to exist; the commission given to the Members by their Constituents is at an end; and whenever a new meeting of Parliament shall happen, they must be elected anew. A prorogation is an adjournment to a time appointed by the King; till which the existence of Parliament is simply interrupted, and the function of the Deputies suspended.

When the Parliament meets, whether it be by virtue of a new summons, or whether, being composed of Members formerly elected, it meets again at the expiration of the term for which it had been prorogued, the King either goes to it in person, invested with the insignia of his dignity, or appoints proper persons to represent him on that occasion, and opens the session by laying before the Parliament the state of the public affairs, and inviting them to take them into consideration. This presence of the King, either real or represented, is absolutely requisite at the first meeting; it is it which gives life to the Legislative Bodies, and puts them in action.

The King having concluded his declaration, withdraws. The Parliament, which is then legally intrusted with the care of the National concerns, enters upon its functions, and continues to exist till it is prorogued, or dissolved. The House of Commons, and that of Peers, assemble separately: the latter, under the presidence of the Lord Chancellor; the former, under that of their Speaker, and both separately adjourn to such days as they respectively think proper to appoint.

As each of the two Houses has a negative on the propositions made by the other, and there is, consequently, no danger of their encroaching on each other's rights, nor on those of the King, who has likewise his negative upon them both, any queſtion judged by them conducive to the public good, without exception, may be made the ſubjeſt of their reſpeſtive deliberations. Such are, for inſtance, new limitations, or extenſions, to be given to the authority of the King; the eſtabliſhing of new laws, or making changes in thoſe already in being. Laſtly, the different kinds of public proviſions, or eſtabliſhments, the various abuſes of adminiſtration, and their remedies, become, in every Seſſion, the objeſt of the attention of Parliament.

Here, however, an important obſervation muſt be made. All Bills for granting Money muſt have their beginning in the Houſe of Commons : the Lords cannot take this objeſt into their conſideration but in conſequence of a bill preſented to them by the latter ; and the Commons have at all times been ſo anxiouſly tenacious of this privilege, that they have never ſuffered the Lords even to make any change in the Money Bills which they have ſent to them ; and the Lords are expeſted ſimply and ſolely either to accept or rejeſt them.

This excepted, every Member, in each Houſe, may propoſe whatever queſtion he thinks proper. If, after being conſidered, the matter is found to deſerve attention, the perſon who made the propoſition, uſually with ſome others adjoined to him, is deſired to ſet it down in writing. If, after more complete diſcuſſions of the ſubjeſt, the propoſition is carried in the affirmative, it is ſent to the other Houſe, that they may, in their turn, take it into conſideration. If the other Houſe rejeſt the Bill, it remains without any effeſt : if they agree to it, nothing remains wanting to its complete eſtabliſhment, but the Royal Aſſent.

When there is no buſineſs that requires immediate diſpatch, the King uſually waits till the end of the Seſſion, or at leaſt till a certain number of bills are ready for him, before he declares his royal pleaſure. When the time is come, the King goes to Parliament in the ſame ſtate with which he opened it : and while he is ſeated on the Throne, a Clerk, who has a lift of the Bills, gives, or refuses, as he reads the Royal Affent.

When the Royal Affent is given to a public Bill, the Clerk fays, *le Roy le veut*. If the Bill be a private Bill, he fays, *foit fait comme il eft défiré*. If the Bill has fubfidies for its object, he fays *le Roy remercie fes loyaux Sujects, accepte leur bénévolence & auffi le veut*. Laftly, if the King does not think proper to affent to the Bill, the Clerk fays, *le Roy s' advifera;* which is a mild way of giving a refufal.

It is, however, pretty fingular, that the King of England fhould make ufe of the French language to declare his intentions to his Parliament. This cuftom was introduced at the Conqueft *, and has been centinued, like other matters of form, which fometimes fubfift for ages after the real fubftance of things has been altered ; and Judge Blackftone expreffes himfelf, on this fubject, in the following words : " A badge, it muft be owned (now the " only one remaining), of Conqueft; and which one " would with to fee fall into total-oblivion, unlefs it be " referved as a folemn memento to remind us that our " liberties are mortal, having once been deftroyed by a " foreign force."

When the King has declared his different intentions, he prorogues the Parliament. Thofe Bills which he has rejected, remain without force : thofe to which he has affented, become the expreffion of the will of the higheft power acknowledged in England : they have the fame binding force as the *Edits enrégiftrés* have in France †,

---

* William the Conqueror added to the other changes he introduced, the abolition of the Englifh language in all public, as well as judicial tranfactions, and fubftituted to it the French that was fpoke in his time; hence the number of old French words that are met with in the ftyle of the Englifh laws. It was only under Edward III. that the Englifh language began to be re-eftablifhed in the Courts of juftice.

† They call in France, *Edits enérgiftrés*, thofe Edicts of the King which have been regiftered in the Court of Parlia-

and as the *Populiscit* had in ancient Rome: in a word, they are LAWS. And though each of the conftituent parts of the Parliament might, at firft, have prevented the exiftence of thofe laws, the united will of all the Three is now neceffary to repeal them.

CHAP. V.

Of the Executive Power.

WHEN the Parliament is prorogued or diffolved, it ceafes to exift; but its laws ftill continue to be in force: the King remains charged with the execution

ment. The word Parliament does not, however, exprefs in France, as it does in England, the Affembly of the Eftates of the Kingdom. The French *Parlemens* are only Courts of Juftice: that of Paris was inftituted in the fame manner, and for the fame purpofes, as the *Aula Regis* was afterwards in England, viz. for the adminiftration of public Juftice, and for deciding the differences between the King and his Barons: it was in confequence of the Judgments awarded by that Court, that the King proceeded to feize the dominions of thofe Lords or Princes againft whom a fentence had been paffed, and when he was able to effect this, united them to the Crown. The *Parliament* of Paris, as do the other Courts of Law, grounds its judgments upon the *Edicts* or *Ordonnances* of the King, when it has once regiftered them. When thofe *Ordonnances* are looked upon as grievous to the Subject, the Parliament refufes to regifter them: but this they do not from any pretenfion they to have a fhare in the Legiflative authority; they only object that they are not fatisfied that the *Ordonnance* before them is really the will of the King, and then proceed to make remonftrances againft it: fometimes the King defers to thefe; or, if he is refolved to put an end to all oppofition, he comes in perfon to the *Parliament*, there holds what they call *un Lit de juftice*, declares that the *Ordonnance* before them is actually his will, and orders the proper Officer to regifter it.

of them, and is supplied with the neceſſary power for that purpoſe.

It is however to be obſerved, that, though in his political capacity of one of the conſtituent parts of the Parliament, that is, with regard to the ſhare allotted to him in the legiſlative authority, the King is undoubtedly Sovereign, and only needs allege his will when he gives or refuſes his aſſent to the bills preſented to him; yet, in the exerciſe of his powers of Government, he is no more than a Magiſtrate, and the laws, whether thoſe that exiſted before him, or thoſe to which, by his aſſent, he has given being, muſt direct his conduct, and bind him equally with his ſubjects.

The firſt prerogative of the King, in his capacity of Supreme Magiſtrate, has for its object the adminiſtration of Juſtice.

1°. He is the ſource of all judicial power in the State; he is the Chief of all the Courts of Law, and the Judges are only his Subſtitutes: every thing is tranſacted in his name; the Judgments muſt be with his Seal, and are executed by his Officers.

2°. By a fiction of the law, he is looked upon as the univerſal proprietor of the kingdom; he is in conſequence deemed directly concerned in all offences; and for that reaſon proſecutions are to be carried on, in his name, in the Courts of law.

3°. He can pardon offences, that is, remit the puniſhment that has been awarded in conſequence of his proſecution.

II. The ſecond prerogative of the King, is, to be the *fountain of honour*, that is, the diſtributor of titles and dignities: he creates the Peers of the realm, as well as beſtows the different degrees of inferior Nobility. He moreover diſpoſes of the different offices, either in the Courts of law, or elſewhere.

III. The King is the ſuperintendent of Commerce; he has the prerogative of regulating weights and meaſures: he alone can coin money, and can give a currency to foreign coin.

IV. He is the Supreme Head of the Church. In this capacity he appoints the Bishops, and the two Archbishops; and he alone can convene the Assembly of the Clergy. This Assembly is formed, in England, on the model of the Parliament: the Bishops form the upper House: Deputies from the Dioceses, and from the several Chapters; form the lower House: the assent of the King is likewise necessary to the validity of their Acts, or Canons; and the King can prorogue, or dissolve, the Convocation.

V. He is, in right of his Crown, the Generalissimo of all sea or land forces whatever; he alone can levy troops, equip fleets, build fortresses, and fill all the posts in them.

VI. He is, with regard to foreign Nations, the representative and the depository of all the power and collective majesty of the Nation: he sends and receives ambassadors; he contracts alliances; and has the prerogative of declaring war, and of making peace, on whatever conditions he thinks proper.

VII. In fine, what seems to carry so many powers to the height, is, its being a fundamental maxim, that THE KING CAN DO NO WRONG: which does not signify, however, that the King has not the power of doing ill, or, as it was pretended by certain persons in former times, that every thing he did was lawful; but only that he is above the reach of all Courts of law whatever, and that his person is sacred and inviolable.

⋯◄⋯◄⋯◄ ⋯◄ ⋯◄⋯◄⋯◄ ⋯◄⋯✦ ✿ ✦ ✿✥ ⋯►►►⋯►⋯►⋯►⋯►⋯►⋯

C H A P. VI.

The Boundaries which the Constitution has set to the Royal Prerogative.

IN reading the foregoing enumeration of the powers with which the laws of England have intrusted the King, we are at a loss to reconcile them with the idea of a Monarchy, which, we are told, is limited. The King not only unites in himself all the branches of the Executive power,—he not only difposes, without controul, of the whole military power in the State,—but he is moreover, it feems,' Mafter of the Law itfelf, fince he calls up, and difmiffes, at his will, the Legiflative Bodies. We find him, therefore, at firft fight, invefted with all the prerogatives that ever were claimed by the moft abfolute Monarchs; and we are at a lofs to find that liberty which the Englifh feem fo confident they poffefs.

But the Reprefentatives of the people ftill have, and that is faying enough, they ftill have in their hands, now that the Conftitution is fully eftablifhed, the fame powerful weapon which has enabled their anceftors to eftablifh it. It is ftill from their liberality alone that the King can obtain fubfidies; and in thefe days, when every thing is rated by pecuniary eftimation, when gold is become the great moving fpring of affairs, it may be fafely affirmed, that he who depends on the will of other men, with regard to fo important an article, is, whatever his power may be in other refpects, in a ftate of real dependence.

This is the cafe of the King of England. He has, in that capacity, and without the grant of his people, fcarcely any revenue. A few hereditary duties on the exportation of wool, which (fince the eftablifhment of manufactures) are become tacitly extinguifhed; a branch of the excife, which, under Charles the Second, was annexed to the Crown as an indemnification for the military fervices it gave up, and which, under George the Firft, has been fixed to feven thoufand pounds; a duty of two fhillings on every ton of wine imported; the wrecks of fhips of which the owners remain unknown; whales and fturgeons thrown on the coaft; fwans fwimming on public rivers; and a few other feudal relics, now compofe the whole appropriated revenue of the King, and are all that remain of the ancient inheritance of the Crown.

The King of England, therefore, has the prerogative of commanding armies, and equipping fleets—but without the concurrence of his Parliament he cannot maintain them. He can beftow places and employments—but

without his Parliament he cannot pay the salaries attending on them.   He can declare war—but without his Parliament it is impossible for him to carry it on.   In a word,
the Royal Prerogative, destitute as it is of the power of
imposing taxes, is like a vast body, which cannot of itself
accomplish its motions : or, if you please, it is like a ship
completely equipped, but from which the Parliament can
at pleasure draw off the water, and leave it aground,—and
also set it afloat again, by granting subsidies.

And indeed we see that, since the establishment of this
right of the Representatives of the People, to grant, or refuse, subsidies to the Crown, their other privileges have been
continually increasing.   Though these Representatives
were not, in the beginning, admitted into Parliament but
upon the most disadvantageous terms, yet they soon found
means, by joining petitions to their money-bills, to have
a share in framing those laws by which they were in future to be governed ; and this method of proceeding,
which at first was only tolerated by the King, they afterwards converted into an express right, by declaring, under
Henry the Fourth, that they would not, thenceforward,
come to any resolutions with regard to subsidies, before
the King had given a precise answer to their petitions.

In subsequent times we see the Commons constantly
successful, by their exertions of the same privilege, in
their endeavours to lop off the despotic powers which still
made a part of the regal prerogative.   Whenever abuses of
power had taken place, which they were seriously determined to correct, they made *grievances and supplies*, to use the
expression of Sir Thomas Wentworth, *go hand in hand
together*, which always produced the redress of them.
And in general, when a bill, in consequence of its being
judged by the Commons essential to the public welfare,
has been joined by them to a money bill, it has seldom
failed *to pass in that agreeable company* *.

* In mentioning the forcible use which the Commons
have at times made of their power of granting subsidies, by
joining provisions of a different nature to bills that had grant-

CHAP. VII.

The same Subject continued.

BUT this force of the prerogative of the Commons, and the facility with which it may be exerted, however necessary they may have been for the first establishment of the Constitution, might prove too considerable at present, when it is requisite only to support it. There might be the danger, that, if the Parliament should ever exert their privilege to its full extent, the Prince, reduced to despair, might resort to fatal extremities ; or that the Constitution, which subsists only by virtue of its equilibrium, might in the end be subverted.

Indeed this is a case which the prudence of the Parliament has foreseen. They have, in this respect, imposed laws upon themselves ; and without touching the prerogative itself, they have moderated the exercise of it. A custom has for a long time prevailed, at the beginning of every reign, and in the kind of overflowing of affection which takes place between a King and his first Parliament, to grant the King a revenue for his life; a provision which, with respect to the great exertions of his power, does not abridge the influence of the Commons, but yet puts him in a condition to support the dignity of the Crown, and affords him, who is the first Magistrate in the Nation, that independence which the laws insure also to those Magi-

for their object, I only mean to shew the great efficiency of that power, which was the subject of this Chapter, without pretending to say any thing as to the propriety of the measure. The House of Lords have even found it necessary (which confirms what is said here) to form, as it were, a confederacy among themselves, for the security of their Legislative authority, against the unbounded use which the Commons might make of their power of taxation ; and it has been made a standing order of their House, to reject any bill whatsoever to which a money-bill has been *tacked*.

ſtrates who are particularly intruſted with the adminiſtration of Juſtice *.

This conduct of the Parliament provides an admirable remedy for the accidental diſorders of the State. For though, by the wiſe diſtribution of the powers of Government, great uſurpations are become in a manner impracticable, neverthelefs it is impoſſible but that, in conſequence of the continual, though ſilent efforts of the Executive power to extend itſelf, abuſes will at length ſlide in. But here the powers, wifely kept in reſerve by the Parliament, afford the means of remedying them. At the end of each reign, the civil liſt, and conſequently that kind of independence which it procured, are at an end. The ſucceſſor finds a Throne, a Sceptre, and a Crown ; but he finds neither power, nor even dignity ; and before a real poſſeſſion of all theſe things is given him, the Parliament have it in their power to take a thorough review of the State, as well as correct the ſeveral abuſes that may have crept in during the preceding reign ; and thus the Conſtitution may be brought back to its firſt principles.

England, therefore, by this means, enjoys one very great advantage, one that all free States have ſought to procure for themſelves ; I mean that of a periodical reformation. But the expedients which Legiſlators have contrived for this purpoſe in other Countries, have always, when attempted to be carried into practice, been found to be productive of very diſadvantageous conſequences. Thoſe laws which were made in Rome, to

---

* The twelve Judges.—Their commiſſions, which in former times were often given them *durante bene placito*, now muſt always " be made *quamdiu ſe bene geſſerint*, and their ſa" laries aſcertained : but upon an addreſs of both Houſes it " may be lawful to remove them."—Stat. 13 Will. III. c. 2. In the firſt year of the reign of his preſent Majeſty, it has been moreover enacted, that the commiſſions of the Judges ſhall continue in force, notwithſtanding the demiſe of the King ; which has prevented their being dependent, with regard to their continuation in office, on the heir apparent.

K

restore that equality which is the essence of a Democratical Government, were always found impracticable: the attempt alone endangered the overthrow of the Republic; and the expedient which the Florentines called *ripigliar il stato*, proved nowise happier in its consequences. This was because all these different remedies were destroyed beforehand, by the very evils they were meant to cure; and the greater the abuses were, the more impossible it was to correct them.

But the means of reformation which the Parliament of England has taken care to reserve to itself, is the more effectual, as it goes less directly to its end. It does not oppose the usurpations of prerogative, as it were, in front—it does not encounter it in the middle of its career, and in the fullest flight of its exertion: but it goes in search of it to its source, and to the principle of its action. It does not endeavour forcibly to overthrow it; it only enervates its springs.

What increases still more the mildness of the operation, is, that it is only to be applied to the usurpations themselves, and passes by, what would be far more formidable to encounter, the obstinacy and pride of the usurpers.

Every thing is transacted with a new Sovereign, who, till then, has had no share in public affairs, and has taken no step which he may conceive himself bound in honour to support. In fine, they do not wrest from him what the good of the State requires he should give up: he himself makes the sacrifice.

The truth of all these observations is remarkably confirmed by the events that followed the reign of the two last Henries. Every barrier that protected the People against the excursions of Power had been broke through. The Parliament, in their terror, had even enacted that proclamations, that is the will of the King, should have the force of laws *. The Constitution seemed really undone. Yet, on the first opportunity afforded by a new reign, liberty

---

* Stat. 31 Hen. VIII. chap. 8.

began again to make its appearance *. And when the Nation, at length recovered from its long fupinenefs, had, at the acceffion of Charles the Firft, another opportunity of a change of Sovereign, that enormous mafs of abufes, which had been accumulating, or gaining ftrength, during five fucceffive reigns, was removed, and the ancient laws were reftored.

To which add, that this fecond reformation, which was fo extenfive in its effects, and might be called a new creation of the Conftitution, was accomplifhed without producing the leaft convulfion. Charles the Firft, in the fame manner as Edward had done in former times †, affented to every regulation that was paffed; and whatever reluctance he might at firft manifeft, yet the Act called *the Petition of Right* (as well as the Bill which afterwards completed the work) received the Royal Sanction without bloodfhed.

It is true, great misfortunes followed; but they were the effects of particular circumftances. During the time which preceded the reign of the Tudors, the nature and extent of regal authority having never been accurately defined, the exorbitant power of the Princes of that Houfe had gradually introduced political prejudices of even an extravagant kind: thofe prejudices, having had a hundred and fifty years to take root, could not be fhaken off but by a kind of general convulfion; the agitation continued after the action, and was carried to excefs by the religious quarrels that arofe at that time.

* The laws concerning Treafon, paffed under Henry the Eighth, which Judge Blackftone calls "an amazing heap of "wild and new-fangled treafons," were, together with the ftatute juft mentioned, repealed in the beginning of the reign of Edward VI.

† Or, which is equally in point, the Duke of Somerfet his uncle, who was the Regent of the Kingdom, under the name of Protector.

CHAPTER VIII.

New Reſtrictions.

THE Commons, however, have not entirely relied on the advantages of the great prerogative with which the Conſtitution has intruſted them.

Though this prerogative is, in a manner, out of danger of an immediate attack, they have nevertheleſs ſhewn at all times, the greateſt jealouſy on its account. They never ſuffer, as we have obſerved before, a money-bill to begin any where but with themſelves; and any alteration that may be made in it, in the other Houſe, is ſure to be rejected. If the Commons had not moſt ſtrictly reſerved to themſelves the exerciſe of a prerogative on which their very exiſtence depends, the whole might at length have ſlidden into that other body which they might have ſuffered to ſhare in it equally with them. If any other perſons beſides the Repreſentatives of the People, had a right to make an offer of the produce of the labour of the people, the executive Power would ſoon have forgot, that it only exiſts for the advantage of the public *.

* As the Crown had the undiſputed prerogative of aſſenting to, and diſſenting from, what bills it thinks proper, as well as of convening, proroguing, and diſſolving, the Parliament, whenever it pleaſes, the latter have no aſſurance of having a regard paid to their Bills, or even of being allowed to aſſemble, but what may reſult from the need the Crown ſtands in of their aſſiſtance: the danger, in that reſpect, is even greater for the Commons than for the Lords, who enjoy a dignity which is hereditary, as well as inherent to their perſons, and form a permanent Body in the State; whereas the Commons completely vaniſh whenever a diſſolution takes place: there is, therefore, no exaggeration in what has been ſaid above, that their *very being* depends on their power of granting ſubſidies to the Crown.

Moved by theſe conſidérations, and no doubt by a ſenſe

Besides, though this prerogative has of itself, we may say, an irresistible efficiency, the Parliament has neglected nothing that may increase it, or at least the facility of its exercise; and though they have allowed the general prerogatives of the Sovereign to remain undisputed, they have in several cases endeavoured to restrain the use he might make of them, by entering with him into divers express and solemn conventions for that purpose †.

Thus, the King is indisputably invested with the exclusive right of assembling Parliaments: yet he must assemble one, at least once in three years; and this obligation on the King, which was, we find, insisted upon by the People in very early times, has been since confirmed by an act passed in the sixteenth year of the reign of Charles the Second.

Moreover, as the most fatal consequences might ensue,

of their duty towards their Constituents, to whom this right of taxation originally belongs, the House of Commons have at all times been very careful least precedents should be established, which might, in the most distant manner, tend to weaken that right. Hence the warmth, I might say the resentment, with which they have always rejected even the amendments proposed by the Lords in their Money Bills. The Lords, however, have not given up their pretension to make such amendments; and it is only by the vigilance and constant pre-determination of the Commons to reject all alteration whatever made in their Money Bills, without even examining them, that this pretension of the Lords is reduced to be an useless, and only dormant, claim. The first instance of a misunderstanding between the two Houses, on that account, was in the year 1671; and the reader may see at length, in Vol. I. of the *Debates of the House of Commons*, the reasons that were at that time alleged on both sides.

† Laws made to bind such Powers in a state, as have no superior power by which they may be legally compelled to the execution of them (for instance, the Crown, as circumstanced in England), are nothing more than general conventions, or treaties, made with the Body of the People.

if laws which might moſt materially affect public liberty, could be enacted in Parliaments abruptly and imperfectly ſummoned, it has been eſtabliſhed that the Writs for aſſembling a Parliament muſt be iſſued forty days at leaſt before the full meeting of it. Upon the ſame principle it has alſo been enacted, that the King cannot abridge the term he has once fixed for a prorogation, except in the two following caſes, viz. of a rebellion, or of imminent danger of a foreign invaſion; in both which caſes a fourteen days notice muſt be given *.

Again, the King is the head of the Church; but he can neither alter the eſtabliſhed religion, or call individuals to an account for their religious opinions †. He cannot even profeſs the religion which the Legiſlature has particularly forbidden; and the Prince who ſhould profeſs it, is declared incapable of *inheriting, poſſeſſing, or enjoying, the Crown of theſe Kingdoms* ‡.

The King is the firſt Magiſtrate; but he can make no change in the maxims and forms confecrated by law or cuſtom: he cannot even influence, in any caſe whatever, the deciſion of cauſes between ſubject and ſubject; and James the Firſt, aſſiſting at the trial of a cauſe, was reminded by the Judge, that he could deliver no opinion §.

---

* Stat. 30 Geo. II. c. 25.

† The Convocation, or aſſembly of the Clergy, of which the King is the head, can only regulate ſuch affairs as are merely eccleſiaſtical; they cannot touch the Laws, Cuſtoms, and Statutes, of the Kingdom.—Stat. 25. Hen. VIII. c. 19?

‡ 1 Will. and M. Stat. 2. c. 2.

§ Theſe principles have ſince been made an expreſs article of an Act of Parliament; the ſame which aboliſhed the Star-Chamber. " Be it likewiſe declared and enacted, by the
" authority of this preſent Parliament, That neither his
" Majeſty, nor his Privy Council, have, or ought to have any
" juriſdiction, power, or authority, to examine or draw in-
" to queſtion, determine, or diſpoſe of the lands, tenements,
" goods, or chattels, of any of the ſubjects of this Kingdom."
—Stat. A. 16. Ch. I. cap. 10. § 10.

Laſtly, though crimes are proſecuted in his name, he cannot refuſe to lend it to any particular perſons who have complaints to prefer.

The King has the privilege of coining money ; but he cannot alter the ſtandard.

The King has the power of pardoning offenders ; but he cannot exempt them from making a compenſation to the parties injured. It is even eſtabliſhed by law, that, in a caſe of murder, the widow, or next heir, ſhall have a right to proſecute the murderer; and the King's pardon, whether it preceded the Sentence paſſed in conſequence of ſuch proſecution, or whether it be granted after it, cannot have any effect *.

The King has the military power ; but ſtill with reſpect to this, he is not abſolute. It is true, in regard to the ſea-forces, as there is in them this very great advantage, that they cannot be turned againſt the liberty of the Nation, at the ſame time that they are the ſureſt bulwark of the iſland, the King may keep them as he thinks proper ; and in this reſpect he lies only under the general reſtraint of applying to Parliament for obtaining the means of doing it. But in regard to land forces, as they may become an immediate weapon in the hands of Power, for throwing down all the barriers of public liberty, the King cannot raiſe them without the conſent of Parliament. The Guards of Charles the Second were declared anti-conſtitutional † ; and James's army was one of the cauſes of his being dethroned ‡.

In theſe times, however, when it is become a cuſtom

---

* The method of proſecution mentioned here, is called an *Appeal*; it muſt be ſued within a year and a day after the completion of the crime.

† He had carried them to the number of four thouſand men.

‡ A new ſanction has been given to the above reſtriction in the ſixth Article of the Bill of Rights : " A ſtanding ar-" my, without the conſent of Parliament, is againſt law."

with Princes to keep thofe numerous armies which ferve as a pretext and means of oppreffing the People, a State that would maintain its independence, is obliged, in a great meafure, to do the fame. The Parliament has therefore thought proper to eftablifh a ftanding body of troops, which amounts to about thirty thoufand Men, of which the King has the command.

But this army is only eftablifhed for one year; at the end of that term, it is (unlefs re-eftablifhed) to be *ipfo facto* difbanded; and as the queftion which then lies before Parliament, is not, whether the army *fhall be diffolved*, but whether it fhall be *eftablifhed anew*, as if it had never exifted, any one of the three branches of the Legiflature may, by its diffent, hinder its continuance.

Befides, the funds for the payment of this body of troops are to be raifed by taxes that never are eftablifhed for more than one year #; and it becomes likewife necef-fary, at the end of this term, again to eftablifh them †. In a word, this inftrument of defence, which the circum-ftances of modern times have caufed to be judged necef-fary, being capable, on the other hand, of being applied to the moft dangerous purpofes, has been joined to the State by only a flender thread, the knot of which may be flipped, on the firft appearance of danger ‡.

* The land-tax and malt-tax.

† It is alfo neceffary that the Parliament, when they re-new the Act called the *Mutiny Act*, fhould authorife the dif-ferent Courts Martial to punifh military offences, and defer-tion. It can therefore refufe the King even the neceffary power of military difcipline.

‡ To thefe laws, or rather conventions, between King and People, I fhall add here the Oath which the King takes at his Coronation; a compact which, if it cannot have the fame precifion as the laws we have related above, yet in a manner comprehends them all, and has the farther advantage of being declared with more folemnity.

" *The archbifhop or bifhop fhall fay*, Will you folemnly pro-
" mife and fwear to govern the people of this Kingdom of

But these laws which limit the King's authority, would not, of themselves, have been sufficient. As they are after all, only intellectual barriers, which it is possible that the King might not at all times respect, as the check which the Commons have on his proceedings, by a refusal of subsidies, affects too much the whole State, to be exerted on every particular abuse of his power; and lastly, as even this means might in some degree be eluded, either by breaking the promises which have procured subsidies, or by applying them to uses different from those for which they were appointed, the Constitution has besides supplied the Commons with a means of immediate opposition to the misconduct of Government, by giving them a right to impeach the Ministers.

It is true, the King himself cannot be arraigned before Judges; because, if there were any that could pass sentence upon him, it would be they, and not he, who must finally possess the executive power: but, on the other

" England, and the dominion thereto belonging, according
" to the Statutes of Parliament agreed on, and the laws and
" customs of the same ? *The king or queen shall say*, I solemn-
" ly promise so to do.

" *Archbishop or bishop.* Will you to your power cause law
" and justice, in mercy, to be executed in all your judg-
" ments ?—*King or queen.* I will.

" *Archbishop or bishop.* Will you to the utmost of your
" power maintain the laws of God, the true profession of
" the gospel, and the protestant reformed religion established
" by the law ? And will you preserve unto the bishops and
" clergy of this realm, and to the churches committed to
" their charge, all such rites and privileges as by law do or
" shall appertain unto them, or any of them ? *King or queen.*
" All this I promise to do.

" *After this the king or queen, laying his or her hand upon the*
" *holy gospels, shall say,* The things which I have here before
" promised I will perform and keep: so help me God.—
" *And then shall kiss the book.*"

L

hand, the King cannot act without Ministers; it is therefore those Ministers, that is, those indispensable instruments whom they attack.

If, for example, the public money has been employed in a manner contrary to the declared intention of those who granted it, an impeachment may be brought against those who had the management of it. If any abuse of power is committed, or in general any thing done contrary to the public weal, they prosecute those who have been either the instruments, or the advisers of the measure *.

But who shall be the Judges to decide in such a cause? What Tribunal will flatter itself, that it can give an impartial decision, when it shall see, appearing at its bar, the Government itself as the accused, and the Representatives of the People, as the accusers?

It is before the House of Peers that the Law has directed the Commons to carry their accusation; that is, before Judges whose dignity, on the one hand, renders them independent, and who, on the other, have a great honour to support in that awful function where they have all the Nation for spectators of their conduct.

When the impeachment is brought to the Lords, they commonly order the person accused to be imprisoned. On the day appointed, the Deputies of the House of Commons, with the person impeached, make their appearance; the impeachment is read in his presence; Counsel are allowed him, as well as time, to prepare for his defence; and at the expiration of this term, the trial goes on from day to day, with open doors, and every thing is communicated in print to the public.

But whatever advantage the law grants to the person impeached for his justification, it is from the intrinsic

---

* It was upon these principles that the Commons, in the beginning of this century, impeached the Earl of Oxford, who had advised the Treaty of Partition, and the Lord Chancellor Somers, who had affixed, the great seal to it.

merits of his conduct that he muſt draw his arguments and proofs. It would be of no ſervice to him, in order to juſtify a criminal conduct, to allege the commands of the Sovereign ; or, pleading guilty with reſpect to the meaſures imputed to him, to produce the Royal pardon *. It is againſt the Adminiſtration itſelf that the impeachment is carried on ; it ſhould therefore by no means interfere ; the King can neither ſtop nor ſuſpend its courſe, but is forced to behold, as an inactive ſpectator, the diſcovery of the ſhare which he may himſelf have had in the illegal proceedings of his ſervants, and to hear his own ſentence in the condemnation of his Miniſters.

An admirable expedient ! which, by removing and puniſhing corrupt Miniſters, affords an immediate remedy for the evils of the State, and ſtrongly marks out the bounds within which Power ought to be confined : which takes away the ſcandal of guilt and authority united, and calms the People by a great and awful act of Juſtice : an expedient, in this reſpect eſpecially, ſo highly uſeful, that it is to the want of the like, that Machiavel attributes the ruin of his Republic.

* This point in ancient times was far from being clearly ſettled. In the year 1678, the Commons having impeached the Earl of Danby, he pleaded the King's pardon in bar to that impeachment : great altercations enſued on that ſubject, which were terminated by the diſſolution of that Parliament. It has been ſince enacted, (Stat. 12 and 13 W. III. c. 2.) “ that no pardon under the great ſeal can be pleaded in bar “ to an impeachment by the Houſe of Commons.”

I once aſked a gentleman very learned in the laws of this Country, if the King could remit the puniſhment of a Man condemned in conſequence of an impeachment of the Houſe of Commons : he anſwered me, The Tories will tell you the King can, and the Whigs he cannot.—But it is not perhaps very material that the queſtion ſhould be decided : the great public ends are attained when a corrupt Miniſter is removed with diſgrace, and the whole Syſtem of his proceedings unveiled to the public eye.

But all thefe general precautions to fecure the rights of the Parliament, that is, thofe of the Nation itfelf, againft the efforts of the executive Power, would be vain, if the Members themfelves remained perfonally expofed to them. Being unable openly to attack, with any fafety to itfelf, the two legiflative bodies, and by a forcible exertion of its prerogatives, to make, as it were, a general affault, the executive power might, by fubdividing the fame prerogatives, gain an entrance, and fometimes by intereft, and at others by fear, guide the general will, by influencing that of individuals.

But the laws which fo effectually provide for the fafety of the People, provide no lefs for that of the Members, whether of the Houfe of Peers, or that of the Commons. There are not known in England, either thofe *Commiffaries*, who are always ready to find thofe guilty whom the wantonnefs of ambition points out, nor thofe fecret imprifonments which are, in other Countries, the ufual expedients of Government. As the forms and maxims of the Courts of Juftice are ftrictly prefcribed, and every individual has an invariable right to be judged according to Law, he may obey without fear the dictates of public virtue. Laftly, what crowns all thefe precautions, is its being a fundamental maxim, "That the freedom of fpeech, " and debates and proceedings in Parliament, ought not " to be impeached or queftioned in any Court or place " out of Parliament *."

The Legiflators, on the other hand, have not forgot that intereft, as well as fear, may impofe filence on duty. To prevent its effects, it has been enacted, that all perfons concerned in the management of any taxes created fince 1692, commiffioners of prizes, navy, victualling-office, &c. comptrollers of the army accounts, agents for regiments, the clerks in the different offices of the revenue, any perfons that hold any new office under the Crown, created fince 1705, or having a penfion under the Crown,

---

* Bill of Rights. Art. 9.

during pleafure, or for any term of years, are incapable of being elected Members. Befides, if any Member accepts an office under the Crown, except it be an officer in the army or navy accepting a new commiffion, his feat becomes void ; though fuch Member is capable of being re-elected.

Such are the precautions hitherto taken by the Legifla-tors, for preventing the undue influence of the great pre-rogative of difpofing of rewards and places : precautions which have been fucceffively taken, according as circum-ftances have fhewn them to be neceffary ; and which we may thence fuppofe are owing to caufes powerful enough to produce the eftablifhment of new ones, whenever cir-cumftances fhall point out the neceffity of them *.

* Nothing can be a better proof of the efficacy of the cauf-es that produce the liberty of the Englifh, and which will be explained hereafter, than thofe victories which the Parliament from time to time gains over itfelf, and in which the Mem-bers, forgetting all views of private ambition, only think of their intereft as fubjects.

Since this was firft written, an excellent regulation has been made for the decifion of controverted elections. For-merly the Houfe decided them in a very fummary manner, and the witneffes were not examined upon oath. But, by an Act paffed a few years ago, the decifion is now to be left to a Jury, or Committee, of fifteen Members, formed in the following manner. Out of the Members prefent, who muft not be lefs than one hundred, forty-nine are drawn by lots : out of thefe, each candidate ftrikes off one alternately, till there remain only thirteen, who, with two others, named out of the whole Houfe, one by each candidate, are to form the Committee : in order to fecure the neceffary number of a hundred Members, all other bufinefs in the Houfe is to be fuf-pended, till the above operations are completed.

C H A P. IX.

Of private Liberty, or the Liberty of Individuals.

WE have hitherto only treated of general liberty, that is, of the rights of the Nation as a Nation, and of its share in the Government. It now remains that we should treat particularly of a thing without which this general liberty, being absolutely frustrated in its object, would be only a matter of ostentation, and even could not long subsist, I mean the liberty of individuals.

Private Liberty, according to the division of the English Lawyers, consists, first, of the right of *Property*, that is, of the right of enjoying exclusively the gifts of fortune, and all the various fruits of one's industry. Secondly, of the right of *Personal Security*. Thirdly, of the *Locomotive Faculty*, taking the word Liberty in its more confined sense.

Each of these rights, say again the English Lawyers, is inherent in the person of every Englishman : they are to him as an inheritance, and he cannot be deprived of them, but by virtue of a sentence passed according to the laws of the land. And, indeed, as this right of inheritance is expressed in English by one word *(birth-right,)* the same as that which expresses the King's title to the Crown, it has, in times of oppression, been often opposed to him as a right, doubtless of less extent, but of a sanction equal to that of his own.

One of the principal effects of the right of Property is, that the King can take from his subjects no part of what they possess; he must wait till they themselves grant it him ; and this right, which, as we have seen before, is, by its consequences, the bulwark that protects all the others, has moreover the immediate effect of preventing one of the chief causes of oppression.

In regard to the attempts to which the right of property might be exposed from one individual to another, I believe I shall have said every thing, when I have observed, that there is no Man in England who can oppose the irresistible power of the Laws,—that, as the Judges cannot be deprived of their employments but on an accusation by Parliament, the effect of interest with the Sovereign, or with those who approach his person, can scarcely influence their decisions,—that, as the Judges themselves have no power to pass sentence till the matter of fact has been settled by men nominated, we may almost say, at the common choice of the parties *, all private views, and consequently all respect of persons, are banished from the Courts of Justice. However, that nothing may be wanting which may help to throw light on the subject, I have undertaken to treat, I shall relate, in general, what is the law in civil matters, that has taken place in England.

When the Pandects were found at Amalphi, the Clergy, who were then the only Men that were able to understand them, did not neglect that opportunity of increasing the influence they had already obtained, and caused them to be received in the greater part of Europe. England, which was destined to have a Constitution so different from that of other States, was to be farther distinguished by its rejecting the Roman laws.

Under William the Conqueror, and his immediate successors, a multitude of foreign Ecclesiastics flocked to the Court of England. Their influence over the mind of the Sovereign, which, in the other States of Europe, as they were then constituted, might be considered as matter of no great importance, was not so in a country where the Sovereign being all-powerful, to obtain influence over him, was to obtain power itself. The English Nobility saw with the greatest jealousy, Men of a condition so different from their own, vested with a power to the attacks of which they were immmediately exposed, and thought that they would carry that power to the height, if they

---

* Owing to the extensive right of challenging jurymen, which is allowed to every person brought to his trial, though not very frequently used.

were ever to adopt a fyſtem of laws which thoſe ſame men ſought to introduce, and of which they would neceſſarily become both the depoſitaries and the interpreters.

It happened, therefore, by a ſomewhat ſingular conjunction of circumſtances, that, to the Roman laws, brought over to England by Monks, the idea of eccleſiaſtical power became aſſociated, in the ſame manner as the idea of regal Deſpotiſm became afterwards annexed to the Religion of the ſame Monks, when favoured by Kings who endeavoured to eſtabliſh an arbitrary government. The nobility at all times rejected theſe laws, even with a degree of ill humour *; and the uſurper Stephen, whoſe intereſt it was to conciliate their affections, went ſo far as to prohibit the ſtudy of them.

As the general diſpoſition of things brought about, as hath been above obſerved, a ſufficient degree of intercourſe between the Nobility or Gentry, and the People, the averſion to the Roman Laws gradually ſpread itſelf far and wide; and thoſe laws, to which their wiſdom in many caſes, and particularly their extenſiveneſs, ought naturally to have procured admittance when the Engliſh laws themſelves were as yet but in their infancy, experienced the moſt ſteady oppoſition from the Lawyers; and as thoſe perſons who ſought to introduce them, frequently renewed their attempts, there at length aroſe a kind of general combination amongſt the Laity, to confine them to Univerſities and Monaſteries †.

---

* The nobility, under the reign of Richard II. declared in the French language of thoſe times, "Purce que le roialme " d'Engleterre n'étoit devant ces heures ne a l'entent du " Roy notre Seignior, & Seigniors du Parlement, unques " ne ſera, rulé ne governé par la ley civil." viz. Inaſmuch as the Kingdom of England was not before this time, nor according to the intent of the King our Lord and Lords of Parliament, ever ſhall be ruled or governed by the civil law— *In Rich. Parliémento Weſtmenaſterii, Feb. 3. Anno 2.*

† It might perhaps be ſhewn, if it belonged to the ſubject, that the liberty of thinking in religious matters, which has

This oppofiiton was carried fo far, that Fortefcue, Chief Juftice of the King's Bench, and afterwards Chancellor under Henry VI. wrote a Book intitled *De Laudibus Legum Angliæ*, in which he propofes to demonftrate the fuperiority of the Englifh Laws over the Civil; and that nothing might be wanting in his arguments on that fubject, he gives them the advantage of fuperior antiquity, and traces their origin to a period much anterior to the foundation of Rome.

This fpirit has been preferved even to much more modern times; and when we perufe the many paragraphs which Judge Hale has written in his Hiftory of the Common Law, to prove, that in the few cafes in which the Civil Law is admitted in England, it can have no power by virtue of any deference due to the orders of Juftinian (a truth which certainly had no need of proof), we plainly fee that this Chief Juftice, who was alfo a very great Lawyer, had, in this refpect, retained fomewhat of the heat of party.

Even at prefent the Englifh Lawyers attribute the liberty they enjoy, and of which other Nations are deprived, to their having rejected, while thofe Nations have ad-

at all times remarkably prevailed in England, is owing to much the fame caufes as its political liberty : both perhaps are owing to this, that the fame Men, whofe intereft it is in other Countries that the People fhould be influenced by prejudices of a political or religious kind, have been in England forced to inform and unite with them. I fhall here take occafion to obferve, in anfwer to the reproach made to the Englifh, by Prefident Henault, in his much efteemed Chronological Hiftory of France, that the frequent changes of religion which have taken place in England, do not argue any fervile difpofition in the People; they only prove the equilibrium between the then exifting fects : there was none but what might become the prevailing one, whenever the Sovereign thought proper to declare for it : and it was not, England, as people may think at firft fight, it was only its government, which changed its religion.

M .

mitted the Roman law; which is miſtaking the effect for
the cauſe. It is not becauſe the Engliſh have rejected
the Roman laws that they are free; but it is becauſe they
were free, or at leaſt becauſe there exiſted among them
cauſes which were, in proceſs of time, to make them ſo, that
they have been able to reject the Roman laws. But e-
ven though they had admitted thoſe laws, the ſame circumſtances that have enabled them to reject the whole,
would have likewiſe enabled them to reject thoſe parts
which might not have ſuited them; and they would have
ſeen, that it is very poſſible to receive the deciſions of
the civil law on the ſubject of the *ſervitutes urbanæ &
ruſticæ*, without adopting its principles with reſpect to
the power of the Emperors *.

Of this the Republic of Holland, where the Civil Law
is adopted, would afford a proof, if there were not the
ſtill more ſtriking one, of the Emperor of Germany, who,
though in the opinion of his People, he is the ſucceſſor
to the very throne of the *Cæſars* †, has not by a great
deal ſo much power as a King of England; and the reading of the ſeveral treaties which deprived him of the
power of nominating the principal offices of the Empire,
ſufficiently ſhews that a ſpirit of unlimited ſubmiſſion to
Monarchial power, is no neceſſary conſequence of the
admiſſion of the Roman Civil Law.

The Laws therefore that have taken place in England,
are what they call the *Unwritten Law*, alſo termed the
Common Law, and the *Statute Law*.

The *Unwritten Law* is thus called, not becauſe it is only
tranſmitted by tradition from generation to generation;
but becauſe it is not founded on any known act of the Legiſlature. It receives its force from immemorial cuſtom,

* What particularly frightens the Engliſh Lawyers is L.
i. Lib. I. Tit. 4. Dig.—*Quod Principi placuerit legis habet vi-
gorem*.

† The German word to expreſs the Emperor's dignity,
is, *Cæſar*, Kaiſer.

and, for the moſt part, derives its origin from Aẛts of Parliament enaẛed in the times which immediately followed the conqueſt (particularly thoſe anterior to the time of Richard the Firſt) the originals of which are loſt.

The principal objeẛs ſettled by the Common Law, are the rules of deſcent, the different methods of acquiring property, the various forms required for rendering contraẛs valid; in all which points it differs, more or leſs, from the Civil Law. Thus, by the Common Law, lands deſcend to the eldeſt ſon, to the excluſion of all his brothers and ſiſters; whereas, by the Civil Law, they are equally divided between all the children : by the Common Law, property is transferred by *writing*; but by the Civil, Law *trdditiox*, or aẛual delivery, is moreover requiſite, &c.

The ſource from which the deciſions of the Common Law are drawn, is what is called *præteritorum memoria eventorum*, and is found in the colleẛion of judgments that have been paſſed from time immemorial, and which, as well as the proceedings relative to them, are carefully preſerved under the title of *Records*. In order that the principles eſtabliſhed by ſuch a ſeries of judgments may be known, extraẛs from them are, from time to time, publiſhed under the name of *Reports*; and theſe reports reach, by a regular ſeries, ſo far back as the reign of Edward the Second, incluſively.

Beſides this colleẛion, which is pretty voluminous, there are alſo ſome ancient Authors of great authority among Lawyers; ſuch as *Glanvil*, who wrote under the reign of Henry the Second—*Braẛon*, who wrote under Henry the Third—*Fleta*, and *Lyttleton*. Among more modern Authors, is Sir Edward Coke, Lord Chief Juſtice of the King's Bench under James the Firſt, who has written four books of Inſtitutes, and is at preſent the Oracle of the Common Law.

The Common Law moreover comprehends ſome particular cuſtoms, which are fragments of the ancient Saxon laws, efcaped from the difafter of the Conqueft; fuch as that called *Gavelkind*, in the County of Kent, by which lands are divided equally between the Sons; and that called *Borough Englifh*, by which, in fome particular diftricts, lands defcend to the youngeft Son.

The Civil Law, in the few inftances where it is admitted, is likewife comprehended under the Unwritten Law, becaufe it is of force only fo far as it has been authorifed by immemorial cuftom. Some of its principles are followed in the Ecclefiaftical Courts, in the Courts of Admiralty, and in the Courts of the two Univerfities; but it is there nothing more than *lex fub lege graviori;* and thefe different Courts muft conform to Acts of Parliaments, and to the fenfe given to them by the Courts of Common Law; being moreover fubjected to the controul of thefe latter.

Laftly, the Written Law is the collection of the various Acts of Parliament, the originals of which are carefully preferved, efpecially fince the reign of Edward the Third. Without entering into the diftinctions made by Lawyers with refpect to them, fuch as *public* and *private* Acts *declaratory* Acts, or fuch as are made to extend or reftrain the Common Law, it will be fufficient to obferve, that being the refult of the united wills of the Three Conftituent Parts of the Legiflature, they, in all cafes, fuperfede both the Common Law and all former Statutes, and the Judges muft take cognizance of them, and decide in conformity to them, even though they had not been alleged by the parties *.

The different Courts for the adminiftration of Juftice, in England, are,

I. The Court of *Common Pleas*. It formerly made a part of the *Aula Regis;* but as this latter Court was bound by its inftitution always to follow the perfon of the King, and private individuals experienced great difficulties in obtaining relief from a Court that was ambulatory, and al-

---

* Unlefs they be private Acts.

ways in motion, it was made one of the articles of the Great Charter, that the Court of Common Pleas should thenceforward be held in a fixed place *; and since that time it has been seated at Westminster. It is composed of a Lord Chief Justice, with three other Judges; and appeals from its judgments, usually called *Writs of Errour*, are brought before the Court of King's Bench.

II. The Court of Exchequer. It was originally established to determine those causes in which the King or his servants, or accomptants, were concerned, and has gradually become open to all persons. The confining the power of this Court to the above class of persons, is therefore now a mere fiction; only a man must, for form's sake, set forth in his declaration that he is debtor to the King, whether he be so, or no. The Court of Exchequer is composed of the Chief Baron of the Exchequer, and three other Judges.

III. The Court of King's Bench forms that part of the *Aula Regis* which continued to subsist after the dismembering of the Common Pleas. This Court enjoys the most extensive authority of all other Courts: it has the superintendance over all Corporations, and keeps the various jurisdictions in the Kingdom within their respective bounds. It takes cognizance, according to the end of its original institution, of all criminal causes, and even of many causes merely civil. It is composed of the Lord Chief Justice of the Court of King's Bench, and three other Judges. Writs of errour against the judgments passed in that Court in civil matters, are brought before the Court of the Exchequer Chamber; or, in most cases, before the House of Peers.

IV. The Court of the Exchequer Chamber. When this Court is formed by the four Barons, or Judges of the Exchequer, together with the Chancellor and Treasurer of the same, it sits as a court of Equity; a kind of

---

* *Communia Placita non sequantur Curiam nostram, sed teneantur in aliquo loco certo.* Magna Charta, cap. 11.

inftitution on which fome obfervations will be introduced in a following Chapter.   When this Court is formed by the twelve Judges, to whom fometimes the Lord Chancellor is joined, its office is to deliberate, when properly referred and applied to, and give an opinion on important and difficult caufes, before judgments are paffed upon them, in thofe Courts where the caufes are depending.

C H A P. X.

On the Law in regard to Civil Matters, that is obferved in England.

CONCERNING the manner in which Juftice is adminiftered, in civil matters, in England, and the kind of law that obtains in that refpeft, the following obfervations may be made.

In the firft place, it is to be obferved, that the beginning of a civil procefs in England, and the firft ftep ufually taken in bringing an action, is the feizing by public authority the perfon againft whom that action is brought.   This is done with a view to fecure fuch perfon's appearance before a judge, or at leaft make him give fureties for that purpofe.   In moft of the Countries of Europe, where the forms introduced in the Roman Civil Law, in the reigns of the latter Emperors, have been imitated, a different method has been adopted to procure a man's appearance before a Court of Juftice.   The ufual practice is to have the perfon fued, fummoned to appear before the Court, by a public officer belonging to it, a week before hand : if no regard is paid to fuch fummons twice repeated, the Plaintiff, or his Attorney, is admitted to make before the Court a formal reading of his demand, which is then granted him, and he may proceed to execution *.

* A perfon againft whom a judgment of this kind has

In this mode of proceeding, it is taken for granted, that a perfon who declines to appear before a Judge, to anfwer the demand of another, after being properly fummoned, acknowledges the juftice of fuch demand, and this fuppofition is very juft and rational. However, the above-mentioned practice of fecuring before hand the body of a perfon fued, though not fo mild in its execution as that juft now defcribed, nor even more effectual, appears more obvious, and is more readily adopted, in thofe times when Courts of Laws begin to be formed in a Nation, and rules of diftributive juftice to be eftablifhed ; and it is, very likely, followed in England as a continuation of the methods that were adopted when the Englifh laws were as yet in their infancy.

In the times we mention, when laws begin to be form-ed in a Country, the adminiftration of juftice between in-dividuals is commonly lodged in the fame hands which are intrufted with the public and military authority in the State.   Judges invefted with a power of this kind, like to carry on their operations with a high hand : they confider the refufal of a Man to appear before them, not as being barely an expedient to avoid doing that which is juft, but as a contempt of their authority : they of courfe look up-on themfelves as being bound to vindicate it ; and a writ of *Capias* is fpeedily iffued to apprehend the refractory Defendant.   A preliminary Writ, or order, of this kind, becomes in time to be ufed of courfe, and as the firft re-gular ftep of a law-fuit ; and thus, it is likely enough, has it happened that in the Englifh courts of law, if I am right-ly informed, a Writ of *Capias* is either iffued before the *original* Writ itfelf (which contains the fummons of the plaintiff, and a formal delineation of his cafe,) or is joined to fuch Writ, by means of an *ac etiam capias,* and is ferv-

been paffed (which they call in France *un jugement par defaut)* may eafily obtain relief : but as he now in his turn becomes in a manner the Plaintiff, his deferting the caufe, in this fe-cond ftage of it, would leave him without remedy.

ed along with it. It may be remembered that, in England, the *Aula Regis*, at the head of which the King himself presided, was originally the common Court of Justice for the whole Kingdom, in civil as well as criminal matters, and continued so till the Court of Common Pleas was in time separated from it.

In Rome, where the distribution of civil Justice was at first lodged in the hands of the Kings, and afterwards of the Consuls, the method of seizing the person of a man against whom a demand of any kind was preferred, previously to any judgment being passed against him, was likewise adopted, and continued to be followed after the institution of the Prætor's Court, to whom the civil branch of the power of the Consuls was afterwards delegated; and it lasted till very late times; that is, till the times when those capital alterations were made in the Roman civil Law, during the reign of the latter Emperors, which gave it the form it now has in those Codes or collections of which we are in possession.

A very singular degree of violence even took place in Rome, in the method used to secure the persons of those against whom a legal demand was preferred. In England, the way to seize upon the person of a man under such circumstances, is by means of a public Officer, supplied with a writ or order for that purpose, supposed to be directed to him (or to the Sheriff his employer) from the King himself. But in Rome, every one became a kind of public officer in his own cause, to assert the Prætor's prerogative; and, without any ostensible legal licence or badge of public authority, had a right to seize by force the person of his opponent, wherever he met him. The practice was, that the Plaintiff (*Actor*) first summoned the person sued (*Reum*) with a loud voice, to follow him before the Court of the Prætor *. When the Defendant refused to obey the summons, the Plaintiff, by means of the words *licet antestari*, requested the by-standers to be

* *Ad Tribunal sequere, in Ius ambula.*

witneffes of the fact, as a remembrance of which he touched the ears of each of them ; and then proceeded to feize the perfon of his opponent, by throwing his arms round his neck (*obtorto collo*), thus endeavouring to drag him before the Prætor. When the perfon fued was, through age or ficknefs, difabled from following the Plaintiff, the latter was directed by the law of the Twelve Tables to fupply him with a horfe (*jumentum dato*).

The above method of proceeding was however in after-times mitigated, though very late and flowly. In the firft place, it became unlawful to feize a man in his own houfe, as it was the abode of his domeftic Gods. Women of good family (*Matronæ*) were in time protected from the feverity of the above cuftom, and they could no longer be dragged by force before the tribunal of the Prætor. The method of placing a fick or aged perfon by force upon a horfe, feems to have been abolifhed during the latter times of the Republic. Emancipated Sons, and freed Slaves, were afterwards reftrained from fummoning their Parents, or late Mafters, without having exprefsly obtained the Prætor's leave, under the penalty of fifty pieces of gold. However, fo late as the time of Pliny, the whole mode of fummoning, or carrying by force, before a Judge, continued in general to fubfift; though, in the time of Ulpian, the neceffity of exprefsly obtaining the Prætor's leave was extended to all cafes and perfons ; and in Conftantine's reign, the method began to be eftablifhed of having legal fummonfes ferved only by means of a public Officer appointed for that purpofe. After that time, other changes in the former law were introduced, from which the mode of proceeding now ufed on the continent of Europe, has been borrowed.

In England likewife, fome changes, we may obferve, have been wrought in the law and practice concerning the arrefts of fued perfons, though as flowly and late as those effected in the Roman Republic or Empire, if not more so; which evinces the great impediments of various kinds that obstruct the improvement of laws in every Nation. So late as the reign of king George the First, an Act was passed to prohibit the practice of previous personal Arrest, in cases of demands under two pounds sterling; and since that time, those Courts, justly called *of Conscience*, have been established, in which such demands are to be summarily decided, and simple summonses, without arrest, can only be used. And lately, another Bill has been passed on the motion of Lord Beauchamp, whose name deserves to be recorded, by which the like prohibition of arrest is extended to all cases of debt under ten pounds sterling; a Bill the passing of which was of twenty, or even a hundred times, more real importance than the rise or fall of a Favourite or a Minister, though it has perhaps been honoured with a less degree of attention by the Public.

Another peculiarity of the English Civil Law, is the great refinements, formalities, and strictness that prevail in it. Concerning such refinements, which are rather imperfections, the same observation may be made that has been introduced above, in regard to the mode and frequency of civil arrest in England; which is, that they are continuations of methods adopted when the English Law began to be formed, and are the consequences of the situation in which the English placed themselves when they rejected the ready made Code of the Roman civil Law, compiled by order of Justinian, which most nations of Europe have admitted, and rather chose to become their own Law-makers, and raise from the ground the structure of their own national Civil Code; which Code, it may be observed, is as yet in the first stage of its formation, as the Roman Law itself was during the times of the Republic, and in the reigns of the first Emperors.

The time at which the power of adminiſtrating juſtice to individuals, becomes ſeparated from the military power (an event which happens ſooner or later in
different Countries) is the realer of the origin of a
regular ſyſtem of laws in a Nation. Judges being now
deprived of the power of the ſword, or, which amounts
to the ſame, being obliged to borrow that power from
other perſons, endeavour to find their reſources within
their own Courts, and, if poſſible, to obtain ſubmiſſion to their decrees from the great regularity of their
proceedings, and the reputation of the impartiality of
their deciſions.

At the ſame time alſo Lawyers begin to crowd in
numbers to Courts which it is no longer dangerous to
approach, and add their refinements to the rules already ſet down either by the Legiſlature or the Judges.
As the employing of them is, eſpecially in the beginning, matter of choice, and they fear, that, if bare
common-ſenſe were thought ſufficient to conduct a law-
ſuit, every body might imagine he knows as much as
they do, they contrive difficulties to make their aſſiſtance needful. As the true ſcience of the Law, which
is no other than the knowledge of a long ſeries of former rules and precedents, cannot as yet exiſt, they endeavour to create an artificial one, to recommend themſelves by. Formal diſtinction and definitions are in-
vented to expreſs the different kinds of claims Men
may ſet up againſt one another; in which almoſt the
ſame nicety is diſplayed as that uſed by Philoſophers
in claſſing the different ſubjects, or *kingdoms*, of Natural Hiſtory. Settled forms of words, under the name
of *Writs*, or ſuch like, are deviſed to ſet thoſe claims
forth; and, like introductory paſſes, ſerves to uſher
Claimants into the Temple of Juſtice. For fear their
Clients ſhould deſert them after their firſt introduction,
like a ſick man who reſts contented with a ſingle viſit
of the Phyſician, Lawyers contrive other ceremonies

and technical forms for the farther conduct of the procefs and the *pleadings*; and in order ftill more fafely
to bind their Clients to their dominion, they at length
obtain to make every error relating to their profeffional regulations, whether it be a *mifnomer*, a *mifpleading*,
or fuch like tranfgreffion, to be of as fatal a confequence as a failure againft the laws of ftrict Juftice.
Upon the foundation of the above-mentioned definitions and metaphyfical diftinctions of cafes and actions,
a number of ftrict rules of law are moreover raifed,
with which none can be acquainted but fuch as are complete mafters of thofe diftinctions and definitions.

To a perfon who in a pofterior age obferves for the
firft time fuch refinements in the diftribution of Juftice,
they appear very ftrange and even ridiculous. Yet, it
muft be confeffed, that during the times of the firft inftitution of Magiftracies and Courts of a civil nature,
ceremonies and formalities of different kinds are very
ufeful to procure to fuch Courts, both the confidence
of thofe perfons who are brought before them, and the
refpect of the Public at large; and they thereby become
actual fubftitutes for military force, which, till then,
had been the chief fupport of Judges. Thofe fame
forms and profeffional regulations are moreover ufeful
to give uniformity to the proceedings of the Lawyers
and of the Courts of Law, and to infure conftancy and
fteadinefs to the rules they fet down among themfeves.
And if the whole fyftem of the refinements we mention
continues to fubfift in very remote ages, it is in a great
meafure owing (not to mention other caufes) to their
having fo coalefced with the effential parts of the Law
as to make danger, or at leaft great difficulties, to be
apprehended from a feparation; and they may, in that
refpect, be compared with a fcaffolding ufed in the
raifing of a houfe, which, though only intended to fet
the materials, and fupport the builders, happens to be
fuffered for a long time afterwards to ftand, becaufe it

is thought the removing of it might endanger the building.

Very singular law formalities and refined practices
of the kind here alluded to, had been contrived by the
first Jurisconsults in Rome, with a view to amplify
the rules set down in the Laws of the Twelve Tab'es;
which being but few, and engraved on brass, every body could know as well as they : it even was a general
custom to give those laws to children to learn, as we
are informed by Cicero.

Very accurate definitions, as well as distinct branches of cases and actions, were contrived by the first
Roman Jurisconsults ; and when a Man had once made
his election of that peculiar kind of *action* he chose to
pursue his claim by, it became out of his power to
alter it. Settled forms of words, called *Actiones legis*,
were moreover contrived, which Men must absolutely
use to set forth their demands. The party himself was
to recite the appointed words before the Prætor ; and
should he unfortunately happen to miss or add a single
word, so as to seem to alter his real case or demand,
he lost his suit thereby. To this an allusion is made by
Cicero, when he says, " We have a civil law so con-
" stituted, that a Man becomes non-suited, who has
" not proceeded in the manner he should have done *."
An observation of the like nature is also to be found
in Quintilian, whose expressions on the subject are as
follow : " There is besides another danger ; for if
" but one word has been mistaken, we are to be con-
" sidered as having failed in every point of our suit †."
Similar solemnities and appropriated forms of words
were moreover necessary to introduce the reciprocal

---

* *Ita Ius civile habemus constitutum, ut causa cadat is qui non
quemadmodum oportet egerit.* De Invent. II. 19.

† *Est etiam periculosum, quuam si uno verbo sit erratum, totá
causá cecidisse videamur.* Inst. Orat. III. 8. VII. 3.

answers and replies of the Parties, to require and accept surities, to produce witnesses, &c.

Of the above *Actiones legis*, the Roman Jurisconsults and Pontiffs had carefully kept the exclusive knowledge to themselves, as well as of those days on which religion did not allow Courts of law to sit *. One Cn. Flavius, secretary to Appius Claudius, having happened to divulge the secret of those momentous forms (an act for which he was afterwards preferred by the People), Jurisconsults contrived fresh ones, which they began to keep written with secret cyphers; but a member of their own Body again betrayed them, and the new Collection which he published, was called *Ius Ælianum*, from his name, Sex. Ælius, in the same manner as the former collection had been called *Ius Flavianum*. However, it does not seem that the influence of Lawyers became much abridged by those two collections: besides written information of that sort, practice is also necessary: and the public Collections we mention, like the many books that have been published on the English law, could hardly enable a Man to become a Lawyer, at least sufficiently so as to conduct a law-suit †.

Modern Civilians have been at uncommon pains to find out and produce the ancient law *Formulæ* we mention; in which they really have had surprising

---

* *Dies Fasti & Nefasti.*

† The Roman Jurisconsults had extended their skill to objects of *voluntary* jurisdiction as well as to those of *contentious* jurisdiction, and had devised peculiar formalities, forms of words, distinctions and definitions, in regard to the contracting of obligations between Man and Man, in regard to stipulations, donations, spousals, and especially last wills, in regard to all which they had displayed surprising nicety, refinement, accuracy, and strictness. The English Lawyers have not bestowed so much pains on the objects of *voluntary* jurisdiction, nor any thing like it.

fuccefs. Old Comic writers, fuch as Plautus and Te-
rence, have fuppled them with feveral; the fettled
words, for inftance, ufed to claim the property of a
Slave, frequently occur in their Works*.

* The words addreffed to the Plaintiffs by the perfon
fued, when the latter made his appearance on the day for
which he had been compelled to give fureties, were as follow,
and are alluded to by Plaut. *Curcul.* I. 3. v. 5. " Where art
" thou who haft obliged me to give fureties? Where art
" thou who fummoneft me? Here I ftand before thee, do
" thyfelf ftand before me." To which the Plaintiff made
anfwer, " Here I am." The Defendant replied, " What
" doft thou fay?" When the Plaintiff anfwered, I fay . . .
(*Aio*) and then followed the form of words by which he chofe
to exprefs his action. *Ubi tu es, qui me vadatus es? Ubi tu es
qui me citafti? Ecce ego me tibi fifto; tu contra & te mihi fifte, &c.*
If the action, for inftance, was brought on account of
goods ftolen, the fettled penalty or damages for which was
the reftitution of twice the value, the words to be ufed were,
AIO *decem aureos mihi furto tuo abeffe, teque eo nomine viginti
aureos mihi dare oportere.* For work done, fuch as cleaning
of clothes, &c. Aio *te mihi tritici modium de quo inter nos, con-
venit ob polita veftimenta tua, dare oportere.* For recovering the
value of a flave killed by another citizen. Aio *te hominem
meum occidiffe, teque mihi quantum ille hoc anno plurimi fuit dare,
oportere.* For damages done by a vicious animal. Aio *bovem Mævii fervum meum, Stichum, cornu petiiffe & occidiffe, eoque
nomine Mævium, aut fervi æftimationem praeftare, aut bovem mihi
noxae dare, oportere;* or Aio *urfum mevii mihi vulnus intuliffe,
& Mævium quantum aequius melius mihi dare oportere, &c. &c.*
It may be obferved, that the particular kind of remedy
which was provided by the law for the cafe before the Court,
was exprefsly pointed out in the formula, ufed by a Plaintiff; and in regard to this no miftake was to be made.—
Thus, in the laft quoted formula, the words *quantum aequius
melius,* fhew that the Prætor was to appoint inferior Judges
both to afcertain the damage done and determine finally upon
the cafe, according to the direction he previoufly gave them;

Extremely like the above *Actiones legis* are the *Writs* used in the English Courts of law. Those writs are framed for, and adapted to every branch or denomination of actions, such as *detinue, trespass, action upon the case, accompt, and covenant,* &c. the same strictness obtains in regard to them as did in regard to the Roman law *formulæ* above mentioned : there is the same danger in misapplying them, or in failing in any part of them ; and to use the words of an English Law-writer on the subject, " Writs must be rightly directed, or they will be nought.. " .. In all writs, care must be had that they be laid and " formed according to their case, and so pursued in the " process thereof *."

The same formality likewise prevails in the English *pleadings,* and conduct of the process, as obtained in the old Roman Law proceedings; and in the same manner as the Roman Jurisconsults had their *Actionis postulationes & editiones* their *inficiationes, exceptiones, sponsiones, replicationes, duplicationes,* &c. so the English Lawyers have their *counts, bars, replicationes, rejoinders, sur-rejoinders, rebutters, sur-rebutters,* &c. A scrupulous accuracy in observing certain rules, is moreover necessary in the management of those pleadings: the following are the words of an English Law-writer on the subject ; " Though the art and dexterity of pleading, was in its " nature and design only to render the fact plain and in- " telligible, and to bring the matter to judgment with " convenient certainty, it began to degenerate from its " primitive simplicity. Pleaders, yea and Judges, hav- " ing become too curious in that respect, pleadings at

these words being exclusively appropriated to the kind of actions called *Arbitrariae,* from the above-mentioned Judges or Arbitrators. In actions brought to require the execution of conventions that had no name, the convention itself was expressed in the formula ; such is that which is recited above, relating to work done by the Plaintiff &c. &c.

* Jacob's Law Dictionary. See *Writ.*

" length ended in a piece of nicety and curiofity, by
" which the mifcarriage of many a caufe, upon fmall
" trivial objections, has been occafioned *.

There is, however, a difference between the Roman
Actionis leges, and the English Writs; which is, that the
former might be framed when new ones were neceffary,
by the Prætor or Judge of the Court, or, in fome cafes,
by the body of the Jurifconfults themfelves,—whereas
Writs, when wanted for fuch new cafes as may offer, can
only be devifed by a diftinct Judge or Court, exclufively
invefted with fuch power, viz. the High Court of Chancery. The iffuing of Writs already exifting, for the different cafes to which they belong, is alfo exprefsly referved to this Court; and fo important has its office on
thofe two points been deemed by Lawyers, that it has
been called, by way of eminence, the Manufactory of
Juftice *(Officina Juftitiæ)*. Original Writs befides,
when once framed, are not at any time to be altered, except by Parliamentary authority †.

Of fo much weight in the English law are the original delineations of cafes we mention, that no caufe is

* Cunningham's Law Dictionary. See *Pleadings.*

† Writs, legally iffued, are alfo neceffary for executing
the different incidental proceedings that may take place in
the courfe of a law-fuit, fuch as producing witneffes, &c.
The names given to the different kinds of writs, are ufually
derived from the firft Latin words by which they began
when they were written in Latin, or at leaft from fome remarkable word in them; which gives rife to expreffions fufficiently uncouth and unintelligible. Thus a *Pone*, is a writ
iffued to oblige a perfon in certain cafes to give fureties
(Pone per vadium, and *falvos plegios)*. A writ of *Subpœna* is
to oblige witneffes, and fometimes other claffes of perfons,
to appear before a Court. An action of *Qui tam*, is that
which is brought to fue for a proportional fhare of a fine eftablifhed by fome penal Statute, by the perfon who laid an information: the words in the writ being, *Qui tam pro Dom-
ino rege, quam pro feipfo in hac parte fequitur*, &c. &c.

O

suffered to be proceeded upon, unless they first appear as legal introductors to it. However important or interesting the case, the Judge, till he sees the Writ he is used to, or at least a Writ issued from the right Manufactory, is both deaf and dumb. He is without eyes to see, or ears to hear. And when a case of a new kind offers, for which there is as yet no Writ in being, should the Lord Chancellor and Masters in Chancery disagree in creating one, or prove unequal to the arduous task, the Great National Council, that is Parliament themselves, are in such emergency expressly applied to: by means of their collected wisdom, the right mystical words are brought together: the Judge is restored to the free use of his organs of hearing and of speech; and, by the creation of a new *Writ*, a new province is added to the Empire of the Courts of Law.

In fine, those precious Writs, those valuable Briefs *(Brevia)* as they are also called by way of eminence, which are the elixir and quintessence of the Law, have been committed to the special care of the Officers appointed for that purpose, whose offices derive their names from those peculiar instruments they respectively use for the preservation of the deposit with which they are intrusted; the one being called the office of the *Hamper*, and the other, of the *Small bag* *.

To say the truth, however, the creating of a new Writ, upon any new given case, is matter of more difficulty than the generality of Readers are aware of. The very importance which is thought to be in those professional forms of words, renders them really important. As every thing without them is illegal in a Court of Common

---

* *Hanaperium & Parva baga*, the Hanaper Office and the Petty-bag Office: the above two Latin words, it is not improper to observe, do not occur in Tully's works. To the care of the Petty-bag office those writs are trusted in which the King's business is concerned: and to the Hanaper-office, those which relate to the subject.

Law, fo with them every thing becomes legal; that is to fay, they empower the Court legally to determine upon every kind of fuit to which they are made to ferve as introductors. The creating of a new Writ, therefore, amounts in its confequences to the framing of a new law, and a law of a general nature too: now, the creating of fuch a law, on the firft appearance of a new cafe, which law-is afterwards to be applied to all fuch cafes as may be fimilar to the firft, is really matter of difficulty; efpecially, when men are as yet in the dark as to the beft kind of provifion to be made for the cafe in queftion, or even when it is not perhaps yet known whether it be proper to make any provifion at all. The framing of a new Writ under fuch circumftances, is a meafure on which Lawyers or Judges will not very willingly either venture of themfelves, or apply to the Legiflature for that purpofe.

Owing to the above-mentioned real difficulty in creating new Writs on the one hand, and to the abfolute neceffity of fuch Writs in the Court of Common Law on the other, many new fpecies of claims and cafes (the arifing of which is from time to time the unavoidable confequence of the progrefs of trade and civilization) are left unprovided for, and remain like fo many vacant fpaces in the Law, or rather, like fo many inacceffible fpots, which the laws in being cannot reach: now this is a great imperfection in the diftribution of Juftice, which fhould be open to every individual, and provide remedies for every kind of claim which men may fet up againft one another.

To remedy the above inconvenience, or rather in fome degree to palliate it, law fictions have been reforted to, in the Englifh Law, by which Writs, being warped from their actual meaning, are made to extend to cafes to which they in no fhape belong.

Law fictions of the kind we mention were not unknown to the old Roman Jurifconfults; and as an inftance of their ingenuity in that refpect, may be mentioned that kind of action, in which a Daughter

was called a Son *.   Several inftances might alfo be quoted of the fictitious ufe of Writs in the Englifh Courts of
Common Law. A very remarkable expedient of that fort
occurs in the method generally ufed to fue for the payment of certain kinds of debt, before the Court of Common Pleas, fuch, if I am not miftaken, as a falary for
work done, indemnity for fulfilling orders received, &c.
The Writ iffued in thofe cafes is grounded on the fuppofition, that the perfon fued has trefpaffed on the ground
of the Plaintiff, and broken by force of arms through his
fences and inclofures; and under this predicament the
Defendant is brought before the Court : this Writ, which
has been that which Lawyers have found of moft convenient ufe, to introduce before a Court of Common Law
the kinds of claim we mention, is called in technical language a *Claufum fregit.*——In order to bring a perfon
before the Court of King's Bench, to anfwer demands of
much the fame nature with thofe above, a Writ, called a
Latitat, is iffued, in which it is taken for granted that the
Defendant infidioufly conceals himfelf, and is lurking in
fome County, different from that in which the Court is
fitting ; the expreffions ufed in the Writ being, that " he
" runs up and fecretes himfelf ;" though no fuch fact is
ferioufly meant to be advanced either by the Attorney or
the Party.

The fame principle of ftrict adherence to certain forms
long fince eftablifhed, has alfo caufed Lawyers to introduce
into their proceedings, fictitious names of perfons who are
fuppofed to difcharge the office of fureties; and in certain
cafes, it feems, the name of a fictitious perfon is introduced in a Writ along with that of the principal Defendant,
as being joined in a common caufe with him.   Another

---

* From the above inftance it might be concluded that the
Roman Jurifconfults were poffeffed of ftill greater power than
the Englifh Parliament ; for it is a fundamental principle
with the Englifh Lawyers, that Parliament can do every
thing, *except* making a Woman a Man, or a Man a Woman.

inftance of the fame high regard of Lawyers, and Judges too, for certain old forms, which makes them more unwilling to depart from fuch forms than from the truth itfelf of facts, occurs in the above-mentioned expedient ufed to bring ordinary caufes before the Court of Exchequer, in order to be tried there at Common Law ; which is, by making a declaration that the Plaintiff is a King's debtor, though neither the Court nor the Plaintiff's Attorney lay any ferious ftrefs on the affertion *.

CHAP. XI.

The Subject continued. The Courts of Equity.

HOWEVER, there are limits to the law fictions and fubtilties we mention ; and the remedies of the law cannot by their means be extended to all poffible cafes that arife, unlefs to many abfurdities are fuffered to

* Another inftance of the ftrict adherence of the Englifh Lawyers to their old eftablifhed forms in preference even to the truth of facts, occurs in the manner of executing the very Act mentioned in this Chapter, paffed in the reign of George I. for preventing perfonal Arreft for debts under forty fhillings. If the defendant, after being perfonally ferved with a copy of the procefs, does not appear on the appointed days, the method is to fuppofe that he has actually made his appearance, and the caufe is proceeded upon according to this fuppofition : fictitious names of bails are alfo reforted to.

The inhabitants of Bengal, and other Eaft-India provinces, have been prodigioufly furprifed, it is faid, at the refinements, fictions, and intricacy of the Englifh law, in regard to civil matters, which was introduced among them a few years ago ; and it is certainly not to be doubted that they may have been aftonifhed.

be accumulated; nay, there have been instances in which
the improper application of Writs, in the Courts of Law,
has been checked by authority.   In order therefore to remedy the inconveniences we mention, that is, in order to
extend the administration of distributive Justice to all
possible cases, by freeing it from the professional difficulties that have gradually grown up in its way, a new Kind
of Courts has been instituted in England, called *Courts of
Equity*.

The generality of people, missed by this word *Equity*,
have conceived false notions of the office of the Courts
we mention ; and it seems to be generally thought that
the Judges who sit in them, are only to follow the rules
of natural Equity ; by which People appear to understand, that in a Court of Equity, the Judge may follow
the dictates of his own private feelings, and ground his
decisions as he thinks proper, on the peculiar circumstances and situation of those persons who make their appearance before him.   Nay, Doctor Johnson, in his abridged
Dictionary, gives the following definition of the power
of the Court of Chancery, considered as a Court of Equity : " The Chancellor hath power to moderate and tem-
" per the written law, and subjecteth himself only to
" the law of nature and conscience :" for which definition Dean Swift, and Cowell, who was a Lawyer, are
quoted as authorities.   Other instances might be produced of Lawyers who have been inaccurate in their definitions of the true offices of the Judges of Equity.   And
the above-named Doctor himself is on no subject a despicable authority.

Certainly the power of the Judges of Equity cannot
be to alter, by their own private power, the Written Law,
that is, Acts of Parliament, and thus to controul the Legislature.   Their office only consists, as will be proved in
the sequel, in providing remedies for those cases for which
the public good requires that remedies should be provided,
and in regard to which the Courts of Common Law, shac-

kled by their original forms and inftitutions, cannot procure any ;—or, in other words—the Courts of Equity have a power to adminifter Juftice to individuals, unreftrained, not by the Law, but by the profeffional law difficulties which Lawyers have from time to time contrived in the Courts of Common Law, and to which the Judges of thofe Courts have given their fanction.

An office of the kind here mentioned, was foon found neceffary in Rome, for reafons of the fame nature with thofe above delineated. For it is remarkable enough, that the Body of Englifh Lawyers, by refufing admittance to the Code of Roman Laws, as it exifted in the latter times of the Empire, have only fubjected themfelves to the fame difficulties under which the old Roman Jurifconfults laboured, during the time they were raifing the ftructure of thofe fame Laws. And it may alfo be obferved, that the Englifh Lawyers or Judges have fallen upon much the fame expedients as thofe which the Roman Jurifconfults and Prætors had adopted.

This office of a Judge of *Equity* was in time affumed by the Prætor in Rome, in addition to the judicial power he before poffeffed *. At the beginning of the year for which he had been elected, the Prætor made a declaration of thofe remedies for new difficult cafes, which he had determined to afford during the time of his Magiftracy ; in the choice of which he was no doubt directed, either by his own obfervations, while out of office, on the propriety of fuch remedies, or by the fuggeftions of experienced Lawyers on the fubject. This Declaration (*Edictum*) the Prætor produced *in albo*, as the expreffion was. Modern Civilians have made many conjactures on the real meaning of the above words : one of their fuppofitions, which is as likely to be true as any other, is, that the Prætor's

---

* The Prætor thus poffeffed two diftinct branches of judicial authority, in the fame manner as the Court of Exchequer does in England, which occafionally fits as a Court of Common Law, and a Court of Equity.

Edictum, or heads of new law remedies, were written on a whitened wall, by the fide of his tribunal.

Among the provifions made by the Roman Prætors in their capacity of Judges of Equity, may be mentioned thofe which they introduced in favour of emancipated Sons and of relations by the Women's fide *(Cognati,)* in regard to the right of inheriting. Emancipated Sons were fuppofed, by the Laws of the Twelve Tables, to have ceafed to be the children of their Father, and, as a confequence, a legal claim was denied them on the paternal inheritance. Relations by the Woman's fide were taken no notice of, in that article of the fame laws which treated of the right of fucceffion, mention being only made of relations by the Men's fide *(Agnati.)* The former, the Prætor admitted, by the Edict *Unde Liberi*, to fhare the Father's (or Grandfather's) inheritance along with their brother's; and the latter he put in poffeffion of the patrimony of a kinfman deceafed, by means of the Edict *Unde Cognati*, when there were no relations by the Men's fide. Thefe two kinds of inheritance were not however called *hæreditas*, but only *bonorum poffeffio;* thefe words being very accurately diftinguifhed, though the effect was in the iffue exactly the fame *.

---

* As the power of Fathers, at Rome, was unbounded, and lafted as long as their life, the emancipating of Sons was a cafe that occurred frequently enough, either for the fecurity or fatisfaction of thofe who engaged in any undertaking with them. The power of Fathers had been carried fo far by the laws of Romulus, confirmed afterwards by thofe of the Twelve Tables, that they might fell their Sons for flaves as often as three times, if, after a firft or fecond fale, they happened to acquire their liberty. It was only after being fold for the third time, and then becoming again free, that fons could be entirely releafed from the paternal authority. On this law-doctrine were founded the peculiar formality and method of emancipating Sons. A pair of fcales, and fome copper coin were firft brought; without the prefence of thefe ingredients the whole bufinefs would have been void; and the Father ·

'In the fame manner, the Laws of the Twelve Tables had provided relief only for cafes of theft ; and no mention was made in them of cafes of goods taken away by force (a deed which was not looked upon in fo odious a light at Rome as theft, which was confidered as the peculiar guilt of flaves). In procefs of time the Prætor promifed relief to fuch perfons as might have their goods taken from them by open force, and gave them an action for the recovery of four times the value, againft thofe who had committed the fact with an evil intention. *Si cui dolo malo bona rapta effe dicentur, ei in quadruplum* JUDICIUM DABO.

Again, neither the Law of the Twelve Tables, nor the Laws made afterwards in the Affemblies of the People, had provided remedies except for very few cafes of fraud. Here the Prætor likewife interfered in his capacity of Judge of Equity, though fo very late as the time of Cicero ; and promifed relief to defrauded perfons, in thofe cafes in which the laws in being afforded no action. *Quæ dolo malo facta effe dicentur, fi de his rebus alia actio non erit & jufta caufa effe videbitur,* JUDICIUM DABO *. By Edicts of the fame nature, Prætors in procefs of time gave relief in certain cafes to married Women, and like-

then made a formal fale of his fon to a perfon appointed to buy him, who was immediately to free, or *manumit* him : thefe fales and manumiffions were repeated three times. Five witneffes were to be prefent, befides a Man to hold the fcales, *(Libripens,)* and another *(Anteftatus)* occafionally to remind the witneffes to be attentive to the bufinefs before them.

* At the fame time that the Prætor proffered a new Edict, he alfo made public thofe peculiar formulæ by which the execution of the fame was afterwards to be required from him. The name of that Prætor who firft produced the Edict above mentioned, was Aquilius, as we are informed by Cicero, in that elegant ftory well known to Scholars, in which he relates the kind of fraud that was put upon Canius, a Roman Knight, when he purchafed a pleafure-houfe and gardens, near Syracufe in Sicily. This account Cicero

wife to Minors (*Minoribus xxv annis succurrit Prætor,* &c. *

The Courts of Equity eſtabliſhed in England, have in like manner provided remedies for a very great number of caſes, or ſpecies of demand, for which the Courts of Common Law, cramped by their forms and peculiar law tenets, can afford none. Thus, the Courts of Equity may, in certain caſes, give actions for and againſt infants, notwithſtanding their minority—and for and againſt married Women, notwithſtanding their coverture. Married Women may even in certain caſes ſue their huſbands before a Court of Equity. Executors may be made to pay intereſt for money that lies long in their hands. Courts of Equity may appoint Commiſſioners to hear the evidence of abſent witneſſes. When other proofs

concludes with obſerving that Canius was left without remedy, " as Aquilius, his Colleague and friend, had not yet " publiſhed his formulæ concerning fraud." *Quid enim faceret ? nondum enim Aquilius, Collega & familiaris meus, protulerat de dolo malo formulas.* Off. III. 14.

* The Law Collection, or Syſtem that was formed by the ſeries of Edicts publiſhed at different times by Prætors, was called *Jus Prætorium,* and alſo *Jus Honorarium (not ſtrictly binding).* The Laws of the Twelve Tables, together with all ſuch other Laws as had at any time been paſſed in the Aſſembly of the People, were called by way of eminence, *Jus Civile.* The diſtinction was exactly of the ſame nature as that which takes place in England, between the Common and Statute Laws, and the law or practice of the Courts of Equity. The two branches of the Prætor's judicial office were very accurately diſtinguiſhed ; and there was beſides, this capital difference between the remedies or actions which he gave in his capacity of Judge of Civil Law, and thoſe in his capacity of Judge of Equity, that the former, being grounded on the *Jus Civile,* were perpetual ; the latter muſt be preferred within the year, and were accordingly called *Actiones annuæ,* or *Actiones prætoriae ;* in the ſame manner as the former were called *Actiones civiles,* or *Actiones perpetuae.*

fail, they may impofe an oath on either of the Parties; or, in the like cafe of a failure of proofs, they may compel a trader to produce his books of trade. They may alfo confirm a title to land, though one has loft his writings, &c. &c.

The power of the Courts of Equity in England, of which the Court of Chancery is the principal one, no doubt owes its origin to the power poffeffed by this latter, both of creating and iffuing Writs. When new complicated cafes offered, for which a new kind of Writ was wanted, the Judges of Chancery, finding that it was neceffary that juftice fhould be done, and at the fame time being unwilling to make general and perpetual provifions on the cafes before them by creating new Writs, commanded the appearance of both parties, in order to procure as complete information as poffible in regard to the circumftances attending the cafe; and then they gave a decree upon the fame by way of experiment.

To beginnings and circumftances like thefe the Englifh Courts of Equity, it is not to be doubted, owe their prefent exiftence. In our days, when fuch ftrict notions are entertained concerning the power of Magiftrates and Judges, it can fcarcely be fuppofed that thofe Courts, however ufeful, could gain admittance. Nor indeed, even in the times when they were inftituted, were their proceedings free from oppofition; and afterwards, fo late as the reign of Queen Elizabeth, it was adjudged in the cafe of *Colleflon and Gardner*, that the killing a Sequeftrator from the Court of Chancery, in the difcharge of his bufinefs, was no murder, which judgment could only be awarded on the ground that the Sequeftrator's commiffion, and confequently the power of his Employers, were illegal*. However, the authority of the Courts of

---

* When Sir Edward Coke was Lord Chief Juftice of the King's Bench, and Lord Ellefmere Lord Chancellor, during the reign of James I. a very ferious quarrel alfo took place between the Courts of Law, and thofe of Equity, which is

Equity has in procefs of time become fettled; one of the conftituent branches of the Legiflature even receives at prefent appeals from the decrees paffed in thofe Courts; and I have no doubt that feveral Acts of the whole Legiflature might be produced, in which the office of the Courts of Equity is openly acknowledged.

The kind of procefs that has in time been eftablifhed in the Court of Chancery, is as follows. After a petition is received by the Court, the perfon fued is ferved with a writ of *Subpœna*, to command his appearance. If he does not appear, an attachment is iffued againft him; and if a *non inventus* is returned, that is, if he is not to be found, a proclamation goes forth againft him; then a commiffion of rebellion is iffued for apprehending him, and bringing him to the Fleet prifon. If the perfon fued ftands farther in contempt, a Serjeant at arms is to be fent out to take him; and if he cannot be taken, a fequeftration of his land may be obtained till he appears. Such is the power which the Court of Chancery, as a Court of Equity hath gradually acquired to compel appearance before it. In regard to the execution of the Decrees it gives, it feems that Court has not been quite fo fuccefsful; at leaft, thofe Law-writers whofe Works I have had an opportunity to fee, hold it as a maxim, that the Court of Chancery cannot bind the eftate, but only the perfon; and as a confequence, a perfon who refufes to fubmit to its decree, is only to be confined to the Fleet prifon *.

mentioned in the fourth Chapter of the third Book of Judge Blackftone's Commentaries: a Work in which more might have been faid on the fubject of the Courts of Equity.

* The Court of Chancery was very likely the firft inftituted of the two Courts of Equity: as it was the Higheft Court in the Kingdom, it was beft able to begin the eftablifhment of an office, or power, which naturally gave rife at firft to fo many objections. The Court of Exchequer, we may fuppofe, only followed the example of the Court of Chancery:

On this occasion I shall observe, that the authority of the Lord Chancellor, in England, in his capacity of a Judge of Equity, is much more narrowly limited than that which the Prætors in Rome had been able to assume. The Roman Prætors, we are to remark, united in themselves the double office of deciding cases according to the Civil Law (*Jus civile*,) and to the Prætorian Law, or Law of Equity ; nor did there exist any other Court besides their own, that might serve as a check upon them : hence it happened that their proceedings in the career of Equity, were very arbitrary indeed. In the first place, they did not use to make it any very strict rule to adhere to the tenor of their own Edicts, during the whole year which their office lasted ; and they assumed a power of altering them as they thought proper. To remedy so capital a defect in the distribution of Justice, a law was passed so late as the year of Rome 687 (not long before Tully's time,) which was called *Lex Cornelia*, from the name of C. Cornelius, a Tribune of the People, who propounded it under the Consulship of C. Piso, and Man. Glabrio. By this law it was enacted, that Prætors should in future constantly decree according to their own Edicts, without altering any thing in them during the whole year of their Prætorship. Some modern Civilians produce a certain Senatusconsult to the same effect, which, they say, had been passed a few hundred years before, while others are of opinion the same is not genuine : however, supposing it to be really so, the passing of the law we mention, shews that it had not been so well attended to as it ought to have been. -

in order the better to secure the new power it assumed, it found it necessary to bring out the whole strength it could muster ; and both the Treasurer and the Chancellor of the Exchequer sit (or are supposed to sit) in the court of Exchequer, when it is formed as a Court of Equity.

Though the above mentioned arbitrary proceedings of Prætors were put a stop to, they still retained another priviledge, equally hurtful; which was, that every new Prætor, on his coming into office, had it in his power to retain only what part he pleased of the Edicts of his predecessors, and to reject the remainder: from which it followed that the Prætorian Laws or Edicts, though provided for so great a number of important cases, were really in force for only one year, the time of the duration of a Prætors office. * Nor was a regulation made to remedy this capital defect in the Roman Jurisprudence, before the time of the Emperor Hadrian; which is another remarkable proof of the very great slowness with which useful public regulations take place in every Nation. Under the reign of the Emperor we mention, the most useful Edicts of former Prætors were by his order collected, or rather compiled into one general Edict, which was thenceforwards to be observed by all civil Judges in their decision, and was accordingly called the perpetual Edict (*perpetuum Edictum*.) This Edict, though now lost, soon grew into great repute; all the Jurisconsults of those days vied with each other in writing commentaries upon it; and the Emperor himself thought it so glorious an act of his reign, to have caused the same to be framed, and he considered himself on that account as being another Numa. †

* Those Edicts of their predecessors in office, which the New Prætors thought proper to retain, were called *Edicta Tralatitia;* those which they themselves published (as also the alterations they made in former ones) were called *Edicta Nova.* From the above mentioned power exercised by every new Prætor in turn, their Edicts were sometimes distinguished by the appellation of *Leges annuæ,* annual. See Orat. in Ver. 1. 42.

† Several other more extensive law compilations were framed after the perpetual Edict we mention; there having

But the Courts of Equity in England, notwithstand-ing the extensive jurisdiction they have been able in procefs of time to affume, never fuperfeded the other Courts of Law. Thefe Courts ftill continue to exift in the fame manner as formerly, and have proved a lafting check on the innovations, and in general the proceedings of the Courts of Equity. And here we may remark the fingular, and at the fame time effec-tual, means of balancing each other's influence, reci-procally poffeffed by the Courts of the two different fpe-cies. By means of its exclufive privilege both of creating and iffuing writs, the Court of Chancery has been able to hinder the Courts of Common Law from arrogating to themfelves the cognizance of thofe new cafes which were not provided for by any law in being, and thus dangeroufly uniting in themfelves the power of Judges of Equity with that of Judges of Common Law. On the other hand, the Courts of Common Law are alone invefted with the power of punifhing (or allowing da-mages for) thofe cafes of violence by which the pro-ceedings of the Courts of Equity might be oppofed; and by that means they have been able to obftruct the enterprizes of the latter, and prevent their effecting in

been a kind of emulation between the Roman Emperors, in regard to the improvement of the law. At laft, under the reign of Juftinian, that celebrated Compilation was publifhed, called the Code of Juftinian, which, under different titles, comprifes the Roman Laws, the Edicts of the Prætors, to-gether with the *refcripts* of the Emperors; and an equal fanc-tion was given to the whole. This was an event of much the fame nature as that which will take place in England, when-ever a coalition fhall be effected between the Courts of Com-mon Law and thofe of Equity, and both fhall thenceforwards be found alike to frame their judgments from the whole mafs of decided cafes and precedents then exifting, at leaft of fuch as it will be poffible to bring confiftently together into one compilation.

themselves the like dangerous union of the two offices of Judges of Common Law and of Equity.

Owing to the situation of the English Courts of Equity, with respect to the Courts of Common Law, those courts have really been kept within limits that may be called exactly defined, if the nature of their functions be considered. In the first place, they can neither touch Acts of Parliament, nor the established practice of the other Courts, much less reverse the judgments already passed in these latter, as the Roman Prætors sometimes used to do in regard to the decisions of their predecessors in office, and sometimes also in regard to their own. The Courts of Equity are even restrained from taking cognizance of any case for which the other Courts can possibly afford remedies. Nay, so strenuously have the Courts of Common Law defended the verge of their frontier, that they have prevented the Courts of Equity from using in their proceedings the mode of Trial by a Jury; so that, when in a case already begun to be taken cognizance of by the Court of Chancery, the Parties happen to join issue on any particular fact (the truth or falsehood of which a Jury is to determine,) the Court of Chancery, is obliged to deliver up the cause to the Court of King's Bench, there to be finally decided. * In fine, the example of the regularity of the proceedings, practised in the courts of Common Law, has been communicated to the Courts of Equity; and Rolls or Records are carefully kept of the pleadings, determinations, and acts of those Courts, to serve as rules for future decisions. †

* See Cunningham's and Jacob's law dictionaries, passim.

† The Master of the Rolls is the Keeper of those records, as the title of this office expresses. His office in the Court of Chancery is of great importance, as he can hear and determine causes in the absence of the Lord Chancellor.

So far therefore from having it in his power "*to temper and moderate,*" (that is, *to alter*) the Written Law or Statutes, a Judge of Equity, we find, cannot alter the Unwritten Law, that is to say, the established practice of the other Courts, and the judgments grounded thereupon,—nor even can he meddle with those cases for which either the Written or Unwritten Law has already made general provisions, and of which there is a possibility for the ordinary Courts of Law to take cognizance.

From all the above observations it follows, that, of the Courts of Equity as established in England, the following definition may be given; which is, that they are a kind of *inferior experimental* Legislature, continually employed in finding out and providing law remedies for those new species of cases for which neither the Courts of Common Law, nor the Legislature, have as yet found it convenient or practicable to establish any. In doing which, they are to forbear to interfere with such cases as they find already in general provided for. A Judge of Equity is also to adhere in his decisions to the system of decrees formerly passed in his own Court, regular records of which are kept for that purpose.

From this latter circumstance it again follows, that a Judge of Equity, by the very exercise he makes of his power, is continually abridging the arbitrary part of it; as every new case he determines, every precedent he establishes, becomes a land-mark or boundary which both he and his successors in office are afterwards expected to regard.

Here it may be added as a conclusion, that appeals from the Decrees passed in the Courts of Equity are carried to the House of Peers; which bare circumstance might suggest that a Judge of Equity is subjected to certain positive rules, besides those "*of nature and con- science only;*" an appeal being naturally grounded on a fuppofition that fome rules of that kind were neglected.

The above difcuffion on the Englifh Law, has proved much longer than I intended at firft ; fo much as to have fwelled, I find, into two new additional Chapters. However I confefs I have been under the greater temptation to treat at fome length the fubject of the Courts of Equity, as I have found the error (which may be called a conftitutional one) concerning the arbitrary office of thofe Courts, to be countenanced by the apparent authority of Lawyers, and of men of abilities, at the fame time that I have not feen in any book any attempt made profeffedly to confute the fame, nor indeed to point out the nature and true office of the Courts of Equity.

※ ※ ※

C H A P T E R XII.

Of Criminal Juftice.

WE are now to treat of an article, which, though it does not in England, and indeed fhould not in any State, make part of the powers which are properly conftitutional, that is, of the reciprocal rights by means of which the Powers that concur to form the Government conftantly balance each other, yet effentially interefts the fecurity of individuals, and, in the iffue, the Conftitution itfelf ; I mean to fpeak of Criminal Juftice. But, previous to an expofition of the laws of England on this head, it is neceffary to defire the reader's attention to certain confiderations.

When a Nation entrufts the power of the State to a certain number of perfons, or to one, it is with a view to

two points : the one, to repel more effectually foreign attacks, the other, to maintain domeſtic tranquillity.

To accompliſh the former point, each individual ſur-
renders a ſhare of his property, and ſometimes, to a certain degree, even of his liberty. But, though the power
of thoſe who are the Heads of the State, may thereby be
rendered very conſiderable, yet it cannot be ſaid, that liberty is, after all, in any high degree endangered ; becauſe
ſhould ever the Executive Power turn againſt the Nation
a ſtrength which ought to be employed ſolely for its defence, this Nation, if it were really free, by which I mean,
unreſtrained by political prejudices, would be at no loſs
for providing the means of its ſecurity.

In regard to the latter object, that is, the maintenance
of domeſtic tranquillity, every individual muſt, excluſive
of new renunciations of his natural liberty, moreover
ſurrender, which is a matter of far more dangerous conſequence, a part of his perſonal ſecurity.

The Legiſlative power, being, from the nature of human affairs, placed in the alternative, either of expoſing
individuals to dangers which it is at the ſame time able
extremely to diminiſh, or of delivering up the State to
the boundleſs calamities of violence and anarchy, finds itſelf compelled to reduce all its members within reach of
the arm of the public Power, and, by withdrawing in ſuch
caſes the benefit of the Social ſtrength, to leave them expoſed, bare, and defenceleſs, to the exertion of the com-
paratively immenſe power of the Executors of the laws.

Nor is this all ; for, inſtead of that powerful re-action
which the public authority ought in the former caſe to experience, here it muſt find none : and the law is obliged
to proſcribe even the attempt of reſiſtance. It is therefore
in regulating ſo dangerous a power, and in guarding leſt
it ſhould deviate from the real end of its inſtitution, that
Legiſlation ought to exhauſt all its efforts.

But here it is of great importance to obſerve, that the
more powers a Nation has reſerved to itſelf, and the more

it limits the authority of the Executors of the laws, the more induſtriouſly ought its precautions to be multiplied.

In a State where, from a ſeries of events, the will of the Prince has at length attained to hold the place of law, he ſpreads an univerſal oppreſſion, arbitrary and unreſiſted; even complaint is dumb; and the individual, undiſtinguiſhable by him, finds ſafety in his own inſignificance. With reſpect to the few who ſurround him, as they are at the ſame time the inſtruments of his greatneſs, they have nothing to dread but momentary caprices; a danger againſt which, if there prevails a certain general mildneſs of manners, they are in a great meaſure ſecured.

But in a State where the Miniſters of the laws meet with obſtacles at every ſtep, even their ſtrongeſt paſſions are continually put in motion, and that portion of public authority, depoſited with them to be the inſtrument of national tranquillity, eaſily becomes a moſt formidable weapon.

Let us begin with the moſt favourable ſuppoſition, and imagine a Prince whoſe intentions are in every caſe thoroughly upright,—let us even ſuppoſe that he never lends an ear to the ſuggeſtions of thoſe whoſe intereſt it is to deceive him; nevertheleſs, he will be ſubject to error; and this error which, I will farther allow, ſolely proceeds from his attachment to the public welfare, yet may very poſſibly happen to prompt him to act as if his views were directly oppoſite.

When opportunities ſhall offer, (and many ſuch will occur) of procuring a public advantage by overleaping reſtraints, confident in the uprightneſs of his intentions, and being naturally not very earneſt to diſcover the diſtant evil conſequences of actions in which, from his very virtue, he feels a kind of complacency, he will not perceive that, in aiming at a momentary advantage, he ſtrikes at the laws themſelves on which the ſafety of the Nation reſts; and that thoſe acts, ſo laudable when we only conſider the motive of them, make a breach at which tyranny will one day enter.

Yet farther, he will not even underftand the complaints that will be made againft him. To infift upon them will appear to him to the laft degree injurious: pride, when perhaps he is leaft aware of it, will enter the lifts; what he began with calmnefs, he will profecute with warmth; and if the laws fhall not have taken every poffible precaution, he may think he is acting a very honeft part, while he treats as enemies of the State, Men whofe only crime will be that of being more fagacious than himfelf, or of being in a better fituation for judging of the refults of meafures.

But it were mightily to exalt human nature, to think that this cafe of a Prince who never aims at augmenting his power, may in any fhape be expected frequently to occur. Experience, on the contrary, evinces that the happieft difpofitions are not proof againft the allurements of power, which has no charms but as it leads on to new advances; authority endures not the very idea of reftraint, nor does it ceafe to ftruggle till it has beaten down every boundary.

Openly to level every barrier, at once to affume the abfolute Mafter, are, as we faid before, fruitlefs tafks. But it is here to be remembered, that thofe powers of the People which are referved as a check upon the Sovereign, can only be effectual fo far as they are brought into action by private individuals. Sometimes a citizen, by the force and perfeverance of his complaints, opens the eyes of the Nation; at other times, fome member of the Legiflature propofes a law for the removal of fome public abufe: thefe, therefore, will be the perfons againft whom the Prince will direct all his efforts *.

And he will the more affuredly do fo, as, from the error fo ufual among men in power, he will think that the oppofition he meets with, however general, wholly depends

* By the word Prince, I mean thofe who, under whatever appellation and in whatever Government it may be, are at the head of public affairs.

on the activity of but one or two leaders; and amidst the
calculations he will make, both of the fuppofed fmallnefs
of the obftacle which offers to his view, and of the decifive confequence of the fingle blow he thinks he needs to
ftrike, he will be urged on by the defpair of ambition on
the point of being baffled, and by the moft violent of all
hatreds, that which was preceded by contempt.

In that cafe which I am ftill confidering, of a really
free Nation, the Sovereign muft be very careful that military violence do not make the fmalleft part of his plan:
a breach of the focial compact like this, added to the horror of the expedient, would infallibly endanger his whole
authority. But, on the other hand, as he was refolved
to fucceed, he will, in defect of other refources, try the
utmoft extent of the legal powers which the Conftitution
has intrufted with him; and if the laws have not in a manner provided for every poffible cafe, he will avail himfelf
of the imperfect precautions themfelves that have been
taken, as a cover to his tyrannical proceedings; he will
purfue fteadily his particular object, while his profeffions
breathe nothing but the general welfare, and deftroy the
affertors of the laws, under the very fhelter of the forms
contrived for their fecurity *.

This is not all; independently of the immediate mif-
chief he may do, if the Legiflature do not interpofe in
time, the blows will reach the Conftitution itfelf; and
the confternation becoming general among the People,
each individual will find himfelf enflaved in a State which
yet may ftill exhibit all the common appearances of liberty.

---

* If there were any perfon who charged me with calum-
niating human nature, for it is her alone I am accufing here,
I would defire him to caft his eyes on the Hiftory of a Lewis
XI.—of a *Richelieu*, and, above all, on that of England before the Revolution; he would fee the arts and activity of
Government increafe, in proportion as it gradually loft its
means of oppreffion.

Not only, therefore, the safety of the individual, but that of the Nation itself, requires the utmost precautions in the establishment of that necessary, but formidable, prerogative of dispensing punishments. The first to be taken, even without which it is impossible to avoid the dangers above suggested, is, that it never be left at the disposal, nor, if it be possible, exposed to the influence of the Man who is the depositary of the public power.

The next indispensable precaution is, that neither shall this power be vested in the legislative Body; and this precaution, so necessary alike under every mode of Government, becomes doubly so, when only a small part of the Nation has a share in the legislative power.

If the judicial authority were lodged in the legislative part of the People, not only the great inconvenience must ensue of its thus becoming independent, but also, that worst of evils, the suppression of the sole circumstance that can well identify this part of the Nation with the whole, which is a common subjection to the rules which they themselves prescribe. The legislative Body, which could not, without ruin to itself, establish, openly and by direct laws, distinctions in favour of its Members, would introduce them by its judgments; and the People, in electing Representatives, would give themselves Masters.

The judicial power ought therefore absolutely to reside in a subordinate and dependent body; dependent, not in its particular acts, with regard to which it ought to be a sanctuary, but in its rules and in its forms, which the legislative authority must prescribe. How is this body to be composed? In this respect further precautions must be taken.

In a State where the prince is absolute Master, numerous Bodies of Judges are most convenient, inasmuch as they restrain, in a considerable degree, that respect of Persons which is one inevitable attendant on that mode of Government. Besides, those bodies, whatever their outward privileges may be, being at bottom in a state of great weakness, have no other means of acquiring the respect of the people than their integrity, and their constancy in observing certain rules and forms : nay, these circumstances united, in some degree over-awe the Sovereign himself, and discourage the thoughts he might entertain of making them the tools of his caprices *.

But, in an effectually limited Monarchy, that is, where the Prince is understood to be, and in fact is, subject to the laws, numerous Bodies of Judicature would be repugnant to the spirit of the Constitution, which requires that all powers in the State should be as much confined as the end of their institution can allow ; not to add, that in the vicissitudes incident to such a State, they might exert a very dangerous influence.

Besides, that awe which is naturally inspired by such Bodies, and is so useful when it is necessary to strengthen the feebleness of the laws, would not only be superfluous in a State where the whole power of the Nation is on their side, but would moreover have the mischievous tendency to introduce another sort of fear than that which Men must be taught to entertain. Those mighty Tribunals, I am willing to suppose, would preserve, in all situations of affairs, that integrity which distinguishes them in States of a different Constitution ; they would never inquire after the influence, still less the political

---

* The above observations are in a great measure meant to allude to the French *Parlemens*, and particularly that of Paris, which forms such a considerable Body as to have been once summoned as a fourth Order to the General Estates of the kingdom. The weight of that body, increased by the circumstance of the Members holding their places for life, has in general been attended with the advantage just mentioned, of placing them above being over-awed by private individuals in the administration either of civil or criminal Justice ; it has even rendered them so difficult to be managed by the Court, that the Ministers have been at times obliged to appoint particular Judges, or *Commissaries*, to try such Men as they resolve to ruin.

fentiments, of thofe whofe fate they were called to decide; but thefe advantages not being founded in the neceffity of things, and the power of fuch Judges feeming
to exempt them from being fo very virtuous, Men would
be in danger of taking up the fatal opinion, that the fimple exact obfervance of the laws is not the only tafk of
prudence; the Citizen called upon to defend, in the fphere
where fortune has placed him, his own rights, and thofe
of the Nation itfelf, would dread the confequence of even
a lawful conduct, and, though encouraged by the law,
might defert himfelf when he came to behold its Minifters.

In the affembly of thofe who fit as his Judges, the Citizen might poffibly defcry no enemies; but neither would
he fee any Man whom a fimilarity of circumftances
might engage to take a concern in his fate: and their
rank, efpecially when joined with their numbers, would
appear to him, to lift them above that which over-awes
injuftice, where the law has been unable to fecure any
other check, I mean the reproaches of the Public.

And thefe his fears would be confiderably heightened,
if, by the admiffion of the Jurifprudence received among
certain Nations, he beheld thofe Tribunals, already fo formidable, wrap themfelves up in myftery, and be made,
as it were, inacceffible *.

* An allufion is made here to the fecrecy with which the
proceedings, in the adminiftration of criminal Juftice, are
to be carried on, according to the rules of the civil law,
which in that refpect are adopted over all Europe. As foon
as the prifoner is committed, he is debarred of the fight of
every body, till he has gone through his feveral examinations. One or two Judges are appointed to examine him,
with a Clerk to take his anfwers in writing: and he ftands
alone before them in fome private room in the prifon. The
witneffes are to be examined apart, and he is not admitted to
fee them till their evidence is clofed: they are then *confronted*
together before all the Judges, to the end that the witneffes

He could not think, without difmay, of thofe vaft prifons within which he is one day perhaps to be immured—of thofe proceedings, unknown to him, through which he is to pafs—of that total feclufion from the fociety of other Men—nor of thofe long and fecret examinations, in which, abandoned wholly to himfelf, he will have nothing but a paffive defence to oppofe to the artfully varied queftions of Men, whofe intentions he fhall at leaft miftruft, and in which his fpirits, broken down by folitude, fhall receive no fupport, either from the counfels of his friends, or the looks of thofe who fhall offer up vows for his deliverance.

may fee if the prifoner is really the Man they meant in giving their refpective evidences, and that the prifoner may object to fuch of them as he fhall think proper. This done the depofitions of thofe witneffes who are adjudged upon trial to be exceptionable, are fet afide: the depofitions of the others are to be laid before the Judges, as well as the anfwers of the prifoner, who has been previoufly called upon to confirm or deny them in their prefence; and a copy of the whole is delivered to him, that he may, with the affiftance of a Counfel, which is now granted him, prepare for his juftification. The Judges are, as has been faid before, to decide, both upon the matter of law and the matter of fact, as well as upon all incidents that may arife during the courfe of the proceedings, fuch as admitting witneffes to be heard in behalf of the prifoner, &c.

This mode of criminal Judicature may be ufeful as to the bare difcovering of truth, a thing which I do not propofe to difcufs here; but, at the fame time, a prifoner is fo completely delivered up into the hands of the Judges, who can even detain him almoft at pleafure, by multiplying or delaying his examinations, that, whenever it is adopted, Men are almoft as much afraid of being accufed, as of being guilty, and efpecially grow very cautious how they interfere in public matters. We fhall fee prefently how the Trial by Jury, peculiar to the Englifh Nation, is admirably adapted to the nature of a free State.

The security of the individual, and the consciousness of that security, being then equally essential to the enjoyment of liberty, and necessary for the preservation of it, these two points must never be left out of sight, in the establishment of a judicial power; and I conceive that they necessarily lead to the following maxims.

In the first place, I shall remind the reader of what has been laid down above, that the judicial authority ought never to reside in an independent Body; still less in him who is already the trustee of the executive power.

Secondly, the party accused ought to be provided with every possible means of defence. Above all things, the whole proceedings ought to be public. The Courts, and their different forms, must be such as to inspire respect, but never terror; and the cases ought to be so accurately ascertained, the limits so clearly marked, as that neither the executive power, nor the Judges, may ever hope to transgress them with impunity.

In fine, since we must absolutely pay a price for the advantage of living in society, not only by relinquishing some share of our natural liberty (a surrender which, in a wisely framed Government, a wise Man will make without reluctance) but even also by resigning part of our personal security, in a word, since all judicial power is an evil, though a necessary one, no care should be omitted to reduce as far as possible the dangers of it.

And as there is however a period at which the prudence of Man must stop, at which the safety of the individual must be given up, and the law is to resign him over to the judgment of a few persons, that is, to speak plainly, to a decision in some sense arbitrary, it is necessary that this law should narrow as far as possible this sphere of peril, and so order matters, that when the subject shall happen to be summoned to the decision of his fate by the fallible conscience of a few of his fellow-creatures, he may always find in them advocates, and never adversaries.

C H A P. XIII.

The Subject continued.

AFTER having offered to the reader, in the preceding Chapter, such general confiderations as I thought neceffary, in order to convey a jufter idea of the fpirit of the criminal Judicature in England, and of the advantages peculiar to it, I now proceed to exhibit the particulars.

When a perfon is charged with a crime, the Magiftrate who is called in England *a Juftice of the Peace*, iffues a warrant to apprehend him; but this warrant can be no more than an order for bringing the party before him: he muft then hear him, and take down in writing his anfwers, together with the different informations. If it appears on this examination, either that the crime laid to the charge of the perfon who is brought before the Juftice, was not committed, or that there is no juft ground to fufpect him of it, he muft be fet abfolutely at liberty; if the contrary refults from the examination, the party accufed muft give bail for his appearance to anfwer to the charge; unlefs in capital cafes, for then he muft, for fafer cuftody, be really committed to prifon, in order to take his trial at the next Seffions.

But this precaution of requiring the examination of an accufed perfon, previous to his imprifonment, is not the only care which the law has taken in his behalf; it has farther ordained that the accufation againft him fhould be again difcuffed, before he can be expofed to the danger of a trial. At every feffion the Sheriff appoints what is called the *Grand Jury*. This Affembly muft be compofed of more than twelve Men, and lefs than twenty-four; and is always formed out of the moft confiderable perfons in the County. Its function is to examine the evidence that has been given in fupport of every charge: if twelve

of thofe perfons do not concur in the opinion that an accufation is well grounded, the party is immediately difcharged : if, on the contrary, twelve of the Grand Jury
find the proofs fufficient, the prifoner is faid to be indicted, and is detained in order to go through the remaining
proceedings.

On the day appointed for his Trial, the prifoner is
brought to the bar of the Court, where the Judge, after caufing the bill of indictment to be read in his prefence, muft afk him how he would be tried : to which
the prifoner anfwers, *by God and my Country* ; by which
he is underftood to claim to be tried by a Jury, and
to have all the judicial means of defence to which the
law intitles him. The Sheriff then appoints what is
called the Petty Jury : this muft be compofed of twelve
Men, chofen out of the county where the crime was
committed, and poffeffed of a landed income of ten
pounds by the year : their declaration finally decides
on the truth or falfhood of the accufation.

As the fate of the prifoner thus entirely depends on
the Men who compofe this Jury, Juftice requires that
he fhould have a fhare in the choice of them ; and this
he has through the extenfive right which the law has
granted him, of challenging, or objecting to, fuch of
them as he may think exceptionable.

Thefe challenges are of two kinds. The firft, which
is called the challenge to the *array*, has for its object
to have the whole pannel fet afide : it is propofed by
the prifoner when he thinks that the Sheriff who formed the pannel is not indifferent in the caufe ; for inftance, if he thinks he has an intereft in the profecution, that he is related to the profecutor, or in general
to the party who pretends to be injured.

The fecond kind of challenges are called, to the
Polls (*in capita :*) they are exceptions propofed againft
the Jurors, feverally, and are reduced to four heads
by Sir Edward Coke. That which he calls *propter*

honoris respectum, may be proposed against a Lord impannelled on a Jury ; or he might challenge himself. That *propter defectum* takes place when a Juror is legally incapable of serving that office, as, if he was an alien ; if he had not an estate sufficient to qualify him, &c. That *propter delictum* has for its object to set aside any Juror convicted of such crime or misdemeanor as renders him infamous, as felony, perjury, &c. That *propter affectum* is proposed against a Juror who has an interest in the conviction of the prisoner : he, for instance, who has an action depending between him and the prisoner ; he who is of kin to the prosecutor, or his counsel, attorney, or of the same society or corporation with him, &c. *

In fine, in order to relieve even the imagination of the prisoner, the law allows him, independently of the several challenges above mentioned, to challenge peremptorily, that is to say, without shewing any cause, twenty Jurors successively. †

When at length the Jury is formed, and they have taken their oath, the indictment is opened, and the prosecutor produces the proofs of his accusation. But, unlike to the rules of the Civil Law, the witnesses deliver their evidence in the presence of the prisoner : the latter may put questions to them ; he may also produce witnesses in his behalf, and have them examined upon oath. Lastly, he is allowed to have a Counsel to assist him, not only in the discussion of any point of law, which may be complicated with the fact, but al

---

* When a prisoner is an alien, one half of the Jurors must also be aliens ; a Jury thus formed is called a Jury *de medietate linguæ*.

† When these several challenges reduce too much the number of the Jurors on the Pannel, which is forty-eight, new ones are named on a writ of the Judge, who are named the *Tales*, from those words of the writ, *decem* or *octo tales*.

to in the inveſtigation of the fact itſelf, and who points out to him the queſtions he ought to aſk, or even aſks them for him. *

Such are the precautions which the law has deviſed for caſes of common proſecutions; but in thoſe for High Treaſon, and for miſpriſion of treaſon, that is to ſay, for a conſpiracy againſt the life of the King, or againſt the State, and for a concealment of it, † accuſations which ſuppoſe a heat of party and powerful accuſers, the law has provided for the accuſed party farther ſafe-guards.

Firſt, no perſon can be queſtioned for any treaſon, except a direct attempt on the life of the King, after three years elapſed ſince the offence. 2°. The accuſed party may, independently of his other legal grounds of challenging, *peremtorily* challenge thirty-five Jurors. 3°. He may have two Counſel to aſſiſt him through the whole courſe of the proceedings. 4°. That his witneſſes may not be kept away, the Judges muſt grant him the ſame compulſive proceſs to bring them in, which they iſſue to compel the evidences againſt him. 5°. A copy of his indictment muſt be delivered to him ten days at leaſt before the trial, in preſence of two witneſſes, and at the expence of five ſhillings; which copy muſt contain all the facts laid to his charge, the names, profeſſions, and abodes of the Jurors who are to be on the pannel, and of all the witneſſes who are intended to be produced againſt him. ‡

When, either in caſes of high treaſon, or of inferi-or crimes, the proſecutor and the priſoner have cloſed

* This laſt article, however, is not eſtabliſhed by law, except in caſes of treaſon; it is done only through cuſtom and the indulgence of the Judges.

† The penalty of a miſpriſion of treaſon is, the forfeiture of all goods, and impriſonment for life.

‡ Stat. 7 Will. III. c. 3. and 7 Ann. c. 21. The latter was to be in force only after the death of the late Pretender.

their evidence, and the witnesses have answered to their respective questions both of the Bench, and of the Jurors, one of the Judges makes a speech, in which he sums up the facts which have been advanced on both sides.   He points out to the Jury what more precisely constitutes the hinge of the question before them; and he gives them his opinion both with regard to the evidences that have been given, and to the point of law which is to guide them in their decision.   This done, the Jury withdraw into an adjoining room, where they must remain without eating and drinking, and without fire, till they have agreed unanimously among themselves, unless the Court give a permission to the contrary.   Their declaration or verdict (*veredictum*) must (unless they choose to give a special verdict) pronounce expressly, either that the prisoner is guilty, or that he is not guilty, of the fact laid to his charge. Lastly, the fundamental maxim of this mode of proceeding, is, that the Jury must be unanimous.

And as the main object of the institution of the Trial by a Jury, is to guard accused persons against all decisions whatsoever by Men invested with any permanent official authority, * it is not only a settled principle that the opinion which the Judge delivers has no weight but such as the Jury choose to give it; but their verdict must besides comprehend the whole matter in trial, and decide as well upon the fact, as upon the point of law that may arise out of it: in other words, they must pronounce both on the commission of a certain fact, and on the reason which makes such fact to be contrary to law †.

---

* "Laws," as *Junius* says extremely well, " are intended, not to trust to what Men will do, but to guard against " what they may do."

† Unless they choose to give a *special* verdict.—" When " the Jury," says Coke, " doubt of the law, and intend

This is even fo effential a point, that a bill of indictment muft exprefsly be grounded upon thofe two objects. Thus, an indictment for treafon muft charge that the alleged facts were committed with a treafonable intent *(proditorie)*. An indictment for murder, muft exprefs, that the fact has been committed with *malice prepenfe*, or forethought. An indictment for robbery muft charge, that the things were taken with an intention to rob *(animo furandi)*, &c. &c. *

Juries are even fo uncontrollable in their verdict, fo apprehenfive has the Conftitution been left precautions to reftrain them in the exercife of their functions, however fpecious in the beginning, might in the iffue be converted to the very deftruction of the ends of that inftitution, that it is a repeated principle that a Juror, in delivering his opinion, is to have no other rule but his opinion itfelf,—that is to fay, no other rule than the belief which refults to his mind from the facts alleged on both fides, from their probability, from the

" to do that which is juft, they find the *fpecial* matter, and " the entry is, *Et fuper tota materia petunt difcretionem Juftici-* " *ariorum.*" Inft. iv. p. 41.—Thefe words of Coke, we may obferve, confirm beyond a doubt the power of the Jury to determine on the whole matter in trial: a power which in all conftitutional views is neceffary; and the more fo, fince a prifoner cannot in England challenge the Judge, as he can under the Civil Law, and for the fame caufe as he can a witnefs.

* The principle that a Jury is to decide both on the fact and the *criminality* of it, is fo well underftood, that if a verdict were fo framed as only to have for its object the bare exiftence of the fact laid to the charge of the prifoner, no punifhment could be awarded by the Judge in confequence of it. Thus, in the profecution of Woodfall, for printing Junius's Letter to the King, the Jury brought in the following verdict, *guilty of printing and publifhing only*; the confequence of which was the difcharge of the prifoner.

credibility of the witnesses, and even from all such circumstances as he may have a private knowledge of. Lord Chief Justice Hale expresses himself on this subject, in the following terms, in his History of the Common Law of England, chap. 12. § 11.

" In this recess of the Jury, they are to consider
" their evidence, to weigh the credibility of the wit-
" nesses, and the force and efficacy of their testimo-
" nies; wherein (as I before said) they are not pre-
" cisely bound to the rules of the Civil Law, viz. to
" have two witnesses to prove every fact, unless it be
" in cases of treason, nor to reject one witness because
" he is single, or always to believe two witnesses, if
" the probability of the fact does upon other circum-
" stances reasonably encounter them; for the Trial
" is not here simply by witnesses, but *by Jury* : nay,
" it may so fall out, that a Jury upon their own
" knowledge may know a thing to be false that a
" witness swore to be true, or may know a witness to
" be incompetent or incredible, though nothing be ob-
" jected against him—and may give their verdict ac-
" cordingly *."

If the verdict pronounces *not guilty*, the prisoner is set at liberty, and cannot, on any pretence, be tried again for the same offence. If the verdict declares him *guilty*, then, and not till then, the Judge enters upon his function as a Judge, and pronounces the punishment which the law appoints †. But, even in this case, he is not to

---

* The same principles and forms are observed in civil matters; only peremptory challenges are not allowed.

† When the party accused is one of the Lords temporal, he likewise enjoys the universal privilege of being judged by his Peers; though the trial then differs in several respects. In the first place, as to the number of the Jurors: all the Peers are to perform the function of such, and they must be summoned at least twenty days beforehand. II. When the Trial takes place during the session, it is said to be in the

judge according to his own difcretion only; he muft ftrictly adhere to the letter of the law; no conftructive extenfion can be admitted, and however criminal a fact might in itfelf be, it would pafs unpunifhed if it were found not to be pofitively comprehended in fome one of the cafes provided for by the law. The evil that may a-rife from the impunity of a crime, that is, an evil which a new law may inftantly ftop, has not by the Englifh laws been confidered as of magnitude fufficient to be put in comparifon with the danger of breaking through a barri-er on which fo mightily depends the fafety of the indi-vidual *.

To all thefe precautions taken by the law for the fafe-ty of the Subject, one circumftance muft be added, which indeed would alone juftify the partiality of the Englifh Lawyers to their laws in preference to the Civil Law,— I mean the abfolute rejection they have made of torture †. Without repeating here what has been faid on this

High Court of Parliament; and the Peers officiate at once as Jurors and Judges: when the Parliament is not fitting, the trial is faid to be in the Court of the *High Steward of Eng-land;* an office which is not ufually in being, but is revived on thofe occafions; and the High Steward performs the office of Judge. III. In either of thefe cafes, unanimity is not required: and the majority, which muft confift of twelve perfons at leaft, is to decide.

* I fhall give here an inftance of the fcruple with which the Englifh Judges proceed upon occafions of this kind. Sir *Henry Ferrers* having been arrefted by virtue of a warrant, in which he was termed a *Knight,* though he was a Baronet, Nightingale his fervant took his part, and killed the Officer; but it was decided, that as the Warrant " was an ill War-" rant, the killing an Officer in executing that Warrant, " cannot be murder, becaufe no good Warrant: wherefore " he was found not guilty of the murder and manflaughter." —See Croke's Rep. P. III. p. 371.

† Coke fays (Inft. III. p. 35.) that when John Holland, Duke of Exeter, and William de la Poole, Duke of Suffolk,

ſubjeƈt by the admirable Author of the Treatiſe on *Crimes and Puniſhments*, I ſhall only obſerve, that the torture, in itſelf ſo horrible an expedient, would, more eſpecially in a free State, be attended with the moſt fatal conſequences. It was abſolutely neceſſary to preclude, by rejeƈting it, all attempts to make the purſuit of guilt an inſtrument of vengeance againſt the innocent. Even the conviƈted criminal muſt be ſpared, and a praƈtice at all rates exploded, which might ſo eaſily be made an inſtrument of endleſs vexation and perſecution *.

For the farther prevention of abuſes, it is an invariable uſage, that the Trial be public. The priſoner neither makes his appearance, nor pleads, but in places where every body may have free entrance; and the witneſſes when they give their evidence, the Judge when he delivers his opinion, the Jury when they give their verdiƈt, are all under the public eye. Laſtly, the Judge cannot change either the place or the kind of puniſhment ordered by the law; and a Sheriff who ſhould take away the life of a Man in a manner different from that which the

renewed, under Henry VI. the attempts made to introduce the Civil Law, they exhibited the torture as a *beginning thereof*. The inſtrument was called the Duke of Exeter's daughter.

* Judge Foſter relates, from Whitlock, that the Biſhop of London having ſaid to Felton, who had aſſaſſinated the Duke of Buckingham, " If you will not confeſs, you *muſt* " *go to the Rack.*" The Man replied, " If it muſt be ſo, I " know not who I may accuſe in the extremity of the torture; Biſhop Laud perhaps, or any Lord at this Board."

" Sound ſenſe, (adds Foſter) in the mouth of an Enthuſi-" aſt and a Ruffian!"

Laud having propoſed the Rack, the matter was ſhortly debated at the Board, and it ended in a reference to the Judges, who unanimouſly reſolved that the Rack could not be legally uſed.

law prefcribes, would be profecuted as guilty of murder *.

In a word, the Conftitution of England being a free
Conftitution, demanded from that circumftance alone (as
I fhould already have but too often repeated, if fo fundamental a truth could be too often urged) extraordinary precautions to guard againft the dangers which unavoidably
attend the Power of inflicting punifhments; and it is
particularly when confidered in this light, that the Trial
by Jury proves an admirable inftitution.

By means of it, the Judicial Authority is not only
placed out of the hands of the man who is vefted with the
Executive Authority—it is even out of the hands of the
Judge himfelf.   Not only the perfon who is trufted with
the public power cannot exert it, till he has as it were received the permiffion to that purpofe, of thofe who are
fet apart to adminifter the laws; but thefe latter are alfo
reftrained in a manner exactly alike, and cannot make
the law fpeak, but when, in their turn, they have likewife
received permiffion.

And thofe perfons to whom the law has thus exclufively delegated the prerogative of deciding that a punifhment is to be inflicted,—thofe Men without whofe declaration the Executive and the Judicial Powers are both
thus bound down to inaction, do not form among themfelves a permanent Body, who may have had time to ftu-
dy how their power can ferve to promote their private
views or intereft : they are Men felected at once from
among the people, who perhaps never were before called
to the exercife of fuch a function, nor forefee that they
ever fhall be called to it again.

As the extenfive right of challenging, effectually baf-
fles, on the one hand, the fecret practices of fuch as, in

---

* And if any other perfon but the Sheriff, even the Judge
himfelf, were to caufe death to be inflicted upon a Man,
though convicted, it would be deemed homicide. See Blackftone, book iv. chap. 14.

the face of fo many difcouragements, might ftill endeavour to make the Judicial Power fubfervient to their own
views, and on the other excludes all perfonal refentments,
the fole affection which remains to influence the integrity
of thofe who alone are intitled to put the public power into
action, during the fhort period of their authority, is, that
their own fate as fubjects is effentially connected with
that of the Man whofe doom they are going to decide.

In fine, fuch is the happy nature of this inftitution,
that the Judicial Power, a power fo formidable in itfelf,
which is to difpofe, without finding any refiftance, of the
property, honour, and life of individuals, and which,
whatever precautions may be taken to reftrain it, muft in
a great degree remain arbitrary, may be faid in England,
to exift,—to accomplifh every intended end,—and to be
in the hands of nobody *.

In all thefe obfervations on the advantages of the Englifh criminal laws, I have only confidered it as connected with the Conftitution, which is a free one, and it is in
this view alone that I have compared it with the Jurifprudence received in other States. Yet, abftractedly
from the weighty conftitutional confiderations which I
have fuggefted, I think there are ftill other interefting
grounds of pre-eminence on the fide of the laws of England.

In the firft place, they do not permit that a Man fhould
be made to run the rifk of a trial, but upon the declaration of twelve perfons at leaft *(the Grand Jury)*. Whether he be in prifon, or on his Trial, they never for an
inftant refufe free accefs to thofe who have either advice,
or comfort, to give him; they even allow him to fum-
mon all who may have any thing to fay in his favour.

* The confequence of this Inftitution is, that no Man in
England ever meets the Man of whom he may fay, " That
" Man has a power to decide on my death or life." If we
could for a moment forget the advantages of that Inftitution,
we ought at leaft to admire the ingenuity of it.

And laſtly, what is of very great importance, the witneſſes againſt him muſt deliver their teſtimony in his preſence; he may croſs-examine them, and, by one unex-
pected queſtion, confound a whole ſyſtem of calumny:
indulgences theſe, all denied by the laws of other Countries.

Hence, though an accuſed perſon may be expoſed to
have his fate decided by perſons *(the Petty Jury)* who
poſſeſs not, perhaps, all that ſagacity which in ſome delicate caſes it is particularly advantageous to meet with in
a Judge, yet this inconvenience is amply compenſated
by the extenſive means of defence with which the law,
as we have ſeen, has provided him. If a Juryman does
not poſſeſs that expertneſs which is the reſult of long
practice, yet neither does he bring to Judgment that
hardneſs of heart which is, more or leſs, alſo the conſequence of it: and bearing about him the principles, let
me ſay, the unimpaired inſtinct of humanity, he trem-
bles while he exerciſes the awful office to which he finds
himſelf called, and in doubtful caſes always decides for
mercy.

It is to be further obſerved, that in the uſual courſe of
things, Juries pay great regard to the opinions delivered
by the Judges: that in thoſe caſes where they are clear
as to the fact, yet find themſelves perplexed with regard
to the degree of guilt connected with it, they leave it, as
has been ſaid before, to be aſcertained by the diſcretion
of the Judge, by returning what is called a *Special Verdict:* that, whenever circumſtances ſeem to alleviate the
guilt of a perſon againſt whom nevertheleſs the proof
has been poſitive, they temper their verdict by recommending him to the mercy of the King; which ſeldom
fails to produce at leaſt a mitigation of the puniſhment: that, though a Man once acquitted, can never under any pretence whatſoever be again brought into peril
for the ſame offence, yet a new Trial would be granted,
if he had been found guilty upon proofs ſtrongly ſuſpect-
ed of being falſe. (Blackſt. b. iv. c. 27.) Laſtly, what

diftinguifhes the laws of England from thofe of other countries in a very honourable manner, is, that as the torture is unknown to them, fo neither do they know any more grievous punifhment than the fimple depriva- tion of life.

All thefe circumftances have combined to introduce. fuch a mildnefs into the exercife of criminal Juftice, that the trial by Jury is that point of their liberty to which the people of England are moft thoroughly and univerfally wedded; and the only complaint I have ever heard uttered againft it, has been by Men who, more fenfible of the neceffity of public order than a-live to the feelings of humanity, think that too many offenders efcape with impunity.

CHAP. XIV.

The Subject concluded. —— Laws relative to Imprifon-ment.

BUT what completes that fenfe of independence which the laws of England procure to every in-dividual (a fenfe which is the nobleft advantage at-tending liberty) is the greatnefs of their precautions upon the delicate point of imprifonment.

In the firft place, by allowing, in moft cafes, of en-largement upon bail, and by prefcribing, on that arti-cle, exprefs rules for the Judges to follow, they have removed all pretexts which circumftances might af-ford, of depriving a man of his liberty.

But it is againft the Executive Power that the Le-giflature has, above all, directed its efforts : nor has it been but by flow degrees that it has been enabled to wreft from it a branch of power which enabled him to deprive the people of their Leaders, as well as to intimidate thofe who might be tempted to affume the function; and which, having thus all the efficacy of more odious means without the dangers of them, was perhaps the moft formidable weapon with which it might attack public liberty.

The methods originally pointed out by the laws of England for the enlargement of a perfon unjuftly imprifoned, were the writs of *mainprize, de odio & atia,* and *de homine replegiando.* Thofe writs, which could not be denied, were an order to the Sheriff of the County in which a perfon was confined, to inquire into the caufes of his confinement; and, according to the circumftances of his cafe, either to difcharge him completely, or upon bail.

But the moft ufeful method, and which even, by being moft general and certain, has tacitly abolifhed all the others, is the writ of *Habeas Corpus,* fo called becaufe it begins with the words *Habeas Corpus ad fubjiciendum.* This writ being, a writ of high prerogative, muft iffue from the Court of King's Bench: its effects extend equally to every County; and the King by it requires, or is underftood to require, the perfon who holds one of his fubjects in cuftody, to carry him before the Judge, with the date of the confinement, and the caufe of it, in order to difcharge him or continue to detain him, according as the Judge fhall decree.

But this writ, which might be a refource in cafes of violent imprifonment effected by individuals or granted at their requeft, was but a feeble one, or rather was no refource at all, againft the prerogative of the Prince, efpecially under the reigns of the Tudors, and in the beginning of that of the Stuarts. And even in the firft years of Charles the Firft, the Judges of the King's Bench, who, in confequence of the fpirit of the times, and of their holding their places *durante bene*

T

placito, were constantly devoted to the Court, declared, " that they could not, upon a *Habeas Corpus*, either " bail or deliver a prisoner, though committed with- " out any cause assigned, in case he was committed by " the special command of the King, or by the Lords " of the Privy Council."

Those principles, and the mode of procedure which resulted from them, drew the attention of Parliament; and in the Act called the Petition of Right, passed in the third year of the reign of Charles the First, it was enacted, that no person should be kept in custody, in consequence of such imprisonments.

But the Judges knew how to evade the intention of this Act; they indeed did not refuse to discharge a Man imprisoned without a cause; but they used so much delay in the examination of the causes, that they obtained the full effect of an open denial of Justice.

The Legislature again interposed, and in the Act passed in the sixteenth year of the reign of Charles the First, the same in which the Star Chamber was suppressed, it was enacted, that " if any person be com- " mitted by the King himself in person, or by his Pri- " vy Council, or by any of the Members thereof, he " shall have granted unto him, without any delay " upon any pretence whatsoever, a writ of *Habeas Cor-* " *pus;* and that the Judge shall thereupon, within three " Court-days after the return is made, examine and de- " termine the legality of such imprisonment "

This Act seemed to preclude every possibility of future evasion: yet it was evaded still; and by the connivance of the Judges, the person who detained the prisoner could, without danger, wait for a second and third writ, called an *Alias* and a *Pluries*, before he produced him.

All these different artifices gave at length birth to the famous Act *Habeas Corpus*, passed in the thirtieth

year of the reign of Charles the Second, which is confidered in England as a fecond Great Charter, and has
finally fuppreffed all the refources of oppreffion. *

The principal articles of this Act are, to fix the different terms allowed for bringing a prifoner: thofe
terms are proportioned to the diftance, and none can
in any cafe exceed twenty days.

2. That the Officer and Keeper neglecting to make
due returns, or not delivering to the prifoner, or his
agent, within fix hours after demand, a copy of the
warrant of commitment, or fhifting the cuftody of the
prifoner from one to another, without fufficient reafon
or authority (fpecified in the act,) fhall for the firft offence forfeit one hundred pounds, and for the fecond
two hundred, to the party grieved, and be difabled to
hold his office.

3. No perfon, once delivered by *Habeas Corpus*, fhall
be re-committed for the fame offence, on penalty of five
hundred pounds.

4. Every perfon committed for treafon or felony, fhall,
if he require it, in the firft week of the next term, or the
firft day of the next feffion, be indicted in that term or feffion, or elfe admitted to bail, unlefs the King's witneffes
cannot be produced at that time: and if not indicted and
tried in the fecond term or feffion, he fhall be difcharged
of his imprifonment for fuch imputed offence.

5. Any of the twelve Judges, or the Lord Chancellor,
who fhall deny a writ of *Habeas Corpus*, on fight of the
warrant, or on oath that the fame is refufed, fhall forfeit
feverally to the party grieved five hundred pounds.

6. No inhabitant of England (except perfons contracting, or convicts, praying to be tranfported) fhall be fent
prifoner to Scotland, Ireland, Jerfey, Guernfey, or any
place beyond the Seas, within or without the King's dominions,—on pain that the party committing, his advifers,
aiders, and affiftants, fhall forfeit to the party grieved a

* The real title of this Act is, *An Act for better fecuring th
Subject, and for Prevention of Imprifonment beyond the Seas.*

sum not less than five hundred pounds, to be recovered with treble costs,—shall be disabled to bear any office of trust or profit,—shall incur the penalties of a *præmunire* *, and be incapable of the King's pardon.

* The Statutes of *præmunire*, thus called from the writ for their execution, which begins with the words *præmunire* (for *præmonere*) *facias*, were originally designed to oppose the usurpations of the Popes. The first was passed under the reign of Edward the First, and has been followed by several others, which, even before the Reformation, established such effectual provisions as to draw upon one of them the epithet of *Execrabile Statutum*. The offences against which those Statutes were framed, were likewise distinguished by the appellation of *præmunire*; and under that word were included in general all attempts to promote the Pope's authority at the expence of the King's. The punishment decreed for such cases, was also called a *præmunire*: it has since been extended again to several other kinds of offence, and amounts to " the impri-" sonment for life, and forfeiture of all goods and rents of " lands during life." See Blackstone's Com, book iv. ch, 8.

B O O K II.

C H A P. I.

Some Advantages peculiar to the English Constitution.
1. The Unity of the Executive Power.

WE have seen in former Chapters, the resources allotted to the different parts of the English Government for balancing each other, and how their reciprocal actions and re-actions produce the freedom of the Constitution, which is no more than an equilibrium between the ruling Powers of the State. I now propose to shew that the particular nature and functions of these same constituent parts of the Government, which give it so different an appearance from that of other free States, are moreover attended with peculiar and very great advantages, which have not hitherto been sufficiently observed.

The first peculiarity of the English Government, as a free Government, is its having a King,—its having thrown into one place the whole mass, if I may use the expression, of the Executive Power, and having invariably and for ever fixed it there. By this very circumstance also has the *depositum* of it been rendered sacred and inexpugnable ;—by making one great, very great Man, in the State, has an effectual check been put to the pretensions of those who otherwise would strive to become such, and disorders have been prevented, which, in· all Republics, ever brought on the ruin of liberty, and, before it was loft, obftructed the enjoyment of it.

If we caft our eyes on all the States that ever were free, we fhall fee that the People ever turning their jealoufy, as it was natural, againft the Executive Power, but never thinking of the means of limiting it that has fo happily taken place in England *, never employed any other expedient befides the obvious one, of trufting that Power to Magiftrates whom they appointed annually ; which was in a great meafure the fame as keeping the management of it to themfelves. Whence it refulted, that the People, who, whatever may be the frame of the Goverment, always poffefs, after all, the reality of power, thus uniting in themfelves with this reality of power the actual exercife of it, in form as well as in fact, conftituted the whole State. In order therefore legally to difturb the whole State, nothing more was requifite than to put in motion a certain number of individuals.

In a State which is fmall and poor, an arrangement of this kind is not attended with any great inconveniences, as every individual is taken up with the care of providing for his fubfiftence, as great objects of ambition are wanting, and as evils cannot, in fuch a State, ever become much complicated. In a ftate that ftrives for aggrandifement, the difficulties and danger attending the purfuit of fuch a plan, infpire a general fpirit of caution, and every individual makes a fober ufe of his rights as a Citizen.

But when, at length, thofe exterior motives come to ceafe, and the paffions, and even the virtues, which they excited, thus become reduced to a ftate of inaction, the People turn their eyes back towards the interior of the Republic, and every individual, in feeking then to concern himfelf in all affairs, feeks for new objects that may reftore him to that ftate of exertion which habit, he finds, has

---

* The rendering that power dependent on the People for its fupplies.—See on this fubject Chapter, VI. Book I.

rendered neceffary to him, and to exercife a fhare of power which, fmall as it is, yet flatters his vanity.

As the preceding events muft needs have given an influence to a certain number of Citizens, they avail themfelves of the general difpofition of the People to promote their private views :' the legiflative power is thenceforth continually in motion ; and as it is badly informed and falfely directed, almoft every exertion of it is attended with fome injury either to the Laws or the State.

This is not all ; as thofe who compofe the general Affemblies cannot, in confequence of their numbers, entertain any hopes of gratifying their own private ambition, or in general their own private paffions, they at leaft feek to gratify their political caprices, and they accumulate the honours and dignities of the State on fome favourite whom the public voice happens to raife at that time.

But, as in fuch a State there can be, from the irregularity of the determinations of the People, no fuch thing as a fettled courfe of meafures, it happens that men never can exactly tell the prefent ftate of public affairs. The power thus given away is already grown very great, before thofe for whom it was given fo much as fufpect it : and he himfelf who enjoys that power, does not know its full extent : but then, on the firft opportunity that offers, he fuddenly pieces through the cloud which hid the fummit from him, and at once feats himfelf upon it. The People, on the other hand, no fooner recover fight of him than they fee their Favourite now become their Mafter, and difcover the evil, only to find that it is paft remedy.

As this power, thus furreptitioufly acquired, is deftitute of the fupport both of the law and of the ancient courfe of things, and is even but indifferently refpected by thofe who have fubjected themfelves to it, it cannot be maintained but by abufing it. The People at length fucceed in forming fomewhere a centre of union ; they agree in the choice of a Leader ; this Leader in his turn rifes ; in his turn alfo he betrays his engagements ;-power produces its wonted effects, and the protector becomes a tyrant.

This is not all; the same causes which have given a Master to the State, give it two, give it three. All those rival powers endeavour to swallow up each other; the State becomes a scene of endless quarrels and broils, and is in a continual convulsion.

If amidst such disorders the People retained their freedom, the evil must indeed be very great, to take away all the advantages of it; but they are slaves, and yet have not what in other Countries makes amends for political servitude, I mean tranquillity.

In order to prove all these things, if proofs were deemed necessary, I would only refer the reader to what every one knows of Pisistratus and Megacles, of Marius and Sylla, of Cæsar and Pompey. However, I cannot avoid translating a part of the speech which a Citizen of Florence addressed once to the Senate; the reader will find in it a kind of abridged story of all Republics; at least of those which, by the share allowed to the People in the Government, deserved that name, and which, besides, have attained a certain degree of extent and power. .

" And that nothing human may be perpetual and sta-
" ble, it is the will of Heaven that in all States whatso-
" ever, there should arise certain destructive families,
" who are the bane and ruin of them. Of this our own
" Republic affords as many and more deplorable exam-
" ples than any other, as it owes its misfortunes not only
" to one, but to several such families. We had at first
" the *Buondelmonti* and the *Huberti*. We had afterwards
" the *Donati* and the *Cerchi*; and at present, (shameful
" and ridiculous conduct!) we are waging war among
" ourselves for the *Ricci* and the *Albizzi.*

" When in former times the Ghibelins were suppress-
" ed, every one expected that the Guelfs, being then sa-
" tisfied, would have chosen to live in tranquillity; yet,
" but a little time had elapsed, when they again divided them-
" selves into the factions of the *Whites* and the *Blacks.*
" When the Whites were suppressed, new parties arose,
" and new troubles followed. Sometimes battles were

" fought in favour of the Exiles; and at other times,
" quarrels broke out between the Nobility and the People.
" And, as if refolved to give away to others what we
" ourfelves neither could, or would, peaceably enjoy, we
" committed the care of our liberty fometimes to King
" Robert, and at other times to his brother, and at length
" to the Duke of Athens; never fettling nor refting in
" any kind of Government, as not knowing either how
" to enjoy liberty, or fupport fervitude *."

The Englifh Conftitution has prevented the poffibility of misfortunes of this kind. Not only by diminifhing the power, or rather the *actual exercife* of the power, of the People +, and making them fhare in the Legiflature only by their Reprefentatives, the irrefiftible violence has been avoided of thofe numerous and general Affemblies, which, on whatever fide they throw their weight, bear down every thing. Befides, as the power of the People, when they have any kind of power, and know how to ufe it, is at all times really formidable, the Conftitution has fet a counterpoife to it; and the Royal Authority is this counterpoife.

In order to render it equal to fuch a tafk, the Confti-tution has, in the firft place, conferred on the King, as we have feen before, the exclufive prerogative of calling and difmiffing the legiflative Bodies, and of putting a negative on their refolutions.

Secondly, it has alfo placed on the fide of the King the whole Executive Power of the Nation.

Laftly, in order to effect ftill nearer an equilibrium, the Conftitution has invefted the Man whom it has made the fole Head of the State, with all the perfonal privile-ges, all the pomp, all the majefty, of which human digni-ties are capable. In the language of the law, the King

---

* See the Hiftory of Florence, by Machiavel, lib. iii.

† We fhall fee in the fequel, that this diminution of the exercife of the power of the People has been attended with a great increafe of their liberty.

U

is Sovereign Lord, and the People are his fubjects :—he is univerfal proprietor of the whole Kingdom;—he beftows all the dignities and places;—and he is not to be addreffed but with the expreffions and outward ceremony of almoft Eaftern humility. Befides, his perfon is facred and inviolable; and any attempt whatfoever againft it, is, in the eye of the law, a crime equal to that of an attack againft the whole State.

In a word fince, to have too exactly completed the equilibrium between the power of the People, and that of the Crown, would have been to facrifice the end to the means, that is, to have endangered liberty with a view to ftrengthen the Government, the deficiency which ought to remain on the fide of the Crown, has at leaft been in appearance made up, by conferring on the King all that fort of ftrength that may refult from the opinion and reverence of the People; and amidft the agitations which are the unavoidable attendants of liberty, the Royal power, like an anchor that refifts both by its weight and the depth of its hold, infures a falutary fteadinefs to the veffel of the State.

The greatnefs of the prerogative of the King, by its thus procuring a great degree of ftability to the State in general, has much leffened the poffibility of the evils we have above defcribed; it has even, we may fay, totally prevented them, by rendering it impoffible for any Citizen ever to rife to any dangerous greatnefs.

And to begin with an advantage by which the People eafily fuffer themfelves to be influenced, I mean that of birth, it is impoffible for it to produce in England effects in any degree dangerous; for though there are Lords who, befides their wealth, may alfo boaft of an illuftrious defcent, yet that advantage, being expofed to a continual comparifon with the fplendour of the Throne, dwindles almoft to nothing; and in the gradation univerfally received of dignities and titles, that of Sovereign Prince and King places him who is invefted with it, out of all degree of proportion.

The Ceremonial of the Court of England is even formed upon that principle. Thofe perfons who are related
to the King, have the title of Princes of the blood, and,
in that quality, an undifputed pre-eminence over all other
perfons *. Nay, the firft men in the Nation think it an
honourable diftinction to themfelves, to hold the different menial offices, or titles, in his Houfehold. If we
therefore were to fet afide the extenfive and real power
of the King, as well as the numerous means he poffeffes
of gratifying the ambition and hopes of individuals, and
were to confider only the Majefty of his title, and that
kind of ftrength founded on public opinion, which refults
from it, we fhould find that advantage fo confiderable,
that to attempt to enter into a competition with it, with
the bare advantage of high birth, which itfelf has no other
foundation than public opinion, and that too in a very
fubordinate degree, would be an attempt completely extravagant.

If this difference is fo great as to be thoroughly fub-
mitted to even by thofe perfons whofe fituation might incline them to difown it, much more does it influence the
minds of the People. And if, notwithftanding the value
which every Englifhman ought to fet upon himfelf as a
Man, and a free Man, there were any whofe eyes were fo
very tender as to be dazzled by the appearance and the
arms of a Lord, they would be totally blinded when they
came to turn them towards the Royal Majefty.

The only Man, therefore, who, to thofe who are unacquainted with the Conftitution of England, might at
firft fight appear in a condition to put the Government
in danger, would be a Man who, by the greatnefs of his
abilities and public fervices, might have acquired in a
high degree the love of the People, and obtained a great
influence in the Houfe of Commons.

---

* This, by Stat. of the 31ft of Hen. VIII. extends to
the fons, grandfons, brothers, uncles, and nephews, of the
reigning King.

But how great foever this enthufiafm of the public may be, barren applaufe is the only fruit which the Man whom they favour can expect from it. He can hope neither for a Dictatorfhip, nor a Confulfhip, nor in general for any power under the fhelter of which he may at once fafely unmafk that ambition with which we might fuppofe him to be actuated,—or, if we fuppofe him to have been hitherto free from any, grow infenfibly corrupt. The only door which the Conftitution leaves open to his ambition, of whatever kind it may be, is a place in the adminiftration, during the pleafure of the King. If, by the continuance of his fervices, and the prefervation of his influence, he becomes able to aim ftill higher, the only door which again opens to him, is that of the Houfe of Lords.

But this advance of the favourite of the people towards the eftablifhment of his greatnefs, is at the fame time a great ftep towards the lofs of that power which might render him formidable.

In the firft place, the People feeing that he is become much lefs dependent on their favour, begin, from that very moment, to leffen their attachment to him. Seeing him moreover diftinguifhed by privileges which are the object of their jealoufy, I mean their political jealoufy, and member of a body whofe interefts are frequently oppofite to theirs, they immediately conclude that this great and new dignity cannot have been acquired but through a fecret agreement to betray them. Their favourite, thus fuddenly transformed, is going, they make no doubt, to adopt a conduct entirely oppofite to that which has till then been the caufe of his advancement and high reputation, and, in the compafs of a few hours, completely renounce thofe principles which he has fo long and fo loudly profeffed. In this certainly the People are miftaken; but yet neither would they be wrong, if they feared that a zeal hitherto fo warm, fo conftant, I will even add, fo fincere, when it concurred with their Favourite's private interest, would, by being thenceforth often in oppofition to it, become gradually much abated.

Nor is this all; the favourite of the People does not even find, in his new-acquired dignity, all the increafe of greatnefs and eclat that might at firft be imagined.

Hitherto he was, it is true, only a private individual; but then he was the object in which the whole Nation interefted themfelves; his actions and words were fet forth in the public prints; and he every where met with applaufe and acclamation.

All thefe tokens of public favour are, I know, fometimes acquired very lightly; but they never laft long, whatever people may fay, unlefs real fervices are performed: now, the title of Benefactor to the Nation, when deferved, and univerfally beftowed, is certainly a very handfome title, and which does no-wife require the affiftance of outward pomp to fet it off. Befides, though he was only a Member of the inferior body of the Legiflature, we muft obferve, he was the firft; and the word *firft* is always a word of very great moment.

But now that he is made Lord, all his greatnefs, which hitherto was indeterminate, becomes defined. By granting him privileges eftablifhed and fixed by known laws, that uncertainty is taken from his luftre which is of fo much importance in thofe things which depend on imagination; and his value is lowered, juft becaufe it is afcertained.

Befides, he is a Lord; but then there are feveral men who poffefs but fmall abilities, and few eftimable qualifications, who alfo are Lords; his lot is, neverthelefs, to be feated among them; the law places him exactly on the fame level with them; and all that is real in his greatnefs, is thus loft in a crowd of dignities, hereditary and conventional.

Nor are thefe the only loffes which the favourite of the People is to fuffer. Independently of thofe great changes which he defcries at a diftance, he feels around him alterations no lefs vifible, and ftill more painful.

Seated formerly in the Affembly of the Reprefentatives of the People, his talents and continual fuccefs had foon raifed him above the level of his fellow Members ; and, being carried on by the vivacity and warmth of the Public favour, thofe who might have been tempted to fet up as his competitors, were reduced to filence, or even became his fupporters.

Admitted now into an affembly of perfons invefted with a perpetual and hereditary title, he finds Men hitherto his fuperiors,—Men who fee with a jealous eye the fhining talents of the *homo novus*, and who are firmly refolved, that after having been the leading Man in the Houfe of Commons, he fhall not be the firft in theirs.

In a word, the fuccefs of the favourite of the People was brilliant, and even formidable ; but the Conftitution, in the very reward it prepares for him, makes him find a kind of Oftracifm. His advances were fudden, and his courfe rapid ; he was, if you pleafe, like a torrent ready to bear down every thing before it; but this torrent is compelled, by the general arrangement of things, finally to throw itfelf into a vaft refervoir, where it mingles, and lofes its force and direction.

I know it may be faid, that, in order to avoid the fatal ftep which is to deprive him of fo many advantages, the favourite of the People ought to refufe the new dignity which is offered to him, and wait for more important fuccefies, from his eloquence in the Houfe of Commons, and his influence over the People.

But thofe who give him this counfel, have not fufficiently examined it. Without doubt there are men in England, who in their prefent purfuit of a project which they think effential to the public good, would be capable of refufing for a while a dignity which would deprive their virtue of opportunities of exerting itself, or might more or lefs endanger it: but woe to him who fhould perfift in fuch a refufal, with any pernicious defign! and who, in a Government where liberty is eftablifhed on fo folid and extenfive a bafis, fhould endeavour to make the people believe that their fate depends on the perfevering virtue of a fingle citizen. His ambitious views being at laft difcovered (nor could it be long before they were fo,) his obftinate refolution to move out of the ordinary courfe of things, would indicate aims, on his part, of fuch an extraordinary nature, that all Men whatever, who have any regard for their country, would inftantly rife up from all parts to oppofe him, and he muft fall, overwhelmed with fo much ridicule, othat it would be better for him to fall from the Tarpeian rock. *

In fine, even though we were to fuppofe that the new Lord might, after his exaltation, have preferved all his intereft with the People, or, what would be no lefs difficult, that any Lord whatever could, by dint of his wealth and high birth, rival the fplendor of the Crown itfelf, all thefe advantages how great foever we may fuppofe them, as they would not of themfelves be

---

* The Reader will perhaps object, that no Man in England can poffibly entertain fuch views as thofe I have fuggefted here : this is precifely what I intended to prove. The effential advantage of the Englifh government above all thofe that have been called *free*, and which in many refpects were but apparently fo, is, that no perfon in England can entertain fo much as a thought of his ever rifing to the level of the Power charged with the execution of the Laws. All Men in the State, whatever may be their rank, wealth, or influence, are thoroughly convinced that they muft in reality, as well as in name, continue to be *Subjects*; and are thus compelled really to love, to defend, and to promote thofe laws which fecure the liberty of the Subject. This latter obfervation will be again introduced in the fequel.

able to confer on him the least executive authority, must for ever remain mere showy unsubstantial advantages. Finding all the active powers in the State con-centered in that very seat of power which we suppose him inclined to attack, and there secured by formidable provisions, his influence must always evaporate in ineffectual words ; and after having advanced himself, as we suppose, to the very foot of the Throne, finding no branch of independent power which he might appropriate to himself, and thus at last give a reality to his political importance, he would soon see it, however great it might have at first appeared, decline and die away.

God forbid, however, that I should mean that the People of England are so fatally tied down to inaction, by the nature of their Government, that they cannot, in times of oppression, find means of appointing a Leader! No; I only meant to say that the laws of England open no door to those accumulations of power, which have been the ruin of so many Republics ; that they offer to the ambitious no possible means of taking advantage of the inadvertence, or even the gratitude, of the People, to make themselves their Tyrants; and that the public power of which the King has been made the exclusive depository, must remain unshaken in his hands, so long as things continue to keep in the legal order ; which, it may be observed, is a strong inducement to him constantly to endeavour to maintain them in it. *

* There are several events, in the English History, which put in a very strong light this idea of the stability which the power of the Crown gives to the State.

One, is the facility with which the great Duke of Marlborough, and his party at home, were removed from their several employments. Hannibal, in circumstances nearly similar, had continued the war against the will of the Senate of

*The Subject concluded.——The Executive Power is
more easily confined when it is* ONE.

ANOTHER great advantage, and which one would
not at firſt expect, in this *unity* of the public
power in England,—in this union, and, if I may ſo
expreſs myſelf, in this coacervation, of all the branches of the Executive authority, is the greater facility
it affords of reſtraining it.

Carthage : Cæſar had done the ſame in Gaul ; and when at
laſt he was expreſsly required to deliver up his commiſſion, he
marched his army to Rome, and eſtabliſhed a military deſpotiſm.   But the Duke, though ſurrounded, as well as the a-
bove-named Generals, by a victorious army, and by Allies in
conjunction with whom he had carried on ſuch a ſucceſsful
war, did not even heſitate to ſurrender his commiſſion. He
knew that all his ſoldiers were inſeparably prepoſſeſſed in favour of that Power againſt which he muſt have revolted : he
knew that the ſame prepoſitions were deeply rooted in the
minds of the whole nation, and that every thing among them
concurred to ſupport the ſame Power: he knew that the very
nature of the claims he muſt have ſet up, would inſtantly have
made all his Officers and Captains turn themſelves againſt
him ; and, in ſhort, that in an enterprize of that nature, the
arm of the ſea he had to repaſs, was the ſmalleſt of the obſtacles he would have to encounter.

The other event I ſhall mention here, is that of the Revolution of 1689.   If the long eſtabliſhed power of the Crown
had not beforehand prevented the people from accuſtoming
themſelves to fix their eyes on ſome particular Citizens, and
in general had not prevented all Men in the State from attaining any too conſiderable degree of power and greatneſs,
the expulſion of James the Second, might have been followed
by events ſimilar to thoſe which took place at Rome after the
death of Cæſar.

X

In thofe States where the execution of the laws is intrufted to feveral different hands, and to each with different titles and prerogatives, fuch divifion, and the changeablenefs of meafures which muft be the confequence of it, conftantly hide the true caufe of the evils of the State: in the endlefs fluctuation of things, no political principles have time to fix among the People: and public misfortunes happen, without ever leaving behind them any ufeful leffon.

At fome times military Tribunes, and at others, Confuls bear an abfolute fway;—fometimes Patricians ufurp every thing, and at other times, thofe who are called Nobles *;—fometimes the People are oppreffed by Decemvirs, and at others by Dictators.

Tyranny, in fuch States, does not always beat down the fences that are fet around it; but it leaps over them. When men think it confined to one place, it ftarts up again in another;—it mocks the efforts of the People, not becaufe it is invincible, but becaufe it is unknown;—feized by the arm of a Hercules, it efcapes with the changes of a Proteus.

But the indivifibility of the public power in England has conftantly kept the views and efforts of the People directed to one and the fame object; and the permanence of that power has alfo given a permanence and a regularity to the precautions they have taken to reftrain it.

---

* The capacity of being admitted to all places of public truft, at length gained by the Plebeians, having rendered ufelefs the old diftinction between them and the Patricians, a coalition was then effected between the great Plebeians, or Commoners, who got into thefe places, and the ancient Patricians: Hence a new clafs of Men arofe, who were called *Nobiles* and *Nobilitas*. Thefe are the words by which Livy, after that period conftantly diftinguifhes thofe Men and families who were at the head of the State.

Conſtantly turned towards that ancient fortreſs, the Royal power, they have made it, for ſeven centuries, the objeſt of their fear; with a watchful jealouſy they have conſidered all its parts—they have obſerved all its outlets—they have even pierced the earth to explore its ſecret avenues, and ſubterraneous works.

United in their views by the greatneſs of the danger, they regularly formed their attacks. They eſtabliſhed their works, firſt at a diſtance; then brought them ſucceſſively nearer; and, in ſhort, raiſed none but what ſerved afterwards as a foundation or defence to others.

After the Great Charter was eſtabliſhed, forty ſucceſſive confirmations ſtrengthened it. The Aſt called *the Petition of Right*, and that paſſed in the ſixteenth year of Charles the Firſt, then followed; ſome years after, the *Habeus Corpus* Aſt was eſtabliſhed; and the Bill of Rights made at length its appearance. In fine, whatever the circumſtances may have been, they always had, in their efforts, that ineſtimable advantage of knowing with certainty the general ſeat of the evils they had to defend themſelves againſt; and each calamity, each particular eruption, by pointing out ſome weak place has ever gained a new bulwark to public Liberty.

To ſay all in three words: the Executive power in England is formidable, but then it is for ever the ſame; its reſources are vaſt, but their nature is at length known; it has been made the indiviſible and inalienable attribute to one perſon alone; but then all other perſons, of whatever rank or degree, become really intereſted to reſtrain it within its proper bounds *.

* This laſt advantage of the greatneſs and indiviſibility of the executive power, viz. the obligation it lays upon the greateſt Men in the State, ſincerely to unite in a common cauſe with the people, will be more amply diſcuſſed hereaf-

CHAP. III.

A second Peculiarity.—The Division of the Legislative Power.

THE second peculiarity which England, as an un-divided State and a free State, exhibits in its Constitution, is the division of its Legislature. But in order to make the reader more sensible of the advantages of this division, it is necessary to desire him to attend to the following considerations.

It is, without doubt, absolutely necessary, for securing the Constitution of a State, to restrain the Executive power; but it is still more necessary to restrain the Legislative. What the former can only do by successive steps (I mean subvert the laws) and through a longer or shorter train of enterprizes, the latter does in a moment. As its bare will can give being to the laws; so its bare will can also annihilate them: and, if I may be permitted the expression,—the Legislative power can change the Constitution, as God created the light.

In order therefore to insure stability to the Constitution of a State, it is indispensably necessary to restrain the Legislative authority. But here we must observe a difference between the Legislative and Executive powers. The latter may be confined, and even is the more easily so, when undivided: the Legislative, on the contrary, in order to its being restrained, should absolutely be divided. For, whatever laws it may make to restrain itself, they never can be, relatively to it, any thing more than simple resolutions: as those

ter, when a more particular comparison between the English Government and the Republican form, shall be offered to the Reader.

bars which it might erect to stop its own motions, must then be within it, and rest upon it, they can be no bars. In a word, the same kind of impossibility is found, to fix the Legislative power when it is *one*, which Archimedes objected against his moving the earth *.

Nor does such a division of the Legislature only render it possible for it to be restrained, since each of those parts into which it is divided, can then serve as a bar to the motions of the others; but it even makes it to be actually so restrained. If it has been divided into only two parts, it is probable that they will not in all cases unite either for *doing*, or *undoing* :—if it has been divided into three parts, the chance that no changes will be made, is thereby greatly increased.

Nay more; as a kind of point of honour will naturally take place between these different parts of the Legislative, they will therefore be led to offer to each other only such propositions as will at least be plausible ; and all very prejudicial changes will thus be prevented, as it were, before their birth.

If the Legislative and Executive powers differ so greatly with regard to the necessity of their being divided, in order to their being restrained, they differ no less with regard to the other consequences arising from such division.

The division of the Executive power necessarily introduces actual oppositions, even violent ones, between the different parts into which it has been divided : and that part which in the issue succeeds so far as to absorb, and unite in itself, all the others, immediately sets itself above the laws. But those oppositions which take place, and which the public good requires should take place, between the different parts of the Legislature, are never any thing more than oppositions between contrary opinions and in-

* He wanted a spot whereupon to fix his instruments.

tentions; all is tranfacted in the regions of the underftanding; and the only contention that arifes is wholly
carried on with thofe inoffenfive weapons, affents and
diffents, *ayes* and *noes*.

Befides, when one of thefe parts of the Legiflature is
fo fuccefsful as to engage the others to adopt its propofition, the refult is, that a law takes place, which has in it a
great probability of being good: when it happens to be
defeated, and fees its propofition rejected, the worft that
can refult from it is, that a law is not made at that time;
and the lofs which the State fuffers thereby, reaches no
farther than the temporary fetting afide of fome more or
lefs ufeful fpeculation.

In a word, the refult of a divifion of the Executive
power, is either a more or lefs fpeedy eftablifhment of *the
right of the ftrongeft*, or a continued ftate of war * :—that
of a divifion of the Legiflative power, is either truth, or
general tranquillity.

The following maxim will therefore be admitted.
That the laws of a State may be permanent, it is requifite that the Legiflative power fhould be divided:—that
they may have weight, and continue in force, it is neceffary that the Executive power fhould be *one*.

If the reader conceived any doubt as to the truth of the
above obfervations, he need only caft his eyes on the hiftory of the proceedings of the Englifh Legiflature down
to our times, to find a proof of them. He would be
furprifed to fee how little variation there has been in the
political laws of this Country, efpecially during the laft

* Every one knows the frequent hoftilities that took
place between the Roman Senate and the Tribunes. In
Sweden there have been continual contentions between the
King and the Senate, in which they have overpowered each
other by turns. And in England, when the Executive power became double, by the King allowing the Parliament to
have a perpetual and independent exiftence, a civil war almoft immediately followed.

hundred years, though, it is moſt important to obſerve, the Legiſlature has been as it were in a continual ſtate of action, and, no diſpaſſionate Man will deny, has generally promoted the public good.   Nay, if we except the act paſſed under William III. by which it had been enacted, that Parliaments ſhould ſit no longer than three years, and which was repealed by a ſubſequent Act, under George I. which allowed them to ſit for ſeven years, we ſhall not find that any law, which may really be called Conſtitutional, and which has been enacted ſince the Reſtoration, has been changed afterwards.

Now, if we compare this ſteadineſs of the Engliſh Government with the continual ſubverſions of the Conſtitutional laws of ſome ancient Republics, with the imprudence of ſome of the laws paſſed in their aſſembl • . *, and with the ſtill greater inconſiderateneſs with which they ſometimes repealed the moſt ſalutary regulations, as it were the day after they had been enacted,—if we call to mind the extraordinary means to which the Legiſlature of thoſe Republics, at times ſenſible how its very power was prejudicial to itſelf and to the State, was obliged to have recourſe, in order, if poſſible, to tie its own hands †, we ſhall remain convinced of the great advantages which attend the Conſtitution of the Engliſh Legiſlature ‡.

* The Athenians, among other laws, had enacted one to forbid applying a certain part of the public revenues to any other uſe than the expences of the Theatres and public Shews.

† In ſome ancient Republics, when the Legiſlature wiſhed to render a certain law permanent, and at the ſame time miſtruſted their own future wiſdom, they added a clauſe to it, which made it death to propoſe the revocation of it. Thoſe who afterwards thought ſuch revocation neceſſary to the public welfare, relying on the mercy of the People, appeared in the public Aſſembly with an halter about their necks.

‡ We ſhall perhaps have occaſion to obſerve hereafter,

Nor is this division of the English Legislature accompanied (which is indeed a very fortunate circumstance) by an actual division of the Nation ; each constituent part of it possesses strength sufficient to insure respect to its resolutions, yet no real division has been made of the forces of the State. Only a greater proportional share of all those distinctions which are calculated to gain the reverence of the People, has been allotted to those parts of the Legislature which could not possess their confidence, in so high a degree as the others ; and the inequalities in point of real strength between them, have been made up by the magic of dignity.

Thus, the King, who alone forms one part of the Legislature, has on his side the majesty of the kingly title : the two Houses are, in appearance, no more than Councils entirely depenent on him : they are bound to follow his person ; they only meet, as it seems, to advise him ; and never address him but in the most solemn and respectful manner.

. As the Nobles, who form the second order of the Legislature, bear, in point both of real weight and numbers, no proportion to the body of the People *, they have re-

that the true cause of the equability of the operations of the English Legislature, is the opposition that happily takes place between the different views and interests of the several bodies that compose it : a consideration this, without which all political inquiries are no more than airy speculations, and is the only one that can lead to useful practical conclusions.

* It is for want of having duly considered this subject, that Mr. Rousseau exclaims, somewhere, against those who, when they speak of General Estates of France, " dare to " call the People, the *third* Estate." At Rome, where all the order we mention was inverted,—where the *fasces* were laid at the feet of the People,—and where the Tribunes whose function, like that of the King of England, was to oppose the establishment of new laws, were only a subordinate kind of Magistracy, many disorders followed. In Sweden, and in Scotland (before the union), faults of another

ceived as a compensation, the advantage of personal honours, and of hereditary title.

Besides, the established ceremonial gives to their Assembly a great pre-eminence over that of the Representatives of the People. They are the *upper* House, and
the others are the *lower* House. They are in a more special manner considered as the King's Council, and it is in
the place where they assemble that his Throne is placed.

When the King comes to the Parliament, the Commons are sent for, and make their appearance at the bar
of the House of Lords. It is moreover before the Lords,
as before their Judges, that the Commons bring their impeachments. When, after passing a bill in their own
House, they send it to the Lords to desire their concurrence, they always order a number of their own Members to accompany it *: whereas the Lords send down
their bills to them only by some of the Assistants of their
House †. When the nature of the alterations which one
of the two Houses desires to make in a bill sent to it by
the other, renders a conference between them necessary,
the Deputies of the Commons to the Committee, which
is then formed of Members of both Houses, are to remain uncovered. Lastly, those bills which (in which-
ever of the two Houses they have originated) have been
agreed to by both, must be deposited in the House of
Lords, there to remain till the Royal pleasure is signified.

Besides, the Lords are Members of the Legislature

kind prevailed : in the former kingdom, for instance, an overgrown body of two thousand Nobles, frequently overruled
both King and People.

* The Speaker of the House of Lords must come down
from the woolpack to receive the bills which the Members
of the Commons bring to their House.

† The Twelve Judges and the Masters in Chancery.
There is also a ceremonial established with regard to the
manner, and marks of respect, with which those two of them,
who are sent with a bill to the Commons, are to deliver it.

Y

by virtue of a right inherent in their perfons, and they are fuppofed to fit in Parliament on their own account, and for the fupport of their own interefts. In confequence of this they have the privilege of giving their votes by *proxies* *; and, when any of them diffent from the refolutions of their Houfe, they may enter a proteft againft them, containing the reafons of their particular opinion. In a word, as this part of the Legiflature is deftined frequently to balance the Power of the People, what it could not receive in real ftrength, it has received in outward fplendor and greatnefs ; fo that, when it cannot refift by its weight, it overawes by its apparent magnitude.

In fine, as thefe various prerogatives by which the component parts of the Legiflature are thus made to balance each other, are all intimately connected with the fortune of State, and flourifh and decay according to the viciffitudes of public profperity or adverfity, it thence follows, that, though differences of opinions may at fome times take place between thofe parts, there can fcarcely arife any, when the general welfare is really in queftion. And when, to refolve the doubts that may arife on political fpeculations of this kind, we caft our eyes on the debates of the two Houfes for a long fucceffion of years, and fee the nature of the laws which have been propofed, of thofe which have paffed, and of thofe which have been rejected, as well as of the arguments that have been urged on both fides, we fhall remain convinced of the goodnefs of the principles on which the Englifh Legiflature is formed.

* The Commons have not that privilege, becaufe they are themfelves *proxies* for the People.—See Coke's Inft. iv. p. 41.

C H A P. IV.

A third Advantage peculiar to the English Government. The Business of proposing Laws, lodged in the Hands of the People.

A THIRD circumstance which I propose to show to be peculiar to the English Government, is the manner in which the respective offices of the three component parts of the Legislature have been divided, and allotted to each of them.

If the reader will be pleased to observe, he will find that in most of the ancient free States, the share of the People in the business of Legislation, was to approve, or reject, the propositions which were made to them, and to give the final sanction to the laws. The function of those Persons, or in general those Bodies, who were intrusted with the Executive power, was to prepare and frame the Laws, and then to propose them to the People: and in a word, they possessed that branch of the Legislative power which may be called the *initiative,* that is, the prerogative of putting that power in action *.

* This power of previously considering and approving such laws as were afterwards to be propounded to the People was, in the first times of the Roman Republic, constantly exercised by the Senate; laws were made, *Populi jussu, ex autoritate Senatûs.* Even in cases of elections, the previous approbation and *auctoritas* of the Senate, with regard to those persons who were offered to the suffrages of the People, was required. *Tum enim non gerebat is magistratum qui ceperat, si Patres auctores non erant facti.* Cic. pro Plancio, 3.

At Venice the Senate also exercises powers of the same kind, with regard to the *Grand Council* or Assembly of the Nobles. In the Canton of Bern, all propositions must be discussed in the *Little* Council, which is composed of twenty-seven Members, before they are laid before the Council of the *Two hundred,* in whom resides the

This *initiative*, or exclusive right of proposing, in Legislative assemblies, attributed to the Magistrates, is indeed very useful, and perhaps even necessary, in States of a republican form, for giving a permanence to the laws, as well as for preventing the disorders and struggles for power which have been mentioned before; but upon examination we shall find that this expedient is attended with inconveniences of little less magnitude than the evils it is meant to remedy.

These Magistrates, or Bodies, at first indeed apply frequently to the Legislature for a grant of such branches of power as they dare not of themselves assume, or for the removal of such obstacles to their growing authority as they do not yet think it safe for them peremptorily to set aside. But when their authority has at length gained a sufficient degree of extent and stability, as farther manifestations of the will of the Legislature could then only create obstructions to the exercise of their power, they begin to consider the Legislature as an enemy whom they must take great care never to rouse. They consequently convene the Assembly of the People as seldom as they can. When they do it, they carefully avoid proposing any thing favourable to public liberty. Soon they even entirely cease to convene the Assembly at all; and the People, after thus losing the power of legally asserting their rights, are exposed to that which is the highest degree of political ruin, the loss of even the remembrance of them; unless some indirect means are found by which they may from time to time give life to their dormant privileges, means which may be found, and succeed pretty well in small States, where provisions can more easily be made to answer their intended ends, but in States of

sovereignty of the whole Canton. And in Geneva, the law is, " that nothing shall be treated in the *General Council*, or " Assembly of the Citizens, which has not been previously " treated and approved in the Council of the *Two hundred*; " and that nothing should be treated in the *Two hundred*, " which has not been previously treated and approved in the " Council of the *Twenty-five*."

considerable extent, have always been found, in the event,
to give rise to disorders of the same kind with those
which were at first intended to be prevented.

But as the capital principle of the English Constitution
totally differs from that which forms the basis of Republican Governments, so is it capable of procuring to the
People advantages, that are found to be unattainable in
the latter. It is the People in England, or at least those
who represent them, who possess the *initiative* in Legislation, that is to say, who perform the office of framing
laws, and proposing them. And among the many circumstances in the English Government, which would appear
entirely new to the Politicians of antiquity, that of seeing
the person intrusted with the Executive power bear that
share in Legislation which they looked upon as being necessarily the lot of the People, and the People that which
they thought the indispensable office of its Magistrates,
would not certainly be the least occasion of their sur-
prise.

I foresee that it will be objected, that, as the King of
England has the power of dissolving, and even of not
calling Parliaments, he is hereby possessed of a prerogative which in fact is the same with that which I have just
now represented as being so dangerous.

To this I answer, that all circumstances ought to be
combined together. Doubtless, if the Crown had been
under no kind of dependence whatever on the People,
it would long since have freed itself from the obligation of calling their Representatives together; and the
British Parliament, like the National Assemblies of
several other Kingdoms, would most likely have no
existence now, except in History.

But, as we have above seen, the necessities of the
State, and the wants of the Sovereign himself, put him
under a necessity of having frequent recourse to his
Parliament; and then the difference may be seen between the prerogative of not calling an Assembly, when
powerful causes nevertheless render such a measure

neceffary, and the exclufive right, when an Affembly, is convened, of *propofing* laws to it.

In the latter cafe, though a Prince, let us even fuppofe, in order to fave appearances, might condefcend to mention any thing befides his own wants, it would be at moft to propofe the giving up of fome branch of his prerogative upon which he fet no value, or to reform fuch abufes as his inclination does not lead him to imitate ; but he would be very careful not to touch any points which might materially affect his authority.

Befides, as all his conceffions would be made, or appear to be made, of his own motion, and would in fome meafure feem to fpring from the activity of his zeal for the public welfare, all that he might offer, though in fact ever fo inconfiderable, would be reprefented by him as grants of the moft important nature, and for which he expects the higheft gratitude. Laftly, it would alfo be his province to make reftrictions and exceptionsto laws thus propofed by himfelf ; he would alfo be the perfon who were to choofe the words to exprefs them, and it would not be reafonable to expect that he would give himfelf any great trouble to avoid all ambiguity*.

* In the beginning of the exiftence of the Houfe of Commons, bills were prefented to the King under the form of *Petitions*. Thofe to which the King affented were regiftered among the rolls of Parliament, with his anfwer to them ; and at the end of each Parliament, the Judges formed them into Statutes. Several abufes having crept into that method of proceeding, it was ordained that the Judges fhould in future make the Statute before the end of every Seffion. Laftly, as even that became, in procefs of time, infufficient, the prefent method of framing bills was eftablifhed ; that is to fay, both the Houfes now frame the Statutes in the very form and words in which they are to ftand when they have received the Royal affent.

But the Parliament of England is not, as we faid before, bound down to wait paffively, and in filence, for
fuch laws as the Executive power may condefcend to
propofe to them. At the opening of every Seffion, they
of themfelves take into their hands the great book of
the State; they open all the pages, and examine every
article.

When they have difcovered abufes, they proceed to
enquire into their caufes :—when thefe abufes arife
from an open difregard of the laws, they endeavour to
ftrengthen them : when they proceed from their infuf-
ficiency, they remedy the evil by additional provifions.*

* No popular Affembly ever enjoyed the privilege of ftarting, canvaffing, and propofing new matter, to fuch a degree
as the Englifh Commons. In France, when their General
Eftates were allowed to fit, their *remonftrances* were little regarded, and the particular Eftates of the Provinces dare now
hardly prefent any. In Sweden, the power of propofing new
fubjects was lodged in an Affembly called the *Secret Committee*,
compofed of Nobles, and a few of the Clergy ; and is now
poffeffed by the King. In Scotland, until the *Union*, all propofitions to be laid before the Parliament, were to be framed
by the perfons called the *Lords of the Articles.* In regard to
Ireland, all bills muft be prepared by the King in his Privy
Council, and are to be laid before the Parliament by the Lord
Lieutenant, for their affent or diffent : only, they are allowed to difcufs, among them, what they call *Heads of a Bill*,
which the Lord Lieutenant is defired afterwards to tranfmit
to the King, who felects out of them what claufes he thinks
proper, or fets the whole afide ; and is not expected to give,
at any time, any precife anfwer to them. And in Republican Governments, Magiftrates are never at reft till they have
entirely fecured to themfelves the important privilege of *propofing;* nor does this follow merely from their ambition ; it
is alfo the confequence of the fituation they are in, from the
principles of that mode of Government.

Nor do they proceed with lefs regularity and freedom, in regard to that important object, fubfidies. They are to be the fole Judges of the quantity of them, as well as of the ways and means of raifing them; and they need not come to any refolution with regard to them, till they fee the fafety of the Subject completely provided for. In a word, the making of laws is not, in fuch an arrangement of things, a *gratuitous* contract, in which the People are to take juft what is given them, and as it is given them:—it is a contract in which they *buy* and *pay*, and in which they themfelves fettle the different conditions, and furnifh the words to exprefs them.

The Englifh Parliament have given a ftill greater extent to their advantages on fo important a fubject. They have not only fecured to themfelves a right of propofing laws and remedies, but they have alfo prevailed on the executive power to renounce all claim to do the fame. It is even a conftant rule that neither the King, nor his Privy Council can make any amendments to the bills preferred by the two Houfes; but the King is merely to accept or reject them: a provifion this, which, if we pay a little attention to the fubject, we fhall find to have been alfo neceffary for completely fecuring the freedom and regularity of the parliamentary deliberations*.

* The King indeed at times fends meffages to either Houfe; and nobody, I think, can wifh that no means of intercourfe fhould exift between him and his Parliament. But thefe meffages are always expreffed in very general words: they are only made to defire the Houfe to take certain fubjects into their confideration; no particular articles or claufes are expreffed; the Commons are not to declare, at any fettled time, any folemn acceptation or rejection of the propofition made by the King; and, in fhort, the Houfe follows the fame mode of proceeding, with refpect to fuch meffages, as they ufually do in regard to petitions prefented by private

I indeed confefs that it feems very natural, in the modelling of a State, to intruft this very important office of framing laws, to thofe perfons who may be fuppofed to have before acquired experience and wifdom, in the management of public affairs: But events have unfortunately demonftrated, that public employments and power improve the underftanding of Men in a lefs degree than they pervert their views ; and it has been found in the iffue that the effect of a regulation which, at firft fight, feems fo perfectly confonant with prudence, is to confine the People to a mere paffive and defenfive fhare in Legiflation, and to deliver them up to the continual enterprizes of thofe who, at the fame time that they are under the greateft temptations to deceive them, poffefs the moft powerful means of effecting it.

If we caft our eyes on the Hiftory of the ancient Governments, in thofe times when the perfons entrufted with the Executive power were ftill in a ftate of dependence on the Legiflature, and confequently frequently obliged to have recourfe to it, we fhall fee almoft continual inftances of felfifh and infidious laws propofed by them to the Affemblies of the people.

And thofe Men in whofe wifdom the law had at firft placed fo much confidence, became, in the iffue, fo loft to all fenfe of fhame and duty, that when arguments were found to be no longer fufficient, they had recourfe to force ; the legiflative Affemblies became fo many fields of battle, and their power, a real calamity.

I know very well, however, that there are other

individuals. Some Member makes a motion upon the fubject expreffed in the King's meffage ; a bill is framed in the ufual way ; it may be dropt at every ftage of it; and it is never the propofal of the Crown, but the motions of fome of their own Members, which the Houfe difcufs, and finally accept or reject.

important circumftances befides thofe I have juft mentioned, which would prevent diforders of this kind
from taking place in England *. But, on the other
hand, let us call to mind that the perfon who, in England, is invefted with the executive authority, unites
in himfelf the whole public power and majefty. Let
us reprefent to ourfelves the great and fole Magiftrate
of the Nation, preffing the acceptance of thofe laws
which he had propofed, with a vehemence fuited to
the ufual importance of his defigns, with the warmth
of Monarchical pride, which muft meet with no refufal, and exerting for that purpofe all his immenfe
refources.

It was therefore a matter of indifpenfable neceffity,
that things fhould be fettled in England in the manner
they are. As the moving fprings of the Executive
power are, in the hands of the King, a kind of facred
depofitum, fo are thofe of the Legiflative Power in the
hands of the two Houfes. The King muft abftain from
touching them, in the fame manner as all the fubjects
of the kingdom are bound to fubmit to his prerogatives. When he fits in Parliament, he has left, we
may fay, his executive power without doors, and can
only affent or diffent. If the Crown had been allowed to take an active part in the bufinefs of making
laws, it would foon have rendered ufelefs the other
branches of the Legiflature.

* I particularly mean here, the circumftance of the People having entirely delegated their power to their Reprefentatives : the confequences of which Inftitution will be difcuffed in the next chapter.

CHAP. V.

In which an Inquiry is made, whether it would be an Advantage to the public Liberty, that the Laws should be enacted by the Votes of the People at large.

BUT it will be said, whatever may be the wisdom of the English Laws, how great soever their precautions may be with regard to the safety of the individual, the People, as they do not themselves expressly enact them, cannot be looked upon as a free People. The Author of the *Social Contract* carries this opinion even farther; he says, that, " though the " People of England think they are free, they are " much mistaken; they are so only during the elec-" tion of Members for Parliament: as soon as these are " elected, the People are slaves—they are nothing *."

Before I answer this objection, I shall observe, that the word *Liberty* is one of those which have been most misunderstood or misapplied.

Thus, at Rome, where that class of Citizens who were really Masters of the State, were sensible that a lawful regular authority, once trusted to a single Ruler, would put an end to their tyranny, they taught the People to believe, that, provided those who exercised a military power over them, and overwhelmed them with insults, went by the names of *Consules, Dictatores, Patricii, Nobiles*, in a word, by any other appellation than that horrid one of *Rex*, they were free, and that such a valuable situation must be preferred at the price of every calamity.

In the same manner, certain Writers of the present age, misled by their inconsiderate admiration of the Governments of ancient times, and perhaps also by a

---

* See M. Rousseau's Social Contract, chap. xv.

defire of prefenting lively contrafts to what they call the degenerate manners of our modern times, have cried up the governments of Sparta and Rome, as the only ones fit for us to imitate. In their opinions, the only proper employment of a free Citizen is, *to be either inceffantly affembled in the forum*, or *preparing for war.*—*Being valiant, inured to hardfhips, inflamed with an ardent love of one's Country*, which is, after all, nothing more than an ardent defire of injuring all Mankind for the fake of that Society of which we are Members —*and with an ardent love of glory*, which is likewife nothing more than an ardent defire of committing flaughter, in order to make afterwards a boaft of it, have appeared to thefe Writers to be the only focial qualifications worthy of our efteem, and of the encouragement of law-givers *. And while, in order to fupport fuch opinions, they have ufed a profufion of exaggerated expreffions without any diftinct meaning, and perpetually repeated, though without defining them, the words *daftardlinefs, corruption, greatnefs of foul*, and *virtue*, they have never once thought of telling us the only thing that was worth our knowing, which is, whether men were happy under thofe Governments which they fo much exhorted us to imitate.

Nor, while they thus mifapprehended the only rational defign of civil Societies, have they better underftood the true end of the particular inftitutions by which they were to be regulated. They were fatisfied when they faw the few who really governed every thing in the State, at times perform the illufory ceremony of affembling the body of the People, that they might appear to confult them : and the mere giving of votes, under any difadvantage in the

---

* I have ufed all the above expreffions in the fame fenfe in which they were ufed in the ancient Commonwealths, and ftill are by moft of the Writers who defcribe their Governments.

manner of giving them, and how much foever the law might afterwards be neglected that was thus pretended to have been made in common, has appeared to them to be Liberty.

But thofe Writers are in the right : a Man who contributes by his vote to the paffing of a law, has himfelf made the law ; in obeying it, he obeys himfelf,—he therefore is free.   A play on words, and nothing more.   The individual who has voted in a popular legiflative Affembly, has not made the law that has paffed in it; he has only contributed, or feemed to contribute, towards enacting it, for his thoufandth, or even ten thoufandth fhare : he has had no opportunity of making his objections to the propofed law, or of canvaffing it, or of propofing reftrictions to it, and he has only been allowed to exprefs his affent or diffent.   When a law is paffed agreeably to his vote, it is not as a confequence of this his vote, that his will happens to take place ; it is becaufe a number of other men have accidentally thrown themfelves on the fame fide with him :—when a law contrary to his intentions is enacted, he muft neverthelefs fubmit to it.

This is not all ; for though we fhould fuppofe that to give a vote is the effential conftituent of liberty, yet, fuch liberty could only be faid to laft for a fingle moment, after which it becomes neceffary to truft entirely to the difcretion of other perfons, that is, according to this doctrine, to be no longer free.   It becomes neceffary, for inftance, for the Citizen who has given his vote, to rely on the honefty of thofe who collect the fuffrages; and more than once have falfe declarations been made of them.

The Citizen muft alfo truft to other perfons for the execution of thofe things which have been refolved upon in common : and when the Affembly fhall have feparated, and he fhall find himfelf alone, in the prefence of the Men who are invefted with the public power, of the Confuls, for inftance, or of the Dictator, he will have but little fecurity for the continuance of his liberty, if he has only that of having contributed by his ſuffrage towards enacting a law which they are determined to neglect.

What then is Liberty? Liberty, I would anſwer, ſo far as it is poſſible for it to exiſt in a ſociety of Beings whoſe intereſts are almoſt perpetually oppoſed to each other, conſiſts in this, that *every Man, while he reſpects the perſons of others, and allows them quietly to enjoy the produce of their induſtry, be certain himſelf likewiſe to enjoy the produce of his own induſtry, and that his perſon be alſo ſecure.* But to contribute by one's ſuffrage to procure theſe advantages to the Community,—to have a ſhare in eſtabliſhing that order, that general arrangement of things, by means of which an individual, loſt as it were in the crowd, is effectually protected,—to lay down the rules to be obſerved by thoſe who, being inveſted with a conſiderable power, are charged with the defence of individuals, and provide that they ſhould never tranſgreſs them,--- theſe are functions, are acts of Government, but not conſtituent parts of Liberty.

To expreſs the whole in two words :—To concur by one's ſuffrage in enacting laws, is to enjoy a ſhare, whatever it may be, of Power: to live in a ſtate where the laws are equal for all, and ſure to be executed (whatever may be the means by which theſe advantages are attained) is to be free.

Be it ſo : we grant that to give one's ſuffrage is not liberty itſelf, but only a means of procuring it, and a means too which may degenerate to mere form ; we grant alſo, that it is poſſible that other expedients might be found for that purpoſe, and that, for a Man to decide that a State with whoſe Government and interior adminiſtration he is unacquainted, is a State in which the People *are ſlaves, are nothing*, merely becauſe the *Comitia* of ancient Rome are no longer to be met with in it, is a ſomewhat precipitate deciſion. But ſtill we muſt continue to think, that liberty would be much more complete, if the People at large were expreſsly called upon to give their opinion concerning the particular proviſions by

which it is to be fecured, and that the Englifh laws, for
inftance, if they were made by the fuffrages of all, would
be wifer, more equitable, and, above all, more likely to
be executed. To this objeftion, which is certainly fpecious, I fhall endeavour to give an anfwer.

If, in the firft formation of a civil Society, the only
care to be taken was that of eftablifhing, once for all, the
feveral duties which every individual owes to others, and
to the State,—if thofe who are intrufted with the care of
procuring the performance of thefe duties, had neither
any ambition, nor any other private paffions, which fuch
employment might put in motion, and furnifh the means
of gratifying: in a word, if looking upon their funftion
as a mere tafk of duty, they were never tempted to deviate from the intentions of thofe who had appointed them;
I confefs that in fuch a cafe, there might be no inconvenience in allowing every individual to have a fhare in
the government of the community of which he is a
member; or rather I ought to fay, in fuch a Society, and
among fuch Beings, there would be no occafion for any
Government.

But experience teaches us that many more precautions,
indeed, are neceffary to oblige Men to be juft towards
each other; nay, the very firft expedients that may be
expefted to conduce to fuch an end, fupply the moft
fruitful fource of the evils which are propofed to be prevented. Thofe laws which were intended to be equal
for all, are foon warped to the private convenience of
thofe who have been made the adminiftrators of them :
—inftituted at firft for the proteftion of all, they foon are
made only to defend the ufurpations of a few ; and as
the People continue to refpeft them, while thofe to whofe
guardianfhip they were intrufted make little account of
them, they at length have no other effeft than that of fup-
plying the want of real ftrength in thofe few who have
contrived to place themfelves at the head of the community, and of rendering regular and free from danger the
tyranny of the fmaller number over the greater.

To remedy, therefore, evils which thus have a tendency to result from the very nature of things,—to oblige those who are in a manner Masters of the law, to conform themselves to it,—to render ineffectual the silent, powerful, and never active conspiracy of those who govern, requires a degree of knowledge, and a spirit of perseverance, which are not to be expected from the multitude.

The greater part of those who compose this multitude, taking up with the care of providing for their subsistence, have neither sufficient leisure, nor even, in consequence of their more imperfect education, the degree of information requisite for functions of this kind. Nature, besides, who is sparing of her gifts, has bestowed upon only a few Men an understanding capable of the complicated researches of Legislation ; and, as a sick Man trusts to his Physician, a Client to his Lawyer, so the greater number of the Citizens must trust to those who have more abilities than themselves for the execution of things which, at the same time that they so materially concern them, require so many qualifications to perform them with any degree of sufficiency.

To these considerations, of themselves so material, another must be added, which is if possible of still greater weight. This is, that the multitude, in consequence of their very being a multitude, are incapable of coming to any mature resolution.

Those who compose a popular Assembly are not actuated, in the course of their deliberations, by any clear and precise view of any present or positive personal interest. As they see themselves lost as it were in the crowd of those who are called upon to exercise the same function with themselves, as they know that their individual votes will make no change in the public resolution, and that to whatever side they may incline, the general result will nevertheless be the same, they do not undertake to enquire how far the things proposed to them agree with the whole of the law already in being, or with the present circumſtances of the State, becauſe Men will not enter upon a laborious taſk, when they know that it can ſcarcely anſwer any purpoſe.

It is, however, with diſpoſitions of this kind, and each relying on all, that the Aſſembly of the People meets. But as very few among them have previouſly conſidered the ſubjects on which they are called upon to determine, very few carry along with them any opinion or inclination, or at leaſt any inclination of their own, and to which they are reſolved to adhere. As however it is neceſſary at-laſt to come to ſome reſolution, the major part of them are determined by reaſons which they would bluſh to pay any regard to, on much leſs ſerious occaſions. An unuſual ſight, a change of the ordinary place of the Aſſembly, a ſudden diſturbance, a rumour, are, amidſt the general want of a ſpirit of deciſion, the *ſufficiens ratio* of the determination of the greateſt part * ; and from this aſſemblage of ſeparate wills, thus formed haſtily and without reflection, a general will reſults, which is alſo void of reflection.

If, amidſt theſe diſadvantages, the Aſſembly were left to themſelves, and no body had an intereſt to lead them into error, the evil, though very great, would not however be extreme, becauſe ſuch an aſſembly never being called upon but to determine upon an affirmative or negative, that is, never having but two caſes to chooſe between, there would be an equal chance for their chooſing either; and it might be hoped that at every other turn they would take the right ſide.

But the combination of thoſe who ſhare either in the

A a

---

* Every one knows of how much importance it was in the Roman Commonwealth, to aſſemble the People, in one place rather than another. In order to change entirely the nature of their reſolutions, it was often ſufficient to hide from them, or let them ſee, the Capitol.

actual exercise of the public Power, or in its advantages, do not thus allow themfelves to fit down in inaction.   They wake, while the People fleep.   Entirely taken up with the thoughts of their own power, they
live but to increafe it.   Deeply verfed in the management of public bufinefs, they fee at once all the poffible confequences of meafures.   And as they have the
exclufive direction of the fprings of Government, they
give rife, at their pleafure, to every incident that may
influence the minds of a multitude who are not on their
guard, and who wait for fome event or other that may
finally determine them.

It is they who convene the Affembly, and diffolve
it: it is they who offer propofitions, and make fpeeches to it.   Ever active in turning to their advantage
every circumftance that happens, they equally avail
themfelves of the tractablenefs of the People during
public calamities, and its heedlefsnefs in times of profperity.   When things take a different turn from what
they expected, they difmifs the Affembly.   By prefenting to it many propofitions at once, and which are
to be voted upon in the lump, they hide what is deftined to promote their own private views, or give a
colour to it, by joining it with things which they know
will take hold of the mind of the People*.   By prefenting in their fpeeches, arguments and facts, which

---

* It was thus the Senate, at Rome, affumed to itfelf the
power of laying taxes.   They promifed, in the time of the
war againft the Vcientes, to give pay to fuch Citizens as
would enlift : and to that end they eftablifh a tribute.   The
people, folely taken up with the idea of not going to war at
their own expence, were tranfported with fo much joy, that
they crowded at the door of the Senate, and laying hold of
the hands of the Senators, called them their Fathers.—*Nihil
unquam acceptum a plebe tanto gaudio traditur : concurfum itaque
Curiam effe, prehenfatafque exeuntium manus, Patres vere oppel-
latos, &c. *See Tit. Liv. book iv.

Men have no time to examine, they lead the People into grofs, and yet decifive errors; and the common places of rhetoric, fupported by their perfonal influence,
ever enable them to draw to their fide the majority of
votes.

On the other hand, the few (for there are, after all,
fome) who, having meditated on the propofed queftion, fee the confequences of the decifive ftep which is
juft going to be taken, being loft in the crowd, cannot
make their feeble voices to be heard in the midft of the
univerfal noife and confufion. They have it no more
in their power to ftop the general motion, than a Man
in the midft of an army on a march, has it in his power to avoid marching. In the mean time the People
are giving their fuffrages; a majority appears in favour of the propofal; it is finally proclaimed as the
general will of all; and it is at bottom nothing more
than the effect of the artificers of a few defigning Men,
who are exulting among themfelves*.

* I might confirm all thefe things by numberlefs inflances
from ancient Hiftory; but, if I may be allowed in this cafe,
to draw examples from my own Country, *& celebrare domef-
tica facta*, I fhall relate facts which will be no lefs to the purpofe. In Geneva, in the year 1707, a law was enacted, that
a General Affembly of the People fhould be held every five
years, to treat of the affairs of the Republic; but the Magiftrates, who dreaded thofe Affemblies, foon obtained from the
Citizens themfelves the repeal of the law; and the firft refolution of the People, in the firft of thefe periodical Affemblies (in the year 1712) was to abolifh them for ever. The
profound fecrecy with which the Magiftrates prepared their
propofal to the Citizens on that fubject, and the fudden manner in which the latter, when affembled, were acquainted
with it, and made to give their votes upon it, have indeed
accounted but imperfectly for this ftrange determination of
the people; and the confternation which feized the whole
Affembly when the refult of the fuffrages was proclaimed, has

In a word, those who are acquainted with Republican Governments, and, in general, who know the manner in

confirmed many in the opinion that some unfair means had been used. The whole transaction has been kept secret to this day; but the common opinion on this subject, which has been adopted by M. Rousseau in his *Lettres de la Montagne*, is this: the Magistrates, it is said, had privately instructed the Secretaries in whose *ears* the Citizens were to *whisper* their suffrages: when a Citizen said, *approbation*, he was understood to approve the proposal of the Magistrates; when he said, *rejection*, he was understood to reject *periodical Assemblies*.

In the year 1738, the Citizens enacted at once into laws a small Code of forty-four Articles, by one single line of which they bound themselves for ever to elect the four *Syndics* (the Chiefs of the Council, of the twenty-five) out of the Members of the same Council; whereas they were before free in their choice. They at that time suffered also the word *approved* to be slipped into the law mentioned in a preceding Note, which was transcribed from a former Code; the consequence of which was to render the Magistrates absolute masters of the Legislature.

The Citizens had thus been successively stripped of all their *political* rights, and had little more left to them than the pleasure of being called a *Sovereign Assembly*, when they met (which idea, it must be confessed, preserved among them a spirit of resistance which it would have been dangerous for the Magistrates to provoke too far,) and the power of at least *refusing* to elect the four *Syndics*. Upon this privilege the Citizens have, a few years ago (A. 1765, to 1768,) made their last stand: and a singular conjunction of circumstances having happened at the same time, to raise and preserve among them, during three years, an uncommon spirit of union and perseverance, they have in the issue succeeded in a great measure to repair the injuries which they had been made to do to themselves, for these last two hundred years and more. *(A total change has since that time been effected by foreign forces, in the Government of the Republic (A. 1782,) upon which this is not a proper place to make any observation.)*

which bufinefs is transacted in numerous Affemblies, will
not fcruple to affirm, that the few who are united together, who take an active part in public affairs, and whofe
ftation makes them confpicuous, have fuch an advantage
over the many who turn their eyes towards them, and are
without union among themfelves, that, even with a
midling degree of fkill, they can at all times direct, at
their pleafure, the general refolutions ;—that, as a confequence of the very nature of things, there is no propofal, however abfurd, to which a numerous affembly of
Men may not, at one time or other, be brought to affent ;
and that laws would be wifer, and more likely to procure
the advantage of all, if they were to be made by drawing
lots, or cafting dice, than by the fufferings of a multitude.

C H A P T E R VI.

Advantages that accrue to the People from appointing
Reprefentatives.

HOW then fhall the People remedy the difadvantages that neceffarily attend their fituation ? How
fhall they refift the Phalanx of thofe who have engroffed
to themfelves all the honours, dignities, and power in
the State ?

It will be by employing for their defence the fame
means by which their adverfaries carry on their attack : it
will be by ufing the fame weapons as they do, the fame
order, the fame kind of difcipline.

They are a fmall number, and confequently eafily united ;—a fmall number muft therefore be oppofed to them,
that a like union may alfo be obtained. It is becaufe
they are a fmall number, that they can deliberate on every occurrence, and never come to any refolutions but
fuch as are maturely weighed—it is becaufe they are
few, that they can have forms which continually

serve them for general standards to resort to, approved maxims to which they invariably adhere, and plans which they never lose sight of:—here, therefore, I repeat it, oppose to them a small number, and you will obtain the like advantages.

Besides, those who govern, as a farther consequence of their being few, have a more considerable share, consequently feel a deeper concern in the success, whatever it may be, of their enterprizes. As they usually profess a contempt for their adversaries, and are at all times acting an offensive part against them, they impose on themselves an obligation of conquering. They in short, who are all alive from the most powerful incentives, and aim at gaining new advantages, have to do with a multitude, who, wanting only to preserve what they already possess, are unavoidably liable to long intervals of inactivity and supineness. But the People, by appointing Representatives, immediately gain to their cause that advantageous activity which they before stood in need of, to put them on a par with their adversaries; and those passions become excited in their defenders by which they themselves cannot possibly be actuated.

Exclusively charged with the care of public liberty, the Representatives of the People will be animated by a sense of the greatness of the concerns with which they are intrusted. Distinguished from the bulk of the Nation, and forming among themselves a separate Assembly, they will assert the rights of which they have been made the Guardians, with all that warmth which the *esprit de corps* is used to inspire *. Placed on an elevated theatre, they will endeavour to render themselves still more conspicuous; and the arts and ambitious activity of those who govern, will now be encountered by the vivacity and perseverance of opponents actuated by the love of glory.

---

* If it had not been for an incentive of this kind, the English Commons would not have vindicated their right of taxation with so much vigilance as they have done, against all enterprizes, often perhaps involuntary, of the Lords.

Laſtly, as the Repreſentatives of the People will naturally be ſelected from among thoſe Citizens who are moſt favoured by fortune, and will have conſequently much to preſerve, they will, even in the midſt of quiet times, keep a watchful eye on the motions of Power. As the advantages they poſſeſs, will naturally create a kind of rivalſhip between them and thoſe who govern, the jealouſy which they will conceive againſt the latter, will give them an exquiſite degree of ſenſibility on every increaſe of their authority. Like thoſe delicate inſtruments which diſcover the operations of Nature, while they are yet imperceptible to our ſenſes, they will warn the People of thoſe things which of themſelves they never ſee but when it is too late; and their greater proportional ſhare, whether of real riches, or of thoſe which lie in the opinions of Men, will make them, if I may ſo expreſs myſelf, the barometers that will diſcover, in its firſt beginning, every tendency to a change in the Conſtitution †.

CHAPTER VII.

The Subject continued—The advantages that accrue to the People from their appointing Repreſentatives, are very inconſiderable, unleſs they alſo entirely truſt their Legiſlative Authority to them.

THE obſervations made in the preceding Chapter are ſo obvious, that the People themſelves, in popular Governments, have alway been ſenſible of the

† All the above reaſoning eſſentially requires that the Repreſentatives of the People ſhould be united in intereſt with the People. We ſhall ſoon ſee that this union really obtains in the Engliſh Conſtitution, and may be called the maſterpiece of it.

truth of them, and never thought it poffible to remedy by themfelves alone, the difadvantages necefſarily attending their fituation. Whenever the oppreſſions of their Rulers have forced them to refort to fome uncommon exertion of their legal powers, they have immediately put themfelves under the direction of thofe few men who had been inſtrumental in informing and encouraging them; and when the nature of the circumftances has required any degree of firmneſs and perfeverance in their conduct, they have never been able to attain the ends they propoſed to themfelves, except by means of the moſt implicit deference to thofe Leaders whom they had thus appointed.

But as thefe Leaders, thus haſtily chofen, are eaſily intimidated by the continual difplay which is made before them of the terrors of Power, as that unlimited confidence which the People now repofe in them, only takes place when public liberty is in the utmoſt danger, and cannot be kept up, otherwife than by an extraordinary conjunction of circumſtances, and in which thofe who govern feldom fuffer themfelves to be caught more than once, the People have conſtantly fought to avail themfelves of the fhort intervals of fuperiority which the chance of events had given them, for rendering durable thofe advantages which they knew would, of themfelves, be but tranfitory, and for getting fome perfons appointed, whofe peculiar office it may be to protect them, and whom the Conſtitution fhall thenceforwards recognize. Thus it was that the People of Lacedæmon obtained their Ephori, and the People of Rome their Tribunes.

We grant this, will it be faid; but the Roman People never allowed their Tribunes *to conclude any thing definitively;* they, on the contrary, referved to themfelves the right of *ratifying* * any Refolutions the latter fhould take, This, I anfwer, was the very circumſtance that rendered the inſtitution of the Tribunes totally ineffectual in the event. The People thus wanting to interfere with their

---

* See M. Roffeau's Social Contract.

own opinions, in the refolutions of thofe on whom they had, in their wifdom, determined entirely to rely, and endeavouring to fettle with an hundred thoufand votes, things which would have been fettled equally well by the votes of their advifers, defeated in the iffue every beneficial end of their former provifions; and while they meant to preferve an appearance of their fovereignty (a chimerical appearance, fince it was under the direction of others that they intended to vote,) they fell back into all thofe inconveniences which we have before mentioned.

The Senators, the Confuls, the Dictators, and the other great Men in the Republic, whom the People were prudent enough to fear, and fimple enough to believe, continued ftill to mix with them, and play off their political artifices. They continued to make fpeeches to them *, and ftill availed themfelves of their privilege of changing at their pleafure the place and form of the public meetings. When they did not find it poffible by fuch means to direct the refolutions of the Affemblies, they pretended that the omens were not favourable, and under this pretext, or others of the fame kind, they diffolved them †.

* Valerius Maximus relates that the Tribunes of the People having offered to propofe fome regulations in regard to the price of corn, in a time of great fcarcity, Scipio Nafica over-ruled the Affembly merely by faying, " Silence, " Romans; I know better than you what is expedient for " the Republic." Which words were no fooner heard by the People, than they fhewed, by a filence full of veneration, that they were more affected by his authority, than by the neceffity of providing for their own fubfiftence. *Tacete, quæfo, Quirites. Plus enim ego quam vos quid reipublicæ expediat intelligo. Quâ voce auditâ, omnes, pleno venerationis filentio, majorem ejus autoritatis quam alimentorum fuorum curam egerunt.*

† *Quid enim majus eft, fi de jure Augurum quærimus,* fays Tully, who himfelf was an Augur and a Senator into the bargain, *quàm poffe a fummis imperiis & fummis poteftatibus Comitatus & Concilia, vel inftituta dimittere, vel habita refcindere ! Quid gravias, quam rem fufceptam dirimi, fi unus Augur* ALIUM (id eft, alium diem) *dixerit !* See De Legib. lib. ii. § 12.

And the Tribunes, when they had succeeded so far as to effect an union among themselves, thus were obliged to submit to the pungent mortification of seeing those projects which they had pursued with infinite labour, and even through the greatest dangers, irrecoverably defeated by the most despicable artifices.

When, at other times, they saw that a confederacy was carrying on with uncommon warmth against them, and despaired of succeeding by employing expedients of the above kind, or were afraid of diminishing their efficacy by a too frequent use of them, they betook themselves to other stratagems. They then conferred on the Consuls, by the means of a short form of words for the occasion †, an absolute power over the lives of the Citizens, or even appointed a Dictator. The People, at the sight of the State masquerade which was displayed before them, were sure to sink into a state of consternation ; and the Tribunes, however clearly they might see through the artifice, also trembled in their turn, when they thus beheld themselves left without defenders ‡.

At other times, they brought false accusations against the Tribunes before the Assembly itself ; or by privately slandering them with the People, they totally deprived them of their confidence. It was through artifices of this kind, that the People were brought to behold, without concern, the murder of Tiberius Gracchus, the only Roman that was really virtuous,—the only one who truly loved the People. It was also in

---

† *Videat Consul ne quid detrimenti Respublica capiat.*

‡ " The Tribunes of the People," says Livy, who was a great admirer of the Aristocratical power, " and the People " themselves, durst neither lift up their eyes, nor even mut- " ter, in the presence of the Dictator." *Nec adversus Dicta-toriam vim, aut Tribuni plebis aut ipsa Plebs, attollere oculos, aut hifcere, audebant.*——See Tit. Liv. lib. vi. § 16.

the fame manner that Caius, who was not deterred by
his brother's fate from purfuing the fame plan of conduct, was in the end fo entirely forfaken by the People, that nobody could be found among them who
would even lend him a horfe to fly from the fury of
the Nobles ; and he was at laft compelled to lay violent hands upon himfelf, while he invoked the wrath
of the Gods on his inconflant fellow-citizens.

At other times, they raifed divifions among the People. Formidable combinations broke out, on a fudden, on the eve of important tranfactions ; and all moderate Men avoided attending Affemblies, where they
faw that all was to be tumult and confufion.

In fine, that nothing might be wanting to the infolence with which they treated the Affemblies of the
People, they fometimes falfified the declarations of the
number of the votes ; they even once went fo far as to
carry off the urns into which the Citizens were to
throw their fuffrages *.

CHAP. VIII.

*The Subject concluded.—Effects that have refulted in the
English Government, from the People's Power being
completely delegated to their Reprefentatives.*

BUT when the People have entirely trufted their
power to a moderate number of perfons, affairs

* The reader with refpect to all the above obfervations,
may fee Plutarch's Lives, particularly the Lives of the two
Gracchi. I muft add, that I have avoided drawing any in-

immediately take a widely different turn. Those who govern are from that moment obliged to leave off all those stratagems which had hitherto ensured their success. Instead of those Assemblies which they affected to despise, and were perpetually comparing to storms, or to the current of the *Euripus* *, and in regard to which they accordingly thought themselves at liberty to pass over the rules of Justice, they now find that they have to deal with Men who are their equals in point of education and knowledge, and their inferiors only in point of rank and form. They, in consequence, soon found it necessary to adopt quite different methods; and, above all, become very careful not to talk to them any more about the sacred chickens, the *white* or *black* days, and the Sibylline books.—As they see their new adversaries expect to have a proper regard paid to them, that single circumstance inspires them with it:—as they see them act in a regular manner, observe constant rules, in a word, proceed with *form*, they come to look upon them with respect, from the very same reason which makes them themselves to be reverenced by the People.

The Representatives of the People, on the other hand, do not fail soon to procure for themselves every advantage that may enable them effectually to use the powers with which they have been entrusted, and to adopt every

stance from those Assemblies in which one half of the People were made to arm themselves against the other. I have here only alluded to those times which immediately either preceded or followed the third Punic war, that is, of those which are commonly called the *best period* of the Republic.

* Tully makes no end of his similies on this subject. *Quod enim fretum, quem Euripum, tot motus, tantas et tam varias habere putatis agitationes fluctuum, quantas perturbationes & quantos æstus habet ratio Comitiorum?* See Orat. pro Muræna.—*Concio,* says he in another place, *quæ ex imperitissimis constat, &c.* De Amicitia, § 25.

rule of proceeding that may make their refolutions to be truly the refult of reflection and deliberation. Thus it was that the Reprefentatives of the Englifh Nation, foon after their firft eftablifhment, became formed into a fepa‑rate Affembly: they afterwards obtained the liberty of appointing a Prefident:—foon, after, they infifted upon their being confulted on the laft form of the Acts to which they had given rife:—laftly, they infifted on thenceforth, framing them themfelves.

In order to prevent any poffibility of furprize in the courfe of their proceedings, it is a fettled rule with them, that every propofition, or bill, muft be read three times, at different prefixed days, before it can receive a final fanction: and before each reading of the bill, as well as at its firft introduction, an exprefs refolution muft be ta‑ken to continue it under confideration. If the bill be re‑jected, in any one of thofe feveral operations, it muft be dropped, and cannot be propofed again during the fame Seffion *.

The Commons have been, above all, jealous of the freedom of fpeech in their Affembly. They have ex‑prefsly ftipulated, as we have above mentioned, that none of their words or fpeeches fhould be queftioned in any place out of their Houfe. In fine, in order to keep their deliberations free from every kind of influence, they have

---

* It is moreover a fettled rule in the Houfe of Commons, that no Member is to fpeak more than once in the fame day. When the number and nature of the claufes of a Bill require that it fhould be difcuffed, in a freer manner, a committee is appointed for the purpofe, who are to make their report af‑terwards to the Houfe. When the fubject is of importance, this Committee is formed of the whole Houfe, which ftill con‑tinues to fit in the fame place, but in a lefs folemn manner, and under another Prefident, who is called the Chairman of the Committee. In order to form the Houfe again, the mace is replaced on the Table, and the Speaker goes again into his chair.

denied their Prefident the right to give his vote, or even his opinion:—they moreover have fettled it as a rule, not only that the King could not fend to them any exprefs propofal about laws, or other fubjects, but even that his name fhould never be mentioned in the deliberations *.

But that circumftance which, of all others, conftitutes the fuperior excellence of a Government in which the People act only through their reprefentatives, that is, by means of an affembly formed of a moderate number of perfons, and in which it is poffible for every member to propofe new fubjects, and to argue and canvafs the quef-tion that arifes, is that fuch a Conftitution is the only one that is capable of the immenfe advantage, and of which I do not know if I have been able to convey an adequate idea to the reader when I mentioned it before †, I mean that of putting into the hands of the People the moving fprings of the Legiflative authority.

In a Conftitution where the People at large exercife the function of enacting the Laws, as it is only to thofe per-fons towards whom the citizens are accuftomed to turn their eyes, that is to the very Men who govern, that the Affembly have either time or inclination to liften, they acquire, at length, as has conftantly been the cafe in all Republics, the exclufive right of propofing, if they pleafe, when they pleafe, in what manner they pleafe. A pre-rogative this, of fuch extent, that it would fuffice to put an affembly formed of Men of the greateft parts, at the mercy of a few dunces, and renders completely illufory the boafted power of the People. Nay more, as this pre-rogative is thus placed in the very hands of the adver-faries of the People, it forces the People to remain ex-pofed to their attacks, in a condition perpetually paffive,

---

* If any perfon were to mention in his fpeech, what the King *wifhes fhould be*, *would be glad to fee*, &c. he would be immediately *called to order*, for attempting to *influence the debate*.

† See chap. iv. of this Book.

and takes from them the only legal means by which they
might effectually oppofe their ufurpations.

To exprefs the whole in a few words. A *reprefentative*
Conftitution places the remedy in the hands of thofe who
feel the diforder: but a *popular* Conftitution places the
remedy in the hands of thofe who caufe it; and it is neceffarily productive, in the event, of the misfortune—of
the political calamity, ot trufting the care and the means
of repreffing the invafions of power, to the Men who
have the enjoyment of power.

C H A P.   IX.

*A farther Difadvantage of Republican Governments.—The
People are neceffarily betrayed by thofe in whom they
truft.*

HOWEVER, thofe general affemblies of a People
who were made to determine upon things which
they neither underftood nor examined,—that general
confufion in which the ambitious could at all times hide
their artifices, and carry on their fchemes with fafety,
were not the only evils attending the ancient Commonwealths. There was a more fecret defect, and a defect
that ftruck immediately at the very vitals of it, inherent
in that kind of Government.

It was impoffible for the People ever to have faithful
defenders. Neither thofe whom they had exprefsly chofen, nor thofe whom fome perfonal advantages enabled
to govern the Affemblies (for the only ufe, I muft repeat
it, which the People ever make of their power, is either
to give it away, or allow it to be taken from them) could
poffibly be united to them by any common feeling of the
fame concerns. As their influence put them, in a great
meafure, upon a level with thofe who are invefted wi h

the executive authority, they cared little to restrain op-
pressions out of the reach of which they saw themselves
placed. Nay, they feared they should thereby lessen a
power which they knew was one day to be their own ;
if they had not even already an actual share in it *.

Thus, at Rome, the only end which the Tribunes ever
pursued with any degree of sincerity and perseverance,
was to procure to the People, that is to themselves, an
admission to all the different dignities in the Republic.
After having obtained that a law should be enacted for
admitting Plebeians to the Consulship, they procured for
them the liberty of intermarrying with the Patricians.
They afterwards rendered them admissible to the Dictatorship, to the office of military Tribune, to the Censor-
ship : in a word, the only use they made of the power of
the People, was to increase privileges which they called
the privileges of all, though they and their friends alone
were ever likely to have the enjoyment of them.

But we do not find that they ever employed the power of the People in things really beneficial to the People. We do not find that they ever set bounds to the
terrible power of its Magistrate, that they ever repressed that class of Citizens who knew how to make
their crimes pass uncensured ;--in a word, that they e-
ver endeavoured, on the one hand to regulate, and on
the other to strengthen, the judicial power ; precautions these, without which men might struggle to the end
of time, and never attain true liberty†.

* How could it be expected that Men who entertained
views of being Prætors, would endeavour to restrain the power of the Prætors,—that Men who aimed at being one day
Consuls, would wish to limit the power of the Consuls,—that
Men whom their influence among the People made sure of
getting into the Senate, would seriously endeavour to confine
the authority of the Senate ?

† Without such precautions, laws must always be, as
Pope expresses it,

" Still for the strong too weak, the weak too strong."

And indeed the judicial power, that sure *criterion* of the goodnefs of a Government, was always, at Rome, a mere inftrument of tyranny. The Confuls were at all times invefted with an abfolute power over the lives of the Citizens. The Dictators poffeffed the fame right; fo did the Prætors, the Tribunes of the People, the judicial Commiffioners named by the Senate, and fo, of courfe, did the Senate itfelf; and the fact of the three hundred and feventy deferters, whom it commanded to be thrown down at one time, as Livy relates, from the Tarpeian rock, fufficiently fhews that it well knew how to exert its power upon occafion.

It even may be faid, that, at Rome, the power of life and death, or rather the right of killing, was annexed to every kind of authority whatever, even to that which refults from mere influence, or wealth; and the only confequence of the murder of the Gracchi, which was accompanied by the flaughter of three hundred, and afterwards of four thoufand unarmed Citizens, whom the Nobles *knocked on the head*, was to engage the Senate to erect a Temple to *Concord*. The *Lex Porcia de tergo civium*, which has been fo much celebrated, was attended with no other effect, but that of more completely fecuring againft the danger of a retaliation, fuch Confuls, Prætors, Queftors, &c. as, like Verres, caufed the inferior Citizens of Rome to be fcourged with rods, and put to death upon croffes, through mere caprice and cruelty*.

* If we turn our eyes to Lacedæmon, we fhall fee, from feveral inftances of the juftice of the Ephori, that matters were little better ordered there, in regard to the adminiftration of public juftice. And in Athens itfelf, which is the only one of the ancient Commonwealths in which the people feem to have enjoyed any degree of real liberty, we fee the Magiftrates proceed nearly in the fame manner as they now

C c

In fine, nothing can more completely shew to what degree the Tribunes had forsaken the interests of the People, whom they were appointed to defend, than the fact of their having allowed the Senate to invest itself with the power of taxation; they even suffered it to assume to itself the power not only of dispensing with the laws, but also of abrogating them*.

In a word, as the necessary consequence of the *communicability* of power, a circumstance essentially inherent in the republican form of government, it is impossible for it ever to be restrained within certain rules. Those who are in a condition to controul it, from that very circumstance, become its defenders. Though they may have risen, as we may suppose, from the humblest stations, and such as seemed totally to preclude them from all ambitious views, they have no sooner reached a certain degree of eminence, than they begin to aim higher. Their endeavours had at first no other object, as they professed, and perhaps with sincerity, than to see the laws impartially executed: their only view now is to set themselves above them ; and seeing themselves raised to the level of a class of men who possess all the power, and enjoy all the advantages

do among the Turks : and I think no other proof needs to be given than the story of that Barber in the Piræus, who having spread about the town the news of the overthrow of the Athenians in Sicilly, which he had heard from a stranger who had stopped at his shop, was put to the torture, by the command of the Archons, because he could not tell the name of his author.—See *Plut. Life of Nicias*.

* There are frequent instances of the Consuls taking away from the Capitol the tables of the laws passed under their predecessors. Nor was this, as we might at first be tempted to believe, an act of violence which success alone could justify : it was a consequence of the acknowledged power enjoyed by the Senate, *cujus erat gravissimum judicium de jure legum,* as we may see in several places in Tully. Nay, the Augurs

in the State, they make haste to associate themselves
with them*.

Personal power and independence on the laws being,
in such States, the immediate consequence of the favour
of the People, they are under an unavoidable necessity of
being betrayed.   Corrupting, as it were, every thing they
touch, they cannot shew a preference to a Man, but
they thereby attack his virtue ; they cannot raise him,
without immediately losing him and weakening their
own cause ; nay, they inspire him with views directly
opposite to their own, and send him to join and increase the number of their enemies.

Thus, at Rome, after the feeble barrier which ex-

themselves, as Tully informs us, enjoyed the same privelege.
" If laws have not been laid before the people, in the legal
" form, they (the Augurs) may set them aside : as was done
" with respect to the *Lex Tatia*, by the decree of the Col-
" lege, and to the *Leges Livæ*, by the advice of Philip, who
" was Consul and Augur."   *Legem si non jure rogata est, tol*
ere possunt ; ut Tatiam, decreto Collegii, ut Livias, consilio Phi
lippi, Consulis & Auguris.---See *De Legib.* lib. ii. § 12.

* Which always proves an easy thing. It is in Commonwealths the particular care of that class of Men who are at
the head of the State, to keep a watchful eye over the People, in order to draw over to their own party any Man who
happens to acquire a considerable influence among them ;
and this they are (and indeed must be) the more attentive to
do, in proportion as the nature of the Government is more
democratical.

The Constitution of Rome had even made express provisions on that subject.   Not only the Censors could at once remove any Citizen into what Tribe they pleased, and even
into the Senate, and we may easily believe that they made a
political use of this privilege ; but it was moreover a settled rule, that all persons who had been promoted to any
public office by the People, such as the Consulship, the Edile-
ship, or Tribuneship, became *ipso facto*, members of the Senate.—See Middleton's *Dissertation on the Roman Senate*.

cluded the People from offices of power and dignity had been thrown down, the great Plebeians, whom the votes of the People began to raise to those offices, were immediately received into the Senate, as has been just now observed. From that period, their families began to form in conjunction with the ancient Patrician families, a new combination or political association of persons*; and as this combination was formed by no particular class of Citizens, but of all those in general who had influence enough to gain admittance into it, a single overgrown head was now to be seen in the Republic, which consisting of all those who had either wealth or power of any kind, and disposing at will of the laws and the power of the people †, soon lost all regard to moderation and decency.

Every Constitution, therefore, whatever may be its form, which does not provide for inconveniencies of the kind here mentioned, is a Constitution essentially imperfect. It is in Man himself that the source of the evils to be remedied, lies ; general precautions therefore can alone prevent them. If it be a fatal error entirely to rely on the justice and equity of those who govern, it is an error no less dangerous to imagine, that, while virtue and moderation are the constant companions of those who oppose the abuses of Power, all ambition, all thirst after dominion, have retired to the other party.

Though wise Men sometimes may, led astray by the power of names, and the heat of political contentions, lose sight of what ought to be their real aim, they nevertheless know, that it is not against the *Appii*, the

---

* Called *Nobiles* and *Nobilitas*.

† It was, in several respects, a misfortune for the People of Rome, whatever may have been said to the contrary by the Writers on this subject, that the distinction between the Patricians and the Plebeians was ever abolished ; though, to say the truth, this was an event which could not be prevented.

Coruncanii, the *Cethegi*, but against all thofe who can influence the execution of the laws, that precautions ought to be taken,—That it is not the Conful, the Prætor, the Archon, the Minifter, the King, whom we ought to dread, nor the Tribune, or the Reprefentative of the People, on whom we ought implicitly to rely; but that all thofe perfons, without diftinction, ought to be the objects of our jealoufy, who, by any methods, and under any names whatfoever, have acquired the means of turning againft each individual the collective ftrength of all, and have fo ordered things around themfelves, that whoever attempts to refift them, is fure to find himfelf engaged alone againft a thoufand.

CHAP. X.

Fundamental difference between the Englifh Government, and the Governments juft defcribed---In England all Executive Authority is placed out of the hands of thofe in whom the People truft. Ufefulnefs of the Power of the Crown.

IN what manner then has the Englifh Conftitution contrived to find a remedy for evils which, from the very nature of Men and things, feem to be irremediable? How has it found means to oblige thofe perfons to whom the People have given up their power, to make them effectual and lafting returns of gratitude? thofe who enjoy an exclufive authority, to feek the advantge of all?—thofe who make the laws, to make only equitable ones?—It has been by fubjecting themfelves to thofe laws, and for that purpofe excluding them from all fhare in the execution of them.

Thus, the Parliament can eftablifh as numerous a ftanding army as it pleafes; but immediately another power comes forward, which takes the abfolute command of it, which fills all the pofts in it, and directs its motions at its pleafure. The Parliament may lay new taxes, but immediately another power feizes upon the produce of them, and alone enjoys the advantages and glory arifing from the difpofal of it. The Parliament may even, if you pleafe, repeal the laws on which the fafty of the Subject is grounded; but it is not their own caprices and arbitrary humours, it is the caprice and paffions of other Men, which they will have gratified, when they fhall thus have overthrown the columns of public liberty.

And the Englifh conftitution has not only excluded from any fhare in the execution of the laws, thofe in whom the People truft for the enacting of them, but it has alfo taken from them what would have had the fame pernicious influence on their deliberations—the hope of ever invading that executive authority, and transferring it to themfelves.

This authority has been made in England one fingle, indivifible prerogative; it has been made for ever the unalienable attribute of one perfon, marked out and afcertained beforehand by folemn laws and long eftablifhed cuftom, and all the active forces in the State have been left at his difpofal.

In order to fecure this prerogative ftill farther againft all poffibility of invafions from individuals, it has been heightened and ftrengthened by every thing that can attract and fix the attention and reverence of the People. The power of conferring, and withdrawing, places and employments has alfo been added to it, and ambition itfelf has thus been interefted in its defence, and fervice.

A fhare in the Legiflative power has alfo been given to the man to whom this prerogative has been delegated: a paffive fhare indeed, and the only one that can, with fafety to the State, be trufted to him, but by means of which he is enabled to defeat every attempt againſt his conſtitutional authority.

Laſtly, he is the only ſelf-exiſting and permanent Power in the State. The Generals, the Miniſters of State, are ſo only by the continuance of his pleaſure. He would even diſmiſs the Parliament themſelves, if ever he ſaw them begin to entertain dangerous deſigns ; and he needs only ſay one word to diſperſe every power in the State that may threaten his authority. Formidable prerogatives theſe ; but with regard to which we ſhall be inclined to lay aſide our apprehenſions, if we reflect, on the one hand, on the great privileges of the People by which they have been counterbalanced, and on the other, on the happy conſequences that reſult from their being thus united together.

From this unity, and, if I may ſo expreſs myſelf, this total ſequeſtration of the Executive authority, this advantageous conſequence in the firſt place follows, which has been mentioned in a preceding Chapter, that the attention of the whole nation is directed to one and the ſame object. The People, beſides, enjoy this moſt eſſential advantage, which they would vainly endeavour to obtain under the government of many,—they can give their confidence, without giving power over themſelves, and againſt themſelves ; they can appoint Truſtees, and yet not give themſelves Maſters.

Thoſe Men to whom the People have delegated the power of framing the Laws, are thereby made ſure to feel the whole preſſure of them. They can increaſe the prerogatives of the executive authority, but they cannot inveſt themſelves with it :—they have it not in their power to command its motions, they only can unbind its hands.

They are made to derive their importance, nay, they are indebted for their exiſtence, to the need in which that Power ſtands of their aſſiſtance ; and they know that they would no ſooner have abuſed the truſt of the People, and completed the treacherous work, than they would fee themfelves diffolved, fpurned, like inftruments now fpent, and become ufelefs.

This fame difpofition of things alfo prevents, in England, that effential defeft, inherent in the Government of many, which has been defcribed in the preceding Chapter.

In that fort of Government, the caufe of the People, as has been obferved, is continually deferted and betrayed. The arbitrary prerogatives of the governing Powers are at all times either openly or fecretly favoured, not only by thofe in whofe poffeffion they are, not only by thofe who have good reafon to hope that they fhall at fome future time fhare in the exercife of them, but alfo by the whole crowd of thofe Men who, in confequence of the natural difpofition of Mankind to over-rate their own advantages, fondly imagine, either that they fhall one day enjoy fome branch of this governing authority, or that they are even already, in fome way or other, affociated to it.

But as this authority has been made, in England, the indivifible, unalienable attribute of one alone, all other perfons in the State are *ipfo facto*, interefted to confine it within its due bounds. Liberty is thus made the common caufe of all; the laws that fecure it are fupported by Men of every rank and order; and the Habeas Corpus Aft, for inftance, is as zealoufly defended by the firft Nobleman in the Kingdom, as by the meaneft Subjeft.

Even the Minifter himfelf, in confequence of this *inalienability* of the executive authority, is equally interefted with his fellow-citizens to maintain the laws on which public liberty is founded. He knows, in the midft of his fchemes for enjoying or retaining his authority, that a Court-intrigue, or a caprice, may at every inftant confound him with the multitude, and the rancour of a fucceffor long kept out, fend him to linger in the fame jail which his temporary paffions might tempt him to prepare for others.

In confequence of this difpofition of things, great Men, therefore, are made to join in a common caufe with the People, for reftraining the exceffes of the governing power; and, which is no lefs effential to the public welfare, they are alfo, from this fame caufe, compelled to reftrain the excefs of their own private power and influence, and a general fpirit of juftice becomes thus diffufed through all parts of the State.

The wealthy Commoner, the Reprefentative of the People, the potent Peer, always having before their eyes the view of a formidable Power, of a Power from the attempts of which they have only the fhield of the laws to protect them, and which would, in the iffue, retaliate an hundred fold upon them their acts of violence, are compelled, both to wifh only for equitable laws, and to obferve them with fcrupulous exactnefs.

Let then the People dread (it is neceffary to the prefervation of their liberty), but let them never entirely ceafe to love, the Throne, that fole and indivifible feat of all the active powers in the State.

Let them know, it is that, which, by lending an immenfe ftrength to the arm of Juftice, has enabled her to bring to account as well the moft powerful, as the meaneft offender,—which has fuppreffed, and if I may fo exprefs myfelf, weeded out all thofe tyrannies fometimes confederated with, and fometimes adverfe to, each other, which inceffantly tend to grow up in the middle of civil focieties, and are the more terrible in proportion as they feel themfelves to be lefs firmly eftablifhed.

Let them know, it is that, which, by making all honours and places depend on the will of one Man, has confined within private walls thofe projects the purfuit of which, in former times, fhook the foundations of whole States,—has changed into intrigues the conflicts, the outrages of ambition,—and that thofe contentions which, in the prefent times, afford them only matter of amufement, are the Volcanos which fet in flames the ancient Commonwealths.

D d

It is that, which, leaving to the rich no other fecurity for his palace than that which the peafant has for his cottage, has united his caufe to that of this latter, the caufe of the powerful to that of the helplefs, the caufe of the Man of extenfive influence and conneflions, to that of him who is without friends.

It is the throne above all, it is this jealous Power, which makes the People fure that its Reprefentatives never will be any thing more than its Reprefentatives: at the fame time it is the ever-fubfifting Carthage which vouches to it for the duration of their virtue.

C H A P. XI.

The Powers which the People themfelves exercife.—The E-lection of Members of Parliament.

THE Englifh Conftitution having effentially connected the fate of the Men to whom the People truft their power, with that of the People themfelves, really feems, by that caution alone, to have procured the latter a complete fecurity.

However, as the viciffitude of human affairs may, in procefs of time, realize events which at firft had appeared moft improbable, it might happen that the Minifters of the Executive power, notwithftanding the intereft they themfelves have in the prefervation of public liberty, and in fpite of the precautions exprefsly taken, in order to prevent the effect of their influence, fhould, at length, employ fuch efficacious means of corruption as might bring about the furrender of fome of the laws upon which this public liberty is founded. And though we fhould fuppofe that fuch a danger would really be chimerical, it might at leaft happen, that conniving at a vi-

cious Adminiftration, and being over-liberal of the produce of the labours of the People, the Reprefentatives of
the People might make them fuffer many of the evils
which attend worfe forms of Government.

Laftly, as their duty does not confift only in preferving their conftituents againft the calamities of an aibitra-
ry Government, but moreover in procuring them the beft
adminiftration poffible, it might happen that they would
manifeft, in this refpect, an indifference which would, in
its confequences, amount to a real calamity.

It was therefore neceffary that the Conftitution fhould
furnifh a remedy for all the above cafes : now, it is in the
right of electing Members of Parliament, that this remedy lies.

When the time is come at which the commiffion which
the People had given to their delegates expires, they again
affemble in their feveral Towns or Counties : on thefe occafions they have it in their power to elect again thofe
of their Reprefentatives whofe former conduct they approve, and to reject thofe who have contributed to give
rife to their complaints. A fimple remedy this, and
which only requiring, in its application, a knowledge of
matters of fact, is entirely within the reach of the abilities of the People ; but a remedy, at the fame time, which
is the moft effectual that could be applied ; for, as the e-
vils complained of, arife merely from the peculiar difpofitions of a certain number of individuals, to fet afide
thofe individuals, is to pluck up the evil by the roots.

But I perceive, that in order to make the reader fenfible of the advantages that may accrue to the People of
England, from their right of election, there is another of
their rights, of which it is abfolutely neceffary that I fhould
firft give an account.

CHAP. XII.

The Subject continued—Liberty of the Press.

AS the evils that may be complained of in a State, do not always arife merely from the defeat of the laws, but alfo from the non-execution of them, and this non-execution of fuch a kind, that it is often impoffible to fubjeft it to any exprefs punifhment, or even to af-certain by any previous definition, Men, in feveral States, have been led to feek for an expedient that might fupply the unavoidable deficiency of legiflative provifions, and begin to operate, as it were, from the point at which the latter began to fail : I mean here to fpeak of the Cenfo-rial power ; a power which may produce excellent ef-fects, but the exercife of which (contrary to that of the legiflative power) muft be left to the People themfelves.

As the propofed end of Legiflation is not, according to what has been above obferved, to have the particular intentions of individuals, upon every cafe, known and complied with, but folely to have what is moft conduc-ive to the public good on the occafions that arife, found out, and eftablifhed, it is not an effential requifite in legiflative operations, that every individual fhould be called upon to deliver his opinion ; and fince this expedi-ent, which at firft fight appears fo natural, of feeking out by the advice of all that which concerns all, is found li-able, when carried into practice, to the greateft inconve-niences, we muft not hefitate to lay it afide entirely. But as it is the opinion of individuals alone, which con-ftitutes the check of a cenforial power, this power cannot poffibly produce its intended effect any farther than this public opinion is made known and declared : the fenti-ments of the People are the only thing in queftion here : therefore it is neceffary that the People fhould fpeak for themfelves, and manifeft thofe fentiments.   A particular

Court of Cenfure therefore effentially fruftrates its inteand-
ed purpofe : it is attended, befides, with very great inconveniences.

As the ufe of fuch a Court is to determine upon thofe
cafes which lie out of the reach of the laws, it cannot be
tied down to any precife regulations. As a farther confequence of the arbitrary nature of its functions, it cannot
even be fubjected to any conftitutional check : and it continually prefents to the eye the view of a power entirely
arbitrary, and which in its different exertions may affect,
in the moft cruel manner, the peace and happinefs of individuals. It is attended, befides, with this very pernicious confequence, that, by dictating to the people their
judgments of Men or meafures, it takes from them that
freedom of thinking which is the nobleft privilege, as well
as the firmeft fupport of Liberty *.

We may therefore look upon it as a farther proof of
the foundnefs of the principles on which the Englifh con-

---

* M. de Montefquieu, and M. Rouffeau, and indeed all
the Writers on this fubject I have met with, beftow vaft en-
comiums on the Cenforial Tribunal that had been inftituted
at Rome :—they have not been aware that this power of
Cenfure, lodged in the hands of peculiar Magiftrates, with
other difcretionary powers annexed to it, was no other than
a piece of ftate craft, like thofe defcribed in the preceding
Chapters, and had been contrived by the Senate as an additional means of fecuring its authority. Sir Thomas More
has alfo adopted fimilar opinions on the fubject : and he is fo
far from allowing the People to canvafs the actions of their
Rulers, that in his Syftem of Policy, which he calls, *An Account of Utopia* (the happy Region,) he makes it death
for individuals to talk about the conduct of Government.

I feel a kind of Pleafure, I muft confefs, to obferve on
this occafion, that though I have been called by fome an advocate for Power, I have carried my ideas of Liberty farther
than many Writers who have mentioned that word with
much enthufiafm.

ftitution is founded, that it has allotted to the People themfelves the province of openly canvaffing and arraigning the conduct of thofe who are invefted with any branch of public authority; and that it has thus delivered into the hands of the People at large, the exercife of the cenforial power.　Every fubject in England has not only a right to prefent petitions to the King, or to the Houfes of Parliament, but he has a right alfo to lay his complaints and obfervations before the public, by means of an open prefs.　A formidable right this, to thofe who rule mankind; and which, continually difpelling the cloud of majefty by which they are furrounded, brings them to a level with the reft of the people, and ftrikes at the very being of their authority.

And indeed this privilege is that which has been obtained by the Englifh Nation with the greateft difficulty, and lateft in point of time, at the expence of the Executive power.　Freedom was in every other refpect already eftablifhed, when the Englifh were ftill, with regard to the public expreffion of their fentiments, under reftraints that may be called defpotic.　Hiftory abounds with inftances of the feverity of the Court of Star-Chamber, againft thofe who prefumed to write on political fubjects. It had fixed the number of printers and printing preffes, and appointed a *Licenfer*, without whofe approbation no book could be publifhed.　Befides, as this Tribunal, decided matters by its own fingle authority, without the intervention of a Jury, it was always ready to find thofe perfons guilty, whom the Court was pleafed to look upon as fuch; nor was it indeed without ground that Chief Juftice Coke, whofe notions of liberty were fomewhat tainted with the prejudices of the times in which he lived, concluded the eulogiums he has beftowed on this Court, with faying that, " the right inftitution and orders there-" of being obferved, it doth keep all England in quiet."

After the Court of Star-Chamber had been abolifhed, the Long Parliament, whofe conduct and affumed power were little better qualified to bear a fcrutiny, revived the regulations againſt the freedom of the preſs. Charles the Second, and after him James the Second, procured farther renewals of them. Theſe latter acts having expired in the year 1692, were at this æra, although poſterior to the Revolution, continued for two years longer ; ſo that it was not till the year 1694, that, in conſequence of the Parliament's refuſal to continue the prohibitions any longer, the freedom of the preſs (a privilege which the Executive power could not, it ſeemed, prevail upon itſelf to yield up to the people) was finally eſtabliſhed.

In what does then this liberty of the preſs preciſely conſiſt ? Is it a liberty left to every one to publiſh any thing that comes into his head ? to calumniate, to blacken, whomſoever he pleaſes ? No ; the ſame laws that protect the perſon and the property of the individual, do alſo protect his reputation ; and they decree againſt libels, when really ſo, puniſhments of much the ſame kind as are eſtabliſhed in other Countries. But, on the other hand, they do not allow, as in other States, that a Man ſhould be deemed guilty of a crime for merely publiſhing ſomething in print ; and they appoint a puniſhment only againſt him who has printed things that are in their nature criminal, and who is declared guilty of ſo doing by twelve of his equals, appointed to determine upon his caſe, with the precautions we have before deſcribed.

The liberty of the preſs, as eſtabliſhed in England, conſiſts, therefore, to define it more preciſely, in this, That neither the Courts of Juſtice, nor any other Judges whatever, are authoriſed to take any notice of writings intended for the preſs, but are confined to thoſe which are actually printed, and muſt, in theſe caſes, proceed by the Trial by Jury.

It is even this latter circumſtance which more particularly conſtitutes the freedom of the preſs. If the Magiſtrates, though confined in their proceedings to caſes of criminal publications, were to be the ſole Judges of the criminal nature of the things publiſhed, it might eaſily happen that, with regard to a point which, like this, ſo

highly excites the jealoufy of the governing Powers, they
would exert themfelves with fo much fpirit and perfeverance, that they might, at length, fucceed in completely
ftriking off all the heads of the hydra.

But whether the authority of the Judges be exerted at
the motion of a private individual, or whether it be at the
inftance of the Government itfelf, their fole office is to
declare the punifhment eftablifhed by the law :—it is to
the Jury alone that it belongs to determine on the matter
of law, as well as on the matter of faƈt ; that is, to determine, not only whether the writing which is the fubjeƈt
of the charge has really been compofed by the Man
charged with having done it, and whether it be really
meant of the perfon named in the indiƈtment,—but alfo
whether its contents are criminal.

And though the law in England does not allow a Man,
profecuted for having publifhed a libel, to offer to fupport by evidence the truth of the faƈts contained in it (a
mode of proceeding which would be attended with very
mifchievous confequences, and is every where prohibited)
yet * as the indiƈtment is to exprefs that the faƈts are *falfe,
malicious,* &c. and the Jury, at the fame time, are fole
mafters of their verdiƈt, that is, may ground it upon what
confiderations they pleafe, it is very probable that they
would acquit the accufed party, if the faƈt, afferted in the
writing before them, were matter of undoubted truth,
and of a general evil tendency. They, at leaft, would
certainly have it in their power.

And this would ftill more likely be the cafe if the conduƈt of the Government itfelf was arraigned ; becaufe,
befides this conviƈtion which we fuppofe in the Jury, of
the certainty of the faƈts, they would alfo be influenced
by their fenfe of a principle generally admitted in England, and which, in a late celebrated caufe, has been

* In aƈtions for damages between individuals, the cafe, if
I miftake not, is different, and the defendant is allowed to
produce evidence of the faƈts afferted by him.

ftrongly infifted upon, viz. That, " though to fpeak ill of
" individuals was deferving of reprehenfion, yet the pub-
" lic acts of Government ought to lie open to public ex-
" amination, and that it was a fervice done to the State,
" to canvafs them freely *."

And indeed this extreme fecurity with which every
man in England is enabled to communicate his fentiments
to the Public, and the general concern which matters relative to the Government are always fure to create, has
wonderfully multiplied all kinds of public papers. Befides thofe which, being publifhed at the end of every
year, month, or week, prefent to the reader a recapitula-
tion of every thing interefting that may have been done
or faid during their refpective periods, there are feveral
others, which making their appearance every day, or every
other day, communicate to the public the feveral meafures
taken by the Government, as well as the different caufes of
any importance, whether civil or criminal, that occur in the
Courts of Juftice, and fketches from the fpeeches either of
the Advocates, or the Judges, concerned in the management
and decifion of them. During the time the Parliament
continues fitting, the votes, or refolutions of the Houfe of
Commons, are daily publifhed by authority; and the moft
interefting fpeeches in both Houfes are taken down in
fhort hand, and communicated to the Public, in print.

Laftly, the private anecdotes in the Metropolis, and
the Country, concur alfo towards filling the collection;
and as the feveral public papers circulate, or are tranfcri-
bed into others, in the different Country Towns, and even
find their way into the villages, where every Man, down
to the labourer, perufes them with a fort of eagernefs, e-
very individual thus becomes acquainted with the State of
the Nation, from one end to the other, and by thefe
means the general intercourfe is fuch, that the three Kingdoms feem as if they were one fingle Town.

E e

* See Serjeant Glynn's Speech for Woodfall in the profecution againft the latter, by the Attorney-General, for publifhing Junius's letter to the King.

And it is this public notoriety of all things that conſtitutes the ſupplemental power, or check, which, we have above ſaid, is ſo uſeful to remedy the unavoidable inſufficiency of the laws, and keep within their reſpective bounds all thoſe perſons who have any ſhare of public authority.

As they are thereby made ſenſible that all their actions are expoſed to public view, they dare not venture upon thoſe acts of partiality, thoſe ſecret connivances at the iniquities of particular perſons, or thoſe vexatious practices, which the Man in office is but too apt to be guilty of, when, exerciſing his office at a diſtance from the public eye, and as it were in a corner, he is ſatisfied that provided he be cautious he may diſpenſe with being juſt. Whatever may be the kind of abuſe in which perſons in power may, in ſuch a ſtate of things, be tempted to indulge themſelves, they are convinced that their irregularities will be immediately divulged. The Juryman, for example, knows that his verdict, the Judge, that his direction to the Jury, will preſently be laid before the Public: and there is no Man in office, but who thus finds himſelf compelled, in almoſt every inſtance, to chooſe between his duty, and the ſurrender of all his former reputation.

It will, I am aware, be thought that I ſpeak in too high terms, of the effects produced by the public news-papers. I indeed confeſs that all the pieces contained in them are not patterns of good reaſoning, or of the trueſt Attic wit: but, on the other hand, it ſcarcely ever happens that a ſubject in which the laws, or in general the public welfare, are really concerned, fails to call forth ſome able writer, who, under ſome form or other, communicates to the public his obſervations and complaints. I ſhall add here, that, though an upright Man, labouring for a while under a ſtrong popular prejudice, may, ſupported by the conſciouſneſs of his innocence, endure with patience the ſevereſt imputations, the guilty Man, hearing nothing in the reproaches of the Public, but what he knows to be true, and already upbraids himſelf with, is very far from enjoying any ſuch comfort; and that, when a man's own confcience takes part againſt him, the moſt deſpicable weapon is ſufficient to wound him to the quick *.

Even thoſe perſons whoſe greatneſs ſeems moſt to ſet them above the reach of public cenſure, are not thoſe who leaſt feel its effeĉts. They have need of the ſuffrages of that vulgar whom they affeĉt to deſpiſe, and who are, after all, the diſpenſers of that glory, which is the real objeĉt of their ambitious cares. Though all have not ſo much ſincerity as Alexander, they have equal reaſon to exclaim, *O People! what toils do we not undergo in order to gain your applauſe!*

I confeſs that in a ſtate where the People dare not ſpeak their ſentiments, but with a view to pleaſe the ears of their rulers, it is poſſible that either the Prince, or thoſe to whom he has truſted his authority, may ſometimes miſtake the nature of the public ſentiments, or that, for want of that affeĉtion of which they are denied all poſſible marks, they may reſt contented with inſpiring terror, and make themſelves amends in beholding the over-awed multitude ſmother their complaints,

But when the laws give a full ſcope to the People for the expreſſion of their ſentiments, thoſe who go-

---

* I ſhall take this occaſion to obſerve, that the liberty of the preſs is ſo far from being injurious to the reputation of individuals (as ſome perſons have complained), that it is on the contrary, its ſureſt guard. When there exiſts no means of Communication with the Public, every one is expoſed, without defence, to the ſecret ſhafts of malignity and envy. The man in office loſes his reputation, the Merchant his credit, the private individual his charaĉter, without ſo much as knowing either who are his enemies, or which way they carry on their attacks. But when there exiſts a free preſs, an innocent Man immediately brings the matter into open day, and cruſhes his adverſaries, at once, by a public challenge to lay before the public the grounds of their ſeveral imputations.

vern cannot conceal from themfelves the difagreeable truths which refound from all fides. They are obliged to put up even with ridicule, and the coarfeft jefts are not always thofe which give them the leaft uneafinefs. Like the lion in the fable, they muft bear the blows of thofe enemies whom they defpife the moft ; and they are, at length, ftopped fhort in their career, and compelled to give up thofe unjuft purfuits which they find to draw upon them, inftead of that admiration which is the propofed end and reward of their labours, nothing but mortification and difguft.

In fhort, whoever confiders what it is that conftitutes the moving principle of what we call great affairs, and the invincible fenfibility of Man to the opinion of his fellow-creatures, will not hefitate to affirm that, if it were poffible for the liberty of the prefs to exift in a defpotic government, and (what is not lefs difficult) for it to exift without changing the conftitution, this liberty of the prefs would alone form a counterpoife to the power of the Prince. If, for example, in an empire of the Eaft, a fanctuary could be found, which, rendered refpectable by the ancient religion of the people, might enfure fafety to thofe who fhould bring thither their obfervations of any kind, and that from thence printed papers fhould iffue, which, under a certain feal, might be equally refpected, and which in their daily appearance fhould examine and freely difcufs the conduct of the Cadis, the Bafhaws, the Vizir, the Divan, and the Sultan himfelf,—that would introduce immediately fome degree of liberty.

CHAP. XIII.

The Subject continued.

ANOTHER effect, and a very confiderable one, of the liberty of the prefs, is, that it enables the People effectually to exert thofe means which the Conftitution has beftowed on them, of influencing the motions of the Government.

It has been obferved in a former place, how it came to be a matter of impoffibility for any large number of men, when obliged to act in a body, and upon the fpot, to take any well-weighed refolution. But this inconvenience, which is the inevitable confequence of their fituation, does in no wife argue a perfonal inferiority in them, with refpect to the few who, from fome accidental advantages, are enabled to influence their determinations. It is not Fortune, it is Nature, that has made the effential differences between Men : and whatever appellation a fmall number of perfons who fpeak without fufficient reflection, may affix to the general body of their fellow-creatures, the whole difference between the Statefman, and many a Man from among what they call the dregs of the People, often lies in the rough outfide of the latter ; a difguife which may fall off on the firft opportunity ; and more than once has it happened, that from the middle of a multitude in appearance contemptible, there have been feen to rife at once Viriatufes, or Spartacufes.

Time, and a more favourable fituation (to repeat it once more), are therefore the only things wanting to the People ; and the freedom of the prefs affords the remedy to thefe difadvantages. Through its affiftance every individual may, at his leifure and in retirement, inform himfelf of every thing that relates to the queftions on which he is to take a refolution. Through its affistance, a whole Nation as it were holds a Council, and deliberates; flowly indeed (for a Nation cannot be informed like an affembly of Judges), but after a regular manner, and with certainty. Through its affiftance, all matters of fact are, at length, made clear; and, through the conflict of the different anfwers and replies, nothing at laft remains, but the found part of the arguments *.

Hence, though all good Men may not think themfelves obliged to concur implicitly in the tumultuary refolutions of the People whom their Orators take pains to agitate, yet, on the other hand, when this

* This right of publicly difcuffing political Subjects, is alone a great advantage to a People who enjoy it; and if the Citizens of Geneva, for inftance, have preferved their liberty better than the People have been able to do in the other Commonwealths of Switzerland, it is, I think, owing to the extenfive right they poffefs of making public remonftrances to their Magiftrates. To thefe remonftrances the Magiftrates, for inftance, the Council of *Twenty-five*, to which they are ufually made, are obliged to give an anfwer. If this anfwer does not fatisfy the remonftrating Citizens, they take time, perhaps two or three weeks, to make a reply to it, which muft alfo be anfwered; and the number of Citizens who go up with each new remonftrance increafes, according as they are thought to have reafon on their fide. Thus, the remonftrances which were made fome years ago, on account of the fentence againft the celebrated M. Rouffeau, and were delivered at firft by only forty Citizens, were afterwards often accompanied by about nine hundred.—This circumftance, together with the ceremony with which thofe remonftrances, (or *Reprefentations*, as they more commonly call them) are delivered, has rendered them a great check on the conduct of the Magiftrates: they even have been ftill more ufeful to the Citizens of Geneva, as a preventative than as a remedy; and nothing is more likely to deter the Magiftrates from taking a ftep of any kind, than the thought that it will give rife to a *Reprefentation*. -

fame People, left to itfelf, perfeveres in opinions which have for a long time been difcuffed in public writings, and from which (it is effential to add) all errors concerning facts have been removed, fuch perfeverance is certainly a very refpectable decifion; and then it is, though only then, that we may with fafety fay,—"the " voice of the People is the voice of God."

How, therefore, can the People of England *act*, when, having formed opinions which may really be called their own, they think they have juft caufe to complain againft the Adminiftration? It is, as has been faid above, by means of the right they have of electing their Reprefentatives; and the fame method of general intercourfe that has informed them with regard to the objects of their complaints, will likewife enable them to apply the remedy to them.

Through this means they are acquainted with the nature of the fubjects that have been deliberated upon in the Affembly of their Reprefentatives;—they are informed by whom the different motions were made, —by whom they were fupported; and the manner in which the fuffrages are delivered, is fuch, that they always can know the names of thofe who have voted conftantly for the advancement of pernicious meafures.

And the People not only know the particular difpofitions of every Member of the Houfe of Commons; but the general notoriety of all things gives them alfo a knowledge of the political fentiments of a great number of thofe, whom their fituation in life renders fit to fill a place in that Houfe. And availing themfelves of the feveral vacancies that happen, and ftill more of the opportunity of a general election, they purify either fucceffively, or at once, the Legiflative Affembly; and thus, without any commotion or danger to the State, they effect a material reformation in the views of the Government.

I am aware that some persons will doubt these patriotic and systematic views, which I am here attributing to the People of England, and will object to me the disorders that sometimes happen at Elections. But this reproach, which, by the way, comes with but little propriety from Writers who would have the People transact every thing in their own persons, this reproach, I say, though true to a certain degree, is not however so much so as it is thought by certain persons who have taken only a superficial survey of the state of things.

Without doubt, in a Constitution in which all important causes of uneasiness are so effectually prevented, it is impossible but that the People will have long intervals of inattention. Being then called upon, on a sudden, from this state of inactivity, to elect Representatives, they have not examined, before-hand, the merits of those who ask them their votes; and the latter have not had, amidst the general tranquillity, any opportunity to make themselves known to them.

The Elector, persuaded, at the same time, that the person whom he will elect, will be equally interested with himself in the support of public liberty, does not enter into laborious disquisitions, and from which he sees he may exempt himself. Obliged, however, to give the preference to somebody, he forms his choice on motives which would not be excusable, if it were not that some motives are necessary to make a choice, and that, at this instant, he is not influenced by any other: and indeed it must be confessed, that, in the ordinary course of things, and with Electors of a certain rank in life, that Candidate who gives the best entertainment, has a great chance to get the better of his competitors.

But if the measures of Government, and the reception of those measures in Parliament, by means of a too complying House of Commons, should ever be such as to fpread a ferious alarm among the People, the fame caufes which have concurred to eftablifh public liberty, would, no doubt, operate again, and likewife concur in its fupport. A general combination would then be formed, both of thofe Members of Parliament who have remained true to the public caufe, and of perfons of every order among the People. Public meetings, in fuch circumftances, would be appointed, general fub-fcriptions would be entered into, to fupport the expen-ces, whatever they might be, of fuch a neceffary op-pofition; and all private and unworthy purpofes being fuppreffed by the fenfe of the National danger, the choice of the electors would then be wholly determin-ed by the confideration of the public fpirit of the Can-didates, and the tokens given by them of fuch fpirit.

Thus were thofe Parliaments formed, which fup-preffed arbitrary taxes and imprifonments. Thus was it, that, under Charles the Second, the People, when recovered from that enthufiafm of affection, with which they received a King fo long perfecuted, at laft return-ed to him no Parliaments but fuch as were compofed of a majority of Men attached to public liberty. Thus it was, that perfevering in a conduct which the circumftances of the times rendered neceffary, the Peo-ple baffled the arts of the Government; and Charles diffolved three fucceffive Parliaments, without any o-ther effect but that of having thofe fame Men re-cho-fen, and fet again in oppofition to him, of whom he hoped he had rid himfelf for ever.

Nor was James the Second happier in his attempts than Charles had been. This Prince foon experienced that his Parliament was actuated by the fame fpirit as thofe which had oppofed the defigns of his late bro-ther; and having fuffered himfelf to be led into mea-fures of violence, inftead of being better taught by the difcovery he made of the real fentiments of the People,

F f

his reign was terminated by that cataftrophe with which every one is acquainted.

Indeed, if we combine the right enjoyed by the People of England, of electing their Reprefentatives, with the whole of the Englifh Government, we fhall become continually more and more fenfible of the excellent effects that may refult from that right. All Men in the State, are, as has been before obferved, really interefted in the fupport of public liberty ;—nothing but temporary motives, and fuch as are quite peculiar to themfelves, can poffibly induce the Members of any Houfe of Commons to connive at meafures deftructive of this liberty: the People, therefore, under fuch circumftances, need only change thefe Members in order effectually to reform the conduct of that Houfe : and it may fairly be pronounced beforehand, that a Houfe of Commons, compofed of a new fet of perfons, will, from this bare circumftance, be in the interefts of the People.

Hence, though the complaints of the People do not, always meet with a fpeedy and immediate redrefs (a celerity which would be the fymptom of a fatal unfteadinefs in the Conftitution, and would fooner or later bring on its ruin;) yet, when we attentively confider the nature and the refources of this Conftitution, we fhall not think it too bold an affertion to fay, that it is impoffible but that complaints in which the People perfevere, that is, to repeat it once more, well-grounded complaints, will fooner or later be redreffed.

CHAP. XIV.

Right of Resistance.

BUT all those privileges of the People, considered in themselves, are but feeble defences against the real strength of those who govern. All those provisions, all those reciprocal Rights, necessarily suppose that things remain in their legal and settled course: what would then be the resource of the People, if ever the Prince, suddenly freeing himself from all restraint, and throwing himself as it were out of the Constitution, should no longer respect either the person, or the property of the subject, and either should make no account of his conversation with the Parliament, or attempt to force it implicitly to submit to his will?—It would be resistance.

Without entering here into the discussion of a doctrine which would lead us to inquire into the first principles of Civil Government, consequently engage us in a long disquisition, and with regard to which, besides, persons free from prejudices agree pretty much in their opinions, I shall only observe here (and it will be sufficient for my purpose) that the question has been decided in favour of this doctrine by the Laws of England, and that resistance is looked upon by them as the ultimate and lawful resource against the violences of Power.

It was resistance that gave birth to the Great Charter, that lasting foundation of English Liberty; and the excesses of a Power established by force, were also restrained by force *. It has been by the same means that, at

---

* Lord Lyttleton says extremely well, in his Persian Letters, "If the privileges of the People of England be concessions from the Crown, is not the power of the Crown itself, a concession of the People?" It might be said with

different times, the People have procured the confirmation of the fame Charter. Laftly, it has alfo been the Refiftance to a King who made no account of his own engagements, that has, in the iffue, placed on the Throne the family which is now in poffeffion of it.

This is not all; this refource, which till then had only been an act of force, oppofed to other acts of force, was, at that æra, exprefsly recognized by the Law itfelf. The Lords and Commons, folemnly affembled, declared, that
" King James the Second, having endeavoured to fub-
" vert the Conftitution of the Kingdom, by breaking the
" original contract between King and People, and having
" violated the fundamental laws, and withdrawn himfelf,
" had abdicated the Government; and that the Throne
" was thereby vacant *."

And left thofe principles to which the Revolution thus gave a fanction, fhould, in procefs of time, become mere *arcana* of State, exclufively appropriated, and only known to a certain clafs of Subjects, the fame Act, we have juft mentioned, exprefsly infured to individuals the right of publicly preferring complaints againft the abufes of Goverment, and moreover, of being provided with arms for their own defence. Judge Blackftone expreffes himfelf in the following terms, in his Commentaries on the Laws of England, (B. I. Ch. i.)
" And laftly, to vindicate thofe rights, when actually
" violated or attacked, the fubjects of England are enti-
" tled, in the firft place, to the regular adminiftration,
" and free courfe of juftice in the Courts of Law ; next,
" to the right of petitioning the King and Parliament for
" redrefs of grievances ; and, laftly, to the right of ha-
" ving and ufing arms for felf-prefervation and defence."

equal truth, and fomewhat more in point of the fubject of this Chapter,—If the privileges of the People be an encroachment on the power of Kings, the power itfelf of Kings was at firft an encroachment (no matter whether effected by furprize) on the natural liberty of the People.

† The Bill of Rights has fince given a new fanction to all thefe principles.

Laftly, this right of oppofing violence, in whatever fhape, and from whatever quarter it may come, is fo generally acknowledged, that the Courts of Law have sometimes grounded their judgments upon it. I fhall relate on this head a fact which is fomewhat remarkable.

A Conftable, being out of his precinct, arrefted a woman whofe name was *Anne Dekins ;* one *Tooly* took her part, and, in the heat of the fray, killed the affiftant of the Conftable.

Being profecuted for murder, he alleged, in his defence, that the illegality of the imprifonment was a fufficient provocation to make the homicide *excufable*, and intitle him to the benefit of Clergy. The Jury having fettled the matter of fact, left the *criminality* of it to be decided by the Judge, by returning a *fpecial verdict*. The caufe was adjourned to the King's Bench, and thence again to Serjeants Inn, for the opinion of the twelve Judges. Here follows the opinion delivered by Chief Juftice Holt, in giving judgment.

" If one be imprifoned upon an unlawful authority, it
" is a fufficient provocation to all people, out of compaf-
" fion, much more fo when it is done under colour of
" juftice ; and when the liberty of the fubject is invaded,
" it is a provocation to all the fubjects of England. A
" Man ought to be concerned for *Magna Charta* and the
" laws ; and if any one againft law imprifon a Man, he is
" an offender againft Magna Cherta." After fome debate, occafioned chiefly by Tooly's appearing not to have known that the Conftable was out of his precinct, feven of the Judges were of opinion that the prifoner was guilty of Man-flaughter, and he was admitted to the benefit of Clergy *.

But it is with refpect to this right of an ultimate refiftance, that the advantage of a free prefs appears in a moft confpicuous light. As the moft important rights of the

---

* See Reports of Cafes argued, debated, and adjudged in *Banco Reginæ,* in the time of the late Queen Anne.

People, without the profpect of a refiftance which over-awes thofe who fhould attempt to violate them, are little more than mere fhadows,—fo this right of *refifting*, itfelf, is but vain, when there exifts no means of effecting a general union between the different parts of the People.

Private individuals, unknown to each other, are forced to bear in filence injuries in which they do not fee other people take a concern. Left to their own individual ftrength, they tremble before the formidable and ever-ready power of thofe who govern; and as thefe latter well know, nay, are apt to over-rate the advantages of their own fituation, they think that they may venture upon any thing.

But when they fee that all their actions are expofed to public view,—that in confequence of the celerity with which all things become communicated, the whole Nation forms, as it were, one continued *irritable* body, no part of which can be touched without exciting an univerfal *tremor*, they become fenfible that the caufe of each individual is really the caufe of all, and that to attack the loweft among the People, is to attack the whole People.

Here alfo we muft remark the error of thofe who, as they make the liberty of the People to confift in their power, fo make their power confift in their action.

When the People are often called to act in their own perfons, it is impoffible for them to acquire any exact knowledge of the ftate of things. The event of one day effaces the notions which they had begun to adopt on the preceding day; and amidft the continual change of things, no fettled principle, and above all no plans of union, have time to be eftablifhed among them.—You wifh to have the People love and defend their laws of liberty; leave them, therefore, the neceffary time to know what laws and liberty are, and to agree in their opinion concerning them;—you wifh an union, a *coalition*, which cannot be obtained but by a flow and peaceable *procefs*, forbear therefore continually to fhake the veffel.

Nay farther, it is a contradiction, that the People fhould

act and at the fame time retain any real power. Have they, for inftance, been forced by the weight of public oppreffion to. throw off the reftraints of the law, from which they no longer received proteétion, they prefently find themfelves fuddenly become fubjeét to the command of a few Leaders, who are the more abfolute in proportion as the nature of their power is lefs clearly afcertained; nay, perhaps, they muft even fubmit to the toils of war and to military difcipline.

If it be in the common and legal courfe of things that the People are called to move, each individual is obliged, for the fuccefs of the meafures in which he is then made to take a concern, to join himfelf to fome party ; nor can this party be without a Head. The Citizens thus grow divided among themfelves, and contraét the pernicious habit of fubmitting to Leaders. They are, at length, no more than the clients of a certain number of Patrons.; and the latter foon becoming able to command the arms of the Citizens in the fame manner as they at firft governed their votes, make little account of a People with one part of which they know how to curb the other.

But when the moving fprings of Government are placed entirely out of the body of the People, their aétion is thereby difengaged from all that could render it complicated, or hide it from the eye. As the People thenceforwards confider things fpeculatively, and are, if I may may be allowed the expreffion, only fpeétators of the game, they acquire juft notions of things ; and as thefe notions, amidft the general quiet, get round and fpread themfelves far and wide, they at length entertain, on the fubjeét of their liberty, but one opinion.

Forming thus, as it were, one body, the People, at every inftant, have it in their power to ftrike the decifive blow which is to level every thing. · Like thofe mechanical powers the greateft efficiency of which exifts at the inftant which precedes their entering into aétion, it has an immenfe force, juft becaufe it does not yet exert any ;

and in this state of stillness, but of attention, consists its true *momentum.*

With regard to those who (whether from personal privileges, or by virtue of a commission from the People) are intrusted with the active part of Government, as they in the mean while, see themselves exposed to public view, and observed as from a distance by Men free from the spirit of party, and who place in them but a conditional trust, they are afraid of exciting a commotion which, though it might not prove the destruction of all power, yet would surely and immediately be the destruction of their own. And if we might suppose that, through an extraordinary conjunction of circumstances, they should resolve among themselves upon the sacrifice of those laws on which public liberty is founded, they would no sooner lift up their eyes towards that extensive Assembly which views them with a watchful attention, than they would find their public virtue return upon them, and would make haste to resume that plan of conduct out of the limits of which they can expect nothing but ruin and perdition.

In short, as the body of the People cannot act without either subjecting themselves to some Power, or effecting a general destruction, the only share they can have in a Government with advantage to themselves, is not to interfere, but influence,—to be able to act, and not to act.

The power of the People is not when they strike, but when they keep in awe: it is when they can overthrow every thing, that they never need to move; and Manlius included all in four words, when he said to the People of Rome, *Ostendite bellum, pacem habebitis.*

C H A P.   XIV.

Proofs drawn from Facts, of the Truth of the Principles laid down in the present Work.—1. The peculiar Manner in which Revolutions have always been concluded in England.

IT may not be sufficient to have proved by arguments the advantages of the English Constitution: it will perhaps be asked, whether the effects correspond to the theory? To this question (which I confess is extremely proper) my answer is ready; it is the same which was once made, I believe, by a Lacedæmonian, *Come and see.*

If we peruse the English History, we shall be particularly struck with one circumstance to be observed in it, and which distinguishes most advantageously the English Government from all other free governments, I mean the manner in which Revolutions and public commotions have always been terminated in England.

If we read with some attention the History of other free states, we shall see that the public dissensions that have taken place in them, have constantly been terminated by settlements in which the interests of only a few were really provided for; while the grievances of the many were hardly, if at all, attended to. In England the very reverse has happened, and we find Revolutions always to have been terminated by extensive and accurate provisions for securing the general liberty.

The History of the ancient Grecian Commonwealths, but above all of the Roman Republic, of which more complete accounts have been left us, afford striking proof of the former part of this observation.

What was, for instance, the consequence of that great Revolution by which the Kings were driven from Rome, and in which the Senate and Patricians acted as the advisers and leaders of the People? The consequence was, as we find in Dionysius of Halicarnassus, and Livy, that

G g

the Senators immediately affumed all thofe powers lately fo much complained of by themfelves, which the Kings had exercifed. The execution of their future decrees was intruffed to two Magiftrates, taken from their own body, and entirely dependent on them, whom they called *Confuls*, and who were made to bear about them all the enfigns of power which had formerly attended the Kings. Only, care was taken that the axes and *fafces*, the fymbols of the power of life and death over the Citizens, which the Senate now claimed to itfelf, fhould not be carried before both Confuls at once, but only before one at a time, for fear, fays Livy, of doubling the terror of the People *.

Nor was this all: the Senators drew over to their party thofe Men who had the moft intereft at that time among the People, and admitted them as Members into their own body † ; which indeed was a precaution they could not prudently avoid taking. But the interefts of the great Men in the Republic being thus provided for, the Revolution ended. The new Senators, as well as the old, took care not to leffen, by making provifions for the liberty of the People, a power which was now become their own. Nay, they prefently ftretched their power beyond its former tone; and the punifhments which the Conful inflicted in a military manner on a number of thofe who ftill adhered to the former mode of Government, and even upon his own children, taught the People what they had to expect for the future, if they prefumed to oppofe the power of thofe whom they had thus unwarily made their Mafters.

Among the oppreffive laws, or ufages, which the Se-

---

* " Omnia jura (*Regum*) omnia infignia, primi Confules " tenuere ; id modò cautum eft ne fi ambo fafces haberent, " duplicatus terror videretur." *Tit. Liv.* lib. ii. § 1.

† Thefe new Senators were called *confcripti* : hence the name of *Patres Confcripti*, afterwards indifcriminately given to the whole Senate.—*Tit. Liv.* ibid.

nate, after the expulsion of the Kings, had permitted to continue, those which were most complained of by the People, were those by which those Citizens who could not pay their debts with the interest (which at Rome was enormous) at the appointed time, became slaves to their creditors, and were delivered over to them bound with cords, hence the word *Nexi*, by which that kind of Slaves were denominated. The cruelties exercised by Creditors on those unfortunate Men, whom the private calamities caused by the frequent wars in which Rome was engaged, rendered very numerous, at last roused the body of the People: they abandoned both the City and their inhuman fellow-citizens, and retreated to the other side of the river *Anio*.

But this second Revolution, like the former, only procured the advancement of particular persons. A new office was created, called the Tribuneship. Those whom the People had placed at their head when they left the City, were raised to it. Their duty, it was agreed, was for the future to protect the Citizens; and they were invested with a certain number of prerogatives for that purpose. This Institution, it must however be confessed, would have, in the issue, proved very beneficial to the People, at least for a long course of time, if certain precautions had been taken with respect to it, which would have much lessened the future personal importance of the new Tribunes * : but these precautions the latter did not think proper to suggest; and in regard to those abuses themselves which had at first given rise to the complaints of the People, no farther mention was made of them †.

As the Senate and Patricians, in the early ages of the

---

* Their number, which was only Ten, ought to have been much greater; and they never ought to have excepted the power left to each of them, of stopping by his single opposition the proceedings of all the rest.

† A number of seditions were afterwards raised upon the same account.

Commonwealth, kept clofely united together, the Tribunes, for all their perfonal privileges, were not able, however, during the firft times after their creation, to gain an admittance either to the Confulfhip, or into the Senate, and thereby to feparate their condition any farther from that of the People. This fituation of theirs, in which it was to be wifhed they might always haye been kept, produced at firft excellent effects, and caufed their conduct to anfwer in a great meafure the expectations of the People. The Tribunes complained loudly of the exorbitancy of the powers poffeffed by the Senate and Confuls; and here we muft obferve, that the power exercifed by thefe latter over the lives of the Citizens, had never been yet fubjected (which will probably furprife the Reader) to any known laws, though fixty years had already elapfed fince the expulfion of the Kings. The Tribunes therefore infifted, that laws fhould be made in that refpect, which the Confuls fhould thenceforwards be bound to follow; and that they fhould no longer be left, in the exercife of their power over the lives of the Citizens, to their own caprice and wantonnefs *.

Equitable as thefe demands were, the Senate and Patricians oppofed them with great warmth, and either by naming Dictators, or calling in the affiftance of the Priefts, or other means, they defeated for nine years together all the endeavours of the Tribunes. However, as the latter were at that time in earneft, the Senate was at length obliged to comply: and the *Lex Terentilla* was paffed, by which it was enacted, that a general Code of Laws fhould be made.

Thefe beginnings feemed to promife great fuccefs to the caufe of the People. But, unfortunately for them, the Senate found means to have it agreed, that the office of Tribune fhould be fet afide during the whole time that the

---

* " Quod Populus in fe jus dederit, eo Confulem ufur-
" um; non ipfos libidinem ac licentiam fuam pro lege habi-
" turos."—*Tit. Liv.* lib. iii. § 9.

Code should be framing. They moreover obtained, that the ten Men, called Decemvirs, to whom the charge of composing this Code was to be given, should be taken from the body of the Patricians. The same causes, therefore, produced the same effects; and the power of the Senate and Consul was left in the new Code, or laws of the Twelve Tables, undefined as before. As to the laws above mentioned, concerning debtors, which never had ceased to be bitterly complained of by the People, and in regard to which some satisfaction ought, in common justice, to have been given them, they were confirmed, and a new terror added to them from the manner in which they were worded.

The true motive of the Senate, when they thus trusted the framing of the new laws to a new kind of Magistrates, called Decemvirs, was that, by suspending the ancient office of Consul, they might have a fair pretence for suspending also the office of Tribune, and thereby rid themselves of the People, during the time that the important business of framing the Code should be carrying on : they even, in order the better to secure that point, placed the whole power in the Republic, in the hands of these new Magistrates. But the Senate and Patricians experienced then, in their turn, the danger of entrusting Men with an uncontrolled authority. As they themselves had formerly betrayed the trust which the People had placed in them, so did the Decemvirs, on this occasion, likewise deceive them. They retained, by their own private authority, the unlimited power that had been conferred on them, and at last exercised it on the Patricians as well as the Plebeians. Both parties therefore united against them, and the Decemvirs were expelled from the City.

The former dignities of the Republic were restored, and with them the office of Tribune. Those from among the People who had been most instrumental in destroying the power of the Decemvirs, were, as it was natural, raised to the Tribuneship; and they entered upon their offices possessed of a prodigious degree of popularity. The Senate and the Patricians were, at the same time, sunk extremely low in consequence of the long tyranny which had just expired; and those two circumstances united, afforded the Tribunes but too easy an opportunity of making the present Revolution end as the former ones had done, and converting it to the advancement of their own power. They got new personal privileges to be added to those which they already possessed, and moreover procured a law to be enacted, by which it was ordained, that the resolutions taken by the *Comitia Tributa* (an Assembly in which the Tribunes were admitted to propose new laws) should be binding upon the whole Commonwealth :—by which they at once raised to themselves an *imperium in imperio*, and acquired, as Livy expresses it, a most active weapon *.

From that time great commotions arose in the Republic, which, like all those before them, ended in promoting the power of a *few*.—Proposals for easing the People of their debts, for dividing with some equality amongst the Citizens the lands which were taken from the enemy, and for lowering the rate of the interest for money, were frequently made by the Tribunes. And indeed all these were excellent regulations to propose ; but, unfortunately for the People, the proposals of them were only pretences made use of by the Tribunes for promoting schemes of a fatal, though somewhat remote, tendency to public liberty. Their real aims were at the Consulship, the Prætorship, the Priesthood, and other offices of Executive power, which they were intended to controul, and not to share. To these views they constantly made the cause of the People subservient :—I shall relate, among other instances, the manner in which they procured to themselves an admittance to the office of Consul.

Having, during several years, seized every opportunity of making speeches to the People on that subject, and even excited seditions in order to overcome the opposi-

* *Acerrimum telum.*

tion of the Senate, they at laſt availed themſelves of the circumſtance of an *interregnum* (a time during which there happened to be no other Magiſtrates in the Republic beſides themſelves) and propoſed to the Tribes, whom they had aſſembled, to enact the three following laws:—the firſt, for ſettling the rate of intereſt of money; the ſecond, for ordaining that no Citizen ſhould be poſſeſſed of more than five hundred acres of land; and the third, for providing that one of the two Conſuls ſhould be taken from the body of the Plebeians. But on this occaſion it evidently appeared, ſays Livy, which of the laws in agitation were moſt agreeable to the People, and which to thoſe who propoſed them; for the Tribes accepted the laws concerning the intereſt of money, and the lands; but as to that concerning the Plebeian Conſulſhip, they rejected it, and both the former articles would from that moment have been ſettled, if the Tribunes had not declared, that the Tribes were called upon, either to accept, or reject, all their three propoſals at once *. Great commotions enſued thereupon, for a whole year; but at laſt the Tribunes, by their perſeverance in inſiſting that the Tribes ſhould vote on their three *rogations*, jointly, obtained their ends, and overcame both the oppoſition of the Senate, and the reluctance of the People.

In the ſame manner did the Tribunes get themſelves made capable of filling all other places of executive power, and public truſt, in the Republic. But when all their views of that kind were accompliſhed, the Republic did not for all this enjoy more quiet, nor was the intereſt of the People better attended to, than before. New ſtruggles then aroſe for actual admiſſion to thoſe places, for procuring

---

* " Ab Tribunis, velut per interregnum, concilio Plebis " habito, apparuit quæ ex promulgatis Plebi, quæ latoribus, " gratiora eſſent; nam de fœnore atque agro rogationes ju- " bebant, de plebeio Conſulatu antiquabant *(antiquis ſta-* " *bant)*: & perfecta utraque res eſſet, ni Tribuni ſe in omnia ſimul conſulere Plebem dixiſſent."—*Tit. Liv.* lib. vi. § 39.

them to relations, or friends; for governments of provinces, and commands of armies. A few Tribunes, indeed, did at times apply themselves seriously, out of real
virtue and love of their duty, to remedy the grievances of
the People; but both their fellow Tribunes, as we may
see in History, and the whole body of those Men upon
whom the People had, at different times, bestowed Con-
sulships, Ædileships, Censorships, and other dignities
without number, united together with the utmost vehemence against them; and the real Patriots, such as Tiberius Gracchus, Caius Gracchus, and Fulvius, constantly
perished in the attempt.

I have been somewhat explicit on the effects produced
by the different Revolutions that have happened in the
Roman Republic, because its History is much known to
us, and we have, either in Dionysius of Halicarnassus, or
Livy, considerable monuments of the more ancient part
of it. But the History of the Grecian Commonwealths
would also have supplied us with a number of facts to the
same purpose: that Revolution, for instance, by which
the *Pisistratidæ* were driven out of Athens—that by which
the *Four hundred*, and afterwards the *Thirty*, were established, as well as that by which the latter were in their
turn expelled, all ending in securing the power of *a few*.
——The Republic of Syracuse, that of Corcyra, of which
Thucydides has left us a pretty full account, and that of
Florence, of which Machiavel has written the History,
also present us a series of public commotions ended by
treaties, in which, as in the Roman Republic, the grievances of the People, though ever so loudly complained of
in the beginning by those who acted as their defenders,
were, in the issue, most carelessly attended to, or even totally disregarded *.

* The Revolutions which have formerly happened in
France, have all ended like the above mentioned: of this a
remarkable instance may be seen in a former Note, of
this Work. The same facts are also to be observed in the

But if we turn our eyes towards the English History, scenes of a quite different kind will offer to our view ; and we shall find, on the contrary, that Revolutions in England have always been terminated by making such provisions, and only such, as all orders of the People were really and indiscriminately to enjoy.

Most extraordinary facts, these ! and which, from all the other circumstances that accompanied them, we see, all along, to have been owing to the impossibility (a point that has been so much insisted upon in former Chapters) in which those who possessed the confidence of the People, were, of transferring to themselves any branch of the Executive authority, and thus separating their own condition from that of the rest of the People.

Without mentioning the compacts which were made with the first Kings of the Norman line, let us only cast our eyes on *Magna Charta*, which is still the foundation of English liberty. A number of circumstances which have been described in the former part of this work, concurred at that time to strengthen the Regal power to such a degree that no Man in the State could entertain a hope of succeeding in any other design than that of setting bounds to it. How great was the union which thence arose among all orders of the People !—what extent, what caution, do we see in the provisions made by the Great Charter ! All the objects for which Men naturally wish to live in a state of Society, were settled in its thirty-eight Articles. The judicial authority was regulated. The person

H h

History of Spain, Denmark, Sweden, Scotland, &c. ; but I have avoided mentioning States of a Monarchical form, till some observations are made, which the reader will find in the XVIIth Chapter.

and property of the individual were fecured. The safety of the Merchant and ftranger was provided for. The higher clafs of Citizens gave up a number of oppreffive privileges which they had long fince accuftomed themfelves to look upon as their undoubted rights *. Nay, the implements of tillage of the *Bondman*, or Slave, were alfo fecured to him: and for the firft time perhaps in the annals of the World, a civil war was terminated by making ftipulations in favour of thofe unfortunate men to whom the avarice and luft of dominion inherent in human Nature, continued, over the greateft part of the Earth, to deny the common rights of Mankind.

Under Henry the Third great difturbances arofe; and they were all terminated by folemn confirmations given to the Great Charter. Under Edward I. Edward II. Edward III. and Richard II. thofe who were intrufted with the care of the interefts of the People loft no opportunity that offered of ftrengthening ftill farther that foundation of public liberty; of taking all fuch precautions as might render the Great Charter ftill more effectual in the event.—They had not ceafed to be convinced that their caufe was the fame with that of all the reft of the People.

Henry of Lancafter having laid claim to the Crown, the Commons received the law from the victorious party. They fettled the Crown upon Henry, by the name of Henry the Fourth; and added to the Act of Settlement, provifions which the Reader may fee in the fecond Volume of the *Parliamentary Hiftory* of England. Struck with the wifdom of the conditions

---

* All poffeffors of lands took the engagement to eftablifh in behalf of their Tenants and Vaffals *(erga fuos)* the fame liberties which they demanded from the King.—*Mag. Char.* cap. xxxviii.

demanded by the Commons, the Authors of the Book just mentioned obferve (perhaps with fome fimplicity), that the Commons of England *were no fools at that time*. They ought rather to have faid;—The Commons of England were happy enough to form among themfelves an Affembly. in which every one could propofe what matters he pleafed, and freely difcufs them;—they had no poffibility left of converting either thefe advantages, or in general the confidence which the People had placed in them, to any private views of their own: they, therefore, without lofs of time endeavoured to ftipulate ufeful conditions with that power by which they faw themfelves at every inftant expofed to be diffolved and difperfed, and applied their induftry to infure the fafety of the whole People, as it was the only means they had of procuring their own.

In the long contentions which took place between the Houfes of York and Lancafter, the Commons remained fpectators of diforders which, in thofe times, it was not in their power to prevent: they fucceffively acknowledged the title of the victorious parties; but whether under Edward the Fourth, under Richard the Third, or Henry the Seventh, by whom thofe quarrels were terminated, they continually availed themfelves of the importance of the fervices, which they were able to perform, to the new eftablifhed Sovereign, for obtaining effectual conditions in favour of the whole body of the People.

At the acceffion of James the Firft, which, as it placed a new family on the Throne of England, may be confidered as a kind of Revolution, no demands were made by the Men who were at the head of the Nation, but in favour of general liberty.

After the acceffion of Charles the Firft, difcontents of a very ferious nature began to take place, and they were terminated in the firft inftance, by the act called the *Petition of Right*, which is still looked upon as a most precise and accurate delineation of the rights of the People *.

At the Restoration of Charles the Second, the Constitution being re-established upon its former principles, the former consequences produced by it began again to take place; and we see at that æra, and indeed during the whole course of that reign, a continued series of precautions taken for securing the general liberty.

Lastly, the great event which took place in the year 1689, affords a striking confirmation of the truth of the observation made in this Chapter. At this æra the political wonder again appeared—of a Revolution terminated by a series of public acts in which no interests but those of the People at large were considered and provided for; no clause, even the most indirect, was inserted, either to gratify the present ambition, or favour the future views, of those who were personally concerned in bringing those acts to a conclusion. Indeed, if any thing is capable of conveying to us an adequate idea of the soundness, as well as peculiarity, of the principles on which the English Government is founded, it is the attentive perusal of the System of public Compacts to which the Revolution of the year

---

* The disorders which took place in the latter part of the reign of that Prince, seem indeed to contain a complete contradiction of the assertion which is the subject of the present Chapter; but they, at the same time, are a no less convincing confirmation of the truth of the principles laid down in the course of this whole Work. The above mentioned disorders took rise from that day in which Charles the First gave up the power of dissolving his Parliament: that is, from the day in which the Members of that Assembly acquired an independent, personal, permanent authority, which they soon began to turn against the People who had raised them to it.

1689 gave rife,—of the Bill of Rights with all its different claufes, and of the feveral Acts which under two fubfequent Reigns, till the Acceffion of the Houfe of Hanover, were made in order to ftrengthen it.

CHAP. XVI.

Second Difference—The Manner after which the Laws for the Liberty of the Subject are executed in England.

THE fecond difference I mean to fpeak of, between the Englifh Government, and that of other free ftates, concerns the important object of the execution of the Laws. On this article, alfo, we fhall find the advantage to lie on the fide of the Englifh Government ; and, if we make a comparifon between the Hiftory of thofe States and that of England, it will lead us to the following obfervation, viz. that though in other free States the laws concerning the Liberty of the Citizens were imperfect, yet the execution of them was ftill more defective. In England, on the contrary, the laws for the fecurity of the Subject are not only very extenfive in their provifions, but the manner in which they are executed, carries thefe advantages ftill farther ; and Englifh Subjects enjoy no lefs liberty from the fpirit both of juftice and mildnefs, by which all branches of the Government are influenced, than from the accuracy of the laws themfelves.

The Roman Commonwealth will here again fupply us with examples to prove the former part of the above affertion. When I faid, in the foregoing Chapter, in times of public commotion, no provifions were made for the body of the People, I meant no provi-

fions that were likely to prove effectual in the events
When the people were roufed to a certain degree, or
when their concurrence was neceffary to carry into
effect certain refolutions, or meafures, that were particularly interefting to the Men in power, the latter
could not, with any prudence, openly profefs a contempt for the political wifhes of the People ; and fome
declarations, expreffed in the general words, in favour
of public liberty, were indeed added to the laws that
were enacted on thofe occafions. But thefe declarations, and the principles which they tended to eftablifh,
were afterwards even openly difregarded in practice.

Thus, when the People were made to vote, about
a year after the expulfion of the Kings, that the Regal Government never fhould be again eftablifhed in
Rome, and that thofe who fhould endeavour to reftore
it, fhould be devoted to the Gods, an article was added which, in general terms, confirmed to the Citizens
the right they had before enjoyed under the King, of
appealing to the People from the fentences of death
paffed upon them. No punifhment (which will furprife the Reader) was decreed againft thofe who fhould
violate this law ; and indeed the Confuls, as we may
fee in Dionyfius of Halicarnaffus and Livy, concerned
themfelves but little about the appeals of the Citizens,
and in the more than military exercife of their functions, continued to fport with rights which they ought
to have refpected, however imperfectly and loofely they
had been fecured.

An article to the fame purport with the above, was
afterwards alfo added to the laws of the Twelve Tables; but the Decemvirs, to whom the execution of
thofe laws was at firft committed, behaved exactly in
the fame manner and even worfe than the Confuls had
done before them : and after they were expelled,* the

* At the time of the expulfion of the Decemvirs, a law
was alfo enacted, that no Magiftrate fhould be created from

Magistrates who succeeded them appear to have been as little tender of the lives of the Citizens. I shall, among many instances, relate one which will shew upon what slight grounds the Citizens were exposed to have their lives taken away,——Spurius Mælius being accused of endeavouring to make himself King, was summoned by the Master of the Horse, to appear before the Dictator, in order to clear himself of this somewhat extraordinary imputation. Spurius took refuge among the People; the Master of the Horse pursued him, and killed him on the spot. The multitude having thereupon expressed a great indignation, the Dictator had them called to his Tribunal, and declared that Spurius had been lawfully put to death, even though he might be innocent of the crime laid to his charge, for having refused to appear before the Dictator, when summoned to do so by the Master of the Horse *.

About one hundred and forty years after the times we mention, the law concerning the appeals to the People was enacted for the third time. But we do not fee that it was better observed afterwards than it had had been before: we find it frequently violated, since that period, by the different Magistrates of the Republic, and the Senate itself, notwithstanding this

whom no appeal could be made to the People (*Magistratus fine provocatione. Tit. Liv.* lib. iii. § 55.) by which the people expressly meant to abolish the Dictatorship: but, from the fact that will just now be related, and which happened about ten years afterwards, we shall see that this law was not better observed than the former ones had been.

* Tumultuantem deinde multitudinem, incerta existimatione facti, ad concionem vocari jussit, & *Mælium jure cæsum* pronunciavit, *etiamsi regni crimine infons fuerit, qui vocatus a Magistro equitum, ad Dictatorem non venisset.* Tit. Liv. lib. iv. § 15.

same law, at times, made formidable examples of the Citizens. Of this we have an instance in the three hundred soldiers who had pillaged the town of Rhegium. The Senate of its own authority, ordered them all to be put to death. In vain did the Tribune Flaccus remonstrate against so severe an exertion of public justice on Roman Citizens; the Senate, says Valerius Maximus, neverthelefs perfisted in its resolution*.

All these laws for securing the lives of the Citizens, had hitherto been enacted without any mention being made of a punishment against those who should violate them. At last the celebrated *Lex Porcia* was passed, which subjected to banishment those who should cause a Roman Citizen to be scourged and put to death. From a number of instances posterior to this law, it appears, that it was not better observed than those before it had been: Caius Gracchius, therefore, caused the *Lex Sempronia* to be enacted, by which a new sanction was given to it. But this second law did not secure his own life, and that of his friends, better than the *Lex Porcia* had done that of his brother, and those who had supported him: indeed, all the events which took place about those times, rendered it manifest that the evil was such as was beyond the power of any laws to cure.—I shall here mention a fact which affords a remarkable instance of the wantonnefs with which the Roman Magistrates had accustomed themselves to take

---

* Val. Max. book ii. c. 7. This author does not mention the precise number of those who were put to death on this occafion; he only says that they were executed fifty at a time, in different succeffive days; but other Authors make the number of them amount to four thousand. Livy speaks of a whole Legion.—*Legio Campana quæ Rhegium occupaverat, obfeffa, deditione facta, securi percuffa est.—Tit Liv.* lib. xv. *Epit.*—I have here followed Polybius, who says that only three hundred were taken and brought to Rome.

away the lives of the Citizens. A Citizen, named Memmius, having put up for the Confulſhip, and publicly canvaſſing for the ſame, in oppoſition to a Man whom the Tribune Saturnius ſupported, the latter cauſed him to be apprehended, and made him expire under blows in the public Forum. The Tribune even carried his inſolence ſo far, as Cicero informs us, as to give to this act of cruelty, tranſacted in the preſence of the whole People aſſembled, the outward form of a lawful act of public Juſtice *.

Nor were the Roman Magiſtrates ſatisfied with committing acts of injuſtice in their political capacity, and for the ſupport of the power of that Body of which they made a part. Avarice and private rapine were at laſt added to political ambition. The Provinces were firſt oppreſſed and plundered. The calamity in proceſs of time reached Italy itſelf, and the centre of the Republic; till at laſt the *Lex Calpurnia de repetundis* was enacted to put a ſtop to it. By this law an action was given to the Citizens and Allies for the recovery of the money extorted from them by Magiſtrates, or Men in power; and the *Lex Junia* afterwards added the penalty of baniſhment to the obligation of making reſtitution.

I i

* The fatal forms of words (*cruciatus carmina*) uſed by the Roman Magiſtrates when they ordered a Man to be put to death, reſounded (ſays Tully in his ſpeech for *Rabirius*) in the Aſſembly of the People, in which the Cenſors had forbidden the common Executioner ever to appear. *I Lictor, colliga manus. Caput obnubito. Arbori infelici ſuſpendito.*— Memmius being a conſiderable Citizen, as we may conclude from his canvaſſing with ſucceſs for the Confulſhip, all the great Men in the Republic took the alarm at the attrocious action of the Tribune: the Senate, the next day, iſſued out its ſolemn mandate, or form of words, to the Conſuls, *to provide that the Republic ſhould receive no detriment;* and the Tribune was killed in a pitched battle that was fought at the foot of the Capitol.

But here another kind of disorder arose. The Judges proved as corrupt as the Magistrates had been oppressive. They equally betrayed, in their own province, the cause of the Republic with which they had been intrusted; and rather chose to share in the plunder of the Consuls, the Prætors, and the Proconsuls, than put the laws in force against them.

New expedients were, therefore, resorted to, in order to remedy this new evil. Laws were made for judging and punishing the Judges themselves; and above all, continual changes were made in the manner of composing their Assemblies. But the malady lay too deep for common legal provisions to remedy. The guilty Judges employed the same resources in order to avoid conviction, as the guilty Magistrates·had done; and those continual changes at which we are amazed, that were made in the constitution of the judiciary Bodies *, instead of obviating the corruption of the Judges, only transferred to other

---

* The Judges (over the Assembly of whom the Prætor usually presided) were taken from the body of the Senate till some years after the last punic War; when the *Lex Sempronia*, proposed by Caius S. Gracchus, enacted that they should in future be taken from the Equestrian Order. The consul Cæpio procured afterwards a law to·be enacted, by which the Judges were to be taken from both orders equally. The *Lex Survilia* soon after put the Equestrian Order again in possession of the *Judgments;* and, after some years, the *Lex Livia* restored them entirely to the Senate.—— The *Lex Plautia* enacted afterwards, that the Judges should be taken from the three orders; the Senatorian, Equestrian, and Plebeian. The *Lex Cornelia*, framed by the Dictator Sylla, enacted again, that the Judges should be entirely taken from the body of the Senate. The *Lex Aurelia* ordered anew, that they should be taken from the three orders. Pompey made afterwards a change in their number, which he fixed at seventy five, and in the manner of electing them. And lastly, Cæsar entirely restored the Judgments to the Order of the Senate.

Men the profit arifing from becoming guilty of it. It was grown to be a general complaint fo early as the times of the Gracchi, that no Man who had money to give, could be brought to punifhment *. Cicero fays, that in his time, the fame opinion was become fettled and univer-fally received † ; and his Speeches are full of his lamen-tations on what he calls the *levity*, and the *infamy*, of the public Judgments.

Nor was the impunity of corrupt Judges the only evil under which the Republic laboured. Commotions of the whole Empire at laft took place. The horrid vexations, and afterwards the acquittal, of Aquilius, Proconful of Syria, and fome others who had been guilty of the fame crimes, drove the Provinces of Afia to defperation ; and then it was that that terrible war of Mithridates arofe, which was ufhered in by the death of eighty thoufand Romans, maffacred in one day, in all the Cities of Afia ‡.

The Laws and public Judgments not only thus failed of the end for which they had been eftablifhed ; they even became, at length, new means of oppreffion added to thofe which already exifted. Citizens poffeffed of wealth, per-fons obnoxious to particular Bodies, or the few Magi-ftrates who attempted to ftem the torrent of the general corruption, were accufed and condemned ; while Pifo, of whom Cicero in his fpeech againft him relates facts which make the Reader fhudder with horror, and Verres, who had been guilty of enormities of the fame kind, efcaped unpunifhed.

Hence a war arofe ftill more formidable than the for-mer, and the dangers of which we wonder that Rome was able to furmount. The greateft part of the Italians revolted at once, exafperated by the tyranny of the pub-lic Judgments ; and we find in Cicero, who informs us of the caufe of this revolt, which was called the *Social war*,

* App. de Bell. Civ.

† Act, in Verr. i. § i.

‡ Appian.

a very expreſſive account both of the unfortunate condition of the Republic, and of the perverſion that had been
made of the methods taken to remedy it. 'An hundred
' and ten years are not yet elapſed (ſays he) ſince the law
' for the recovery of money extorted by Magiſtrates
' was firſt propounded by the Tribune Calpurnius Piſo.
' A number of other laws to the ſame effect, continually
' more and more ſevere, have followed : but ſo many
' perſons have been accuſed, ſo many condemned, ſo for-
' midable a war has been excited in Italy by the terror
' of the public Judgments, and when the laws and Judg-
' ments have been ſuſpended, ſuch an oppreſſion and
' plunder of our Allies have prevailed, that we may
' truly ſay that it is not by our own ſtrength, but by the
' weakneſs of others, that we continue to exiſt *.'

I have entered into theſe particulars with regard to the
Roman Commonwealth, becauſe the facts on which they
are grounded are remarkable of themſelves, and yet no
juſt concluſion can be drawn from them, unleſs a ſeries
of them were preſented to the Reader. Nor are we to
account for theſe facts, by the Luxury which prevailed in
the latter ages of the Republic, by the corruption of the
manners of the Citizens, their degeneracy from their ancient principles, and ſuch like looſe general phraſes,
which may perhaps be uſeful to expreſs the manner itſelf
in which the evil became manifeſted, but by no means ſet
forth the cauſes of it.

The above diſorders aroſe from the very nature of
the Government of the Republic,—of a Government
in which the Executive and Supreme Power being
made to centre in the Body of thoſe in whom the People had once placed their confidence ; there remained
no other effectual Power in the State that might render it neceſſary for them to keep within the bounds
of juſtice and decency. And in the mean time, as the

* See Cic. de Off. lib. ii. § 75.

People, who were intended as a check over that Body, continually gave a fhare in this Executive authority, to thofe whom they entrufted with the care of their interefts, they increafed the evils they complained of, as it were, at every attempt they made to remedy them ; and inftead of raifing up Opponents to thofe who were become the enemies of their liberty, as it was their intention to do, they continually fupplied them with new Affociates.

From this fituation of affairs, flowed as an unavoidable confequence, that continual defertion of the caufe of the People, which, even in time of Revolutions, when the paffions of the People themfelves were roufed, and they were in a great degree united, manifefted itfelf in fo remarkable a manner. We may trace the fymptoms of the great political defect here·mentioned in the earlieft ages of the Commonwealth, as well as in the laft ftage of its duration. In Rome, while fmall and poor, it rendered vain whatever rights or power the People poffeffed, and blafted all their endeavours to defend their liberty, in the fame manner as, in the more fplendid ages of the Commonwealth, it rendered the moft falutary regulations utterly fruitlefs, and even inftrumental to the ambition and avarice of a few. The prodigious fortune of the Republic, in fhort, did not create the diforder, it only gave full fcope to it.

But if we turn our view towards the Hiftory of the Englifh Nation, we fhall fee how, from a Government in which the above defects did not exift, different confequences have followed :—how cordially all ranks of Men have always united together to lay under proper reftraints this Executive power, which they knew could never be their own. In times of public Revolutions, the greateft care, as we have before obferved, was taken to afcertain the limits of that Power: and after peace had been reftored to the State, thofe who remained at the head of the Nation, continued to manifeſt an unwearied jealouſy in maintaining thoſe ſadvantages which the united efforts of all had obtained.

Thus it was made one of the Articles of Magna Charta, that the Executive Power ſhould not touch the perſon of the Subjeƈt, but in conſequence of a judgment paſſed upon him by his Peers; and ſo great was afterwards the general union in maintaining this law, that the *Trial by Jury*, that admirable mode of proceeding which ſo effeƈtually ſecures the Subjeƈt againſt all the attempts of Power, even (which ſeemed ſo difficult to obtain) againſt ſuch as might be made under the ſanƈtion of the judicial authority, hath been preſerved to this day. It has even been preſerved in all its original purity, though the ſame has been ſucceſſively ſuffered to decay, and then to be loſt, in the other Countries of Europe, where it had been formerly known *. Nay, though this privilege of being tried

---

* The Trial by Jury was in uſe among the Normans long before they came over into England; but it is now utterly loſt in that Province: it even began very early to degenerate there from its firſt inſtitution; we ſee in Hale's Hiſtory of the *Common Law* of England, that the unanimity among Jurymen was not required in Normandy for making a verdiƈt a good verdiƈt; but when Jurymen diſſented, a number of them was taken out, and others added in their ſtead, till an unanimity was procured.—In Sweden, where, according to the opinion of the Learned in that Country, the *Trial by Jury* had its firſt origin, only ſome forms of that inſtitution are now preſerved in the lower Courts in the Chancery, where ſets of Jurymen are eſtabliſhed for life, and have a ſalary accordingly. See *Robertſon's State of Sweden.*—And in Scotland, the vicinity of England, has not been able to preſerve to the Trial by Jury its genuine ancient form: the unanimity among Jurymen is not required, as I have been told, to form a verdiƈt; but the majority is deciſive.

by one's Peers, was at firft a privilege of Conquerors and Mafters, exclufively appropriated to thofe parts
of Nations which had originally invaded and feduced
the reft by arms; it has in England been fucceffively
extended to every Order of the People.

And not only the perfon, but alfo the property, of
the individual, has been fecured againft all arbitrary
attempts from the Executive power, and the latter
has been fucceffively reftrained from touching any
part of the property of the Subject even under pretence of the neceffities of the State, any otherwife than
by the free grant of the Reprefentatives of the People.
Nay, fo true and perfevering has been the zeal of thefe
Reprefentatives in afferting on that account the interefts of the Nation, from which they could not feparate their own, that this privilege of taxing themfelves, which was in the beginning grounded on a
moft precarious tenure, and only a mode of governing
adopted by the Sovereign for the fake of his own convenience, has become, in time, a fettled right of the
People, which the Sovereign has found it at length
neceffary folemnly and repeatedly to acknowledge.

Nay more, the Reprefentatives of the People have applied this right of *Taxation* to a ftill nobler ufe than the
mere prefervation of property ; they have, in procefs of
time, fucceeded in converting it into a regular and conftitutional means of influencing the motions of the Executive Power. By means of this Right, they have gained the advantage of being conftantly called to concur in
the meafures of the Sovereign,—of having the greateft
attention fhown by him to their requefts, as well as the
higheft regard paid to any engagements that he enters into with them. Thus has it become at laft the peculiar
happinefs of Englifh Subjects, to whatever other People
either ancient or modern we compare them, to enjoy a
fhare in the government of their Country, by electing
Reprefentatives, who, by reafon of the peculiar circum-

stances in which they are placed, and of the extensive right they poffefs, are both *willing* faithfully to ferve thofe who have appointed them, and *able* to do fo.

And indeed the Commons have not refted fatisfied with eftablifhing, once for all, the provifions for the liberty of the People which have been juft mentioned; they have afterwards made the prefervation of them the firft object of their care *, and taken every opportunity of giving them new vigour and life.

Thus, under Charles the Firft, when attacks of a moft alarming nature were made on the privilege of the People to grant free fupplies to the Crown, the Commons vindicated, without lofs of time, that great right of the Nation, which is the Conftitutional bulwark of all others, and haftened to oppugn in their beginning, every precedent of a practice that muft in the end have produced the ruin of public liberty.

They even extended their care to abufes of every kind. The judicial authority, for inftance, which the Executive Power had imperceptibly affumed to itfelf, both with refpect to the perfon and property of the individual, was abrogated by the Act which abolifhed the Court of Star-Chamber; and the Crown was thus brought back to its true Conftitutional office; viz. the countenancing, and fupporting with its ftrength, the execution of the Laws.

The fubfequent endeavours of the Legiflature have carried even to a ftill greater extent the above privileges of the People. They have moreover fucceeded in reftraining the Crown from any attempt to feize and confine, even for the fhorteft time, the perfon of the Subject, unlefs it be in the cafes afcertained by the Law, of which the Judges of it are to decide.

* The firft operation of the Commons at the beginning of a Seffion, is to appoint four grand Committees. The one is a Committee of Religion, another of Courts of Juftice, another of Trade, and another of Grievances: they are to be ftanding Committees during the whole Seffion.

Nor has this extensive unexampled freedom, at the expence of the Executive Power, been made, as we might be inclinable to think, the exclusive appropriated privilege of the great and powerful. · It is to be enjoyed alike by all ranks of Subjects. Nay, it was the injury done to a common Citizen that gave existence to the act which has completed the security of this interesting branch of public liberty.—*The oppression of an obscure individual,* says Judge Blackstone, *gave rise to the famous Habeas Corpus Act:* Junius has quoted this observation of the Judge; and the same is well worth repeating a third time, for the just idea it conveys of that readiness of all orders of Men, to unite in defence of common liberty, which is a characteristic circumstance in the English Government *.

And this general union in favour of public liberty, has not been confined to the framing of laws for its security: it has operated with no less vigour in bringing to punishment such as have ventured to infringe them; and the Sovereign has constantly found it necessary to give up the violators of those laws, even when his own servants, to the Justice of their Country.

Thus we find, so early as the reign of Edward the First, Judges who were convicted of having committed exactions in the exercise of their offices, to have been condemned by a sentence of Parliament †. From the immense fines which were laid upon them, and which it

K k

* The individual here alluded to was one Francis Jenks, who having made a motion at Guildhall, in the year 1676, to petition the King for a new Parliament, was examined before the Privy Council, and afterwards committed to the Gate-House, where he was kept about two months, through the delays made my the several Judges to whom he applied, in granting him a *Habeas Corpus*.—See the *State Trials*, vol. vii. anno 1676.

† Sir Ralph de Hengham, Chief Justice of the King's Bench, was fined 7000 marks; Sir Thomas Wayland, Chief

feems they were in a condition to pay, we may indeed conclude that, in thofe early ages of the Conftitution, the remedy was applied rather late to the diforder; but yet it was at laft applied.

Under Richard the Second, examples of the fame kind were renewed. Michael de la Pole, Earl of Suffolk, who had been Lord Chancellor of the kingdom, the Duke of Ireland, and the Archbifhop of York, having abufed their power by carrying on defigns that were fubverfive of public liberty, were declared guilty of High-treafon; and a number of Judges who, in their judicial capacity, had acted as their inftruments, were involved in the fame condemnation *.

Under the reign of Henry the Eighth, Sir Thomas

Juftice of the Common Pleas, had his whole eftate forfeited; and Sir Adam de Stratton, Chief Baron of the Exchequer, was fined 3400 marks.

* The moft confpicuous among thefe Judges were Sir Robert Belknap, and Sir Robert Trefilien, Chief Juftice of the King's Bench. The latter had drawn up a ftring of queftions calculated to confer a defpotic authority on the Crown, or rather on the Minifters above named, who had found means to render themfelves entire Mafters of the perfon of the King. Thefe queftions Sir Robert Trefilian propofed to the Judges, who had been fummoned for that purpofe, and they gave their opinion in favour of them. One of thefe opinions of the Judges, among others, tended to no lefs than to annihilate, at one ftroke, all the rights of the Commons, by taking from them that important privilege mentioned before, of ftarting and freely difcuffing whatever fubjects of debate they think proper: the Commons were to be reftrained, under pain of being punifhed as traitors, from proceeding upon any articles befides thofe limitted to them by the King. All thofe who had had a fhare in the above declarations of the Judges, were attainted of high-treafon. Some were hanged; among them was Sir Robert Trefilian; and the others were only banifhed, at the interceffion of the Bifhops.—See the Parl. Hiftory of England, vol. i.

Empſon, and Edmund Dudley, who had been the promoters of the exactions committed under the preceding reign, fell victims to the zeal of the Commons for vindicating the cauſe of the People. Under King James the Firſt, Lord Chancellor Bacon experienced that neither his high dignity, nor great perſonal qualifications, could ſcreen him from having the ſevereſt cenſure paſſed on him, for the corrupt-practices of which he had ſuffered himſelf to become guilty. And under Charles the Firſt, the Judges having attempted to imitate the example of the Judges under Richard the Second, by delivering opinions ſubverſive of the rights of the People, found the ſame ſpirit of watchfulneſs in the Commons, as had proved the ruin of the former. Lord Finch, Keeper of the Great Seal, was obliged to fly beyond ſea. The Judges Davenport and Crawley were impriſoned: and Judge Berkeley was ſeized while ſitting upon the Bench, as we find in Ruſhworth.

In the reign of Charles the Second, we again find freſh inſtances of the vigilance of the Commons. Sir William Scroggs, Lord Chief Juſtice of the King's Bench, Sir Francis North, Chief Juſtice of the Common Pleas, Sir Thomas Jones, one of the Judges of the King's Bench, and Sir Richard Weſton, one of the Barons of the Exchequer, were impeached by the Commons, for partialities ſhewn by them in the adminiſtration of juſtice; and Chief Juſtice Scroggs, againſt whom ſome poſitive charges were well proved, was removed from his employments.

The ſeveral examples offered here to the Reader, have been taken from ſeveral different periods of the Engliſh Hiſtory, in order to ſhew that neither the influence, nor the dignity of the infractors of the laws, even when they have been the neareſt Servants of the Crown, have ever been able to check the zeal of the Commons in aſſerting the rights of the People. Other examples might perhaps be related to the ſame purpoſe; though the whole number of thoſe to be met with, will, upon enquiry, be found the fmaller, in proportion as the danger of infringing the laws has always been indubitable.

So much regularity has even (from all the circumftances above mentioned) been introduced into the operations of the Executive Power in England,—fuch an exact Juftice have the People been accuftomed, as a confequence, to expect from that quarter, that even the Sovereign, for his having once fuffered himfelf perfonally to violate the fafety of the Subject, did not efcape fevere cenfure. The attack made by order of Charles the Second, on the perfon of Sir John Coventry, filled the nation with aftonifhment; and this violent gratification of private paffion, on the part of the Sovereign (a piece of felf-indulgence with regard to inferiors, which whole claffes of individuals in certain Countries almoft think that they have a right to) excited a general ferment. " This event (fays Bifhop " Burnet) put the Houfe of Commons in a furious up- " roar . . . . It gave great advantages to all thofe who " oppofed the Court; and the names of the *Court* and " *Country* party, which till now had feemed to be for- " gotten, were again revived*."

Thefe are the limitations that have been fet, in the Englifh Government, on the operations of the Executive Power : limitations to which we find nothing comparable in any other free States, ancient or modern; and which are owing, as we have feen, to that very circumftance which feemed at firft fight to prevent the poffibility of them, I mean the greatnefs and unity of that Power ; the effect of which has been, in the event, to unite upon the fame object, the views and efforts of all Orders of the People.

From this circumftance, that is, the *unity* and peculiar ftability of the Executive Power in England, another

---

* See Burnet's Hiftory, vol. i. anno 1669.—An Act of Parliament was made on this occafion, for giving a farther extent to the provifions before made for the perfonal fecurity of the Subject ; which is ftill called the *Coventry* Act.

moſt advantageous conſequence has followed, that has been before noticed, and which it is not improper to mention again here, as this Chapter is intended to confirm the principles laid down in the former ones,—I mean the unremitted continuance of the ſame general union among all ranks of Men, and the ſpirit of mutual juſtice which thereby continues to be diffuſed through all orders of Subjeƈts.

Though ſurrounded by the many boundaries that have juſt now been deſcribed, the Crown, we muſt obſerve, has preſerved its prerogative undivided: it ſtill poſſeſſes its whole effeƈtive ſtrength, and is only tied by its own engagements, and the conſideration of what it owes to its deareſt intereſts.

The great, or wealthy men in the Nation, who, aſſiſted by the body of the People, have ſucceeded in reducing the exerciſe of its authority within ſuch well defined li-mits, can have no expeƈtation that it will continue to con-fine itſelf to them any longer than they themſelves conti-nue, by the juſtice of their own conduƈt, to deſerve that ſupport of the People, which alone can make them ap-pear of conſequence in the eye of the Sovereign,—no probable hopes that the Crown will continue to obſerve thoſe laws by which their wealth, dignity, liberty, are pro-teƈted, any longer than they themſelves alſo continue to obſerve them.

Nay more, all thoſe claims of their rights which they continue to make againſt the Crown, are encouragements which they give to the reſt of the People to aſſert their own rights againſt them. Their conſtant oppoſition to all arbitrary proceedings of that Power, is a continual de-claration they make againſt any aƈts of oppreſſion which the ſuperior advantages they enjoy, might entice them to commit on their inferior fellow-ſubjeƈts. Nor was that ſevere cenſure, for inſtance, which they concurred in paſſing on an unguarded violent aƈtion of their Sove-reign, only a reſtraint put upon the perſonal aƈtions of future Engliſh Kings; no, it was a much more extenſive

provifion for the fecuring of public liberty;—it was a folemn engagement entered into by all the powerful Men
in the State to the whole body of the People, fcrupuloufly
to refpect the perfon of the loweft among them.

And indeed the conftant tenor of the conduct even of
the two Houfes of Parliament fhews us, that the above
obfervations are not matters of mere fpeculation. From
the earlieft times we fee the Members of the Houfe of
Commons to have been very cautious not to affume any
diftinction that might alienate from them the affections of
the reft of the People *. Whenever thofe privileges
which were neceffary to them for the difcharge of their
truft have proved burdenfome to the Community, they
have retrenched them. And thofe of their Members
who have applied either thefe privileges, or in general
that influence which they derived from their fituation, to
any oppreffive purpofes, they themfelves have endeavoured to bring to punifhment.

Thus, we fee, that in the reign of James the Firft, Sir
Giles Mompeffon, a Member of the Houfe of Commons,
having been guilty of monopolies, and other acts of great
oppreffion on the People, was not only expelled, but impeached and profecuted with the greateft warmth by the
Houfe, and finally condemned by the Lords to be publicly degraded from his rank of a Knight, held for ever an
infamous perfon, and imprifoned during life.

In the fame reign, Sir John Bennet, who was alfo a

* In all cafes of public offences, down to a fimple breach
of the peace, the Members of the Houfe of Commons have
no privilege whatever above the reft of the People : they may
be committed to prifon by any Juftice of the Peace ; and are
dealt with afterwards in the fame manner as any other Subjects. With regard to civil matters, their only privilege is
to be free from Arrefts during the time of a Seffion, and forty days before, and forty days after ; but they may be fued,
by procefs againft their goods, for any juft debt during that
time.

Member of the House of Commons, having been found to have been guilty of several corrupt practices, in his capacity of Judge of the *Prerogative* Court of Canterbury, such as taking exorbitant fees, and the like, was expelled the House, and prosecuted for these offences.

In the year 1641, Mr. Henry Benson, Member for Knaresborough, having been detected in selling protections, experienced likewise the indignation of the House, and was expelled.

In fine, in order as it were to make it completely notorious, that neither the condition of Representative of the People, nor even any degree of influence in their House, could excuse any one of them from strictly observing the rules of Justice, the Commons did on one occasion pass the most severe censure they had power to inflict, upon their Speaker himself, for having, in a single instance attempted to convert the discharge of his duty as Speaker into a means of private emolument. Sir John Trevor, Speaker of the House of Commons, having, in the sixth year of the reign of King William, received a thousand guineas from the City of London, " as a gratuity for the trouble he had taken with regard to the " passing of the *Orphan Bill*," was voted guilty of a High crime and misdemeanor, and expelled the House. Even the inconsiderable sum of twenty guineas which Mr. Hungerford, another Member, had been weak enough to accept on the same score, was looked upon as deserving the notice of the House, and he was likewise expelled *.

* Other examples of the attention of the House of Commons to the conduct of their Members, might be produced either before, or after, that which is mentioned here. The reader may, for instance, see the relation of their proceedings in the affair of the *South Sea Company* Scheme ; and a few years after, in that of the *Charitable Corporation* ; a fraudulent scheme particularly oppressive to the poor, for which several Members were expelled.

If we turn our view towards the House of Lords, we shall find that they have also constantly taken care that their peculiar privileges should not prove impediments to the common justice which is due to the rest of the People *. They have constantly agreed to every just proposal that has been made to them on that subject by the Commons : and indeed, if we consider the numerous and oppressive privileges claimed by the *Nobles* in most other Countries, and the vehement spirit with which they are commonly asserted, we shall think it no small praise to the body of the Nobility in England (and also to the nature of that Government of which they make a part) that it has been by their free consent that their privileges have been confined to what they now are ; that is to say, to no more, in general, than what is necessary to the accomplishment of the end and constitutional design of that House.

In the exercise of their Judicial authority with regard to civil matters, the Lords have manifested a spirit of equity nowise inferior to that which they have shewn in their Legislative capacity. They have, in the discharge of that function (which of all others is so liable to create temptations), shewn an uncorruptness really superior to what any judicial Assembly in any other Nation can boast. Nor do I think that I run any risk of being contradicted, when I say that the conduct of the House of Lords, in their civil judicial capacity, has constantly been such as has kept them above the reach of even suspicion or slander.

* In case of a public offence, or even a simple breach of the peace, a Peer may be committed, till he finds bail, by any Justice of the Peace : and Peers are to be tried by the com- com course of law, for all offences under felony. With regard to civil matters, they are at all times free from *arrest* ; but execution may be had against their effects, in the same manner as against those of other Subjects.

Even that privilege which they enjoy, of exclufively trying their own Members in cafe of any accufation that may affect their life (a privilege which we
might at firft fight think repugnant to the idea of a regular Government, and even alarming to the reft of
the People) has conftantly been made ufe of by the
Lords to do juftice to their fellow-fubjects ; and if we
caft our eyes either on the collection of the *State Trials*, or on the Hiftory of England, we fhall find very
few examples, if any, of a Peer, really guilty of the
offence laid to his charge, that has derived any advantage from his not being tried by a Jury of *Commoners*.

Nor has this juft and moderate conduct of the two
Houfes of Parliament in the exercife of their power (a
moderation fo unlike what has been related of the
conduct of the powerful Men in the Roman Republic) been the only happy confequence of that falutary
jealoufy which thofe two Bodies entertain of the power of the Crown. The fame motive has alfo engaged
them to exert their utmoft endeavours to put the Courts
of Juftice under proper reftraints : a point of the higheft importance to public liberty.

They have, from the earlieft times, preferred complaints againft the influence of the Crown over thefe
Courts, and at laft procured Laws to be enacted by
which fuch influence has been entirely prevented : all
which meafures, we muft obferve, were at the fame
time ftrong declarations that no Subjects, however exalted their rank might be, were to think themfelves
exempt from fubmitting to the uniform courfe of the
Law, or hope to influence or over-awe it. The fevere
examples which they have united to make on thofe
Judges who had rendered themfelves the inftruments
of the paffions of the Sovereign, or of the defigns of
the Minifters of the Crown, are alfo awful warnings
to the Judges who have fucceeded them, never to attempt to deviate in favour of any, the moft powerful

individuals, from that ftrait line of Juftice which the joint wifdom of the Legiflature has once marked out to them...

. This fingular fituation of the Englifh Judges relatively to the three Conftituent Powers of the State (and alfo the formidable fupport which they are certain to receive from them as long as they continue to be the faithful Minifters of Juftice) has at laft created fuch an impartiality in the diftribution of public Juftice in England, has introduced into the Courts of Law the practice of fuch a thorough difregard of either the influence or wealth of the contending Parties, and procured to every individual, both fuch an eafy accefs to thefe Courts, and fuch a certainty of redrefs, as are not to be paralleled in any other Government.—Philip de Comines, fo long as three hundred years ago, commended in ftrong terms the exactnefs with which Juftice is done in England to all ranks of Subjects *; and the impartiality with which the fame is adminiftered in thefe days, will with ftill more reafon create the furprife of every Stranger who has an opportunity of obferving the cuftoms of this Country †.

* See page 14 of this Work.

† A little after I came to England for the firft time (if the Reader will give me leave to make mention of myfelf in this cafe) an action was brought in a Court of Juftice againft a Prince very nearly related to the Crown : and a noble Lord was alfo, much about that time, engaged in a law-fuit for the property of fome valuable lead-mines in Yorkfhire. I could not but obferve, that in both thefe cafes a decifion was given againft the two moft powerful parties though I wondered but little at this, becaufe I had before heard much of the impartiality of the law proceedings in England, and was prepared to fee inftances of that kind. But what I was much furprifed at, was that no body appeared to be in the leaft fo, not even at the ftrictnefs with which the ordinary courfe of the law had, particularly in the former cafe, been

Indeed to fuch a degree of impartiality has the administration of Public Juftice been brought in England, that it is faying nothing beyond the exact truth, to affirm that any violation of the laws, though perpetrated by Men of the moft extenfive influence, nay, though committed by the fpecial direction of the very firft fervants of the Crown, will be publicly and completely redreffed. And the very loweft of Subjects will obtain fuch redrefs, if he has but fpirit enough to ftand forth, and appeal to the laws of his Country. —Moft extraordinary circumftances thefe! which thofe who know the difficulty that there is in eftablifhing juft laws among Mankind, and in providing afterwards for their due execution, only find credible becaufe they are matters of fact, and can begin to account for, only when they look up to the conftitution of the Government itfelf; that is to fay, when they confider the circumftances in which the Executive Power, or the Crown, is placed in relation to the two Bodies that concur with it to form the Legiflature,--the circumftances in which thofe two Affemblies are placed in relation to the Crown, and to each other, and the fituation in which all the Three find themfelves with refpect to the whole body of the People *.

adhered to,—and that thofe proceedings which I was difpofed to confider as great inftances of juftice, to the production of which fome circumftances peculiar to the times, at leaft fome uncommon virtue of fpirit on the part of the Judges, muft have more or lefs co-operated, were looked upon by all thofe whom I heard fpeak about it, as being nothing more than the common and expected courfe of things. This circumftance became a ftrong inducement to me to enquire into the nature of a Government by which fuch effects were produced.

* The affertion above made with refpect to the impartiality with which Juftice is, in all cafes, adminiftered in England, not being of a nature to be proved by alleging fingle.

In fine, a very remarkable circumstance in the English Government (and which alone evinces something pecu-

facts, I have entered into no particulars on that account.——However, I have subjoined here two cases which, I think, cannot but appear remarkable to the Reader.

The first is the case of the prosecution commenced in the year 1763, by some Journeymen Printers, against the King's Messengers, for apprehending and imprisoning them for a short time, by virtue of a *General Warrant* from the Secretaries of State; and that which was afterwards carried on by another private individual, against one of the Secretaries themselves.——In these actions all the ordinary forms of proceeding used in cases of actions between private Subjects, were strictly adhered to; and both the Secretary of State, and the Messengers, were, in the end, condemned. Yet, which it is proper the Reader should observe, from all the circumstances that accompanied this affair, it is difficult to propose a case in which Ministers could, of themselves, be under greater temptations to exert an undue influence to hinder the ordinary course of Justice. Nor were the Acts for which those Ministers were condemned, Acts of evident oppression, which nobody could be found to justify. They had done nothing but follow a practice of which they found several precedents established in their Offices: and their case, if I am well informed, was such that most individuals, under similar circumstances, would have thought themselves authorised to have acted as they had done.

The second case I propose to relate, affords a singular instance of the confidence with which all Subjects in England claim what they think their just rights, and of the certainty with which the remedies of the law are in all cases open to them. The fact I mean, is the arrest executed in the reign of Queen Anne, in the year 1708, on the person of the Russian Ambassador, by taking him out of his Coach for the sum of fifty pounds—And the consequences that followed this fact are still more remarkable. The Czar highly resented the affront, and demanded that the Sheriff of Middlesex, and all others concerned in the Arrest, should be punished with instant death. "But the Queen," (to the

liar and excellent in its Nature) is that fpirit of extreme
mildnefs with which Juftice, in criminal cafes, is adminiftered in England; a point with regard to which England
differs from all other Countries in the World.

When we confider the punifhments in ufe in the other
States in Europe, we wonder how Men can be brought
to treat their fellow-creatures with fo much cruelty; and
the bare confideration of thofe punifhments would fufficiently convince us (fuppofing we did not know the fact
from other circumftances) that the Men in thofe States
who frame the laws, and prefide over their execution,
have little apprehenfion that either they, or their friends,
will ever fall victims to thofe laws which they thus rafhly
eftablifh.

In the Roman Republic, circumftances of the fame nature with thofe juft mentioned, were alfo productive of
the greateft defects in the kind of criminal Juftice which
took place in it. That clafs of Citizens who were at the
head of the Republic, and who knew how mutually to
exempt each other from the operation of any too fevere
laws or practice, not only allowed themfelves great liberties, as we have feen, in difpofing of the lives of the inferior Citizens, but had alfo introduced into the exercife of
the illegal powers they affumed to themfelves in that refpect, a great degree of cruelty *.

amazement of that defpotic Court, fays Juftice Blackftone,
from whom I borrow this fact) " the Queen directed the
" Secretary of State to inform him that fhe could inflict no
" punifhment upon any, the meaneft of Her Subjects un-
" lefs warranted by the law of the land,"—An Act was afterwards paffed to free from arrefts the perfons of foreign
Minifters, and fuch of their fervants as they have delivered a
lift of to the Secretary of State. A copy of this act elegant-
ly engroffed and illuminated, continues Judge Blackftone,
was fent to Mofcow, and an Ambaffador extraordinary com-
miffioned to deliver it.

* The common manner in which the Senate ordered Citizens to be put to death, was by throwing them headlong

Nor were things more happily conducted in the Grecian Republics. From their Democratical nature, and the frequent Revolutions to which they were subject, we naturally expect to see that authority to have been used with mildness, which those who enjoyed it must have known to have been but precarious; yet, such were the effects of the violence attending those very Revolutions, that a spirit both of great irregularity and cruelty had taken place among the Greeks, in the exercise of the power of inflicting punishments. The very harsh laws of *Draco* are well known, of which it was said that they were not written with ink, but with blood. The severe laws of the Twelve Tables among the Romans, were in great part brought over from Greece. And it was an opinion commonly received in Rome, that the cruelties practised by the Magistrates on the Citizens, were only imitations of the examples which the Greeks had given them *.

In fine, the use of Torture, that method of administering Justice in which folly may be said to be added to cruelty, had been adopted by the Greeks, in consequence of the same causes which had concurred to produce the irregularity of their criminal Justice. And the same practice continues, in these days, to prevail on the continent of Europe, in consequence of that general arrangement of things which creates there such a carelessness about remedying the abuses of public Authority.

---

from the top of the Tarpeian Rock. The Consuls, or other particular Magistrates, sometimes caused Citizens to expire upon a cross; or, which was a much more common case, ordered them to be beaten to death, with their heads fastened between the two branches of a fork: which they called *cervicem furcæ inserere*.

* Cæsar expressly reproaches the Greeks with this fact in his speech in favour of the accomplices of Catiline, which Sallust has transmitted to us—*Sed eodem illo tempore Graciæ morem imitati [Majorus nostri], verberibus animadvertebant in civeis; de condemnatis ultimum supplicium sumptum.*

· But the nature of that fame Government which has procured to the People of England all the advantages we have before defcribed, has, with ftill more reafon, freed them from the moft oppreffive abufes, which prevail in other countries.

· That wantonnefs in difpofing of the deareft rights of Mankind, thofe infults upon human Nature, upon which the frame of the Governments eftablifhed in other States, unavoidably becomes more or lefs productive, are entirely banifhed from a Nation which has the happinefs of having its interefts taken care of by Men, who continue to be themfelves expofed to the preffure of thofe laws which they concur in making, and of every tyrannic practice which they fuffer to be introduced,—by Men whom the advantages which they poffefs above the reft of the People, render only more expofed to the abufes they are appointed to prevent, only more alive to the dangers againft which it is their duty to defend the Community *.

Hence we fee that the ufe of Torture has, from the earlieft times, been utterly unknown in England. And all attempts to introduce it, whatever might be the power of thofe who made them, or the circumftances in which they renewed their endeavours, have been ftrenuoufly oppofed and defeated †.

* Hiftorians take notice that the commons, in the reign of Charles II. made hafte to procure the abolition of the old Statute, *De Hæretico comburendo* (For burning Heretics), as foon as it became to be publicly known that the prefumptive Heir to the Crown was a Roman Catholic. Perhaps they would not have been fo diligent and earneft if they had not been fully convinced that a Member of the Houfe of Commons, or his friends, may be brought to trial as eafily as any other individuals among the people, fo long as an exprefs and written law may be produced againft them.

† The Reader may on this fubject fee again the Note in page 140 of this Work, where the oppofition is mentioned, that was made to the Earl of Suffolk, and the Duke of Exe-

From the fame caufe alfo arofe that remarkable forbearance of the Englifh Laws, to ufe any cruel feverity in the punifhments which experience fhewed it was neceffary for the prefervation of Society to eftablifh : and the utmoft vengeance of thofe laws, even againft the moft enormous Offenders, never extends beyond the fimple deprivation of life *.

Nay, fo anxious has the Englifh Legiflature been to eftablifh mercy, even to convicted offenders, as a fundamental principle of the Government of England, that they made it an exprefs article of that great public Compact which was framed at the important æra of the Revolution, that " no cruel and unufual punifhments fhould " be ufed †."—They even endeavoured, by adding a claufe for that purpofe to the Oath which Kings were thenceforward to take at their Coronation, as it were to

ter, when they attempted to introduce the practice of Torture : this even was one of the caufes for which the latter was afterwards impeached.—The Reader is alfo referred to the Note following that which has juft been quoted, in which the folemn declaration is related, that was given by the Judges againft the practice of Torture, in the cafe of Felton, who had affaffinated the Duke of Buckingham.

* A very fingular inftance occurs in the Hiftory of the year 1605, of the care of the Englifh Legiflator not to fuffer precedents of cruel practices to be introduced. During the time that thofe concerned in the gun-powder plot were under fentence of death, a motion was made in the Houfe of Commons to petition the King that the execution might be ftaid, in order to confider of fome extraordinary punifhment to be inflicted upon them : but this motion was rejected. A propofal of the fame kind was alfo made in the Houfe of Lords, where it was dropped.—See the Parliamentary Hiftory of England, vol. v. anno 1605.

† See the Bill of rights, Art. x. —" Exceffive bail ought not to be required, nor exceffive fines impofed ; nor cruel and unufual punifhments inflicted."

render it an everlasting obligation of English Kings, to make Justice to be " executed with mercy *."

C H A P. XVII.

A more inward View of the English Government than has hitherto been offered to the Reader in the course of this Work.—Very essential differences between the English Monarchy, as a Monarchy, and all those with which we are acquainted.

THE Doctrine constantly maintained in this Work, and which has, I think, been sufficiently supported by facts and comparisons drawn from the History of other Countries, is that the remarkable liberty enjoyed by the English Nation, is essentially owing to the impossibility under which their Leaders, or in general all Men of power among them, are placed, of invading and transferring to themselves any branch of the Governing Executive authority; which authority is exclusively vested, and firmly secured, in the Crown. Hence the anxious care with which those Men continue to watch the exercise of that authority. Hence their perseverance in observing every

* Those same dispositions of the English Legislature, which have led them to take such precautions in favour even of convicted offenders, have still more engaged them to make provisions in favour of such persons as are only suspected and accused of having committed offences of any kind. Hence the zeal with which they have availed themselves of every important occasion, such for instance as that of the Revolution, to procure new confirmations to be given to the institution of the Trial by Jury, to the laws on imprisonments, and in general to that system of criminal Jurisprudence of which a description has been given in the first part of this Work, to which I refer the Reader.

M m

kind of engagement which themselves may have entered into with the rest of the People.

But here a confideration of the moft important kind prefents itfelf.—How comes the Crown in England thus conftantly to preferve to itfelf (as we fee it does) the Executive authority in the State, and moreover to preferve it fo completely as to infpire the great Men in the Nation with that conduct fo advantageous to public Liberty, which has juft been mentioned? All thefe are effects which we do not find, upon examination, that the power of *Crowns* has hitherto been able to produce in other Countries.

In all States of a Monarchical form, we indeed fee that thofe Men whom their rank and wealth, or their perfonal power of any kind, have raifed above the reft of the People, have formed combinations among themfelves to oppofe the Power of the Monarch. But their views, we muft obferve, in forming thefe combinations, were not by any means to fet general and impartial limitations on the Sovereign authority. They endeavoured to render themfelves entirely independent of that authority; or even utterly to annihilate it, according to circumftances.

Thus we fee that in all the States of ancient Greece, the Kings were at laft deftroyed and exterminated. The fame event happened in Italy, where in remote times there exifted for a while feveral kingdoms, as we learn both from the ancient Hiftorians and the Poets. And in Rome, we even know the manner and circumftances in which fuch a revolution was brought about.

In more modern times, we fee the numerous Monarchical Sovereignties which had been raifed in Italy on the ruins of the Roman Empire, to have been fucceffively deftroyed by powerful factions; and events of much the fame nature have at different times taken place in the Kingdoms eftablifhed in the other parts of Europe.

In Sweden, Denmark, and Poland, for inftance, we find that the *Nobles* have commonly reduced their Sovereigns to the condition of fimple Prefidents over their Affemblies,—of mere oftenfible Heads of the Government.

In Germany and in France, Countries where the Monarchs being poffeffed of confiderable demefnes, were better able to maintain their independence than the Princes juft mentioned, the Nobles waged war againft them, fometimes fingly and fometimes jointly ; and events fimilar to thefe have fuccefsfully happened in Scotland, Spain, and the Modern Kingdoms of Italy.

In fine, it has only been by means of ftanding armed forces that the Sovereigns of moft of the Kingdoms we have mentioned, have been able in a courfe of time to affert the prerogatives of the Crown. And it is only by continuing to keep up fuch forces, that, like the Eaftern Monarchs, and indeed like all the Monarchs that ever exifted, they continue to be able to fupport their authority.

How therefore can the Crown of England, without the affiftance of any armed force, maintain, as it does, its numerous prerogatives? How can it, under fuch circumftances, preferve to itfelf the whole Executive power in the State? For here we muft obferve, the Crown in England does not derive any fupport from what regular forces it has at its difpofal; and if we doubted this fact, we need only look to the aftonifhing fubordination in which the military is kept to the civil power, to become convinced that an Englifh King is not indebted to his army for the prefervation of his authority[*].

If we could fuppofe that the armies of the Kings of Spain or of France, for inftance, were, through fome

***

[*] Henry VIII. the moft abfolute Prince, perhaps, who ever fat upon a Throne, kept no ftanding army.

very extraordinary circumftance, all to vanifh in one night, the power of thofe Sovereigns, we muft not doubt, would, ere fix months, be reduced to a mere fhadow. They would immediately behold their pre-rogatives, however formidable they may be at prefent, invaded and difmembered *: and fuppofing that regu-lar Governments continued to exift, they would be re-duced to have little more influence in them than the Doges of Venice, or of Genoa, poffefs in the Govern-ments of thofe Republicst.

How, therefore, to repeat the queftion once more, which is one of the moft interefting that can occur in politics, how can the Crown in England, without the affiftance of any armed force, avoid thofe dangers to which all other Sovereigns are expofed ?

How can it, without any fuch force, accomplifh even incomparably greater works than thofe Sovereigns, with their powerful armies, are, we find in a condi-tion to perform ?—How can it bear that univerfal ef-fort (unknown in other Monarchies) which, we have feen, is continually and openly exerted againft it? How can it even continue to refift it fo powerfully as to pre-clude all individuals whatever, from ever entertaining any views befides thofe of fetting juft and *general* limit-ations to the exercife of its authority ? How can it en-force the laws upon all Subjects, indifcriminately, with-out injury or danger to itfelf? How can it, in fine, im-prefs the minds of all the great Men in the State with fo lafting a jealoufy of its power, as to neceffitate them, even in the exercife of their undoubted rights and pri-

---

* As was the cafe in the feveral Kingdoms into which the Spanifh Monarchy was formerly divided; and, in no very remote times, in France itfelf.

† Or than the Kings of Sweden were allowed to enjoy, be-fore the laft Revolution in that Country.

vileges, to continue to court and deferve the affection of the reft of the people?

Thofe great Men, I fhall anfwer, who even in quiet times prove fo formidable to other Monarchs, are in England divided into two Affemblies ; and fuch, it is neceffary to add, are the principles upon which this divifion is made, that from its refults, as a neceffary confequence, the folidity and indivifibility of the power of the Crown*.

The Reader may perceive that I have led him, in the courfe of this Work, much beyond the line within which Writers on the fubject of Government have confined themfelves, or rather, that I have followed a tract entirely different from that which thofe Writers have purfued. But as the obfervation juft made on the ftability of the power of the Crown in England, and the caufe of it, is new in its kind, fo do the principles from which its truth is to be demonftrated, totally differ from what is commonly looked upon as the foundation of the fcience of Politics. To lay thefe principles here before the Reader, in a manner completely fatisfactory to him, would lead us into philofophical difcuffions on what really conftitutes the bafis of governments and Power amongft Mankind, both extremely long, and in a great meafure foreign to the fubject of this book. I fhall therefore content myfelf with proving the above obfervations by facts ; which is more, after all, than political Writers ufually undertake to do with regard to their fpeculations.

As I chiefly propofed to fhew how the extenfive liberty the Englifh enjoy, is the refult of the peculiar frame of their Government, and occafionally to compare the fame with the Republican form, I even had

---

* I have not flattered myfelf, in writing this Chapter, that it would be perfectly underftood, nor is it defigned for the generality of readers.

at firſt intended to confine myſelf to that circumſtance, which both conſtitutes the eſſential difference between thoſe two forms of Government, and is the immediate cauſe of Engliſh liberty; I mean the having placed all the executive authority in the State out of the hands of thoſe in whom the People truſt. With regard to the remote cauſe of that ſame liberty, that is to ſay the ſtability of the power of the Crown, this ſingular ſolicity without the aſſiſtance of any armed force, by which this executive authority is ſo ſecured, I ſhould perhaps have been ſilent, had I not found it abſolutely neceſſary to mention the fact in this place, in order to obviate the objections which the more reflecting part of Readers might otherwiſe have made, both to ſeveral of the obſervations before offered to them, and to a few others which are ſoon to follow.

Beſides, I ſhall confeſs here, I have been ſeveral times under apprehenſions, in the courſe of this Work, leſt the generality of Readers, miſled by the ſimiliarity of names, ſhould put too extenſive a conſtruction upon what I ſaid with regard to the uſefulneſs of the power of the Crown in England;—leſt they ſhould think, for inſtance, that I attributed the ſuperior advantages of the Engliſh mode of Government over the Republican form, merely to its approaching nearer to the nature of the Monarchies eſtabliſhed in the other parts of Europe, and that I looked upon every kind of Monarchy, as being in itſelf preferable to a Republican Government: an opinion, which I do not by any means or in any degree entertain; I have too much affection, or if you pleaſe, prepoſſeſſion, in favour of that form of Government under which I was born; and as I am ſenſible of its defects, ſo do I know how to ſet a value upon the advantages by which it compenſates for them.

I therefore have, as it were, made haſte to avail myſelf of the firſt opportunity of explaining my meaning on this fubject,—of indicating that the power of the Crown in England ftands upon foundations entirely different from thofe on which the fame Power refts in other Countries,—and of engaging the Reader to ob-ferve (which for the prefent will fuffice) that as the En-glifh Monarchy differs, in its nature and main foun-dations, from every other, fo all that is faid here of its advantages is peculiar and confined to it.

But to come to the proofs (derived from facts) of the folidity accruing to the power of the Crown in En-gland from the *co-exiftence* of the two Affemblies, which concur to form the Englifh Parliament; I fhall firft point out to the Reader feveral open acts of thefe two Houfes, by which they have by turns effectually de-feated the attacks of each other upon its prerogative.

Without looking farther back for examples than the reign of Charles the Second, we fee that the Houfe of Commons had, in that reign, begun to adopt the me-thod of adding (or tacking, as it is commonly expreff-ed) fuch bills as they wanted more particularly to have paffed, to their money bills. This forcible ufe they made of their undoubted privilege of granting money, if fuffered to have grown into common practice, would have totally deftroyed the æquilibrium that ought to fubfift between them and the Crown. But the Lords took upon themfelves the tafk of maintaining that æ-quilibrium : they complained with great warmth of the feveral precedents that were made by the Commons, of the practice we mention : they infifted that bills fhould be framed " *in the old and decent way of Par-* " *liament ;*" and at laft have made it a ftanding order of their Houfe, to reject, upon the fight of them, all bills that are tacked to money bills.

Again, about the thirty-firft year of the fame reign, a ftrong party prevailed in the Houfe of Commons ; and their efforts were not entirely confined, if we may credit the Hiftorians of thofe times, to ferving their

Conftituents faithfully, and providing for the welfare of the State. Among other bills which they propofed in their Houfe, they carried one to exclude from the Crown the immediate Heir to it; an affair this, of a very high nature and with regard to which it may well be queftioned whether the legiflative Affemblies have a right to form a refolution, without the exprefs and declared concurrence of the body of the People. But both the Crown and the Nation were delivered from the danger of eftablifhing fuch a precedent, by the interpofition of the Lords, who threw out the bill on the firft reading.

In the reign of King William the Third, a few years after the Revolution, attacks were made upon the Crown from another quarter. A ftrong party was formed in the Houfe of Lords; and, as we may fee in Bifhop Burnet's Hiftory of his Own Times, they entertained very deep defigns. One of their views, among others, was to abridge the prerogative of the Crown of calling Parliaments, and judging of the proper times of doing it *. They accordingly framed and carried in their Houfe a bill for afcertaining the fitting of Parliament every year: but the bill, after it had paffed in their Houfe, was rejected by the Commons †.

---

* They, befides, propofed to have all money bills ftopped in their Houfe, till they had procured the right of taxing, themfelves, their own eftates; and to have a Committee of Lords, and a certain number of the Commons, appointed to confer together concerning the State of the Nation; ‘ which ‘ Committee (fays Bifhop Burnet) would foon have grown ‘ to have been a Council of State, that would have brought ‘ all affairs under their infpection, and never had been propo- ‘ fed but when the Nation was ready to break into civil wars.’ —See Burnet's Hiftory, anno 1693.

† Nov. 28, 1693.

. Again, we find, a little after the acceſſion of King George the Firſt, an attempt was alſo made by a party in the Houſe of Lords, to wreſt from the Crown a prerogative which is one of its fineſt flowers ; and is, beſides, the only check it has on the dangerous views which that Houſe (which may ſtop both money bills and all other bills) might be brought to entertain ; I mean the right of adding new members to it ; and judging of the times when it may be neceſſary to do ſo. A bill was accordingly preſented and carried, in the Houſe of Lords, for limiting the members of that Houſe to a fixed number, beyond which it ſhould not be increaſed ; but after great pains taken to inſure the ſucceſs of this bill, it was at laſt rejected by the Houſe of Commons.

In fine, the ſeveral attempts which a majority in the Houſe of Commons have in their turn made to reſtrain, farther than it now is, the influence of the Crown ariſing from the diſtribution of preferments and other advantages, have been checked by the Houſe of Lords ; and all place-bills have, from the beginning of this Century, conſtantly miſcarried in that Houſe.

Nor have theſe two powerful Aſſemblies only ſucceeded in thus warding off the open attacks of each other, on the power of the Crown. Their co-exiſtence, and the principles upon which they are ſeverally framed, have been productive of another effect much more extenſive, though at firſt leſs attended to, I mean the preventing even the making of ſuch attacks ; and in times too, when the Crown was of itſelf incapable of defending its authority: the views of each of theſe two Houſes deſtroying, upon theſe occaſions, the oppoſite views of the other, like thoſe poſitive and negative equal quantities (if I may be allowed the compariſon) which deſtroy each other on the oppoſite ſides of an equation.

Of this we have ſeveral remarkable examples: as

for inftance, when the Sovereign has been a minor. If we examine the Hiftory of other Nations, efpecially before the invention of ftanding armies, we fhall find that the event we mention never failed to be attended with open invafions of the Royal authority, or even fometimes with complete and fettled divifions of it. In England, on the contrary, whether we look at the reign of Richard II. or that of Henry VI. or of Edward VI. we fhall fee that the Royal authority has been quietly exercifed by the Councils that were appointed to affift thofe Princes; and when they came of age, the fame has been delivered over to them undiminifhed.

But nothing fo remarkable can be alleged on this fubject, as the manner in which thefe two Houfes have acted upon thofe occafions when the Crown being without any prefent poffeffor, they had it in their power both to fettle it on what perfon they pleafed, and to divide and diftribute its effectual prerogatives, in what manner, and to what fet of Men, they might think proper. Circumftances like thofe we mention, have never failed, in other Kingdoms, to bring on a divifion of the effectual authority of the Crown, or even of the State itfelf. In Sweden, for inftance (to fpeak of that kingdom which has borne the greateft outward refemblance to that of England), when Queen Chriftina was put under a neceffity of abdicating the Crown, and it was transferred to the Prince who ftood next to her in the line of fucceffion, the Executive authority in the State was immediately divided, and either diftributed among the Nobles, or affigned to the Senate, into which the Nobles alone could be admitted; and the new King was only to be a Prefident over it.

After the death of Charles the Twelfth, who died without male heirs, the difpofal of the Crown (the power of which Charles the Eleventh had found means to render again abfolute) returned to the States, and was fettled on the Princefs Ulrica, and the Prince her hufband. But the Senate, at the fame time it thus fettled the poffeffion of the Crown, again affumed to itfelf the effectual authority which had formerly belonged to it. The privilege of affembling the States was vefted in that body. They alfo fecured to themfelves the power of making war and peace, and treaties with foreign powers,—the difpofal of places,—the command of the army and of the fleet,—and the adminiftration of the public revenue. Their number was to confift of fixteen Members. The majority of votes was to be decifive upon every occafion. The only privilege of the new King was, to have his vote reckoned for two; and if at any time he fhould refufe to attend their meetings, the bufinefs was neverthelefs to be done as effectually and definitively without him *.

* The Senate had procured a Seal to be made, to be affixed to their official refolutions, in cafe the King fhould refufe to lend his own. The reader will find a few more particulars concerning the former government of Sweden, in the nineteenth Chapter.

Regulations of a fimilar nature had been made in Denmark, and continued to fubfift, with fome variations, till the Revolution which, in the laft Century, placed the whole power in the State in the hands of the Crown, without controul. The different Kingdoms into which Spain was formerly divided, were governed in much the fame manner.

And in Scotland, that Seat of anarchy and ariftocratical feuds, all the great offices in the State were not only taken from the Crown; but they were moreover made hereditary in the principal families of the Body of the Nobles;—fuch were the offices of High Admiral, High Steward, High Conftable, Great Chamberlain, and Juftice General; this latter office implied powers analogous to thofe of the Lord Chancellor, and the Lord Chief Juftice of the King's Bench, united.

But in England, the Revolution of the year 1689 was terminated in a manner totally different. Thofe who at that interefting epoch had the guardianfhip of the Crown—thofe in whofe hands it lay *vacant*, did not manifeft fo much as a thought to fplit and parcel out its prerogative. They tendered it to a fingle indivifible poffeffor, impelled as it were by fome fecret power that was, unfeen, operating upon them without any falvo, without any article to eftablifh the greatnefs of themfelves, or of their families. It is true thofe prerogatives deftructive of public liberty which the late King had affumed, were retrenched from the Crown ; and thus far the two Houfes agreed. But as to any attempt to transfer to other hands any part of the authority of the Crown, no propofal was even

---

The King's minority, or perfonal weaknefs, or in general the difficulties in which the State might be involved, were circumftances in which the Scotch Leaders never failed to avail themfelves for invading the governing authority ; a remarkable inftance of the claims they were ufed to fet forth on thofe occafions, occurs in a Bill that was framed in the year 1703, for fettling the Succeffion to the Crown, after the demife of the Queen, under the title of *An Act for the Security of the Kingdom*.

The Scotch Parliament was to fit by its own authority, every year, on the firft day of November, and adjourn themfelves as they fhould think proper.

The King was to give his affent to all laws agreed to, and offered by, the Eftates ; or commiffion proper officers for doing the fame.

A Committee of one and thirty members chofen by the Parliament, were to be called the King's Council, and govern, during the recefs, being accountable to the Parliament.

The King not to make any foreign treaty without the confent of Parliament.

All places and offices, both civil and military, and all penfions formerly given by the King, fhall ever after be given by Parliament. See *Parliamentary Debates*, A. 1703.

made about it.   Thofe branches of prerogative which
were taken from the kingly office, were annihilated
and made to ceafe to exift in the ftate; and all the
Executive authority that was thought neceffary to be
continued in the Government, was, as before, left undivided in the Crown.

In the very fame manner was the whole authority of
the Crown transferred afterwards to the Princefs who
fucceeded King William the Third, and who had no
other claim to it but what was conferred on her by the
Parliament.   And in the fame manner again was it fettled, a long time beforehand, on the Princefs of Hanover
who have fince fucceeded her *.

Nay, one more extraordinary fact, and to which I defire the Reader to give attention—Notwithftanding all
the Revolutions we mention, and although Parliament,
hath fat every year fince the beginning of this century,
and though they have conftantly enjoyed the moft unli-

* It may not be improper to obferve here, as a farther
proof of the indivifibility of the power of the Crown (which
has been above faid to refult from the peculiar frame of the
Englifh Government), that no part of the Executive authority of the King is vefted in his privy Council, as we have
feen it was in the Senate of Sweden : the whole bufinefs cen-
tres in the Sovereign ; the votes of the members are not even
counted, if I am well informed : and in fact the conftant
ftyle of the Law is, the King *in* Council, and not the King
and Council.   A provifo is indeed fometimes added to fome
Bills that certain acts mentioned in them are to be tranfacted by the King in Council : but this is only a precaution
taken in the view that the moft important affairs of a great
Nation may be tranfacted with proper folemnity, and to
prevent, for inftance, all objections that might in procefs of
time, be drawn from the uncertainty whether the King has
affented, or not, to certain particular tranfactions.   The
King names the Members of the Privy Council ; or excludes them, by caufing their names to be ftruck out of the
Book.

mited freedom both as to the subjects and the manner of their deliberations, and numberless proposals have in confequence been made,—yet, fuch has been the efficiency of each Houfe, in deftroying, preventing, or qualifying, the views of the other, that the Crown has not been obliged during all that time to make ufe, even once, of its negative voice; and the laft Bill rejected by a King of England, has been that rejected by King William the Third, in the year 1692, for Triennial Parliaments *.

There is another inftance yet more remarkable of this forbearing conduct of the Parliament in regard to the Crown, to whatever open or latent caufe it may be owing, and how little their *efprit de corps* in reality leads them, amidft the apparent heats fometimes of their ftruggles, to invade its governing executive authority; I mean, the facility with which they have been prevailed upon to give up any effential branch of that authority, even after a conjunction of preceding circumftances had caufed them to be actually in poffeffion of it; a cafe this, however, that has not frequently happened in the Englifh Hiftory. After the Reftoration of Charles the Second, for inftance, we find the Parliament to have of their own accord paffed an Act, in the firft year that followed that event, by which they annihilated, at one ftroke, both the independent legiflative authority, and all claims to fuch authority, which they had affumed during the preceding difturbances:—by the Stat. 13 Car. II. c. 1. it was forbidden, under the penalty of a *premunire*, (fee p. 84.) to affirm that either of the two Houfes of Parliament, or both jointly, poffefs, without the concurrence of the King, the Legiflative authority. In the fourth year after the Reftoration, another capital branch of the governing authority of the Crown was alfo reftored to it, without any manner of ftruggle:—by the Stat. 16 Car. II. c. 1. the Act was repealed by which it had been enacted, that in cafe the

* He affented a few years afterwards to that Bill, after feveral amendments had been made in it.

King fhould negle&t to call a Parliament once at leaft in
three years, the Peers fhould iffue the writs for an ele&tion ;
and that fhould they negle&t to iffue the fame, the Conftituents fhould of themfelves affemble to ele&t a Parliament.

It is here to be obferved, that, in the fame reign we
mention, the Parliament paffed the *Habeas Corpus* A&t,
as well as the other A&ts that prepared the fame, and in
general fhewed a jealoufy in watching over the liberty of
the fubje&t, fuperior perhaps to what has taken place at
any other period of the Englifh Hiftory; this is another
ftriking confirmation of what has been remarked in a preceding Chapter, concerning the manner in which public
difturbances have always been terminated in England.
Here we find a feries of Parliaments to have been tenaci-
oufly and perfeverantly jealous of thofe kinds of popular univerfal provifions which great Men in other States
ever difdained ferioufly to think of, or give a place to, in
thofe treaties by which internal peace was reftored to the
Nation ; and at the fame time thefe Parliaments cordially
and fincerely gave up thofe high and fplendid branches
of Governing authority, which the Senates or Affemblies
of great Men who furrounded the Monarchs in other limited Monarchies, never ceafed anxioufly to ftrive to
affume to themfelves,—and which the Monarchs, after
having loft them, never were able to recover but by military violence aided by furprife, or through National commotions. All thefe are political fingularities, certainly
remarkable enough. It is a circumftance in no fmall degree conducive to the folidity of the executive authority
of the Englifh Crown (which is the fubje&t of this Chapter,) that thofe perfons who feem to have it in their
power to wreft the fame from it, are, fomehow, prevented from entertaining thoughts of doing fo *.

* I will mention another inftance of this real difinterefted-
nefs of the Parliament in regard to the power of the Crown,
nay, of the ftrong bent that prevails in that Affembly, to

As another proof of the peculiar solidity of the power of the Crown, in England, may be mentioned the facility, and safety to itself, and to the State, with which it has

make the Crown the general depository of the executive authority to the Nation ; I mean to speak of the manner in which they use to provide for the execution of those resolutions of an active kind they may at times come to : it is always by addressing the Crown for that purpose, and desiring it to interfere with its own executive authority. Even in regard to the printing of their Journals, the Crown is applied to by the Commons, with a promise of making good to it the necessary expences. Certainly, if there existed in that Body any latent anxiety, any real ambition (I speak here of the general tenor of their conduct) to invest themselves with the executive authority in the State, they would not give up the providing by their own authority at least for the object just mentioned : it might give them a pretence for having a set of Officers belonging to them, as well as a Treasury of their own, and, in short, for establishing in their favour some sort of beginning or precedent : at the same time that a wish on their part, to be the publishers of their own Journals, could not be decently opposed by the Crown, nor would be likely to be found fault with by the public. To some readers the fact we are speaking of may appear trifling : to me it is not so : I confess I never happen to see a paragraph in the newspapers, mentioning an address to the Crown for borrowing its executive prerogative in regard to the inconsiderable object here alluded to, without pausing for half a minute on the article.- Certainly there must needs exist causes of a very peculiar nature which produce in an Assembly possessed of so much weight, that remarkable freedom from any serious ambition to push their advantages farther,—which inspire it with the great political forbearance we have mentioned, with so sincere an indifference in general, in regard to arrogating to themselves any branch of the executive authority of the Crown :—they really seem as if they did not know what to do with it after having acquired it, nor of what kind of service it may be to them.

at all times been able to deprive any particular Subjects of their different offices, however overgrown, and even dangerous, their private power may seem to be. A very remarkable instance of this kind occurred when the great Duke of Marlborough was suddenly removed from all his employments: the following is the account given by Dean Swift, in his, " History of the Four last years of " the Reign of Queen Anne."

" So that the Queen found herself under a necessity, " by removing one person from so great a trust, to get " clear of all her difficulties at once: her Majesty deter- " mined upon the latter expedient, as the shorter and " safer course ; and during the recess at Christmas, sent " the Duke a letter to tell him she had no farther occa- " sion for his service.

" There has not perhaps in the present age been a " clearer instance to shew the instability of power, which " is not founded on virtue: and it may be an instruction " to Princes who are well in the hearts of their People, " that the overgrown power of any particular person, al- " though supported by exorbitant wealth, can, by a little " resolution, be reduced in a moment, without any dan- " gerous consequences. This Lord, who was, beyond " all comparison, the greatest subject in Christendom, " found his power, credit, and influence crumble away " on a sudden; and except a few friends and followers, " the rest dropped off in course, &c." (B. I. near the " end.)

The ease with which such a Man as the Duke was suddenly removed, Dean Swift has explained by the necessary advantages of Princes who possess the affection of their People, and the natural weakness of power which is not founded on virtue. However, these are very unsatisfactory explanations. The History of Europe, in former times, offers us a continued series of examples to the contrary. We see in it numberless instances of Princes incessantly engaged in resisting in the field the competition of Subjects invested with the eminent dignities of the Realm, who were not by any means superior to them in point of virtue,—or at other times, living in a continued state of vassalage under some powerful Man whom they durst not resist, and whose *power, credit, and influence* they would have found it far from possible to *reduce in a moment, or crumble on a sudden*, by the sending of a single letter, even though assisted *by a little resolution*, to use Dean Swift's expressions, and without any dangerous consequences.

Nay, certain Kings, such as Henry the Third of France, in regard to the Duke of Guise, and James the Second of Scotland, in regard to the two Earls of Douglas successively, had at last recourse to plot and assassination; and expedients of a similar sudden violent kind, are the settled methods adopted by the Eastern monarchs; nor is it very sure they can always easily do otherwise *.

Even in the present Monarchies of Europe, notwithstanding, the awful force by which they are outwardly supported, a discarded Minister is the cause of more or less anxiety to the governing Authority; especially if, through the length of time he has been in office, he happens to have acquired a considerable degree of influence. He is generally sent and confined to one of his estates in the country, which the Crown names to him: he is not

---

* We might also mention here the case of the Emperor Ferdinand II. and the Duke of Walstein, which seems to have at the time made a great noise in the world.—The Earls of Douglas were sometimes attended by a retinue of two thousand horse. See Dr. Robertson's History of Scotland.—The Duke of Guise was warned, some hours before his death, of the danger of trusting his person into the King's presence or house; he answered, *On n'oseroit*—They durst not.

If Mary, Queen of Scots, had possessed a power analogous to that exerted by Queen Anne, she might perhaps have avoided being driven into those instances of ill-conduct which were followed by such tragical consequences.

allowed to appear at Court, nor even in the Metropolis; much less is he suffered to appeal to the People in loud complaints, to make public speeches to the great Men in the State, and intrigue among them, and in short to vent his resentment by those bitter, and sometimes desperate methods, which, in the Constitution of this Country, prove in a great measure harmless.

But a dissolution of the Parliament, that is, the dismission of the whole body of the great Men in the Nation, assembled in Legislative capacity, is a circumstance in the English Government, in a much higher degree remarkable and deserving our notice, than the depriving any single individual, however powerful, of his public employments. When we consider in what an easy and complete manner such a dissolution is effected in England, we must needs become convinced, that the power of the Crown bears upon foundations of very uncommon, though perhaps hidden, strength; especially, if we attend to the several facts that take place in other Countries.

In France, for example, we find the Crown, notwithstanding the immense outward force by which it is surrounded, to use the utmost caution in its proceedings towards the Parliament of Paris: an Assembly only of a judiciary Nature, without any Legislative authority or avowed claim, and which, in short, is very far from having the same weight in the kingdom of France, as the English Parliament has in England. The King never repairs to that Assembly; to signify his intentions, or hold a *Lit de Justice*, without the most over-awing circumstances of military apparatus and preparation, constantly choosing to make his appearance among them rather as a military General, than as a King.

And when the late King, having taken a serious alarm at the proceedings of this Parliament, at length resolved upon their dismission, he fenced himself, as it were, with his army; and military Messengers were sent with every circumstance of secrecy and dispatch, who, at an early part of the day, and at the same hour, surprised each

Member in his own house, causing them severally to depart for distant parts of the country which were prescribed to them, without allowing them time to consider, much less to meet, and hold any consultation together.

But the Person who is invested with the kingly office, in England, has need of no other weapon, no other artillery, than the Civil *Insignia* of his dignity, to effect a dissolution of the Parliament. He steps into the middle of them, telling them they are dissolved ; and they are dissolved :—he tells them, they are no longer a Parliament ; and they are no longer so. Like Popilius's wand, * a dissolution instantly puts a stop to their warmest debates and most violent proceedings. The wonderful words by which it is expressed have no sooner met their ears, than all their legislative faculties are benumbed : though they may, still be sitting on the same benches, they look no longer upon themselves as forming an Assembly ; they no longer consider each other in the light of Associates or of Colleagues. As if some strange kind of weapon, or a sudden magical effort, had been exerted in the midst of them, all the bonds of their union are cut off: and they hasten away, without having so much as the thought of continuing for a single minute the duration of their Assembly †.

* He who stopped the army of King Antiochus.

† Nor has London post-horses enough to drive them far and near into the Country, in case the declaration by which the Parliament is dissolved, also mentions the calling of a new one.

A Dissolution, when proclaimed by a common Crier assisted by a few Beadles, is attended by the very same effects.

To the account of the expedient used by the late King of France, to effect the dismission of the Parliament of Paris, we may add the manner in which the Crown of Spain, in a higher degree arbitrary perhaps than that of France, undertook, some years ago, to rid itself of the religious Society of the Jesuits, whose political influence and intrigues had grown to give it umbrage. They were seized by an armed force, at

To all thefe obfervations concerning the peculiar folidity of the authority of the Crown, in England, I fhall add another that is fupplied by the whole feries of the Englifh Hiftory; which is, that though bloody broils and difturbances have often taken place in England, and war often made againft the King, yet it has fcarcely ever been done, but by perfons who pofitively and exprefsly laid claim to the Crown. Even while Cromwell contended with an armed force againft Charles the Firft, it was, as every one knows who has read that part of the Englifh hiftory, in the King's own name he waged war againft him.

The fame objection might be exprefled in a more general manner, and with ftrict truth, by faying, that no war has been waged, in England, againft the governing authority, except upon national grounds ; that is to fay, either when the title to the Crown has been doubtful, or when general complaints, either of a political or religious kind, have arifen from every part of the Nation : as inftances of fuch complaints may be mentioned thofe that gave rife to the war againft King John, which ended in the paffing of the Great Charter,—the civil wars in the reign of Charles

the fame minute of the fame day, in every Town or Borough of that extenfive Monarchy where they had refidence, in order to their being hurried away to fhips that were waiting to carry them into another Country : the whole bufinefs being conducted with circumftances of fecrecy, furprife, and of preparation far fuperior to what is related of the moft celebrated confpiracies mentioned in Hiftory.

The Diffolution of the Parliament which Charles the Second had called at Oxford, is an extremely curious event ; a very lively account of it is to be found in Oldmixon's Hiftory of England.

If certain alterations, however imperceptible they may perhaps be, at firft, to the public eye, ever take place, the period may come at which the Crown will no longer have it in its power to diffolve the Parliament ; that is to fay, a diffolution will no longer be followed by the fame effects that it is at prefent.

the Firſt,—and the Revolution of the year 1689. From the facts juſt mentioned it may alſo be obſerved as a concluſion, that the Crown cannot depend on the great ſecurity we have been deſcribing any longer than it continues to fulfil its engagements to the Nation, and to reſpect thoſe laws which form the compact between it and the People.   And the imminent dangers, or at leaſt the alarms and perplexities, in which the Kings of England have conſtantly involved themſelves, whenever they have attempted to ſtruggle againſt the general ſenſe of the Nation, manifeſtly ſhew that all that has been above obſerved, concerning the ſecurity and remarkable ſtability ſomehow annexed to their Office, is to be underſtood, not of the capricious power of the Man, but of the lawful authority of the Head of the State *.

* One more obſervation might be made on the ſubject; which is, that when the kingly dignity has happened in England to be wreſted from the poſſeſſor, through ſome revolution, it has been recovered, or ſtruggled for, with more difficulty than in other Countries: in all the other Countries upon earth, a King *de jure* (by claim) poſſeſſes advantages in regard to the King in being, much ſuperior to thoſe of which the ſame circumſtances may be productive in England.   The power of the other ſovereigns in the World, is not ſo ſecurely eſtabliſhed as that of an Engliſh King: but then their character is more indelible; that is to ſay,—till their antagoniſts have ſucceeded in cutting them off and their families, they poſſeſs in a high degree a power to renew theſe claims, and diſturb the State.   Thoſe family pleas or claims of priority, and in general thoſe arguments to which the bulk of Mankind have agreed to allow ſo much weight, ceaſe almoſt entirely to be of any effect, in England, againſt the perſon actually inveſted with the kingly office, as ſoon as the conſtitutional parts and ſprings have begun to move, and in ſhort as ſoon as the machine of the Government has once begun to be in full play.   An univerſal national ferment, ſimilar to that which produced the former diſturbances, is the only time of real danger.

Second Part of the same Chapter.

THERE is certainly a very great degree of fingularity in all the circumſtances we have been deſcribing here: thoſe perſons who are acquainted with the Hiſtory of other Countries, cannot but remark with ſurpriſe, that ſtability of the power of the Engliſh Crown,—that myſterious ſolidity,—that inward binding ſtrength with which it is able to carry on with certainty its legal operations, amidſt the clamorous ſtruggle and uproar with which it is commonly ſurrounded, and without the medium of any armed threatening force. To give a demonſtration of the manner in which all theſe things are brought to bear and operate, is not, as I ſaid before, my deſign to attempt here; the principles from which ſuch demonſtration is to be derived, ſuppoſe an inquiry into the nature of Man, and of human affairs, which rather belongs to Philoſophy (though a branch hitherto unexplored) than to Politics: at leaſt ſuch an inquiry certainly lies out of the ſphere of the common Science of Politics *. However, I had a very material reaſon in introducing all the above-mentioned faćts concerning the peculiar ſtability of the governing authority of England, in

The remarkable degree of internal national quiet, which, for very near a century paſt, has followed the Revolution of the year 1689, is a remarkable proof of the truth of the obſervations above made; nor do I think, that, all circumſtances being conſidered, any other Country can produce the like inſtance.

* It may, if the reader pleaſes, belong to the Science of *Metapolitics*; in the ſame ſenſe as we ſay *Metaphyſics*; that is, the ſcience of thoſe things which lie beyond phyſical, or ſubſtantial, things. A few more words are beſtowed upon the ſame ſubjećt, in the Advertiſement, or Preface, at the head of this Work.

that they lead to an obfervation of a moſt important political nature ; which is, that this ſtability allows ſeveral eſſential branches of Engliſh liberty to take place which without it could not exiſt.   For there is a very eſſential conſideration to be made in every Science, though ſpeculators are ſometimes apt to loſe ſight of it, which is, that in order that things may have exiſtence,   they muſt be *poſſible* ; in order that political regulations of any kind may obtain their effect, they muſt imply no direct contradiction, either open or hidden, to the nature of things, or to the other circumſtances of the government.   In reaſoning from this principle, we ſhall find that the ſtability of the Governing executive authority in England, and the weight it gives to the whole machine of the State, have actually enabled the Engliſh Nation, conſidered as a free Nation, to enjoy ſeveral advantages which would really have been totally unattainable in the other States we have mentioned in former Chapters, whatever degree of public virtue we might even ſuppoſe to have belonged to thoſe who acted in thoſe States as the adviſers of the People, or in general who were truſted with the buſineſs of framing laws *.

One of theſe advantages reſulting from the Solidity of the Government, is, the extraordinary perſonal freedom which all ranks of individuals in England enjoy . at the expence of the governing authority.   In the Roman Commonwealth, for inſtance, we ſee the Senate to have been veſted with a number of powers totally deſtructive of the liberty of the Citizens : and the continuance of theſe powers, was, no doubt, in a great meaſure owing to the treacherous remiſſneſs of thoſe

---

* I ſhould be very well ſatisfied though only the more reflecting claſs of readers were fully to underſtand the tendency of this Chapter : in the mean time it is conſiderably illuſtrated beyond what it was in the former Editions.

Men in whom the People trufted for repreffing them, or even to their determined refolution not to abridge thofe prerogatives. Yet, if we attentively confider the conftant fituation of affairs in that Republic, we fhall find that though we might fuppofe thofe perfons to have been ever fo truly attached to the caufe of the People, it would not really have been poffible for them to procure to the People an entire fecurity. The right enjoyed by the Senate, of fuddenly naming a Dictator with a power unreftrained by any law, or of invefting the Confuls with an authority of much the fame kind, and the power it at times affumed of making formidable examples of arbitrary Juftice, were refources of which the Republic could not, perhaps, with fafety have been totally deprived: and though thefe expedients frequently were ufed to deftroy the juft liberty of the People, yet they were alfo very often the means of preferving the Commonwealth.

Upon the fame principle we fhould poffibly find that the *Oftracifm*, that arbitrary method of banifhing Citizens, was a neceffary refource in the Republic of Athens. A Venetian Noble would perhaps alfo confefs, that however terrible the State Inquifition eftablifhed in his Republic may be even to the Nobles themfelves, yet it would not be prudent entirely to abolifh it. And we do not know but a Minifter of State in France, though we might fuppofe him ever fo virtuous and moderate a Man, would fay the fame with regard to the fecret imprifonments, the *lettres de cachet*, and other arbitrary deviations from the fettled courfe of law, which often take place in that kingdom, and in the other Monarchies of Europe. No doubt, if he was the Man we fuppofe, he would confefs the expedients we mention have in numberlefs inftances been villainoufly proftituted to gratify the wantonnefs and private revenge of Minifters, or of thofe who had any

P p

interest with them; but still perhaps he would continue to give it as his opinion, that the Crown, notwithstanding its apparent immense strength, cannot avoid
recurring at times to expedients of this kind; much
less could it publicly and absolutely renounce them for
ever.

It is therefore a most advantageous circumstance in
the English Government, that its security renders all such
expedients unnecessary, and that the Representatives of the
People have not only been constantly willing to promote
the public liberty, but that the general situation of affairs
has also enabled them to carry their precautions so far as
they have done. And indeed, when we consider what
prerogatives the Crown, in England, has sincerely renounced—that in consequence of the independence conferred on the Judges, and of the method of *Trial by Jury*,
it is deprived of all means of influencing the settled course
of the law both in civil and criminal matters,—that it has
renounced all power of seizing the property of individuals, and even of restraining in any manner whatsoever,
and for the shortest time, the liberty of their persons, we
do not know what we ought most to admire, whether the
public virtue of those who have deprived the supreme
Executive Power of all those dangerous prerogatives, or
the nature of that same Power, which has enabled it to
give them up without ruin to itself—whether the happy
frame of the English Government, which makes those in
whom the People trust, continue so faithful in the discharge of their duty, or the solidity of that same Government, which really can afford to leave to the People so
extensive a degree of freedom *.

* At the times of the invasions of the pretender, assisted by
the forces of hostile nations, the *Habeas Corpus* Act was indeed suspended (which by the bye may serve as one proof,
that in proportion as a Government is any how in danger, it
becomes necessary to abridge the liberty of the subject;) but
the executive power did not thus of itself stretch its own au-

Again, the Liberty of the Prefs, that great advantage enjoyed by the Englifh Nation, does not exift in any of the other Monarchies of Europe, however well eftablifhed their power may at firft feem to be ; and it might even be demonftrated that it cannot exift in them. The moft watchful eye, we fee, is conftantly kept in thofe Monarchies upon every kind of publication ; and a jealous attention is paid even to the loofe and idle fpeeches of individuals. Much unneceffary trouble (we may be apt at firft to think) is taken upon this fubject ; but yet if we confider how uniform the conduct of all thofe Governments is, how conftant and unremitted their cares in thofe refpects, we fhall become convinced, without looking farther, that there muft be fome fort of neceffity for their precautions.

In Republican States, for reafons which are at bottom the fame as in the before-mentioned Governments, the People are alfo kept under the greateft reftraints by thofe who are at the head of the State. In the Roman Commonwealth, for inftance, the liberty of writing was curbed by the fevereft laws * : with regard to the freedom of

thority ; the precaution was deliberated upon and taken by the Reprefentatives of the People ; and the detaining of individuals in confequence of the fufpenfion of the Act, was limited to a certain fixed time. Notwithftanding the juft fears of internal and hidden enemies which the circumftances of the times might raife, the deviation from the former courfe of the law was carried no farther than the fingle point we have mentioned : Perfons detained by order of the Government, were to be dealt with in the fame manner as thofe arrefted at the fuit of private individuals : the proceedings againft them were to be carried on no otherwife than in a public place : they were to be tried by their Peers, and have all the ufual legal means of defence allowed to them, fuch as calling of witneffes, preremptory challenge of Juries, &c.

* The Law of the Twelve Tables had eftablifhed the punifhment of death againft the author of a Libel : nor was it by a *Trial by Jury* that they determined what was to be called a

ſpeech, things were, but little better, as we may conclude
from ſeveral facts; and many inſtances may even be produced of the dread with which the private Citizens, upon
certain occaſions, communicated their political opinions
to the Conſuls, or to the Senate. In the Venitian Republic, the preſs is moſt ſtrictly watched: nay, to forbear
to ſpeak in any matter whatſoever on the conduct of the
Government, is the fundamental maxim which they inculcate on the minds of the People throughout their dominions *.

Libel. SIQUIS CARMEN OCCENTASSIT, ACTITASSIT, CONDI-
DISSIT, QUOD ALTERI FLAGITIUM FAXIT, CAPITAL ESTO.
* Of this I have myſelf ſeen a proof ſomewhat ſingular,
which I beg leave of the Reader to relate. Being, in the
year 1768, at Bergamo, the firſt town of the Venetian State,
as you come into it from the State of Milan, about an hundred
and twenty miles diſtant from Venice, I took a walk in the
evening in the neighbourhood of the Town; and wanting to
know the names of ſeveral places which I ſaw at a diſtance,
I ſtopped a young Countryman to aſk him information.——
Finding him to be a ſenſible young man, I entered into ſome
farther converſation with him; and as he had himſelf a
great inclination to ſee Venice, he aſked me whether I propoſed to go there? I anſwered that I did: on which he immediately warned me, when I was at Venice not to ſpeak of
the Prince (del Prencipe,) an appellation aſſumed by the Venetian Government, in order, as I ſuppoſe, to convey to the
People a greater idea of their union among themſelves. As
I wanted to hear him talk farther on the ſubject, I pretended
to be entirely ignorant in that reſpect, and aſked for what
reaſon I muſt not ſpeak of the Prince? But he (after the
manner of the common people in Italy, who, when ſtrongly
affected by any thing, rather chooſe to expreſs themſelves by
ſome vehement geſture, than by words) ran the edge of his
hand, with great quickneſs, along his neck, meaning thereby
to expreſs, that being ſtrangled, or having one's throat cut,
was the inſtant conſequence of taking ſuch liberty.

With refpect therefore to this point, it may again be looked upon as a moft advantageous circumftance in the Englifh Government, that thofe who have been at the head of the People, have not only been conftantly difpofed to procure the public liberty, but alfo that they have found it poffible for them to do fo; and that the remarkable ftrength and fteadinefs of the Government has admitted of that extenfive freedom of fpeaking and writing which the People of England enjoy. A moft advantageous privilege, this! which, affording to every Man a means of laying his complaints before the Public, procures him almoft a certainty of redrefs againft any act of oppreffion that he may have been expofed to: and which leaving, moreover, to every Subject a right to give his opinion on all public matters, and, by thus influencing the fentiments of the Nation, to influence thofe of the Legiflature itfelf (which is fooner or later obliged to pay a deference to them,) procures to him a fort of Legiflative authority of a much more efficacious and beneficial nature than any formal right he might enjoy of voting by a mere *yea* or *nay*, upon general propofitions fuddenly offered to him, and which he could have neither a fhare in framing, nor any opportunity of objecting to, and modifying.

A privilege which, by raifing in the People a continual fenfe of their fecurity, and affording them undoubted proofs that the Government, whatever may be its form, is ultimately deftined to enfure the happinefs of thofe who live under it, is both one of the greateft advantages of Freedom, and its fureft characteriftic. The kind of fecurity as to their perfons and poffeffions which Subjects who are totally deprived of that privilege, enjoy at particular times, under other Governments, perhaps may intitle them to look upon themfelves as the well adminiftered property of Mafters who rightly underftood their own interefts; but it is the right of canvaffing without faar the conduct of thofe who are placed at their head, which conftitutes a free Nation *.

The unbounded freedom of debate poffeffed by the Englifh Parliament, is alfo a confequence of the peculiar ftability of the Government. All Sovereigns have agreed in their jealoufy of Affemblies of this kind, in their dread of the privileges of Affemblies who attract in fo high a degree the attention of the reft of the People, who in a courfe of time become connected by fo many effential ties with the bulk of the Nation, and acquire fo much real influence by the effential fhare they muft needs have in the management of public affairs, and by the eminent fervices, in fhort, which they are able to perform to the Community †. Hence it has happened that Monarchs, or fingle Rulers, in all Countries, have endeavoured to difpenfe with the Affiftance of Affemblies like thofe we mention, notwithftanding the capital advantages they might have derived from their fervices towards the good government of the State; or if the circumftances of the times have rendered it expedient for them to call fuch Affemblies together, they have ufed the utmoft endeavours in abridging thofe privileges and legiflative claims which they foon found to prove fo hoftile to their fecurity: in fhort, they have ever found it impracticable to place any unreferved truft in public Meetings of this kind.

We may here name Cromwell, as he was fupported by

* If we confider the great advantages to public liberty which refult from the inftitution of the Trial by Jury, and from the Liberty of the Prefs, we fhall find England to be in reality a more Democratical State than any other we are acquainted with. The Judicial power, and the Cenforial power, are vefted in the People.

† And which they do actually perform, till they are able to throw off the reftraints of impartiality and moderation; a thing which, being Men, they never fail to do when their influence is generally eftablifhed, and proper opportunities offer. Sovereigns know thefe things, and dread them.

a numerous army, and poffeffed more power than any
foreign Monarch who has not been fecured by an armed
force. Even after he had *purged*, by the agency of Colonel Pride, and two regiments, the Parliament that was
fitting when his power became fettled, thereby thrufting
out all his opponents to the amount of about two hundred, he foon found his whole authority endangered by
their proceedings, and was at laft under a neceffity of
turning them out in the military manner with which every one is acquainted. Finding ftill a Meeting of this
kind highly expedient to legalize his military authority,
he called together that Affembly which was called *Bare-*
bone's Parliament. He had himfelf chofen the Members
of this Parliament, to the number of about an hundred
and twenty, and they had feverally received the fummons
from him : yet notwithftanding this circumftance, and
the total want of perfonal weight in moft of the Members, he began in a very few months, and in the midft of
his powerful victorious army, to feel a ferious alarm at
their proceedings ; he foon heard them talk of their own
divine commiffion, and of the authority they had received
from the *Lord ;* and, in fhort, finding he could not truft
them, he employed the offices of a fecond Colonel, to
effect their difmiffion. Being now dignified with the legal appellation of *Protector*, he ventured to call a Parliament elected by confiderable parts of the People; but
though the exiftence of this Parliament was grounded,
we might fay grafted, upon his own ; and though bands
of Soldiers were even pofted in the avenues to keep out
all fuch Members as refufed to take certain perfonal engagements to him, he made fuch hafte, in the iffue, to rid
himfelf of their prefence, as to contrive a mean quibble
or device to fhorten the time of their fitting by ten or
twelve days *. To a fourth Affembly he again applied ;
but, though the elections had been fo managed as to pro-

---

* They were to have fat five months ; but Cromwell pretended that the months were to confift of only twenty-eight.

cure him a formal tender of the Crown during the firſt ſitting, he put a final end to the ſecond with reſentment and precipitation *.

The example of the Roman Emperors, whoſe power was outwardly ſo prodigious, may alſo be introduced here. They uſed to ſhow the utmoſt jealouſy in their conduct with reſpect to the Roman Senate; and that Aſſembly, which the prepoſſeſſion of the People, who looked upon it as the ancient remains of the Republic, had made it expedient to continue, were not ſuffered to aſſemble but under the drawn ſcymitars of the Prætorian guards.

Even the Kings of France, though their authority is ſo unqueſtioned, ſo univerſally reſpected, as well as ſtrongly ſupported, have felt frequent anxiety from the claims and proceedings of the Parliament of Paris; an Aſſembly of ſo much leſs weight than the Engliſh Parliament. The alarm has been mentioned which the late King at laſt expreſſed concerning their meaſures, as well as the expedient to which he reſorted to free himſelf from their preſence. And when the preſent King thought proper to call again this Parliament together, a meaſure highly prudent in the beginning of his reign, every jealous precaution was at the ſame time taken to abridge thoſe privileges of deliberating and remonſtrating upon which any diſtant claim to, or ſtruggle for, a ſhare of the ſupreme authority might be grounded.

It may be objected that the pride of Kings, or ſingle Rulers, makes them averſe to the exiſtence of Aſſemblies

days; as this was the way of reckoning time uſed in paying the army, and the fleet.

* The hiſtory of the conduct of the deliberating and debating Aſſemblies we are alluding to, in regard to the Monarchs, or ſingle Rulers of any denomination, who ſummon them together, may be expreſſed in a very few words. If the Monarch is unarmed, they over-rule him ſo as almoſt entirely to ſet him aſide: if his power is of a military kind, they form connections with the army.

like thofe we mention, and defpife the capital fervices which they might derive from them for the good govern- ment of their Kingdoms. I grant it may in fome mea- fure be fo. But if we examine into the general fituation of affairs in different States, and into the examples with which their Hiftory fupplies us, we fhall alfo find that the pride of thofe Kings agrees in the main with the intereft and quiet of their Subjects, and that their preventing the Affemblies we fpeak of from meeting, or, when met, from affuming too large a fhare in the management of public affairs, is, in a great meafure, matter of neceffity.

We may therefore reckon it as a very great advantage, that, in England, no fuch neceffity exifts. Such is the frame of the Government, that the Supreme executive authority can both give leave to affemble, and fhew the moft unreferved truft, when affembled, to thofe two Houfes which concur together to form the Legiflature.

Thefe two Houfes, we fee, enjoy the moft complete freedom in their debates, whether the fubject be *grievances*, or regulations concerning government matters of any kind: no reftriction whatever is laid upon them ; they may ftart any fubject they pleafe. The Crown is not to take any notice of their deliberations : its wifhes, or even its name, are not to be introduced in the debates. And, in fhort, what makes the freedom of deliberating, exer- cifed by the two Houfes, really to be unlimited, unbound- ed, is the privilege, or fovereignty we may fay, enjoyed by each within its own walls, in confequence of which nothing done or faid in Parliament, is to be queftioned in any place out of Parliament. Nor will it be pretended by thofe perfons who are acquainted with the Englifh Hiftory, that thofe privileges of Parliament we mention are nominal privileges, only privileges upon paper, which the Crown has difregarded whenever it has thought proper, and to the violations of which the Parliament have ufed very tamely to fubmit. That thefe remarkable advantages,—that this total freedom from any compulfion or even fear, and in fhort this unlimited liberty of debate, fo ſtrictly claimed by the Parliament, and ſo ſcrupulouſly allowed by the Crown, ſhould be exerciſed year after year during a long courſe of time, without producing the leaſt relaxation in the execution of the laws, the ſmalleſt degree of anarchy, are certainly very ſingular political phenomena.

It may be ſaid that the remarkable Solidity of the governing executive authority, in England, operates to the advantage of the People with reſpect to the objects we mention, in a two-fold manner. In the firſt place, it takes from the great Men in the Nation all ſerious ambition to invade this authority, thereby preventing thoſe anarchical and more or leſs bloody ſtruggles to reſult from their debates, which have ſo conſtantly diſturbed other Countries. In the ſecond place, it inſpires thoſe Great Men with that ſalutary jealouſy of the ſame authority which leads them to frame ſuch effectual proviſions for laying it under proper reſtraints. On which I ſhall obſerve, by way of a ſhort digreſſion, that this diſtinguiſhed *ſtability* of the executive authority of the Engliſh Crown, affords an explanation for the peculiar manner in which public commotions have conſtantly been terminated in England, compared with the manner in which the ſame events have been concluded in other Kingdoms. When I mentioned, in a former Chapter, this peculiarity, in the Engliſh Government, I mean the accuracy, impartiality, and univerſality, of the proviſions by which peace, after internal diſturbances, has been reſtored to the Nation, I confined my compariſons to inſtances drawn from Republican Governments, purpoſely poſtponing to ſay any thing of Governments of a Monarchical form, till I had introduced the very eſſential obſervation contained in this Chapter, which is, that the power of *Crowns*, in other Monarchies, has not been able, by itſelf, to produce the ſame effects it has in England, that is, has not been able to inſpire the

Great Men in the State with any thing like that falutary jealoufy we mention, nor of courfe to induce them to unite in a real common caufe with the reft of the People.   In other Monarchies*, thofe Men, who, during the continuation of the public difturbances, were at the head of the People, finding it in their power, in the iffue, to parcel out, more or lefs, the Supreme governing authority (or even the State itfelf) and to transfer the fame to themfelves, conftantly did fo, in the fame manner, and from the very fame reafons, as it conftantly happened in the ancient Commonwealths ; thofe Monarchical Governments being in reality, fo far as that, of a Republican nature : and the governing authority was left, at the conclufion, in the fame undefined extent it had before†.   But in England, the great Men in the Nation finding themfelves in a fituation effentially different, loft no time in purfuits like thofe in which the great Men of other countries ufed to indulge themfelves on the occafion we mention.   Every Member of the Legiflature plainly perceived, from the general afpect of affairs and his feelings, that the Supreme executive authority in the State muft in the iffue fall fomewhere undivided, and continue fo ; and being moreover fenfible, that neither perfonal advantages of any kind, nor the power of any faction, but the law alone, could afterwards be an effectual reftraint upon its motions, they had no thought or aim left, except

* I mean, before the introduction of thofe numerous ftanding armies which are now kept by all the Crowns of Europe : fince that epoch, which is of no very ancient date, no Treaty has been entered into by thofe Crowns with any fubjects.

† As a remarkable inftance of fuch a Treaty may be mentioned that by which the War *for the Public good* was terminated in France.   It is quoted in page 30 of this Work.

the framing with care thofe laws on which their own
liberty was to continue to depend, and to reftrain a
power which they, fomehow, judged it fo impracticable to transfer to themfelves or their party, or to render themfelves independent of. Thefe obfervations I
thought neceffary to be added to thofe in the fifteenth
Chapter, to which I now refer the reader.

Nor has the great freedom of canvaffing political
fubjects we have defcribed, been limited to the Members of the Legiflature, or confined to the walls of
Weftminfter, that is, to that exclufive fpot on which
the two Houfes meet: the like privilege is allowed to
the other orders of the people; and a full fcope is
given to that fpirit of party, and a complete fecurity
infured to thofe numerous and irregular meetings,
which, efpecially when directed to matters of government, create fo much uneafinefs in the Sovereigns of
other countries. Individuals even may, in fuch meetings take an active part for procuring the fuccefs of
thofe public fteps which they wifh to fee purfued; they
may frame petitions to be delivered to the Crown, or
to both Houfes, either to procure the repeal of meafures already entered upon by Government, or to prevent the paffing of fuch as are under confideration, or
to obtain the enacting of new regulations of any kind:
they may feverally fubfcribe their names to fuch petitions: the law fets no reftriction on their numbers;
nor has it, we may fay, taken any precaution to prevent even the abufe that might be made of fuch freedom.

That mighty political engine, the prefs, is alfo at
their fervice; they may avail themfelves of it to advertife the time and place, as well as the intent of the
meetings, and moreover to fet off and inculcate the
advantages of thofe notions which the wifh is to fee adopted.

Such meetings may be repeated ; and every individual may deliver what opinion he pleafes on the propofed fubjects, though ever fo directly oppofite to the
views or avowed defigns of the Government. The
Member of the Legiflature may, if he choofes, have
admittance among them, and again enforce thofe to-
pics which have not obtained the fuccefs he expected,
in that houfe to which he belongs. The difappointed
Statefman, the Minifter turned out, alfo find the door
open to them : they may bring in the whole weight of
their influence and of their connections : they may exert every nerve to enlift the Affembly in the number of
their fupporters : they are bid to do their worft : they
fly through the Country from one place of meeting to
another : the clamour increafes : the Conftitution, one
may think, is going to be fhaken to its very foundations :—but thefe mighty ftruggles, by fome means or
other, always find a proportinate degree of re-action :
new difficulties, and at laft infuperable impediments,
grow up in the way of thofe who would take advantage of the general ferment to raife themfelves on the
wreck of the governing authority : a fecret force exerts itfelf, which gradually brings things back to a
ftate of moderation and calm ; and that fea fo ftormy,
to appearance fo deeply agitated, conftantly ftops at
certain limits which it feems as if it wanted the power
to pafs.

The impartiality with which juftice is dealt to all
orders of Men in England, is alfo in great meafure owing to the peculiar ftability of the Government: the
very remarkable, high degree, to which this impartiality is carried, is one of thofe things which, being impoffible in other Countries, are poffible under the Government of this Country. In the ancient Commonwealths, from the inftances that have been introduced
in a former place, and from others that might be quoted, it is evident that no redrefs was to be obtained for

the acts of injuftice or oppreffion committed by the Men poffeffed of influence or wealth upon the inferior Citizens. In the Monarchies of Europe, in former times, abufes of a like kind prevailed to a moft enormous degree. In our days, notwithftanding the great degrees of ftrength acquired by the different Governments, it is matter of the utmoft difficulty for fubjects of the inferior claffes to obtain the remedies of the law againft certain individuals: in fome Countries it is impoffible, let the abufe be ever fo flagrant; an open attempt to purfue fuch remedies being moreover attended with danger. Even in thofe Monarchies of Europe in which the Government is fupported both by real ftrength, and by civil inftitutions of a very advantageous nature, great differences prevail between individuals in regard to the facility of obtaining the remedies of the law; and to feek for redrefs is at beft, in many cafes, fo arduous and precarious an attempt as to take from injured individuals all thoughts of encountering the difficulty. Nor are thefe abufes we mention, in the former or prefent Governments of Europe, to be attributed only to the want of refolution in the Heads of thefe Governments. In fome Countries, the Sovereign, by an open defign to fupprefs thefe abufes, would have endangered at once his whole authority; and in others, he would find obftructions multiply fo in his way as to compel him, and perhaps foon enough too, to drop the undertaking. How can a Monarch make, alone, a perfevering ftand againft the avowed expectations of all the great Men by whom he is furrounded, and againft the loud claims of powerful claffes of individuals? In a Commonwealth, what is the Senate to do when they find that their refufing to protect a powerful offender of their own clafs, or to indulge fome great Citizen with the impunity of his friends, is likely to be productive of

ferious divifions among themfelves, or perhaps to difturbances among the People?

If we caft our eyes on the ftrict and univerfal impartiality with which juftice is adminiftered in England, we fhall foon become convinced that fome inward effential difference exifts between the Englifh
Government, and thofe of other Countries, and that
its power is founded on caufes of a diftinct nature. Individuals of the moft exalted rank do not entertain fo
much as the thought to raife the fmalleft direct oppofition to the operation of the law. The complaint of
the meaneft Subject, if preferred and fupported in the
ufual way, immediately meets with a ferious regard.
The Oppreffor of the moft extenfive influence, though
in the midft of a train of retainers, nay, though in the
fulleft flight of his career and pride, and furrounded
by thoufands of applauders and partifans, is ftopped
fhort at the fight of the legal paper, which is delivered into his hands, and a Tipftaff is fufficient to bring
him away, and produce him before the Bench.

Such is the *greatnefs* and uninterrupted *prevalence* of
the law, * fuch is in fhort the continuity of omnipo-
tence, of refiftlefs fuperiority, it exhibits, that the extent of its effects at length ceafes to be a fubject of obfervation to the Public.

Nor are great or wealthy Men to feek for redrefs or
fatisfaction of any kind, by any other means than fuch
as are open to all: even the Sovereign has bound himfelf to refort to no other: and experience has fhewn
that he may, without danger, truft the protection of
his perfon, and of the places of his refidence, to the
flow and litigious affiftance of the law.†

---

* *Lex magna eft & prævalebit.*

† I remember, during the time after my firft coming to
this Country, I took notice of the boards fet up from place to
place behind the inclofure of Richmond Park. " Whoever
" trefpaffes upon this ground will be *profecuted.*"

Another very great advantage attending this remarkable stability of the English Government we are describing, is, that the same is operated without the assistance of an armed standing force: the constant expedient this, of all other Governments. On this occasion I shall introduce a passage of Doctor Adam Smith *, in a Work published since the present Chapter was first written, in which passage an opinion certainly erroneous is contained: the mistakes of persons of his very great abilities deserve attention. This Gentleman, struck with the necessity of a sufficient power of re-action, of a sufficient strength on the side of Government, to resist the agitations attending on liberty, has looked round, and judged the English Government derived the singular stability it manifests from the standing force it has at its disposal: the following are his expressions. " To a Sovereign " who feels himself supported, not only by the natural " Aristocracy of the Country, but by a well-regulated " standing army, the rudest, the most groundless, and the " most licentious remonstrances can give little disturb- " ance. He can safely pardon or neglect them, and his " consciousness of his superiority naturally disposes him " to do so. *That degree of liberty which approaches to li-* " *centiousness, can be tolerated only in Countries where the* " *Sovereign is secured by a well-regulated standing army†."*
The above positions are grounded on the notion that an army places in the hand of the Sovereign an united irresistible strength, a strength liable to no accident, difficulties, or exceptions; a supposition this, which is not conformable to experience. If a Sovereign was endued

* An *Inquiry into the Nature and Causes of the Wealth of Nations.* Book V. Chap. I. Vol. II. p. 313, 314.

† The Author's design in the whole passage, is to shew that standing armies, under proper restrictions, cannot be hurtful to public liberty; and may in some cases be useful to it, by freeing the Sovereign from any troublesome jealousy in regard to this liberty.

with a kind of extraordinary power attending on his perfon, at once to lay under water whole legions of infur-
gents, or to repulfe and fweep them away by flafhes and
fhocks of the electrical fluid, then indeed he might ufe the
great forbearance above defcribed :—though it is not
perhaps very likely he would put up with the *rude* and
groundlefs remonftrances of his fubjects, and with their
licentious freedom, yet he might, with fafety, do or not do
fo, at his own choice. But an army is not that fimple
weapon which is here fuppofed. It is formed of Officers
and Soldiers who feel the fame paffions with the reft of
the people, the fame difpofition to promote their own intereft and importance, when they find out their ftrength,
and proper opportunities offer. What will therefore be
the refource of the Sovereign, if, into that army on the
affiftance of which he relies, the fame party fpirit creeps
by which his other Subjects are actuated ? Whereto
will he take his refuge, if the fame political caprices,
abetted by the ferious ambition of a few leading Men, the
fame reftleffnefs, and at laft perhaps the fame difaffection,
begin to pervade the fmaller kingdom of the army, by
which the main Kingdom or nation are agitated ?

. The prevention of dangers like thofe juft mentioned,
conftitutes the moft effential part of the precautions and
ftate craft of Rulers, in thofe governments which are fecured by ftanding armed forces. Mixing the troops
formed of natives with foreign auxiliaries, difperfing them
in numerous bodies over the country, and continually
fhifting their quarters, are among the methods that are
ufed ; which it does not belong to our fubject to enume-
rate, any more than the extraordinary expedients employed by the Eaftern Monarchs for the fame purpofes. But
one caution very effential to be mentioned here, and
which the Governments we allude to never fail to take
before every other, is to retrench from their unarmed
Subjects, a freedom which, tranfmitted to the Soldiery,
would be attended with fo fatal confequences : hindering
fo bad examples from being communicated to thofe in

whofe hands their power and life are trufted, is what eve-ry notion of felf-prefervation fuggefts to them : every weapon is accordingly exerted to fupprefs the rifing and fpreading of fo awful a contagion.

In general, it may be laid down as a maxim, that, where the Sovereign looks to his army for the fecurity of his perfon and authority, the fame military laws by which this army is kept together, muft be extended over the whole Nation : not in regard to military duties and exercifes ; but certainly in regard.to all that relates to the refpect due to the Sovereign and to his orders. The mar-tial law concerning thefe tender points, muft be univer-fal. The jealous regulations concerning mutiny and contempt of orders, cannot be feverely enforced on that part of the Nation which fecures the fubjection of the reft, and enforced too through the whole fcale of military fubordination, from the Soldier to the Officer, up to the very Head of the military Syftem,—while the more nu-merous and inferior part of the People are left to enjoy an unreftrained freedom :—that fecret difpofition which prompts Mankind to refift and counteract their Superi-ors, cannot be furrounded by fuch formidable checks on the one fide, and be left to be indulged to a degree of li-centioufnefs and wantonnefs on the other.

In a Country where an army is kept, capable of com-manding the obedience of the Nation, this army will both imitate for themfelves the licentioufnefs above men-tioned, and check it in the People. Every Officer and Soldier, in fuch a Country, claims a fuperiority in regard to other individuals ; and, in proportion as their affiftance is relied upon by the Government, expect a greater or lefs degree of fubmiffion from the reft of the People *.

* In the beginning of the paffage which is here examined, the Author fays, " Where the Sovereign is himfelf the Gen-" eral, and the principal Nobility and Gentry of the Coun-" try, the chief Officers of the army,—where the military " force is placed under the command of thofe who have the

The same Author concludes his above quoted obfer-vations concerning the fecurity of the power of an arm-ed Sovereign, by immediately adding, " It is in fuch " Countries only that it is unneceffary that the Sove-

" greateft intereft in the fupport of the civil authority, be-" caufe they have the greateft fhare of that authority, a " ftanding army can never be dangerous to liberty. Ou " the contrary, it may in fome cafes be favourable to liberty, " &c. &c."—in a Country fo circumftanced, a ftanding ar-my can never be dangerous to liberty : no, not the liberty of thofe principal Nobility and Gentry, efpecially if they have wit enough to form combinations among themfelves againft the Sovereign. Such an union as is here mentioned, of the civil and military powers, in the Ariftocratical body of the Nation, leaves loth the Sovereign and the People without re-fource. If the former Kings of Scotland had imagined to adopt the expedient of a ftanding army, and had trufted this army, thus defrayed by them, to thofe Noblemen and Gen-tlemen who had rendered themfelves hereditary Admirals, he-reditary High Stewards, hereditary High Conftables, here-ditary Great Chamberlains, hereditary Juftices General, he-reditary Sherriffs of Counties, &c. they would have but bad-ly mended the diforders under which the Government of their Country laboured, they would only have fupplied thefe No-bles with frefh weapons againft each other, againft the Sove-reign, and againft the People.

If thofe Members of the Britifh Parliament, who fome-times make the whole Nation refound with the clamour of their diffenfions, had an army under their command which they might engage in the fupport of their pretenfions, the reft of the People would not be the better for it. Happily the fwords are fecured, and force is removed from their De-bates.

The Author we are quoting, has deemed a Government to be a fimpler machine, and an army a fimpler inftrument, than they in reality are. Like many other perfons of great abilities, while ftruck with a certain peculiar confideration, he has overlooked others no lefs important.

" reign should be trusted with any discretionary power
" for suppressing even the wantonness of this licentious
" liberty." The idea here expressed coinciding with those
already discussed, I shall say nothing farther on the sub‑
ject. My reason for introducing the above expressions,
has been, that they lead me to take notice of a remarkable
circumstance in the English Government. From the ex‑
pression, *it is unnecessary the Sovereign should be trusted
with any discretionary power*, the Author appears to think
that a Sovereign at the head of an army, and whose pow‑
er is secured by this army, uses to wait to set himself in
motion, till he has received leave for that purpose, that
is, till he has been trusted with a power for so doing.
This notion in the Author we quote, is borrowed from
the steady and thoroughly legal Government of this
Country; but the like law doctrine, or principle, obtains
under no other Government. In all Monarchies (and
it is the same in Republics) the Executive power in the
State is supposed to possess, originally and by itself, all
manner of lawful authority : every one of its exertions
is deemed to be legal; and they do not cease to be so,
till they are stopped by some express and positive regula‑
tion. The Sovereign, and also the civil Magistrate, till
so stopped by some positive law, may come upon the Sub‑
ject when they choose; they may question any of his ac‑
tions; they may construe them into unlawful acts; and
inflict a penalty, as they please: in these respects they may
be thought to abuse, but not to exceed, their power. The
authority of the Government, in short, is supposed to be
unlimited so far as there are no visible boundaries set up
against it : behind and within these boundaries, lies what‑
ever degree of liberty the Subject may possess.

In England, the very reverse obtains. It is not the
authority of the Government, it is the liberty of the
Subject, which is supposed to be unbounded. All the
Individual's actions are supposed to be lawful, till that
law is pointed out which makes them to be otherwise.
The *onus probandi* is here transferred from the Subject

to the Prince. The Subject is not at any time to shew the grounds of his conduct. When the Sovereign or Magistrate think proper to exert themselves, it is their businefs to find out and produce the law in their own favour, and the prohibition againft the Subject*.

* I fhall take the liberty to mention another fact respecting myself, as it may serve to elucidate the above obfervations ; or at leaft my manner of expreffing them. I remember when I was beginning to pay attention to the operations of the Englifh Government, I was under a prepoffeffion of quite a contrary nature to that of the Gentleman whofe opinions have been above difcuffed : I ufed to take it for granted that every article of liberty the Subject enjoys in this Country, was grounded upon fome pofitive law by which this liberty was infured to him. In regard to the freedom of the prefs I had no doubt but it was fo, and that there exifted fome particular law, or rather feries of laws or legiflative paragraphs, by which this freedom was defined and carefully fecured : and as the liberty of writing happened at that time to be carried very far, and to excite a great deal of attention (the noife about the Middlefex election had not yet fubfided,) I particularly wifhed to fee thofe laws I fuppofed, not doubting but there muft be fomething remarkable in the wording of them. I looked into thofe law books I had opportunities to come at, fuch as Jacob's and Cunningham's *Law Dictionaries*, Wood's *Inftitutes*, and Judge Blackftone's *Commentaries*. I alfo found means to have a fight of Comyns's *Digeft of the Laws of England*, and I was again difappointed ; this Author, though this Work confifts of five folio Volumes, had not had, any more than the Authors juft mentioned, any room to fpare for the interefting law I was in fearch of. At length it occurred to me, though not immediately, that this liberty of the Prefs was grounded upon its not being prohibited,—that this want of prohibition was the fole, and at the fame time folid, foundation of it. This led me, when I afterwards thought of writing fomething upon the Government of this Country, to give the definition of the freedom of the prefs,

This kind of law principle, owing to the general spirit by which all parts of the Government are influenced, is even carried so far, that any quibble, or trifling circumstance, by which an Offender may be enabled to step aside, and escape, though ever so narrowly, the reach of the law, are sufficient to screen him from punishment, let the immorality or intrinsic guilt of his conduct be ever so openly admitted*.

Such a narrow circumscription of the exertions of the Government, is very extraordinary : it does not exist in any Country but this, nor could it. The situation of other Governments is such that they cannot thus allow themselves to be shut out of the unbounded space unoccupied by any law, in order to have their motions confined to that spot which express and previously declared provisions have chalked out. The power of these Governments being constantly attended with more or less precariousness, there must be a degree of discretion answerable to it†.

which is contained in p. 214, 215 : adding to it the important consideration of all actions respecting publications being to be decided by a Jury.

* A number of instances, some even of a ludicrous kind, might be quoted in support of the above observation. Even only a trifling flaw in the words of an Indictment, is enough to make it void. The reader is also referred to the fact mentioned in the note, p. 139. and to that in p. 329, 330, of this Work.

I do not remember the name of that Party Writer who, having published a treasonable writing in regard to which he escaped punishment, used afterwards to answer to his friends when they reproached him with his rashness, *I know I was writing within an inch of the gallows.* The law being both ascertained and strictly adhered to, he had been enabled to bring his words and positions so nicely within compass.

† It might perhaps also be proved, that the great lenity used in England in the administration of criminal justice, both

The foundation of that law principle, or doctrine, which confines the exertion of the power of the Government to fuch cafes only as are expreffed by a law in being, was laid when the Great Charter was paffed: this reftriction was implied in one of thofe general impartial articles which the Barons united with the People to obtain from the Sovereign. The Crown, at that time, derived from its foreign dominions, that ftability and inward ftrength in regard to the Englifh Nation, which is now in a fecret hidden manner annexed to the Civil branch of its office, and which, though operating by different means, continues to maintain that kind of confederacy againft it, and union between the different orders of the People. By the article in *Magna Charta* here alluded to, the Sovereign bound himfelf neither to *go*, nor *fend*, upon the Subject, otherwife than by the Trial of Peers, and the Law of the Land.* This article was however afterwards difregarded in practice, in confequence of the lawful efficiency which the King claimed for his *Proclamations*, and efpecially by the inftitution of the Court of *Star-Chamber*, which grounded its proceedings not only upon thefe proclamations, but alfo upon the particular rules it chofe to frame within itfelf. By the abolition of this Court (and alfo of the Court of High Commiffion) in the reign of Charles the Firft, the above provifion of the Great Charter was put in actual force ;

in regard to the mildnefs, and to the frequent remitting of punifhments, is effentially connected with the fame circumftance of the *ftability* of the Government. Experience fhews that it is needlefs to ufe any great degree of harfhnefs and feverity in regard to Offenders ; and the Supreme governing authority is under no neceffity of fhewing the fubordinate Magiftracies any bad example in that refpect.

* .... *Nec fuper eum ibimus, nec fuper eum mittemus, nifi per legale judicium parium vel per legem terræ.* Cap. XXIX.

and it has appeared by the event, that the very extraordinary reſtriction of the governing authority we are alluding to, and its execution, are no more than what the intrinſic ſituation of things, and the ſtrength of the Conſtitution, can bear*.

The law doctrine we have above deſcribed, and its being ſtrictly regarded by the High governing authority, I take to be the moſt characteriſtic circumſtance in the Engliſh Government, and the moſt pointed proof that can be given of the true freedom which is the conſequence of its frame. The practice of the Executive authority thus to ſquare its motions upon ſuch laws, and ſuch only, as are aſcertained and declared beforehand, cannot be the reſult of that kind of ſtability which the Crown might derive from being ſupported by an armed force, or, as the above-mentioned Author has expreſſed, from the Sovereign being the General of an army: ſuch a rule of acting is even contradictory to the office of a General: the operations of a General eminently depend for their ſucceſs, on their being ſudden, unforeſeen, attended by ſurpriſe.

In general, that ſtability of the power of the Engliſh

* The Court of Star Chamber was like a Court of Equity in regard to criminal matters; it took upon itſelf to decide upon thoſe caſes of offence upon which the uſual Courts of Law, when uninfluenced by the Crown, refuſed to decide, either on account of the ſilence of the laws in being, or of the particular rules they had eſtabliſhed within themſelves; which is exactly the office of the Court of Chancery (and of the Exchequer) in regard to matters of property. (See back, p. 112.) The great uſefulneſs of Courts of this kind has cauſed the Courts of Equity in regard to civil matters, to be ſupported and continued: but experience has ſhewn, as is above obſerved, that no eſſential inconvenience can ariſe from the Subject being indulged with the very great freedom he has acquired by the total abolition of all arbitrary or proviſional Courts in regard to criminal matters.

Crown we have defcribed, cannot be the refult of that kind of ftrength which arifes from an armed force : the kind of ftrength which is conferred by fuch a weapon as an army, is too uncertain, too complicate, too liable to accidents : in a word, it falls infinitely fhort of that degree of fteadinefs which is neceffary to counterbalance, and at laft quiet, thofe extenfive agitations in the People which fometimes feem to threaten the deftruction of Order and Government. An army, if its fupport be well directed, may be ufeful to prevent this reftleffnefs in the People from beginning to exift ; but it cannot keep it within bounds, when it has once taken place.

If from general arguments and confiderations, we pafs to particular facts, we fhall actually find that the Crown, in England, does not rely for its fupport, nor ever has relied, upon the army of which it has the command. From the earlieft times, that is, long before the invention of ftanding armies among European Princes, the Kings of England poffeffed an authority certainly as full and extenfive as that which they do now enjoy. After the weight they derived from their poffeffions beyond fea had been loft, a certain arrangement of things began to be formed at home, which fupplied them with a ftrength of another kind, though not lefs folid : and they began to derive from the Civil branch of their regal Office that fecure power which no other Monarchs had ever poffeffed, except through the affiftance of Legions and Prætorian guards, or of armies of Janiffaries, or of Strelitzes.

The Princes of the Houfe of Tudor, to fpeak of a very remarkable period in the Englifh Hiftory, though they had no other vifible prefent force than inconfiderable retinues of fervants, were able to exert a power equal to that of the moft abfolute Monarchs who ever did reign, equal to that of the Domitians or

Commoduſes, or of the Amuraths or Bajazets ; nay, it even was ſuperior, if we conſider the ſlow ſteadineſs and outward ſhow of legality with which it was attended throughout.

The ſtand which the Kings of the Houſe of Stuart were able to make, though unarmed, and only ſupported by the civil authority of their Office, during a long courſe of years, againſt the reſtleſs ſpirit which began to actuate the Nation, and the vehement political and religious notions that broke out in their time, is ſtill more remarkable than even the exorbitant power of the Princes of the Houſe of Tudor, during whoſe reign prepoſſeſſions of quite a contrary nature were univerſal.

The ſtruggle opened with the reign of James the Firſt ; yet he peaceably weathered the beginning ſtorm, and tranſmitted his authority undiminiſhed to his ſon. Charles the Firſt was indeed at laſt cruſhed under the ruins of the Conſtitution : but if we conſider that, after making the important national conceſſions contained in the *Petition of Right*, he was able, ſingle and unarmed, to maintain his ground without loſs or real danger during a ſpace of eleven years, that is, till the year 1640 and thoſe that followed, we ſhall be inclined to think that, had he been better adviſed, he might have avoided the misfortunes that befel him at length.

Even the events of the reign of James the Second afford a proof of that ſolidity which is annexed to the authority of the Engliſh Crown. Notwithſtanding the whole Nation, not excepting the army, were in a manner unanimous againſt him, he was able to reign full four years, ſtanding ſingle againſt all, without meeting with any open reſiſtance. Nor was ſuch juſtifiable and neceſſary reſiſtance eaſily brought about at length *. Though

* Mr. Hume is rather too anxious in his wiſh to exculpate James the Second. He begins the concluſive character he gives of him, with repreſenting him as a Prince *whom we may ſafely pronounce more unfortunate than criminal.* If we conſider

it is not to be doubted that the dethroning of James the Second would have been effected in the issue, and perhaps in a very tragical manner, yet, if had not been for the assistance of the Prince of Orange, the event would certainly have been postponed till a few years later. That authority on which James relied with so much confidence, was not annihilated at the time it was, otherwise than by a ready and considerable armed force being brought against it from the other side of the Sea, like a solid Fortress, which, though without any visible out-works, requires, in order to be compelled to surrender, to be battered with cannon.

If we look into the manner in which this Country has been governed since the Revolution, we shall evidently see that it has not been by means of the army the Crown has under its command, that it has been able to preserve and exert its authority. It is not by means of their Soldiers that the Kings of Great Britain prevent the manner in which elections are carried on, from being hurtful to them; for these Soldiers must move from the places of elections one day before such elections are begun, and not return till one day after they are finished. It is not by means of their military force that they prevent the several kinds of civil Magistracies in the Kingdom from invading and lessening their prerogative; for this military force is not to act till called for by these latter, and under their direction. It is not by means of their army that they lead the two Branches of the Legislature into that respect of their regal authority we have before de-

the solemn engagements entered into, not by his predecessors only, but by himself, which this Prince endeavoured to break, how cool and deliberate his attack on the liberties and religion of the people was, how unprovoked the attempt, and in short how totally destitute he was of any plea of self-defence or necessity, a plea to which most of the Princes who have been at variance with their Subjects had some sort of more or less distant claim, we shall look upon him as being perhaps the guiltiest Monarch that ever existed.

scribed; since each of these two Branches, severally, is possessed with an annual power of disbanding this army *.

There is another circumstance, which, abstractedly of all others, makes it evident that the executive authority of the Crown is not supported by the army : I mean the very singular subjection in which the military is kept in regard to the civil power in this Country.

In a Country where the governing authority in the State is supported by the army, the military profession, who, in regard to the other professions, have on their side the advantage of present force, being now moreover countenanced by the law, immediately acquire, or rather assume, a general ascendancy ; and the Sovereign, far from wishing to discourage their claims, feels an inward happiness in seeing that instrument on which he rests his authority, additionally strengthened by the respect of the People, and receiving a kind of legal sanction from the general outward consent.

And not only the military profession at large, but the individuals belonging to it, also claim personally a pre-eminence: chief Commanders, Officers, Soldiers or Janissaries, all claim, in their own spheres, some sort of exclusive privilege : and these privileges, whether of an honorific, or of a more substantial kind, are violently asserted, and rendered grievous to the rest of the Community, in proportion as the assistance of the military force is more evidently necessary to, and more frequently employed by, the Government.   These things cannot be otherwise.

* The generality of the People have from early times been so little accustomed to see any display of force used to influence the debates of the Parliament, that the attempt made by Charles the First to seize the *five members*, attended by a retinue of about two hundred Servants, was the actual spark that set in a blaze the heap of combustibles which the preceding contests had accumulated.   The Parliament, from that fact, took a pretence to make military preparations in their turn ; and then the Civil war began.

Now, if we look into the facts that take place in England, we shall find that a quite different order prevails from what is above described. All Courts of a military kind are under a conftant fubordination to the ordinary Courts of Law. Officers who have abufed their private power, though only in regard to their own Soldiers, may be called to account before a Court of Common Law, and compelled to make proper fatisfaction. Even any flagrant abufe of authority committed by Members of Courts Martial, when fitting to judge their own people, and determine upon cafes of a bare military kind, makes them liable to the animadverfion of the civil judge *.

* A great number of inftances might be produced to prove the above-mentioned fubjection of the Civil to the Military power. I fhall introduce one which is particularly remarkable : I meet with it in the periodical publications of the year 1746.

A Lieutenant of Marines, whofe name was *Frye,* had been charged, while in the Weft Indies, with contempt of orders, for having refufed, when ordered by the Captain, to affift another Lieutenant in carrying another Officer prifoner on board the Ship : the two Lieutenants wanted to have the Captain give the order in writing. For this Lieutenant *Frye* was tried at Jamaica by a Court Martial, and fentenced to fifteen years imprifonment, befides being declared incapable of ferving the King. He was brought home ; and his cafe, after being laid before the Privy Council, appearing in a juftifiable light, he was releafed. Some time after he brought an action againft Sir *Chaloner Ogle,* who had fat as Prefident to the above Court Martial, and had a verdict in his favour for one thoufand pounds damages (it was alfo proved that he had been kept fourteen months in the moft fevere confinement before he was brought to his Trial.) The Judge moreover informed him, that he was at liberty to bring his action againft any of the Members of the faid Court Martial he could meet with. The following part of the affair is ftill more remarkable,

To the above facts concerning the pre-eminence of the Civil over the Military Power at large, it is needless to add, that all offences committed by persons of the milita-

Upon application made by Lieutenant *Frye*, Sir *John Willes*, Lord Chief Justice of the Common Pleas, issued his Writ against Admiral *Mayne* and Captain *Rentone*, two of the Persons who had sat in the above Court Martial, who happened to be at that time in England, and were Members of the Court Martial that was then sitting at Deptford, to determine on the affair between Admirals Matthews and Lestock, of which Admiral *Mayne* was moreover President; and they were arrested immediately after the breaking up of the Court. The other Members resented highly what they thought the insult; they met twice on the subject; and came to certain *Resolutions*, which the Judge Advocate was directed to deliver to the Board of Admiralty, in order to their being laid before the King. In these resolutions they demanded " satisfaction for the high insult on their President, from " all persons how high soever in office, who have set on foot " this arrest, or in any degree advised or promoted it :"— moreover complaining, that, by the said arrest, " the order, " discipline, and government of his Majesty's armies by Sea " was dissolved, and the Statute 13 Car. II. made null and " void."

The altercations on that account lasted some months. At length the Court Martial thought it necessary to submit; and they sent to Lord Chief Justice Willes, a letter signed by the seventeen Officers, Admirals and Commanders, who composed it, in which they acknowledged that " *the resoluti-* " *ons of the 16 and 21 May were unjust and unwarrantable, and* " *do ask pardon of his Lordship and the whole Court of Common* " *Pleas, for the indignity offered to him and the Court.*"

This letter Judge Willes read in the open Court, and directed the same to be registered in the *Remembrance* Office, " as a memorial *to the present and future ages, that whoever* " *set themselves above the Law, will, in the end, find themselves* " *mistaken.*" The letter from the Court Martial, together with Judge Willes's acceptation, were inserted in the next Gazettee, 15th November 1746.

ry profeffion, in regard to individuals belonging to the
other claffes of the People, are to be determined upon by
the Civil Judge.　Any ufe they may make of their force,
unlefs exprefsly applied to, and directed by, the Civil Magiftrate, let the occafion be what it may, makes them liable to be convicted of murder for any life that may have
been loft.　Pleading the duties or cuftoms of their profeffion in extenuation of any offence, is a plea which the
Judge will not fo much as underftand.　Whenever
claimed by the Civil power, they muft be delivered up
immediately.　Nor can it, in general, be faid, that the
countenance fhewn to the military profeffion by the Ruling power in the State, has conftantly been fuch as to
infpire the bulk of the People with a difpofition tamely
to bear their acts of oppreffion, or to raife in Magiftrates
and Juries any degree of prepoffeffion fufficient to lead
them always to determine with partiality in their favour*.

The fubjection of the Military to the Civil power,
carried to that extent it is in England, is another characteriftic and diftinctive circumftance in the Englifh
Government.

It is fufficiently evident that a king does not look
to his army for his fupport, who takes fo little pains
to bribe and unite it to his intereft.

In general, if we confider all the different circum-

* The Reader may fee in the publications of the year
1770, the clamour that was raifed on account of a General
in the army (Gen. Ganfell) having availed himfelf of the
vicinity of his Soldiers to prevent certain Sheriff's Officers
from executing an arreft upon his perfon, at Whitehall. It however appeared that the General had done nothing more than
put forth a few of his Men in order to perplex and aftonifh
the Sheriff's Officers; and in the mean time he took an opportunity for himfelf to flip out of the way.　The violent
clamour we mention was no doubt owing to the party fpirit
of the time; but it neverthelefs fhews what the notions of
the bulk of the People were on the fubject.

stances in the English Government, we shall find that the army cannot possibly procure to the Sovereign any permanent strength, any strength upon which he can rely, and from it expect the success of any future and distant measures,

The public notoriety of the Debates in Parliament, induces all individuals, Soldiers as well as others, to pay some attention to political subjects: and the liberty of speaking, printing and intriguing, being extended to every order of the Nation by whom they are surrounded, makes them liable to imbibe every notion that may be directly contrary to the views of that power which keeps them.

The case would be still worse if the Sovereign was engaged in a contest with a very numerous part of the Nation. The general concern would increase in proportion to the vehemence of the Parliamentary Debates: Individuals, in all the different classes of the Public, would try their eloquence on the same subjects; and this eloquence would be in great measure exerted, during such interesting times, in making converts of the Soldiery: these evils the Sovereign could not obviate, nor even know, till it should be in every respect too late. A prince engaged in the contest we suppose, would scarcely have completed his first preparations, —his project would scarcely be half ripe for execution, before his army would be taken from him. And the more powerful this army might be, the more adequate, seemingly, from its numbers, to the task it is intended for, the more open it would be to the danger we mention.

Of this, James the Second made a very remarkable experiment. He had augmented his army to the number of thirty thousand. But when the day finally came in which their support was to have been useful to him, some deserted to the enemy; others threw down their arms; and those who continued to stand together, shewed more inclination to be spectators of, than agents in, the contest. In short, he gave all over for lost, without making any manner of trial of their assistance*. Tt

* The army made loud rejoicings on the day of the *acquittal of the Bishops*, even in the presence of the King, who had purposely repaired to Hounflow Heath on that day. He had not been able to bring a single regiment to declare an approbation of his measures in regard to the Test and Penal Statutes. The celebrated ballad, *lero lero lillibulero*, which is reported to have had such an influence on the minds of the People at that time, and of which Bishop Burnet says, " ne- " ver perhaps *fo flight a thing had fo great an effect*," originated in the army : " *the whole army, and at laft People both in* " *City and Country, were perpetually finging it.* "

To a King of England engaged in a project against public liberty, a numerous army, ready formed before hand, must, in the present situation of things, prove a very great impediment ; he cannot possibly give his attention to the proper management of it : the less so, as his measures for that purpose must often be contradictory to those he is to pursue with the rest of the People.

If a King of England, wishing to set aside the present Constitution, and to assimilate his power to that of the other Sovereigns of Europe, was to do me the honour to consult me as to the means of obtaining success, I would recommend to him, as his first preparatory step, and before his real project is even suspected, to disband his army, keeping only a strong guard, not exceeding twelve hundred men. This done, he might, by means of the weight and advantages of his place, set himself about undermining such constitutional laws as he diflikes ; using as much temper as he can, that he may have the more time to proceed. And when at length things should be brought to a crisis, then I would advise him to form another army, out of those friends or class of People whom the turn and incidents of the preceding contests will have linked and riveted to his interest : with this army he might now take his chance : the rest would depend on his general-

From all the facts before introduced, it is evident that the power of the Crown, in England, bears upon foundations that are quite peculiar to it, and that its security and strength are obtained by means totally different from those by which the same advantages are so incompletely procured, and so deeply paid for in other Countries.

It is without the assistance of an armed force that the Crown, in England, is able to manifest that fearlessness of particular individuals, or whole classes of them, with which it discharges its legal functions and duties. It is without the assistance of an armed force it is able to counterbalance the extensive and unrestrained freedom of the People, it is able to exert that resisting strength which constantly keeps increasing in a superior proportion to the force by which it is opposed, that ballasting power by which, in the midst of boisterous winds and gales, it recovers and rights again the Vessel of the State*.

ship; and even in a great measure on his bare reputation in that respect.

This advice to the King of England I suppose: I would, however, conclude with observing to him, that his situation is as advantageous to the full, as that of any King upon earth; and upon the whole, that all the advantages that can possibly arise from the success of his plan, cannot make it worth his while to undertake it.

* There is a number of circumstances in the English Government which those persons who wish for speculative meliorations, such as Parliamentary reform, or other changes of a like kind, do not perhaps think of taking into consideration. If so, they are, in their proceedings, in danger of meddling with a number of strings, the existence of which they do not suspect. While they only mean reformation and improvements, they are in danger of removing the *Talisman* on which the existence of the Fabric depends, or, like King *Nisus's* daughter, of cutting off the fatal hair with which the fate of the city is connected.

It is from the Civil branch of its Office the Crown derives that ſtrength by which it ſubdues even the Military power, and keeps it in a ſtate of ſubjection to the Laws, unexampled in any other Country. It is from an happy arrangement of things it derives that uninterrupted ſteadineſs, that indiviſible ſolidity, which procures to the Subject both ſo certain a protection, and ſo extenſive a freedom. It is from the Nation it receives the force with which it governs the Nation. Its reſources are, accord, and not compulſion,—free action, and not fear,—and it continues to reign through the play, the ſtruggle, of the voluntary paſſions of thoſe who pay obedience to it*.

⊰⋅⊰⋅⊰⋅⊰⋅⊰⋅⊰⋅⊰⋅⊰⋅⊰⋅⊰⋅❖❖❖⊱⋅⊳⋅⊳⋅⊳⋅⊳⋅⊳⋅⊳⋅⊳⋅⊳⋅⊳

C H A P. XVIII.

How far the Examples of Nations who have loſt their Liberty, are applicable to England.

EVERY Government, thoſe Writers obſerve who have treated on theſe ſubjects, containing within itſelf the efficient cauſe of its ruin, a cauſe which is eſſentially connected with thoſe very circumſtances that had produced its proſperity; the advantages attending the Engliſh Government cannot therefore, according to theſe Writers, exempt it from that hidden defect

---

* Many perſons, ſatisfied with ſeeing the elevation and upper parts of a building, think it immaterial to give a look under ground, and notice the foundation. Thoſe Readers therefore who chooſe, may conſider the long Chapter that has juſt been concluded, as a kind of foreign digreſſion, or parentheſis, in the courſe of the Work.

which is secretly working its ruin ; and M. de Montesquieu, giving his opinion both on the effect and the
cause, says, the English Constitution will lose its liberty, will perish : " Have not Rome, Lacedæmon, and
" Carthage, perished ? It will perish when the Legis-
" lative power shall have become more corrupt than
" the Executive."

Though I do by no means pretend that any human
establishment can escape the fate to which we see every thing in Nature is subject, nor am so far prejudi-
ced by the sense I entertain of the great advantages
of the English Government, as to reckon among them
that of Eternity ; I will however observe in general,
that as it differs by its structure and resources from
all those with which History makes us acquainted, so
it cannot be said to be liable to the same dangers. To
judge of the one from the other, is to judge by analogy where no analogy is to be found ; and my respect
for the author I have quoted will not hinder me from
saying, that his opinion has not the same weight with
me on this occasion, that it has on many others.

Having neglected, as indeed all systematic Writers
upon Politics have done, very attentively to inquire
into the real foundations of Power, and of Government,
among Mankind, the principles he lays down are not
always so clear, or even so just, as we might have expected from a Man of so true a genius. When he
speaks of England, for instance, his observations are
much too general : and though he had frequent opportunities of conversing with Men who had been personally concerned in the public affairs of this Country,
and he had been himself an eye-witness of the operations of the English Government, yet, when he attempts to describe it, he rather tells us what he con-
jectured than what he saw.

The examples he quotes, and the causes of dissolution which he assigns, particularly confirm this observa-

tion. The Government of Rome, to speak of the one which, having gradually, and as it were of itself, fallen to ruin, may afford matter for exact reasoning, had no relation to that of England. The Roman People were not, in the latter ages of the Commonwealth, a people of Citizens, but of Conquerors. Rome was not a State, but the head of a State. By the immensity of its conquests, it came in time to be in a manner only an accessory part of its own Empire. Its power, became so great, that, after having conferred it, it was at length no longer able to resume it: and from that moment it became itself subjected to it, from the same reason that the Provinces themselves were to.

The fall of Rome, therefore, was an event peculiar to its situation; and the change of manners which accelerated this fall, had also an effect which it could not have had but in that same situation. Men who had drawn to themselves all the riches of the World, could no longer content themselves with the supper of Fabricius, and the cottage of Cincinnatus. That People, who were masters of all the corn of Sicily and Africa, were no longer obliged to plunder their neighbours of theirs. All possible Enemies, besides, being exterminated, Rome, whose power was military, became to be no longer an army; and that was the æra of her corruption; if, indeed, we ought to give that name to what was the inevitable consequence of the nature of things.

In a word, Rome was destined to lose her Liberty when she lost her Empire, and she was destined to lose her Empire, whenever she should begin to enjoy it.

But England forms a Society founded upon principles absolutely different. All liberty, and power, are not accumulated as it were on one point, so as to leave, every where else, only slavery and misery, consequently only seeds of division and secret animosity. From the one end of the island to the other the same laws take place, and the same interests prevail : the whole Nation, besides, equally concurs in the formation of the Government : no part, therefore, has cause to fear that the other parts will suddenly supply the necessary forces to destroy its liberty : and the whole have, of course, no occasion for those ferocious kinds of virtue which are indispensably necessary to those who, from the situation in which they have brought themselves, are continually exposed to such dangers, and, after having invaded every thing, must abstain from every thing,

The situation of the People of England, therefore, essentially differs from that of the People of Rome. The form of the English Government does not differ less from that of the Roman Republic : and the great advantages it has over the latter for preserving the liberty of the People from ruin, have been described at length in the course of this Work.

Thus, for instance, the total ruin of the Roman Republic was principally brought about by the exorbitant power to which several of its Citizens were successively enabled to rise. In the latter age of the Commonwealth, those Citizens went so far as to divide among themselves the dominions of the Republic, in much the same manner as they might have done lands of their own. And to them others in a short time succeeded, who not only did the same, but who even proceeded to that degree of tyrannical insolence, as to make cessions to each other, by express and formal compacts, of the lives of thousands of their Fellow-citizens. But the great and constant authority and weight of the Crown, in England, prevent, in thir very beginning, as we have seen, all misfortunes of this kind ; and the Reader may recollect what has been said before on that subject.

At last the ruin of the Republic, as every one knows, was completed. One of those powerful Citizens we mention, in process of time found means to exterminate all his competitors: he immediately affumed to himfelf the whole power of the State; and eftablifhed for ever after an arbitrary Monarchy. But fuch a fudden and violent eftablifhment of a Monarchical power, with all the fatal confequences that would refult from fuch an event, are calamities which cannot take place in England; that fame kind of power we fee is already in being; it is afcertained by fixed laws, and eftablifhed upon regular and well-known foundations.

Nor is there any great danger that that power may, by means of thofe legal prerogatives it already poffeffes, fuddenly affume others, and at laft openly make itfelf abfolute. The important privilege of granting to the Crown its neceffary fupplies, we have before obferved, is vefted in the Nation: and how extenfive foever the prerogatives of a King of England may be, it conftantly lies in the power of his People either to grant or deny him the means of exercifing them.

This right poffeffed by the People of England, conftitutes the great difference between them and all the other Nations that live under Monarchical Governments. It likewife gives them a great advantage over fuch as are formed into Republican States, and confers on them a means of influencing the conduct of the Government, not only more effectual, but alfo (which is more in point to the fubject of this Chapter) incomparably more lafting and fecure than thofe referved to the People in the States we mention.

In thofe States, the political rights which ufually fall to the fhare of the People, are thofe of voting in general Affemblies, either when laws are to be enacted, or Magiftates to be elected. But as the advantages arifing from thefe general rights of giving votes, are never very clearly afcertained by the generality of the People, fo neither are the confequences attending particular forms or modes of giving thefe votes, generally and completely underftood. They accordingly never entertain any strong and constant preference for one method rather than another; and it hence always proves but too easy a thing in Republican States, either by insidious proposals made at particular times to the People, or by well-contrived precedents, or other means, first to reduce their political privileges to mere ceremonies and forms, and at last entirely to abolish them.

Thus, in the Roman Republic, the mode which was constantly in use for about one hundred and fifty years, of dividing the Citizens into *Centuriæ* when they gave their votes, reduced the right of the greater part of them, during that time, to little more than a shadow. After the mode of dividing them by Tribes had been introduced by the Tribunes, the bulk of the Citizens indeed were not, when it was used, under so great a disadvantage as before; but yet the great privileges exercised by the Magistrates in all the public assemblies, the power they assumed of moving the Citizens out of one Tribe into another, and a number of other circumstances, continued to render the rights of the Citizens more and more ineffectual; and in fact we do not find that, when those rights were at last entirely taken from them, they expressed any very great degree of discontent.

In Sweden (the former Government of which partook much of the Republican form) the right allotted to the People in the Government, was that of sending Deputies to the General States of the Kingdom, who were to give their votes on the resolutions that were to be taken in that Assembly. But the privilege of the People of sending such Deputies was, in the first place, greatly diminished by several essential disadvantages under which these Deputies were placed with respect to the Body, or *Order*, of the Nobles. The same privilege of the People was farther lessened by their Deputies being deprived of the right of freely laying their different propofals before the States, for their affent or diffent, and attributing the exclufive right of framing fuch propofals, to a private Affembly which was called the *Secret Committee*. Again, the right allowed to the Order of the Nobles, of having a number of Members in this Secret Committee, double to that of all the other Orders taken together, rendered the rights of the People ftill more ineffectual. At the laft Revolution thofe rights we mention have been in a manner taken from the People; and they do not feem to have made any great efforts to preferve them *.

But the fituation of affairs in England is totally different from that which we have juft defcribed. The political rights of the People are infeparably connected with the right of Property—with a right which it is as difficult to invalidate by artifice, as it is dangerous to attack by force, and which we fee that the moft arbitrary Kings, in the full career of their power, have never offered to violate without the greateft precautions. A King of England who would enflave his People, muft begin with doing, for his firft act, what all other Kings referve for the laft; and he cannot attempt to deprive his Subjects of their political privileges, without declaring war againft the whole Nation at the fame time, and attacking every individual at once in his moft permanent and beft underftood intereft.

And that means poffeffed by the People of England, of influencing the conduct of the Government, is not only in a manner fecure againft any danger of being taken

U u.

* I might have produced examples of a number of Republican States in which the People have been brought, at one time or other, to fubmit to the lofs of their political privileges. In the Venetian Republic, for inftance, the right, now exclufively vefted in a certain number of families, of enacting laws, and electing the Doge and other Magiftrates, was originally vefted in the whole People.

from them: it is moreover attended with another advantage of the greateſt importance; which is that of conferring naturally, and as it were neceſſarily, on thoſe to
whom they truſt the care of their intereſts, the great privilege we have before deſcribed, of debating among themſelves whatever queſtions they think conducive to the
good of their Conſtituents, and of framing whatever bills
they think proper, and in what terms they chooſe.

This privilege of ſtarting new ſubjeƈts for deliberation,
and, in ſhort, of *propounding* in the buſineſs of legiſlation,
which, in England, is allotted to the Repreſentatives of
the People, ſets another capital difference between the
Engliſh Conſtitution, and the government of other free
States, whether limited Monarchies or Commonwealths,
and prevents that which, in thoſe States, proves a moſt
effeƈtual means of ſubverting the laws favourable to public liberty: I mean the undermining of theſe laws by the
precedents and artful praƈtices of thoſe who are inveſted
with the Executive Power in the Government.

In the States we mention, the *aƈtive* ſhare, or the buſineſs of *propounding*, in legiſlation, being ever allotted
to thoſe perſons who are inveſted with the Executive authority, they not only poſſeſs a general power, by means
of inſidious and well-timed propoſals made to the People, of getting thoſe laws repealed which ſet bounds to
their authority; but when they do not chooſe openly to
diſcover their wiſhes in that reſpeƈt, or perhaps even fear
to fail in the attempt, they have another reſource, which,
though ſlower in its operation, is not leſs effeƈtual in the
iſſue. They negleƈt to execute thoſe laws which they
diſlike, or deny the benefit of them to the ſeparate ſtrag-
gling individuals who claim them, and in ſhort introduce
praƈtices that are direƈtly derogatory to them. Theſe
praƈtiſes in a courſe of time become reſpeƈtable *Uſes*,
and at length obtain the force of *Laws*.

The People, even where they are allowed a ſhare in
legiſlation, being ever *paſſive* in the exerciſe of it, have
no opportunities of framing new proviſions by which
to remove theſe ſpurious praƈtices or regulations, and

declare what the law in reality is. The only refource
of the Citizens, in fuch a ftate of things, is either to
be perpetually cavilling, or openly to oppofe : and always exerting themfelves, either too foon, or too late,
they cannot come forth to defend their liberty, without incurring the charge, either of difaffection, or of
rebellion.

And while the whole clafs of politicians, who are
conftantly alluding to the ufual forms of limited Governments, agree in deciding that freedom, when once
loft, cannot be recovered*, it happens that the maxim, *principiis obfta*, which they look upon as the fafe-
guard of liberty, and which they accordingly never
ceafe to recommend, befides its requiring a degree of
watchfulnefs incompatible with the fituation of the
People, is in a manner impracticable.

But the operation of preferring grievances, which
in other Governments is a conftant fore-runner of public commotions, and that of framing new law remedies, which is fo jealoufly fecured to the Ruling power of the State, are, in England, the conftitutional and
appropriated offices of the Reprefentatives of the People.

How long foever the People may have remained in
a ftate of fupinenefs as to their moft valuable interefts,
whatever may have been the neglect and even the errors of their Reprefentatives, the inftant the latter
come either to fee thefe errors, or to have a fenfe of
their duty, they proceed, by means of the privilege we
mention, to fet afide thofe abufes or practices which,
during the preceding years, had become to hold the
place of the laws. To how low foever an eftate public liberty may happen to be reduced, they take it
where they find it, lead it back through the fame path,
and to the fame point, from which it had been compel-

* "Ye free Nations, remember this maxim : Freedom
" may be acquired, but cannot be recovered." *Rouff.*
Social Compact, Chap. VIII.

led to retreat; and the ruling power, whatever its u-
surpations may have been, how far foever it may have
overflowed its banks, is ever brought back to its old
limits.

To the exertions of the privilege we mention, were
owing the frequent confirmations and elucidations of
the Great Charter that took place in different reigns.
By means of the fame privilege the Act was repealed,
without public commotion, which had enacted that the
King's proclamation fhould have the force of law: by
this Act public liberty feemed to be irretrievably loft;
and the Parliament who paffed it, feemed to have done
what the Danifh Nation did about a century afterwards. The fame privilege procured the peaceable
abolition of the Court of Star-Chamber: a Court
which, though in itfelf illegal, had grown to be fo
refpected through the length of time it had been fuffered to exift, that it feemed to have for ever fixed
and riveted the unlawful authority it conferred on
the Crown. By the fame means the power was fet
afide which the Privy Council had affumed, of impri-
foning the Subject without admitting to bail, and even
mentioning any caufe: this power was in the firft inftance declared illegal by the *Petition of Right*; and
the attempts of both the Crown and the Judges to invalidate this declaration by introducing, or maintaining, practices that were derogatory to it, were as often
obviated, in a peaceable manner, by frefh declarations,
and, in the end, by the celebrated *Habeas Corpus* Act*.

* The cafe of the General Warrants, may alfo be mentioned as an inftance. The iffuing of fuch Warrants, with
the name of the perfon to be arrefted left blank, was a practice that had been followed in the Secretaries of State's office
for above fixty years. In a Government differently conftituted, that is, in a Government in which the Magiftrates,
or Executive Power, fhould have been poffeffed of the *Key*
of Legiflation, it is difficult to fay how the conteft might
have been terminated: thefe Magiftrates would have been

And I fhall take this opportunity to make the Reader obferve, in general, how the different parts of the Englifh Government mutually affift and fupport each other. It is becaufe the whole executive authority in the State is vefted in the Crown, that the People may without danger delegate the care of their liberty to Reprefentatives :—it is becaufe they fhare in the Government only through thefe Reprefentatives, that they are enabled to poffefs the great advantage arifing from framing and propofing new laws : but for this purpofe, it is again abfolutely neceffary that the *Crown*, that is to fay, a *Veto* of extraordinary power, fhould exift in the State.

It is, on the other hand, becaufe the balance of the People is placed in the right of granting to the Crown its neceffary fupplies, that the latter may, without danger, be intrufted with the great authority we mention; and that the right, for inftance, which is vefted in it of judging of the proper time for ealling and diffolving Parliaments (a right abfolutely neceffary to its prefervation) may exift without producing, *ipfo facto*, the ruin of public Liberty. The moft fingular Government upon Earth, and which has carried fartheft the liberty of the individual, was in danger of total deftruction, when Bartholomew Columbus was on his paffage to England, to teach Henry the Seventh the way to Mexico and Peru *.

but indifferently inclined to frame and bring forth a declaration by which to abridge their affumed authority. In the Republic of Geneva, the Magiftracy, inftead of refcinding the judgment againft M. Rouffeau, of which the Citizens complained, chofe rather openly to avow the maxim, that ftanding *Ufes* were valid derogations to the written Law, and ought to fuperfede it. This rendered the clamour more violent than before.

* As affairs are fituated in England, the diffolution of a

As a conclusion of this subject (which might open a field for speculations without end,) I shall take notice of an advantage peculiar to the English Government, and which, more than any other we could mention must contribute to its duration.   All the political passions of Mankind, if we attend to it, are satisfied and provided for in the English Government; and whether we look at the Monarchical, or the Aristocratical, or the Democratical part of it, we find all those powers already settled in it in a regular manner, which have an unavoidable tendency to arise at one time or other in all human Societies.

If we could for an instant suppose that the English form of Government, instead of having been the effect of a lucky concurrence of fortunate circumstances, had been established from a settled plan by a Man who had discovered, beforehand and by reasoning, all those advantages resulting from it which we now perceive from experience, and had undertaken to point them out to other men capable of judging of what he said to them, the following is, most likely, the manner in which he would have expressed himself.

' Nothing is more chimerical, he would have said,
' than a state either of total equality, or total liberty,
' amongst Mankind. In all societies of men, some Pow-
' er will necessarily arise. This power, after gradually
' becoming confined to a smaller number of persons,
' will, by a like necessity, at last fall into the hands
' of a single Leader: and these two effects (of which
' you may see constant examples in History) arising
' from the ambition of the one part of Mankind, and
' from the various affections and passions of the other;
' are absolutely unavoidable.

' Let us, therefore, admit this evil at once, since it

Parliament on the part of the Crown, is no more than an appeal either to the People themselves, or to another Parliament.

‘ is impoffible to avoid it. Let us, of ourfelves, efta-
‘ blifh a Chief among us, fince we muft, fome time
‘ or other, fubmit to one : we fhall by this means ef-
‘ fectually prevent the conflicts that would arife a-
‘ mong the competitors for that ftation. But let us,
‘ above all, eftablifh him fingle ; left, after fucceffively
‘ raifing himfelf on the ruins of his Rivals, he fhould
‘ finally eftablifh himfelf whether we will or not, and
‘ through a train of the moft difadvantageous incidents.

‘ Let us even give him every thing we can poffibly
‘ give without endangering our fecurity. Let us call
‘ him our Sovereign ; let us make him confider the
‘ State as being his own patrimony ; let us grant him,
‘ in fhort, fuch perfonal privileges as none of us can
‘ ever hope to rival him in, and we fhall find thofe
‘ things which we were at firft inclined to confider as
‘ a great evil, will be in reality a fource of advantages
‘ to the Community. We fhall be the better able to
‘ fet bounds to that Power which we fhall have thus
‘ afcertained and fixed in one place. We fhall have
‘ the more interefted the Man whom we fhall have
‘ put in poffeffion of fo many advantages, in the faith-
‘ ful difcharge of his duty. And we fhall have thus
‘ procured for each of us, a powerful protector, at
‘ home, and for the whole Community, a defender
‘ againft foreign enemies, fuperior to all poffible
‘ temptation of betraying his Country.

‘ You may alfo have obferved (he would continue,)
‘ that in all States, there naturally arifes around the
‘ perfon, or perfons, who are invefted with the public
‘ power, a clafs of Men, who, without having any
‘ actual fhare in that power, yet partake of its luftre :
‘ who, pretending to be diftinguifhed from the reft of
‘ the Community, do, from that very circumftance,
‘ become diftinguifhed from it : and this diftinction,
‘ though only matter of opinion, and at firft thus fur-

‘ reptitiously obtained, yet may become in time the
‘ source of very grievous effects.

‘ Let us therefore regulate this evil which we can-
‘ not entirely prevent. Let us establish this class of
‘ Men who would otherwise grow up among us with-
‘ out our knowledge, and gradually acquire the most
‘ pernicious privileges. Let us grant them distinctions
‘ that are visible and clearly ascertained: their nature
‘ will, by this means, be the better understood, and
‘ they will of course be much less likely to become
‘ dangerous. By this means, also, we shalt preclude
‘ all other persons from the hopes of usurping them.
‘ As to pretend to distinctions can thenceforward be
‘ no longer a title to obtain them, every one who shall
‘ not be expressly included in their number, must con-
‘ tinue to confess himself one of the People ; and just
‘ as we said before, let us choose ourselves one Master
‘ that we may not have fifty, so let us again say here,
‘ let us establish three hundred Lords, that we may
‘ not have ten thousand Nobles.

‘ Besides, our pride will better reconcile itself to a
‘ superiority which it will no longer think of disput-
‘ ing. Nay, as they will themselves see us to be be-
‘ forehand in acknowledging it, they will think them-
‘ selves under no necessity of being insolent to furnish
‘ us a proof of it. Secure as to their privileges, all
‘ violent measures on their part for maintaining, and
‘ at last perhaps extending them, will be prevented :
‘ they will never combine together with any degree
‘ of vehemence, but when they really have cause to
‘ think themselves in danger ; and by having made
‘ them indisputably great Men, we shall have a chance
‘ of often seeing them behave like modest and virtuous
‘ Citizens.

‘ In fine, by being united in a regular Assembly,
‘ they will form an intermediate Body in the State,
‘ that is to say, a very useful part of the Government.

‘ It is alfo neceffary, our Lawgiver would farther
‘ add, that We, the People, fhould have an influence up-
‘ on Government: it is neceffary for our own fecurity;
‘ it is no lefs neceffary for the fecurity of the Government
‘ itfelf. But experience muft have taught you, at the fame
‘ time, that a great body of Men cannot act, without be-
‘ ing, though they are not aware of it, the inftruments
‘ of the defigns of a fmall number of perfons; and that
‘ the power of the People is never any thing but the pow-
‘ er of a few Leaders, who (though it may be impoffible
‘ to tell when or how) have found means to fecure to
‘ themfelves the direction of its exercife.

‘ Let us, therefore, be alfo before-hand with this other
‘ inconvenience. Let us effect openly what would, other-
‘ wife, take place in fecret. Let us intruft our power,
‘ before it be taken from us by addrefs. Thofe whom we
‘ fhall have exprefsly made the depofitaries of it, being
‘ freed from any anxious care about fupporting them-
‘ felves, will have no object but to render it ufeful:
‘ They will ftand in awe of us the more, becaufe they will
‘ know that they have not impofed upon us; and inftead
‘ of a fmall number of Leaders, who would imagine they
‘ derive their whole importance from their own dexterity,
‘ we fhall have exprefs and acknowledged Reprefenta-
‘ tives, who will be accountable to us, for the evils of
‘ the State.

‘ But above all, by forming our Government with a
‘ fmall number of perfons, we fhall prevent any diforder
‘ that may take place in it, from ever becoming danger-
‘ oufly extenfive. Nay more, we fhall render it capable
‘ of ineftimable combinations and refources, which would
‘ be utterly impoffible in that Government of all, which
‘ never can be any thing but uproar and confufion.

‘ In fhort, by exprefsly divefting ourfelves of a power
‘ of which, we fhould, at beft, have only an apparent
‘ enjoyment, we fhall be entitled to make conditions for
‘ ourfelves: we will infift that our liberty be augmented;

X x

' we will, above all, referve to ourfelves the right of
' watching and cenfuring that adminiftration which will
' have been eftablifhed by our own confent. We fhall
' the better fee its faults, becaufe we fhall be only Specta-
' tors of it; we fhall correct them the better, becaufe we
' fhall not have perfonally concurred in its operations*.

The Englifh Conftitution being founded upon fuch principles as thofe we have juft defcribed, no true comparifon can be made between it, and the Governments of any other States: and fince it evidently affures, not only the liberty, but the general fatisfaction in all refpects, of thofe who are fubject to it, in a much greater degree than any other Government ever did, this confideration alone affords fufficient ground to conclude, without looking further, that it is alfo more likely to be preferved from ruin.

And indeed we may obferve the remarkable manner in which it has been maintained in the midft of fuch general commotions as feemed unavoidably to prepare its deftruction. It rofe again, we fee, after the wars between Henry the Third and his Barons: after the ufurpation of Henry the Fourth: and after the long and bloody contentions between the Houfes of York and Lancafter. Nay, though totally deftroyed in appearance after the fall of Charles the Firft, and though the greateft efforts had been made to eftablifh another form of government in its ftead, yet, no fooner was Charles the Second called over, than the Conftitution was re-eftablifhed upon all its ancient foundations.

* He might have added,—" As we will not feek to coun-
" teract nature, but rather to follow it, we fhall be able to pre-
" cure ourfelves a mild Legiflation.   Let us not be without
" caufe afraid of the power of one Man; we fhall have no
" need either of a Tarpeian Rock, or of a Council of *Ten*.
" Having exprefsly allowed to the People a liberty to inquire
" into the conduct of Government, and to endeavour to cor-
" rect it, we fhall need neither State-prifons, nor fecret In-
" formers."

However, as what has not happened at one time may happen at another, future Revolutions (events which no form of Government can totally prevent) may perhaps end in a different manner from that in which paſt ones have been terminated. New combinations may poſſibly take place among the then ruling Powers of the State, of ſuch a nature as to prevent the Conſtitution, when peace ſhall be reſtored to the Nation, from ſettling again upon its ancient and genuine foundations; and it would certainly be a very bold aſſertion to decide, that both the outward form, and the true ſpirit of the Engliſh Government, would again be preſerved from deſtruction, if the ſame dangers to which they have in former times been expoſed, ſhould again happen to take place.

Nay, ſuch fatal changes as thoſe we mention may be introduced even in quiet times, or, at leaſt, by means in appearance peaceable and conſtitutional. Advantages, for inſtance, may be taken by particular factions, either of the feeble temper, or of the miſconduct, of ſome future King. Temporary prepoſſeſſions of the People may be made uſe of, to make them concur in doing what will prove afterwards the ruin of their own liberty. Plans of apparent improvement in the Conſtitution, forwarded by Men who, though with good intentions, ſhall proceed without a due knowledge of the true principles and foundations of Government, may produce effects quite contrary to thoſe which were deſigned, and in reality prepare its ruin *. The Crown, on the other hand, may, by the

---

* Inſtead of looking for the principles of Politics in their true ſources, that is to ſay, in the nature of the affections of Mankind, and of thoſe ſecret ties by which they are united together in a ſtate of Society, Men have treated that ſcience in the ſame manner as they did natural Philoſophy in the times of Ariſtotle, continually recurring to occult cauſes, and principles, from which no uſeful conſequence could be drawn. Thus, in order to ground particular aſſertions,

acquifition of foreign dominions, acquire a fatal independency on the People ; and if, without entering into any farther particulars on this fubject, I were required to point out the principal events which would, if they were ever to happen, prove immediately the ruin of the Englifh Government, I would fay,—The Englifh Government will be no more, either when the Crown fhall become independent on the Nation for its fupplies, or when the Reprefentatives of the People fhall begin to fhare in the Executive authority *.

they have much ufed the word Conftitution, in a perfonal fenfe, *the Conftitution loves, the Conftitution forbids,* and the like. At other times they have had recourfe to *Luxury,* in order to explain certain events ; and at others, to a ftill more occult caufe, which they have called *Corruption ;* and abundance of comparifons drawn from the human Body, have been alfo ufed for the fame purpofes : continued inftances of fuch defective arguments and confiderations occur in the Works of M. *de Montefquieu ;* though a man of fo much genius, and from whofe writings fo much information is neverthelefs to be derived. Nor is it only the obfcurity of the writings of Politicians, and the impoffibility of applying their fpeculative Doctrines to practical ufes, which prove that fome peculiar and uncommon difficulties lie in the way of the inveftigation of political truths ; but the remarkable perplexity which men in General, even the ableft, labour under, when they attempt to defcant and argue upon abftract queftions in politics, alfo juftifies this obfervation, and proves that the true firft principles of this fcience, whatever they are, lie deep both in the human feelings, and underftanding.

* And if at any time, any dangerous changes were to take place in the Englifh Conftitution, the pernicious tendency of which the People were not able at firft to difcover, reftrictions on the Liberty of the Prefs, and on the Power of Juries, will give them the firft information.

CHAP. XIX.

A few additional thoughts on the attempts that at particular times may be made to abridge the power of the Crown, and some of the dangers by which such attempts may be attended.

THE power of the Crown is supported by deeper, and more numerous, roots, than the generality of people are aware of, as has been observed in a former Chapter ; and there is no cause anxiously to fear that the wresting any capital branch of its prerogative, may be effected, in common peaceable times, by the mere theoretical speculations of Politicians. However, it is not equally impracticable that some event of the kind we mention may be brought about through a conjunction of several circumstances. Advantage may, in the first place, be taken of the minority, or even also the inexperience or the errors, of the person invested with the kingly authority. Of this a remarkable instance happened under the reign of King George the First, while that bill, by which the number of Peers was in future to be limited to a certain number, was under consideration in the House of Commons, to whom it had been sent from that of the Lords, where it had been passed. So unacquainted was the King at that time with his own interest, and with the constitution of that Government over which he was come to preside, that, having been persuaded by that party who wished success to the Bill, that the objection made against it by the House of Commons, was only owing to an opinion they entertained of the Bill being disagreeable to him, he was prevailed upon to send a message to them, to let them know that such an opinion was ill-grounded, and that should the Bill pass in their

House, it would meet with his assent *.   Considering the prodigious importance of the consequences of such a Bill, the fact is certainly very remarkable †.

With those personal disadvantages under which the Sovereign may lie for defending his authority, other causes or difficulty may concur :—such as popular discontents of long continuance in regard to certain particular abuses of influence or authority. The generality of the Public, bent, at that time, both upon remedying the abuses that are complained of, and preventing the like from taking place in future, will perhaps wish to see that branch of the prerogative which gave rise to them, taken from the Crown : a general disposition to applaud such a measure, if effected, will be manifested from all quarters ; and at the same time Men may not be aware that the only material consequence that may arise from depriving the Crown of that branch of power which has caused the public complaints, will perhaps be the having transposed that branch of power from its former seat to another, and having trusted it to new hands, which will be still more likely to abuse it than those in which it was formerly lodged.

In general, it may be laid down as a maxim, that Power, under any form of Government, must exist and be trusted somewhere. If the Constitution does not admit of a King, the governing authority is lodged in the hands of Magistrates. If the Government, at the same time it is a limited one, bears a Monarchical form, those shares of power that are retrenched from the King's prerogative, most likely continue to subsist, and are vested in a Senate, or Assembly of great Men, under some other name of the like kind.

* See the Collection of *Parliamentary Debates* ; I do not remember exactly what Volume.

† This Bill has been mentioned in the preceding part of this work.

Thus, in the Kingdom of Sweden, which, having been a limited Monarchy, may supply examples very applicable to the Government of this Country, we find that the power of convoking the General States (or Parliament) of that Kingdom, had been taken from the Crown; but at the same time we also find that the Swedish Senators had invested themselves with that essential branch of power which the Crown had lost.—I mean here to speak of the Government of Sweden as it stood before the last revolution.

The power of the Swedish King to confer offices and employments, had been also very much abridged. But what was wanting to the power of the King, the Senate enjoyed: it had the nomination of three persons for every vacant office, out of whom the King was to choose one.

The King of Sweden had but a limited power in regard to pardoning offenders; but the Senate likewise possessed what was wanting to that branch of its prerogative; and it appointed two persons, without the consent of whom the King could not remit the punishment of any offence.

The King of England has an exclusive power in regard to foreign affairs, war, peace, treaties;—in all that relates to military affairs; he has the disposal of the existing army, of the fleet, &c. The King of Sweden had no such extensive powers; but they neverthelefs existed; every thing relating to the above-mentioned objects was transacted in the Assembly of the Senate; the majority decided; the King was obliged to submit to it; and his only privilege consisted in his vote being accounted two*.

---

* The Swedish Senate was usually composed of sixteen Members. In regard to affairs of smaller moment, they formed themselves into two divisions; in either of these, when they did sit, the presence of seven Members was required for the effectual transacting of business: in affairs of

If we purfue farther our inquiry on the fubject, we fhall find that the King of Sweden could not raife whom he pleafed to the office of Senator, as the King of England can, in regard to the office of member of the Privy Council; but the Swedifh States, in the Affembly of whom the Nobility enjoyed moft capital advantages poffeffed a fhare of the power we mention, in conjunction with the King; and in cafes of vacancies in the Senate, they elected three perfons, out of whom the King was to return one.

The King of England may, at all times, deprive his Minifters of their employments. The King of Sweden could remove no man from his office; but the States enjoyed the power that had been denied to the King; and they might deprive of their places both the Senators, and thofe perfons in general who had a fhare in the Adminiftration.

The King of England has the power of diffolving, or keeping affembled as long as he pleafes, his Parliament. The King of Sweden had not that Power; but the State might, of themfelves, prolong their duration as they thought proper.

Thofe perfons who think that the prerogative of a King

importance, the Affembly was formed of the whole Senate; and the prefence of ten Members was required to give force to the refolutions. When the King could not, or would not, take his feat, the Senate proceeded neverthelefs, and the majority continued to be equally decifive.

As the Royal Seal was neceffary for putting in execution the refolutions of the Senate, King Adolphus Frederick, father to the prefent King, tried, by refufing to lend the fame, to procure that power which he had not by his fuffrage, and to ftop the proceedings of the Senate. Great debates, in confequence of that pretenfion, arofe, and continued for a while; but, at laft, in the year 1756, the King was overruled by the Senate, who ordered a feal to be made, that was named the *King's Seal*, which they affixed to their official refolutions, when the King refufed to lend his own.

cannot be too much abridged, and that power lofes all its influence on the difpofitions and views of thofe who poffefs it, according to the kind of name ufed to exprefs thofe offices by which it is conferred, may be fatisfied, no doubt, to behold thofe branches of power that were taken from a King, diftributed to feveral bodies, and fhared in by the Reprefentatives of the People: but thofe who think that Power, when parcelled and diffufed, is never fo well repreffed and regulated as when it is confined to a fole indivifible feat, that keeps the Nation united and awake,—thofe who know that, names by no means altering the intrinfic nature of things, the Reprefentatives of the People, as foon as they are vefted with independent authority, become *ipfo facto* its Mafters,—thofe perfons, I fay, will not think it a very happy regulation in the former Conftitution of Sweden, to have deprived the King of prerogatives formerly attached to his office in order to veft the fame either in a Senate, or in the Deputies of the People, and thus to have trufted with a fhare in the exercife of the public power, thofe very Men whofe Conftitutional office fhould have been to watch and reftrain it.

To the indivifibility of the governing authority in England, the community of intereft which takes place among all orders of Men, is owing; and from this community of intereft rifes, as a neceffary confequence, the liberty enjoyed by all ranks of fubjects. This obfervation has been infifted upon at length in the courfe of this Work. The fhorteft reflection on the frame of the human heart fuffices to convince us of its truth, and at the fame time manifefts the danger that would refult from making any changes in the form of the exifting Government by which this general community of intereft might be leffened,— unlefs we are at the fame time alfo determined to believe, that partial Nature forms men in this Ifland, of quite other ftuff than the felfifh and ambitious one of which fhe ever made them in other Countries*.

Y y

* Such regulations as may capitally affect, through their confequences, the equipoife of a Government, may be

But paſt experience does not by any means allow us to entertain ſo pleaſing an opinion. The peruſal of the Hiſtory of this Country will ſhew us, that the care of its Legiſlators for the welfare of the ſubject, always kept

brought about, even though the promoters themſelves of thoſe regulations are not aware of their tendency. At the ſame time the bill was paſſed in the laſt century, by which it was enacted that the Crown ſhould give up its prerogative of diſſolving the Parliament then ſitting, the generality of People had no thought of the calamitous conſequences that were to follow: very far from it. The King himſelf certainly felt no very great apprehenſion on that account; elſe he would not have given his aſſent: and the Commons themſelves, it appears, had but very faint notions of the capital changes which the Bill would ſpeedily effect in their political ſituation.

When the Crown of Sweden was, in the firſt inſtance, ſtripped of all the different prerogatives we have mentioned, it does not appear that thoſe meaſures were effected by ſudden, open proviſions for that purpoſe: it is very probable they had been prepared by indirect regulations formerly made, the whole tendency of which ſcarcely any body perhaps could foreſee at the time they were framed.

When the Bill was in agitation, that has been mentioned in the former part of this work, by which the Houſe of Peers was in future to be limited to a certain number that was not to be exceeded, the great conſtitutional conſequences of the Bill were ſcarcely attended to by any body. The King himſelf certainly ſaw no harm in it, ſince he ſent an open meſſage to promote the paſſing of it: a meaſure which I cannot ſay how far it was in itſelf regular. The Bill was, it appears, generally approved out of doors. Its fate was for a long time doubtful in the houſe of Commons; nor did they acquire any glory with the bulk of the People by finally rejecting it: and Judge Blackſtone, as I find in his Commentaries, does not ſeem to have thought much of the Bill and its being rejected, as he only obſerves that the Commons " wiſh-
" ed to keep the door of the Houſe of Lords as open as
" poſſible." Yet, no Bill of greater conſtitutional import-

pace with the exigencies of their own fituation. When, through the minority, or eafy temper of the reigning Prince, or other circumftances, the dread of a fuperior power began to be overlooked, the public caufe was immediately deferted in a greater or lefs degree, and purfuit after private influence and lucrative offices took the place of patriotifm. When, under the reign of Charles the Firft, the authority of the Crown was for a while utterly annihilated, thofe very Men who, till then, had talked of nothing but Magna Charta and liberty, inftantly endeavoured openly to trample both under foot.

Since the time we mention, the former Conftitution of the Government having been reftored, the great outlines of public liberty have indeed been warmly and ferioufly defended: but if any partial unjuft laws or regulations have been made, efpecially fince the Revolution of the year 1689, if any abufes injurious to particular claffes of individuals have been fuffered to continue (facts into the truth of which I do not propofe to examine here,) it will certainly be found upon enquiry, that thofe laws and thofe abufes were fuch as that from them the

ance was ever agitated in Parliament; fince the confequences of its being paffed would have been the freeing the Houfe of Lords, both in their Judicial and Legiflative capacities, from all conftitutional check whatever, either from the Crown, or the Nation. Nay, it is not to be doubted they would have acquired, in time, the right of electing their own Members: though it would be ufelefs to point out here by what feries of intermediate events the meafure might have been brought about. Whether there exifted any actual project of this kind, among the firft framers of the Bill, does not appear: but a certain number of the Members of the Houfe we mention, would have thought of it foon enough, if the Bill in queftion had been enacted into a law; and they would certainly have met with fuccefs, had they been but contented to wait, and had they taken time. Other equally important changes in the fubftance, and perhaps the outward form, of the Government, would have followed.

Members of the Legiflature well knew, that neither they, nor their friends, would ever be likely to fuffer.

If through the unforefeen operation of fome new regulation made to reftrain the royal prerogative, or through fome fudden public revolution, any particular bodies or claffes of individuals were ever to acquire a perfonal independent fhare in the exercife of the governing authority, we fhould behold the public virtue and patriotifm of the Legiflators and Great Men immediately ceafe with its caufe, and Ariftocracy, as it were watchful of the opportunity, burft out at once, and fpread itfelf over the Kingdom.

The Men who are now the Minifters, then the Partners of the Crown, would inftantly fet themfelves above the reach of the law, and foon after enfure the fame privilege to their feveral fupporters or dependants.

Perfonal and independent power being become the only kind of fecurity of which Men would now fhew themfelves ambitious, the *Habeas Corpus* Act, and in general all thofe laws which fubjects of every rank mention with love, and to which they look up for protection and fafety, would be fpoken of with contempt, and mentioned as remedies fit only for Countrymen and Cits:—it even would not be long before they were fet afide, as obftructing the wife and falutary fteps of the Senate.

The pretenfions of an equality of right in all Subjects, of whatever rank and order, to their property and to perfonal fafety, would foon be looked upon as an old-fafhioned doctrine, which the Judge himfelf would ridicule from the Bench. And the liberty of the prefs, now fo univerfally and warmly vindicated, would without lofs of time, be cried down and fuppreffed, as only ferving to keep up the infolence and pride of a refractory People.

And let us not believe that the miftaken People, whofe Reprefentatives we now behold making fuch a firm ftand againft the *indivifible* power of the Crown, would, amidft the general devaftation of every thing they hold dear, eafily find Men equally difpofed to reprefs the encroaching while *attainable*, power of a Senate and Body of Nobles.

The time would be no more when the People, upon whatever Men they let their choice fall, are sure to find them ready sincerely to join in the support of every important branch of public liberty.

Present or expected, personal power and independance on the laws being now the consequence of the trust of the People, wherever they should apply for servants, they would only meet with betrayers. Corrupting as it were every thing they should touch, they could confer no favour upon an individual but to destroy his public virtue; and to repeat the words used in a former Chapter, " their raising a Man would on- " ly be immediately inspiring him with views direct- " ly opposite to their own, and sending him to in- " crease the number of their enemies."

All these considerations strongly point out the very great caution which is necessary to be used in the difficult business of laying new restraints on the governing authority. Let therefore the less-informed part of the People, whose zeal requires to be kept up by visible objects, look if they choose upon the Crown as the only seat of the evils they are exposed to; mistaken notions on their part are less dangerous than political indifference, and they are more easily directed than roused,—but at the same time, let the more enlightened part of the Nation constantly remember, that the Constitution only subsists by virtue of a proper equilibrium,—by a line being drawn between Power and Liberty.

Made wise by the examples of several other Nations, by those which the History of this very Country affords, let the People, in the heat of their struggles in the defence of liberty, always take heed, only to reach, never to overshoot, the mark,—only to repress, never to transfer and diffuse, Power.

Amidst the alarms that may, at particular times,

arife from the really awful authority of the Crown, let it, on the one hand, be remembered, that even the power of the Tudors was oppofed and fubdued,—and on the other. let it be looked upon as a fundamental maxim, that, whenever the profpect of perfonal power and independance on the governing authority, fball offer to the view of the Members of the Legiflature, or in general of thofe Men to whom the People muft truft, even Hope itfelf is deftroyed. The Hollander, in the midft of a ftorm, though trufting to the experienced ftrength of the mounds that protect him, fhudders no doubt at the fight of the foaming Element that furrounds him; but they all gave themfelves over for loft, when they thought the worm had got into their dykes *.

C H A P. XX.

A few additional Obfervations on the right of Taxation which is lodged in the hands of the Reprefentatives of the People. What kind of danger this Right may be expofed to.

THE generality of Men, or at leaft of Politicians, feem to confider the right of taxing themfelves, enjoyed by the Englifh Nation, as being no more than a means of fecuring their property againft the attempts

* Such new forms as may prove deftructive of the real fubftance of a Government, may be unwarily adopted, in the fame manner as the fuperftitious notions and practices defcribed in my Work, entitled *Memorials of Human Superftition*, may be introduced into a Religion, fo as to entirely fubvert the true fpirit of it.

of the Crown ; while they overlook the nobler and more extensive efficiency of that privilege.

The right to grant subsidies to the Crown, possessed by the People of England, is the safeguard of all their other liberties, religious and civil : it is a regular means conferred on them by the Constitution, of influencing the motion of the Executive power ; and it forms the tie by which the latter is bound to them. In short, this privilege is a sure pledge in their hands, that their Sovereign, who can dismiss their Representatives at his pleasure, will never entertain thoughts of ruling without the assistance of these.

If, through unforeseen events, the Crown could attain to be independant on the People in regard to its supplies, such is the extent of its Prerogative, that, from that moment, all the means the People possess to vindicate their liberty, would be annihilated. They would have no resource left,—except indeed that uncertain and calamitous one, of an appeal to the sword ; which is no more, after all, than what the most enslaved Nations enjoy.

Let us suppose, for instance, that abuses of power should be committed, which, either by their immediate operation, or by the precedents they might establish, should undermine the liberty of the subject. The People, it will be said, would then have their remedy in the Legislative power possessed by their Representatives. The latter would, at the first opportunity, interfere, and frame such Bills as would prevent the like abuses for the future. But here we must observe, that the Assent of the Sovereign is necessary to make those Bills become Laws; and if, as we have just now supposed, he had no need of the support of the Commons, how could they obtain his assent to laws thus purposely framed to abridge his authority ?

Again, let us suppose that, instead of contenting itself with making slow advances to despotism, the Ex-

ecutive power, or its Minifters, fhould at once openly
invade the liberty of the fubject. Obnoxious Men,
Printers for inftance, or political Writers, are deftroyed, either by military violence, or, to do things with
more fecurity, with the forms of law. Then, it will
be faid, the Reprefentatives of the People would impeach the perfons concerned in thofe meafures. Though
unable to reach a King who perfonally *can do no wrong*,
they at leaft would lay hold of thofe Men who were
the immediate inftruments of his tyrannical procced-
ings, and endeavour, by bringing them to condign
punifhment, to deter future Judges or Minifters from
imitating them. All this I grant ; and I will even
add, that circumftanced as the Reprefentatives of the
People now are, and having to do with the Sovereign
who can enjoy no dignity without their affiftance, it
is moft likely that their endeavours in the purfuit of
fuch laudable objects would prove fuccefsful. But if,
on the contrary, the King, as we have fuppofed, ftood
in fo need of their affiftance, and moreover knew that
he fhould never want it, it is impoffible to think that
he would then fuffer himfelf to remain a tame fpecta-
tor of their proceedings. The impeachments thus
brought by them would immediately prove the fignal
of their difmiffion ; and the King would make hafte,
by diffolving them, both to revenge what would then
be called the infolence of the Commons, and to fecure
his Minifters.

But even thofe are vain fuppofitions : the evil would
reach much farther ; and we may be affured, that if
ever the Crown was to be in a condition to govern
without the affiftance of the Reprefentatives of the
People, it would difmifs them for ever, and thus rid
itfelf of an Affembly which, while it continued to be
a clog on its power, could no longer be of any fervice
to it. This Charles the Firft attempted to do when
he found his Parliaments grew refractory, and the

Kings of France really have done, with refpect to the General Eftates of their Kingdom.

And indeed if we confider the extent of the Prerogative of the King of England, and efpecially the circumftance of his completely uniting in himfelf all the executive and active powers of the State, we fhall find that it is no exaggeration to fay, that he has power fufficient to be as arbitrary as the Kings of France, were it not for the right of taxation, which in England is poffeffed by the People; and the only conftitutional difference between the French and Englifh Nations is, that the former can neither confer benefits on their Sovereign, nor hinder his meafures; while the latter, how extenfive foever the prerogative of their King may be, can deny him the means of exerting it.

But here a moft important obfervation is to be made; and I intreat the Reader's attention to the fubject. This right of granting fubfidies to the Crown, can only be effectual when it is exercifed by one Affembly alone. When feveral diftinct Affemblies have it equally in their power to fupply the wants of the Prince, the cafe becomes totally altered. The competition which fo eafily takes place between thofe different Bodies, and even the bare confcioufnefs which each entertains of its inability to hinder the meafures of the Sovereign, render it impoffible for them to make any effectual conftitutional ufe of their privilege. " Thofe different Parliaments or Eftates (to repeat the " obfervation introduced in the former part of this " Work) having no means of recommending them- " felves to their Sovereign, but their fuperior readi- " nefs in complying with his demands, vie with each " other in granting what it would not only be fruit- " lefs, but even dangerous to refufe. And the King " in the mean time, foon comes to demand as a tri- " bute, a gift which he is confident to obtain." In fhort, it may be laid down as a maxim, that when a

Sovereign is made to depend, in regard to his supplies, on more Assemblies than one, he, in fact, depends upon none. And indeed the King of France is not independent on his People for his necessary supplies, any otherwise than by drawing the same from several different Assemblies of their Representatives: the latter have in appearance a right to refuse all his demands: and as the English call the grants they make to their Kings, Aids or Subsidies, so do the Estates of the French Provinces call their *Dons gratuits*, or free gifts.

What is it, therefore, that constitutes the difference between the political situation of the French and English Nations, since their rights thus seem outwardly to be the same? The difference lies in this, that there has never been in England more than one Assembly that could supply the wants of the Sovereign. This has always kept him in a state, not of a seeming, but of a real dependance on the Representatives of the People for his necessary supplies; and how low soever the liberty of the Subject may, at particular times, have sunk, they have always found themselves possessed of a most effectual means of restoring it, whenever they have thought proper so to do. Under Henry the Eighth, for instance, we find the Despotism of the Crown to have been carried to an astonishing height: it was even enacted that the Proclamations of the King should have the force of law; a thing which even in France never was so expressly declared: yet, no sooner did the Nation recover from its long state of supineness, than the exorbitant power of the Crown was reduced within its constitutional bounds.

To no other cause than the disadvantage of their situation, are we to ascribe the low condition in which the Deputies of the People in the Assembly called the General Estates of France, were always forced to remain.

Surrounded as they were by the particular Estates

of thofe Provinces into which the Kingdom had been formerly divided, they never were able to ftipulate conditions with their Sovereign ; and inftead of making their right of granting fubfides to the crown ferve to gain them in the end a fhare in Legiflation, they ever remained confined to the naked privilege of " humble Supplication and Remonftrance."

Thofe Eftates, however, as all the great Lords in France were admitted into them, began at length to appear dangerous ; and as the King could in the mean time do without their affiftance, they were fet afide. But feveral of the particular Eftates of the Provinces are preferved to this day : fome, which for temporary reafons had been abolifhed, have been reftored : nay, fo manageable have popular Affemblies been found by the Crown when it has to do with many, that the kind of Government we mention is that which it has been found moft convenient to affign to Corfica ; and Corfica has been made *un pays d'Etats* *.

* An idea of the manner in which the bufinefs of granting fupplies to the Crown, was conducted by the States of the Province of Britany, under the reign of Lewis the Fourteenth, may be formed from feveral lively ftrokes to be met with in the Letters of Mad. de Sévigné, whofe Eftate lay in that Province, and who had often affifted at the holding of thofe States. The granting of fupplies was not, it feems, looked upon as any ferious kind of bufinefs. The whole time the States were fitting, was a continued fcene of feftivity and entertainment ; the canvaffing of the demands of the Crown was chiefly carried on at the table of the Nobleman who had been deputed from Court to hold the States ; and every thing was commonly decided by a kind of acclamation. In a certain Affembly of thofe States, the Duke of Chaulnes, the Lord Duputy, had a prefent of fifty thoufand crowns made to him, as well as a confiderable one for his Duchefs, befides obtaining the demand of the Court : and the Lady we quote here, commenting fomewhat jocularly

That the Crown in England should, on a sudden, render itself independant on the Commons for its supplies, that is, should on a sudden successfully assume to itself a right to lay taxes, on the subject, by its own authority, is not certainly an event in any degree likely to take place, nor indeed that should, at this present time, raise any kind of political fear. But it is not equally impracticable that the right of the Representatives of the People might become invalidated, by being divided in the manner that has been just described.

Such a division of the right of the People might be effected several different ways. National calamities for instance, unfortunate foreign wars attended with loss of public credit, might suggest methods for raising the necessary supplies, different from those which have hitherto been used. Dividing the Kingdom into a certain number of parts, which should severally vote subsidies to the Crown, or even distinct assessments to be made by the different Counties into which England is now divided, might, in the circumstances we suppose, be looked upon as adviseable expedients; and these being once introduced, might be continued afterwards.

on these grants, says, *Ce n'st pas que nous soyons riches ; mais nous sommes honnêtes, nous avons du courage, & entre midi & une heure, nous ne savons rienrefuser à nos amis.* " It is not " that we are rich ; but we are civil, we are full of courage, "'and, between twelve and one o'clock, we are unable to deny any thing to our friends."

The different Provinces of France, it may be observed, are liable to pay several taxes besides those imposed on them by their own States. Dean Tucker, in one of his Tracts, in which he has thought proper to quote this Work, has added to the above instance of the French Provinces, that of the States of the Austrian Netherlands, which is very conclusive. And examples to the same purpose might be supplied by all those Kingdoms of Europe in which Provincial States are held.

Another divifion of the right of the People, much more likely to take place than thofe juft mentioned, might be fuch as might arife from acquifitions of foreign dominions, the inhabitants of which fhould in time claim and obtain a right to treat directly with the Crown, and grant fupplies to it, without the interference of the Britifh Legiflature.

Should any Colonies acquire the right we mention—fhould, for inftance, the American Colonies have acquired it, as they claimed it, it is not to be doubted that the confequences that have refulted from a divifion like that we mention in moft of the Kingdoms of Europe, would alfo have taken place in the Britifh dominions, and that that fpirit of competition which has been above defcribed, would in time have manifefted itfelf between the different Colonies. This defire of ingratiating themfelves with the Crown, by means of the privilege of granting fupplies to it, has even been openly confeffed by an Agent of the American provinces*, when, on his being examined by the Houfe of Commons, in the year 1766, he faid, " *the* " *granting Aids to the Crown, is the only means the Ame-* " *ricans have of recommending themfelves to their Sove-* " *reign.*" And the events that have of late years taken place in America, render it evident that the Colonies would not have fcrupled going any lengths to obtain favourable conditions at the expence of Britain and the Britifh Legiflature.

That a fimilar fpirit of competition might be raifed in Ireland, is alfo fufficiently plain from certain late events. And fhould the American Colonies have obtained their demands, and at the fame time fhould Ireland and America have increafed in wealth to a certain degree, the time might have come at which the Crown might have governed England with the fup-

* Doctor Franklin

plies of Ireland and America—Ireland with the supplies of England and of the American Colonies—and the American Colonies with the money of each other, and of England and Ireland.

To this it may be objected, that the supplies granted by the Colonies, even though joined with those of Ireland, never could have risen to such a height as to have counterbalanced the importance of the English Commons.—I answer, in the first place, that there would have been no necessity that the aids granted by Ireland and America should have risen to an equality with those granted by the British Parliament: it would have been sufficient, to produce the effects we mention, that they had only borne a certain proportion with these latter, so far as to have conferred on the Crown a certain degree of independance, and at the same time have raised in the English Commons a correspondent sense of self-diffidence in the exercise of their undoubted privilege of granting, or rather *refusing*, subsidies to the Crown.—Here it must be remembered, that the right of granting, or refusing, supplies to the Crown, is the only ultimate, forcible, privilege the British Parliament possess : by the Constitution they have no other, as hath been observed in the begiming of this Chapter : this circumstance ought to be combined with the absolute exclusiveness of the executive powers lodged in the Crown—with its prerogative of dissenting from the Bills framed by Parliament, and even of dissolving it*.

* Being with Doctor Franklin at his house in Craven-street, some months before he went back to America, I mentioned to him a few of the remarks contained in this Chapter, and in general, that the claim of the American Colonies directly clashed with one of the vital principles of the English Constitution. The observation, I remember, struck him very much : it led him afterwards to speak to me of the ex-

I shall mention in the second place, a remarkable fact in regard to the subject we are treating (which may serve to shew that Politicians are not always confistent, or even sagacious in their arguments;) which is, that the same persons who are the most strenuous advocates for granting to the American Colonies their demands, were at the same time the most sanguine in their predictions of the future wealth and greatness of America, and at the same time, also, used to make frequent complaints of the undue influence which the Crown derives from the scanty supplies granted to it by the kingdom of Ireland*.

Had the American Colonies fully obtained their demands, both the essence of the present English Government, and the condition of the English People, would

amination he had undergone in the House of Commons; and he concluded with lending me the volume of the Collection of *Parliamentary Debates*, in which an account of it is contained. Finding the constitutional tendency of the claim of the Americans to be a subject not very generally understood, I added a few paragraphs concerning it, in the English edition I some time after gave of this work ; and on publishing a third Edition of the same, I thought it might not be amiss to write something more compact on the subject, and have according added the present new Chapter, into which I have transferred the few additional paragraphs I mention, leaving in the place where they stood only the general observations on the right of granting subsidies, which were formerly in the French work. Several of the ideas, and even expressions contained in this Chapter, made their appearance in the *Public Advertiser*, about the time I was preparing the first Edition: I sent them myself to that Newspaper, under the signature of *Advena*. I mention this for the sake of those persons who may perchance remember having seen the sketch I allude to.

* For instance, the complaints made in regard to the pensions on the Irish establishment.

certainly have been altered thereby: nor would such a change have been inconsiderable, but in proportion as the Colonies should have remained in a state of national poverty*.

* When I observe that no Man who wished for the preservation of the form and spirit of the English Constitution, ought to have desired that the claim of the American Colonies might be granted them, neither do I mean to say that the American Colonies should have given up their claim.—— The wisdom of Ministers, in regard to American affairs, ought to have been constantly employed in making the Colonies useful to this Country, and at the same time in hiding their subjection from them (a caution which is, after all, more or less used in every government upon earth ;) it ought to have been exerted in preventing the opposite interests of Britain, and of America, from being brought to an issue, to any such clashing dilemma as would render disobedience on the one hand, and the resort to force on the other, almost surely unavoidable. The generality of people fancy that Ministers use a great depth of thought, and much forecast in their operations ; whereas the truth is, that Ministers in all Countries never think but of providing for present, immediate, contingencies ; in doing which they constantly follow the open track before them. This method does very well for the common course of human affairs, and even is the safest ; but whenever cases and circumstances of a new and unknown nature occur, sad blunders and uproar are the consequences. The celebrated Count Oxenstiern, Chancellor of Sweden, one day when his Son was expressing to him his diffidence of his own abilities, and the dread with which he thought of ever engaging in the management of public affairs, made the following Latin answer to him : *Nescis, mi fili, quam parvâ cum sapientiâ regitur mundus.* " You do not know, my Son, " with what little wisdom the World is governed."

Matters having come to an eruption, it was no longer to be expected they could be compromised by the palliative offers sent at different times from this Country to America. When the Earl of Carlisle solicited to be at

C H A P. XXI.

Conclufion.—A few Words on the Nature of the Divi-
fions that take place in England.

I SHALL conclude this Work with a few Obfervations on the total freedom from violence with
which the political difputes and contentions in England are conducted and terminated, in order both to
give a farther proof of the foundnefs of the principles
on which the Englifh Government is founded, and to
confute in general the opinion of foreign Writers or
Politicians, who, mifled by the apparent heat with
which thofe difputes are fometimes carried on, and
the clamour to which they give occafion, look upon
England as a perpetual fcene of civil broils and diffenfions.

In fact, if we confider, in the firft place, the conftant tenor of the conduct of the Parliament, we fhall
fee that whatever different views the feveral Branches

3 A

the head of the folemn Commiffion that failed for the purpofe
we mention, he did not certainly fhew modefty equal to that
of the Son of Chancellor Oxenftiern. It has been faid that, in
that ftage of the conteft the Americans could not think that
the propofals thus fent to them were ferioufly meant : however, this cannot have been the principal caufe of the mifcarriage of the Commiffion. The fact is, that after the
Americans had been once made to open their eyes on their
political fituation, and rendered fenfible of the local advantages of their Country, it was become in a manner impoffible
to have ftruck with them any bargain at which either Nation would have afterwards had caufe to rejoice, or even to
have made any bargain at all. It would be needlefs to fay
here any thing more on the fubject of the American conteft.
The motto of one of the Englifh Nobility fhould have
been that of Minifters, in their regulations for rendering the
Colonies ufeful to the Mother Country,—*Fairs fans dire.*

that compose it may at times pursue, and whatever use they may accordingly make of their privileges, they never go, in regard to each other, beyond the terms, not only of decency, but even of that general good understanding which ought to prevail among them.

Thus the King, though he preserves the style of his Dignity, never addresses the two Houses but in terms of regard and affection; and if at any time he chooses to refuse their Bills, he only says that he will consider of them *(le Roy s'advisera ;)* which is certainly a gentler expression than the word *Veto*.

The two Houses on their part, though very jealous, each within their own walls, of the freedom of speech, are, on the other hand, careful that that liberty shall never break out into unguarded expressions with regard to the person of the King. It is even a constant rule among them never to mention him, when they mean to blame the administration; and those things which they may choose to censure even in the Speeches made by the King in person, and which are plainly his own acts, are never considered but as the deed of his Ministers, or in general of those who have advised him.

The two Houses are also equally attentive to prevent every step that may be inconsistent with that respect which they mutually owe to one another. The examples of their differences with each other are very rare, and were, for the most part, mere misunderstandings. Nay, in order to prevent all subject of altercation, the custom is, that when one of the two Houses refuses to consent to a Bill presented by the other, no formal declaration is made of such refusal; and that House whose Bill is rejected, learns its fate only from their hearing no more of it, or by what the Members may be told as private persons.

In each House, the Members take care, even in the heat of debate, never to go beyond certain bounds in their manner of speaking of each other: if they were to offend in that refpeſt, they would certainly incur the cenfure of the Houfe.   And as reafon has taught Mankind to refrain, in their wars, from all injuries to each other that have no tendency to promote the main objeſt of their contentions, fo a kind of Law of Nations (if I may fo exprefs myfelf) has been introduced among the perfons who form the Parliament, and take part in the debates : they have difcovered that they may very well be of oppofite parties, and yet not hate and perfecute one another. Coming frefh from debates carried on even with confiderable warmth, they meet without reluſtance in the ordinary intercourfe of life; and, fufpending all hoftilities, they hold every place out of Parliament to be neutral ground.

In regard to the generality of the People, as they never are called upon to come to a final decifion with refpeſt to any public meafures, or exprefsly to concur in fupporting them, they preferve themfelves ftill more free from party fpirit than their reprefentatives themfelves fometimes are. Confidering, as we have obferved, the affairs of Government as only matter of fpeculation, they never have occafion to engage in any vehement contefts among themfelves on that account: Much lefs do they think of taking an aſtive and violent part in the differences of particular faſtions, or the quarrels of private individuals. And thofe family feuds, thofe party animofities, thofe victories and confequent outrages of faſtions alternately fuccefsful; in fhort, all thofe inconveniences which in fo many other States have conftantly been the attendants of liberty, and which Authors tell us we muft fubmit to, as the price of it, are things in very great meafure unknown in England.

But are not the Englifh perpetually making complaints againft the Adminiftration ? and do they not fpeak and write as if they were continually expofed to grievances of every kind ?

Undoubtedly, I fhall anfwer, in a Society of Beings

subject to error, diffatisfactions will neceffarily arife from fome quarter or other; and in a free Society, they will be openly manifefted by complaints. Befides, as every Man in England is permitted to give his opinion upon all fubjects, and as to watch over the Adminiftration, and to complain of grievances, is the proper duty of the Reprefentatives of the People, complaints muft neceffarily be heard in fuch a Government, and even more frequently, and upon more fubjects, than in any other.

But thofe complaints, it fhould be remembered, are not, in England, the cries of oppreffion forced at laft to break its filence. They do not fuppofe hearts deeply wounded. Nay, I will go farther, they do not even fuppofe very determinate fentiments; and they are often nothing more than the firft vent which Men give to their new, and yet unfettled conceptions.

The agitation of Men's minds is not therefore in England what it would be in other States: it is not the fymptom of a profound and general difcontent, and the forerunner of violent commotions. Forefeen, regulated, even hoped for by the Conftitution, this agitation animates all the different parts of the State, and is to be confidered only as the beneficial viciffitude of the feafons. The governing Power being dependent on the Nation, is often thwarted, but fo long as it continues to deferve the affection of the People, can never be endangered. Like a vigorous tree, which ftretches its branches far and wide, the flighteft breath can put it in motion; but it acquires and exerts at every minute a new degree of force, and refifts the winds, by the ftrength and elafticity of its fibres, and the depth of its roots.

In a word, whatever Revolutions may at times happen among the perfons who conduct the public affairs in England, they never occafion the fhorteft ceffation of the power of the Laws, nor the fmalleft diminution of the fecurity of individuals. A Man who fhould have incurred the enmity of the moft powerful Men in the State,—what do I fay!—though he had, like another *Vatinius*, drawn upon himfelf the united deteftation of all parties, might, under the protection of the Laws, and by keeping within the bounds required by them, continue to fet both his enemies and the whole Nation at defiance.

The limits prefcribed to this book do not admit of entering into any farther particulars on the fubject we are treating here; but if we were to purfue this inquiry, and examine into the influence which the Englifh Government has on the manners and cuftoms of the People, perhaps we fhould find that, inftead of infpiring them with any difpofition to diforder or anarchy, it produces in them a quite contrary effect. As they fee the higheft Powers in the State conftantly fubmit to the Laws, and they receive, themfelves, fuch a certain protection from thofe Laws, whenever they appeal to them, it is impoffible but they muft infenfibly contract a deep-rooted reverence for them, which can at no time ceafe to have fome influence on their actions. And, in fact, we fee that even the lower clafs of the People, in England, notwithftanding the apparent exceffes into which they are fometimes hurried, poffefs a fpirit of juftice and order, fuperior to what is to be obferved in the fame rank of men in other Countries. The extraordinary indulgence which is fhewn to accufed perfons of every degree, is not attended with any of thofe pernicious confequences which we might at firft be apt to fear from it. And it is perhaps to the nature of the Englifh Conftitution itfelf (however remote the caufe may perhaps feem,) and to the fpirit of juftice it continually and infenfibly diffufes throughout all orders of the People, that we are to attribute the fingular advantage poffeffed by the Englifh Nation, of employing an incomparably milder mode of adminiftering Juftice in criminal matters than any other Nation, and at the fame time of affording perhaps fewer inflances of violence of cruelty.

Another confequence which we might obferve here, as flowing alfo from the principles of the Englifh Government, is the moderate behaviour of all thofe who are invefled with any branch of public authority. And if we look at the conduct of all public Officers in England, from the Minifters of State, or the Judge, down to the loweft Officers of Juftice, we find a fpirit of forbearance and lenity prevailing in England, among all perfons in power, which cannot but create fome furprife in thofe who have vifited other Countries.

One circumftance more I fhall obferve here, as peculiar to England, which is the conftant attention of the Legiflature in providing for the interefts and welfare of the People, and the indulgences fhewn by them to their very prejudices. Advantages thefe, which are no doubt the confequence of the general fpirit which animates the whole Englifh Government, but are alfo particularly owing to that circumftance peculiar to it, of having lodged the active part of Legiflation in the Hands of the Reprefentatives of the Nation, and committed the care of alleviating the grievances of the People to perfons who either feel them, or fee them nearly, and whofe fureft path to advancement and glory is to be active in finding remedies for them.

Not that I mean, however, that no abufes take place in the Englifh Government, and that all poffible good laws are made in it ; but that there is a conftant tendency in it, both to correct the one, and improve the other. And that all the laws that are in being are certainly executed, whenever appealed to, is what I look upon as the characteriftic and undifputed advantage of the Englifh Conftitution. A Conftitution the more likely to produce all the effects we have mentioned, and to procure in general the happinefs of the People, in that it has taken Mankind as they are, and has not endeavoured to prevent every thing, but to regulate every thing : I shall add, the more difficult to discover, because its form was complicated, while its principles were natural and simple.   Hence it is that the Politicians of Antiquity, sensible of the inconveniences of the Governments they had opportunities of knowing, wished for the establishment of such a Government, without much hopes of ever seeing it effected*. Nay, Tacitus, the best judge of them all, considered it as a project entirely chimerical†.   Nor was it because he had not thought of it, had not reflected on it, that he was of this opinion : he had sought for such a government, had had a glimpse of it, and yet continued to pronounce it impracticable.

Let us not, therefore, ascribe to the confined views of Man, to his imperfect sagacity, the discovery of this important secret.   The world might have grown old, generations might have succeeded generations, still seeking it in vain.   It has been by a fortunate conjunction of circumstances, I shall add, by the assistance of a favourable situation, that liberty has at last been able to erect herself a Temple.

Invoked by every Nation, but of too delicate a nature, as it should seem, to subsist in Societies formed of such imperfect beings as Mankind, she shewed, and but just shewed, herself to the ingenious Nations of antiquity who inhabited the south of Europe.   They were constantly mistaken in the form of the worship they paid to her.   As they continually aimed at extending dominion and conquest over other Nations, they were no less mistaken in

---

" * Statuo esse optimè constitutam Rempublicam quaæ ex
" tribus generibus illis, regali, optimo, et populari, modice
" confusa."—Cic. *Fragm.*

† " Cunctas Nationes & Urbes, Populus, aut Priores,
" aut Singuli, regunt.   Delecta ex his & constituta Rei-
" publicæ forma, laudari facilius quàm evenire ; vel si evenit,
" haud diuturna esse potest."—Tac. Ann. lib. iv.

the spirit of that worship; and though they continued for ages to pay their devotions to her, she still continued, with regard to them, to be the *unknown* Goddess.

Excluded, since that time, from those places to which she had seemed to give a preference, driven to the extremity of the Western World, banished even out of the Continent, she has taken refuge in the Atlantic Ocean. There it is, that freed from the dangers of external disturbance, and assisted by a happy pre-arrangement of things, she has been able fully to display the form that suited her; and she has found six centuries to have been necessary to the completion of her Work.

- Being sheltered, as it were, within a Citadel, she there reigns over a Nation which is the better entitled to her favours as it endeavours to extend her Empire, and carries with it, to every part of its dominions, the blessings of industry and equality. Fenced in on every side, to use the expressions of Chamberlayne, with a wide and deep ditch, the sea, guarded with strong outworks, its ships of war, and defended by the courage of her Seamen, she preserves that important secret, that sacred fire, so difficult to be kindled, and which, if it were once extinguished, would perhaps never be lighted again. When the World shall have been again laid waste by Conquerors, she will still continue to shew Mankind, not only the principle that ought to unite them, but what is of no less importance, the form under which they ought to be united. And the Philosopher, when he considers the constant fate of civil Societies amongst Men, and observes the numerous and powerful causes which seem as it were unavoidably to conduct them all to a state of incurable political Slavery, takes comfort in seeing that Liberty has at length disclosed her secret to Mankind, and secured an Asylum to herself.

I N D E X.

I N D E X.

able treaty by which the war for the *public good* was terminated, 44. General eſtates, how conſtituted, 45. A remarkable inſurrection, 47. What they call *Edits enrégiſtrés*, 67. French parliament, what, ibid. Late king's expedient for diſmiſſing the parliament of Paris, 292. The jealouſy of the crown againſt that aſſembly, 304.

Franklin, Dr. quoted, 365.

French language, introduced into the Engliſh laws by William the Conqueror, 66.

G

George I. king, led into an imprudent ſtep, 281, 349, 354, 355.

General warrants, ſet aſide, 341.

Geneva, republic of, mentioned, 172, 187, 222, 341.

Germany, by what cauſe the growth of the power of the crown has been checked there, 48.

Grand Jury, its office, 132, 133.

Guiſe, duke of, ſlain by order of King Henry III. of France, 190.

H

Habeas Corpus act, when paſſed, and for what purpoſe, 146. The tenor of it, 147.

Hale, judge, his deſcription of the office of a jury, 138.

Henry I. grants a charter to his ſubjects, what condition he annexes to it, 38.

Henry VIII. his great power, 52.

Holt, judge, remarkable opinion delivered by him, 229.

Hugh Capet, the firſt hereditary king in France, 32.

Hume, Mr. a few words on the character given by him of James II. 322, 323.

I

Jacob's Law Dictionary quoted, 104, 120.

James I. keeps his ground againſt the reſtleſs ſpirit of the times, 322.

James II. how his dethronement was effected, 58.

Jeſuits, how expelled from Spain, 292.

money-bill, 65. The great pre-eminence allowed them in point of ceremony over the commons, 169, 170. Can vote by proxy, 170. Their impartiality in their judicial capacity, 264. A bill is framed to limit their number, 281, 349.

Lyttelton, lord, quoted, 227, 228.

M

Machiavel's history of the republic of Florence quoted, 153.

Marlborough, duke of, easily dismissed from his employments, 161, 289.

Martial, courts, a remarkable dispute between one and a court of law, 325, 326.

Military power, its needlessness to support the power of the crown in England, 276, 320, 324. The surprising subjection of it to the civil power in England, 276, 324, 327.

Minister, equally interested with other subjects in maintaining the laws concerning personal security, 208.

Monarchies, revolutions always concluded in them by provisions for the advantage of great men and leaders, not of the people, the same as in commonwealths, 240, 284, 306, 307. The monarchs are afraid of powerful subjects, 290. Cannot do without some arbitrary means of asserting their authority, 297. Very jealous of the liberty of the press, and perhaps are really obligated to be so, 299, 300. The military superior to the civil power, 324.

Money Bills, not to be tacked to other bills, 72, 280.

Montesquieu, quoted, 213, 332.

More's Utopia quoted, 213.

O

Ostracism, an arbitrary unjust expedient, but perhaps necessary in the republic of Athens, 297.

Oxenstiern, chancellor, his words to his son, 368.

P

Parliament, English, the constitution of, 62—70.

Peers, how to be tried, 138.

Pope, Mr. quoted, 200.

Præmunire, the different meanings of the word, 148.

Prætor, his office in Rome, 96. His provisions, 111--113.

Press, liberty of the, is a real cenforial power lodged in the people, 212, 213. A definition of it, 215. How extensive its use has become, 217. The real foundation on which it rests in England, 317, 318.

Prisoner, how to be committed, 132.

Privy council, its real office in the English government, 285.

Prorogation, its effects, 64. The term not to be afterwards shortened, 78.

Propounding, in legislation, the privilege of, reserved to the executive power in commonwealths, 171. Allotted in the English constitution to the representatives of the people, 173—176. How the same was formerly settled in France, Sweden, Scotland, and Ireland, 175.

R

Representatives, qualifications for being one, 62. Advantages that accrue to the people from acting through representatives, 189—191.

Resistance, right of, admitted by the English laws, 227, 229. Recognized even by the courts of law, 229.

Revolutions, have always been concluded in England in an advantageous manner to public liberty, 233.

Rome, wrong notions of liberty the patricians and senate give to the people, 179. Who were called *nobiles*, 162, 204. Remarkable instance of insolence and cruelty in a magistrate, 249. Corruption of the judges, 250, 251. How the final overthrow of the republic was operated, 334. The political rights allotted to the people, 335.

Rousseau, quoted, 168, 179, 213, 339.

Russian ambassador, the case of his arrest, 268.

S

Saxon government, abolished in England by the Nor-

F I N I S.